KU-509-199

THE SECRET LOVERS

Charles McCarry

THE SHERIDAN
BOOK COMPANY

This edition published in 1993 by
The Sheridan Book Company

First published in Great Britain by Hutchinson 1977
Random House, 20 Vauxhall Bridge Road, London SW1V 2SA

Coronet edition
Arrow edition 1985

Set in Baskerville

Printed and bound in Great Britain by
Cox & Wyman Ltd, Reading, Berkshire

ISBN 1–85501–451–3

For my father,
in loving memory

One

I

As the car moved through the wet streets of Berlin in the hour after dawn, Horst Bülow fussed with his briefcase. It was a pigskin satchel, strapped and buckled, so old that it had lost the smell of leather. The night before, Bülow had carried it out of East Germany. Now he arranged on the seat of the car the things he had brought in his briefcase: a safety razor and a tube of shaving cream, a heel of bread, half a sausage, a bit of hard cheese with tooth marks on it, a flask of schnapps – and, finally, a thick manuscript, hundreds of flimsy pages covered with tiny handwriting. 'You'll need a cryptanalyst to read this,' Bülow said, 'it looks as if this Russian writes with his fingernails.'

Paul Christopher smiled at the agent. 'Did you read it on the train?' he asked.

Bülow looked shocked, then realized the American was joking. 'Not a chance,' he said. 'There is only one thing more boring than Russians in the flesh, and that is Russians in a novel, tormented by their own stupidity, called by three different names. What is Russian literature? One universal genius, Tolstoy, and six provincial bores.'

Risk made Bülow talkative. He had been chattering, giving his

7

opinions, ever since Christopher picked him up three hours earlier near the Wannsee. They had walked together in the dark on the deserted beach. Bülow, his long greying hair blown by a wind filled with rain, told Christopher about the Wannsee beach between the wars. He had brought girls to a lakeside restaurant called the Swedischer Pavillon and fed them trout and strawberries and cream and a drink called *Bowle*, a mixture of Rhine wine and champagne, with fruit and herbs and sugar. 'Afterwards, we would lie down in the Grunewald,' Bülow had said, 'but none of that exists any more. I haven't heard of anyone drinking *Bowle* for twenty years.'

In the car, he shivered violently and drank from his flask. He registered his complaints. The manuscript had been handed to him in Dresden by a man, clearly not a professional, who had brought it from Warsaw. Bülow wanted to know why the package had not been delivered in a more secure manner. 'I asked for a dead-drop,' he said. 'I don't like to see faces and I don't like my face to be seen.' He had been in the Abwehr, he had operated against the OSS. He believed that Americans knew nothing about tradecraft. He thought himself in constant danger because of his employers' clumsiness. Once, he had almost been taken at the frontier with a strip of microfilm. The border guard had taken Bülow's sandwich apart, but had somehow missed the evidence, smeared with mustard, concealed between two slices of cheese. Afterwards, he had seized Christopher by the shoulders and cried, 'Why do you think I work for you? It's the money, only the money. I'd work for the British for one-tenth the price – they're professionals!' Christopher had said, 'I don't think the English want people who hide microfilm in sandwiches – the mustard is bad for the film.' Bülow drew danger to himself by the excessive use of technique; he behaved like a spy because he enjoyed the trappings of conspiracy. He had been making the same furtive mistakes for such a long time that he believed they had preserved his life. No one else doubted that sooner or later they would kill him.

Christopher did not like to stay with Bülow any longer than was necessary. But the German required handling. At each meeting he talked more compulsively than at the last. As he became less valuable, he demanded more money. He wanted reassurance. He wanted to come over to the West and stay there, to be given a quiet job. He had been twenty years old in 1930, and the following ten years had been the best in his life. In Bonn and Hamburg and Munich, he thought, Germans had regained the past he had believed lost for ever. They went to restaurants in the park on Sunday and walked together under the trees and owned things. He wanted that again.

Christopher watched the mirror carefully. There was no surveillance, nothing in the long street behind the rented car except the first tram of the day, howling to a stop to pick up a small group of old women, night-cleaners on their way home. Christopher gave Bülow two thick books, novels in German. 'Put these in with your lunch,' he said. 'You'll want your briefcase to look as full going back as it looked coming over.' Bülow repacked his satchel, buckled its straps, held it on his lap. The sun shone feebly through the overcast, like a lamp covered by a woman's scarf in a shabby hotel room. The S-Bahn sign for the Zoo station was just visible through the fogged windscreen. 'On Sundays we used to dance in the Zoo,' Bülow said, 'there were endless gardens, orchestras, the girls came in droves. You'd buy one beer and share it with a girl.' He looked out the back window, making certain that the street was empty. 'I'll get down here,' he said.

He opened the door and held it slightly ajar while the car pulled to the kerb. He turned his long face, the bony jaw covered with stubble, towards Christopher and nodded once, crisply, before stepping out. The war had been over for fifteen years but Berlin still smelled of dead fires when it rained and Horst Bülow still carried himself like a German officer. He strode over the wet pavement as if he wore the tailored jacket and the polished boots of a cavalry lieutenant, as if the bent old women waiting for the tram were once again the girls who had drunk beer from the same glass with him in the gardens of the Zoo.

At the corner, Bülow stepped down into Kant Strasse and raised the rolled newspaper that he carried to signal the tram. In the mirror Christopher saw a black Opel sedan, tyres slipping as it accelerated in first gear, flash past the tram, then past his own parked automobile. The Opel, gears shrieking, splashed through a pool of water and struck Bülow. His upraised newspaper popped open like a magician's trick bouquet. His body was thrown twenty feet, pages of the newspaper sailing after it. The corpse fell to the pavement in the path of another car, an old Mercedes

9

whose driver braked after running over it; Christopher heard the thud of the tyres like four rapid gunshots.

Bülow's briefcase lay in the street. The black Opel reversed with its door open. A man's arm reached out and took the briefcase into the car. The Opel moved away at normal speed, gears changing smoothly.

No one approached the dead man. The old women who had seen the murder gazed for a moment at Horst Bülow as blood leaked through his clothes and mixed with a rainbow of spilled oil in a puddle of rainwater. Then they walked away.

While the eyes of the witnesses were still on the black Opel, Christopher backed his own car into a side street, turned it around, and drove away, towards the Wannsee to the west. Again he wasn't followed. He didn't attempt to call the Berlin base. Bülow was not their agent. The base would want to know what Bülow had brought to Berlin, why the opposition had waited to break the chain of couriers when it was almost at its last link, what was so valuable. It was not so usual in Berlin to run people like Horst Bülow down with cars as it had been a few years earlier. They would want to know why this had happened on their territory. They had no need to know.

Christopher left the car in a parking space near the new Hilton Hotel, and loosened the coil wire. At the airport, Christopher told the Hertz girl that the car had broken down, and where it was. She apologized and deducted the cost of the taxi from his bill.

Christopher got aboard the early flight to Paris. He had no luggage except an attaché case. In it he carried a clean shirt, a toothbrush and razor, and the manuscript in Russian that had been handed from idealist to idealist in a long line that had begun in Moscow and had not quite ended in Berlin. Was Bülow the first of them to die, or the last? None of the others had been agents. They had been friends of the author, men with a higher opinion of Russian literature than Horst Bülow had had. They were unknown to Christopher and his people. They would disappear unnoticed as soon as they were known to the Soviet security apparatus.

On the aeroplane Christopher refused breakfast and went into the toilet to escape the smell of food. He shaved and brushed his teeth, and put his shirt, sweaty from being worn all night, on top of the smeared manuscript. The title, CMEPTEHEKA – THE LITTLE DEATH – was printed in large cyrillic capitals in the careless hand of the Russian who had begun all this by wanting to write the truth.

2

'Bülow,' said David Patchen, 'at least had the satisfaction of dying a professional death.'

Christopher described the look of Bülow as he died. 'It would be a mercy if that were true,' he said. 'Horst always wanted to be important enough to be killed. But I don't think he had time.'

'He didn't see it coming?'

'I don't think so. It was very quick. One second he was waiting for the tram, the next he was ten feet in the air with a broken spine. I'd never seen it done before.'

'Stupid.'

'Yes. Why didn't they just pull him into the car? He would have told them where their package went. Now they have a dead end to deal with.'

Patchen and Christopher were strolling in the Tuileries Gardens. Two young men had taken the manuscript into the Embassy on the other side of the Place de la Concorde. Christopher had handed it to them inside the Jeu de Paume while Patchen, at the other end of the long gallery, limped from painting to painting. He didn't linger; the Impressionists annoyed him. 'Picnics *explain* nothing,' he said, when he joined Christopher in the open air.

Now considering the death of Bülow, Patchen sighed. 'This is going to be a pain,' he said. 'Berlin is going to see it as a security problem. *I* see it as a security problem. If you had no surveillance, if no one followed you, if you hadn't made a habit of dropping him by the Zoo, how did they know?'

'There are ways. Maybe Horst told them. He was a born security problem. Maybe they bugged my car and followed on parallel streets. Maybe Horst told someone who told them. He was hell-bent on getting off at the Zoo station. I couldn't talk him into taking the S-Bahn from a quieter neighbourhood.'

Christopher described Bülow's behaviour in the moments before he died: the untidy clothes, the unshaven cheeks, the giddy speech, the military manners copied from Nazis who had copied them from films. 'The Zoo,' Horst had said, voice trembling with anxiety; he had to get back to his office in East Berlin before 7 a.m. 'Only the Zoo will give me time, the S-Bahn line is direct to my stop.' Patchen cut Christopher off; even in death Bülow had the power to exasperate.

'I wanted a quieter operation than this,' Patchen said. 'That's why I used Bülow and you to bring the book the last few miles. Now we'll have gumshoes from Security all over us. I wish I knew who was responsible for this.'

A street photographer snapped a picture of a couple walking ten yards ahead of them. Patchen and Christopher turned into a path that led towards the Seine. It was not quite spring. The trees were bare, the fallow flower beds beside the walk were cold mud. Patchen coughed. In the war he had been wounded in the lungs. He was subject to colds and always caught one when he came from Washington to Europe in winter. He and Christopher could not talk inside. They continued to walk in the bitter wind.

'There's no understanding this,' Patchen said. 'Why run over that poor ass *after* he had been with you for three hours, and then let you go, not even following? If they wanted the manuscript, the Russians could have taken both of you. It would have been easy.'

'Why does it have to be the Russians?'

'No one else has an interest.'

Christopher put out a hand, showing Patchen which way to turn. 'Now that I've let a man be killed,' he said, 'maybe you can tell me what exactly their interest is.'

Patchen turned his stiff body to stare at Christopher. 'You'll have to know,' he said. 'I want this kept among three people – you, and me, and Otto Rothchild.'

'I thought Otto was going to retire.'

'Not quite yet. As Otto will tell you, he has ghosts in his past, and more ghosts. One of them wrote him a letter, and that's why you went to Berlin, and why poor old Bülow . . .' Patchen broke off the sentence with a shrug.

3

Grinning, Christopher reproduced Patchen's gesture and mimicked the self-mocking tone in which the other man had spoken Otto Rothchild's name. It was an old joke, and Patchen was tired of it; shivering in the soaking cold, he looked beyond Christopher to the dome of Sacré Cœur, white as an erasure on the smudged winter horizon. Too much talk of Rothchild embarrassed Patchen. He had a weakness for this agent, and he was overcoming it more slowly than he usually did. Rothchild was old now, and sick but in his day he had been a legendary operative; his successes, coup after brilliant coup, had made the careers of other men, hidden away in Headquarters, brighter than they would otherwise have been. Rothchild had temperament. He insisted, as the price of his work and friendship, that others see him as he saw himself. He hunted down and destroyed those who insulted his idea of himself; time after time, he had forced Headquarters to make a choice between him and a case officer who had tried to control him. Headquarters had always chosen Rothchild. He named some of Rothchild's old agents: 'Lazarus. Rainbow. Sailmaker. Thinkingcap.' These were the cryptonyms of famous men; Rothchild had recruited and handled them all. To the unwitting, they were prime ministers and statesmen. In fact they were aspects of Rothchild. Patchen said, 'Otto may be a bastard, but he gets results. I know you think we love him too much.' Christopher didn't want to go over the old ground onto which Patchen was leading him; Rothchild's secret fame, the more delicious because it was known only to a handful of the most trusted men in America, fascinated Patchen. Once again he wanted to explain it. 'An intelligence service is like a frigid woman,' he told Christopher. 'It waits such a long time between orgasms that it thinks of nothing else. When a man is found who, like Otto, can give consistent results, the outfit tends to be blind to his faults.'

Patchen saw the danger in admiring any human being, and he wanted to be reminded of Rothchild's flaws. Four years before, he had made Christopher Rothchild's case officer. Christopher, as Patchen had expected, saw Rothchild as he was, and kept Rothchild from realizing it. Like many daring men, Rothchild was a hypochondriac. As he grew older, his illnesses became real; he had severe hypertension, and his physical weakness reduced his intellectual power. Rothchild sought to conceal this condition as an alcholic, moving and speaking with exaggerated care, attempts to hide the signs of drunkenness.

Christopher and Rothchild met once a month. In the past year, the physical change in Rothchild had accelerated; over the course of a dozen meetings he had turned, stage by stage, into an old man. He could no longer handle his agents; his physical weakness took away the illusion that he could protect them, and one by one they were reassigned to Christopher and other case officers.

Rothchild, when he saw Christopher, had little to report. He spoke about himself constantly, watching Christopher's face for some flicker of impatience. Nothing bored Christopher; he had learned to accept all experience and all information, false or true, without emotion. Rothchild's past was very deep, and only he knew everything about it. 'If I talk too much about my life, I don't mean to weary you,' Rothchild had said to Christopher. 'I'm getting older. I've spent all my life in this work. I've lived so many cover stories that I feel a need, Paul, to describe my real life, my original self, over and over again. It's a way of keeping these things alive. Someday, if you go on living in secret, you'll feel this need too.'

Rothchild had been born in Russia. He was just old enough for the Great War, and he was commissioned at eighteen and invalided out of the Imperial Army before he was twenty as a result of a wound. Recovering in Moscow, he and other young wounded officers spoke to one another of the shame of defeat after defeat. 'It was incomprehensible,' Rothchild told Christopher forty years afterwards. 'How could the Germans, who were already fighting the French, the English, the Italians, and finally the Americans, still thrash the Imperial Russian Army? Russia was like some great whale attacked by clever savages with stone spearheads. By the time news of a wound had travelled through the nervous system to the brain, it was too late. It was fatal.'

Rothchild, born into the nobility, became a man of the Left, a socialist, plotting against the Czar, fighting in the streets. He had a sabre wound running into his scalp, delivered, he said, by one of the Imperial Horse Guards during a riot. He and others like him brought an end to the Czarist autocracy. They brought Kerensky to power. Otto had no kind memories of this man. 'He looked sick all the time, and everyone thought him a dying man. But he's still alive in America. I had a friend, a lady's man, who was his aide-de-camp. Kerensky would tease girls who called this young man on the phone. He'd change his voice, baby talk. No wonder Lenin chewed him up and spat him out.'

In those days, Rothchild's name had not been Rothchild. He changed his Russian name when he went to Berlin after the Bolsheviks took power. 'I had lost my house, my family, my political cause, my emperor, my birch forests, my connection with the soil – this means a lot to a Russian, though foreigners smile, you, Paul, can smile. Losing all that, what good was my name? I thought it comic to take a Jewish name. I was beyond the pale. That was in 1920. Ten years later, in Berlin, it wasn't so funny to be a Social Democrat with a Jewish name.'

In Paris, Rothchild had an apartment on the Île Saint-Louis. Christopher had been sent there by Patchen to see if he and Rothchild, whose contacts had begun to overlap, could work together.

Rothchild, for their first meeting, had invited him to lunch. They sat on a small balcony overlooking the Seine. The flow of the river gave the illusion, after they had drunk wine in the mild autumn sun, that Rothchild's apartment building was under way, like a ship. Rothchild was pleased when Christopher remarked on the effect; he was proud of this trompe l'œil. On the white tablecloth by his plate, Rothchild had a row of pill bottles. He took several before the meal, several more afterwards, making an apologetic face as he washed them down with Evian water.

His skin was very red and there was a pulse in his forehead. Wine excited him; he told anecdote after anecdote. Christopher realized how interesting Rothchild must once have been. He was still a handsome man, fine-boned, with a thin arched nose and melancholy eyes. He ate very lightly – two pieces of tinned white asparagus, four bites of cold chicken – but he drank most of the two bottles of wine he and Christopher shared. When the sun grew hotter he removed his jacket and sat opposite Christopher in a short-sleeved shirt. Arteries throbbed in his forearms and the skin moved as if unable to interpret incessant signals from the nerves beneath it.

So that Christopher would not be seen by an outsider, Rothchild had sent the maid away. Lunch was served by Rothchild's wife, an American many years younger than he. She was an Agency person; Christopher had helped to train her when she had come to Paris from Vassar. He had worked with her later. She had been an officer, not a secretary, and when she had been assigned to Rothchild's project she had fallen in love with him. No one was surprised: Maria did not like young men.

She and Rothchild had married only the year before, and she spoke to Christopher about their honeymoon in Spain. Rothchild had not been on Spanish soil since the civil war. All his friends had been on the losing side. The Rothchilds stayed at the Hotel de Madrid in Seville. 'The entire downstairs is a garden, a greenhouse,' said Maria Rothchild. 'I sneezed the whole time, but it was heaven, wasn't it, Otto?' He smiled and covered her hand with his long grey fingers. Maria was happiest when she and Rothchild were in the company of someone who knew, as Christopher knew, who Rothchild really was. She loved his importance, and charged the atmosphere with it; living with him, she became part of it. 'I *exult* in being Otto's wife; Otto doesn't mind that at all,' she had told Christopher on her wedding day. Maria treated her husband with joshing equality, but made him see that she never forgot for a moment who he was, and what he had been. ('The second Mrs Wilson must have treated Woodrow in about the same way,' Patchen had said. 'Maria has a lot of the nurse in her. That's why I sent her to Otto in the first place.')

As she left the table to fetch dessert, Christopher said something that made her snort with laughter. 'I almost didn't marry her because of that laugh,' Rothchild said. 'Her father paid a fortune to send her to Miss Porter's. You'd think they would have cured her.'

Throughout the lunch the Rothchilds had flirted. Maria gave Otto the best pieces of asparagus, a special cut of glazed chicken. Now she brought strawberries and *crème fraîche*. 'Berries are out of season,' Maria said, 'God bless the expense account.'

Rothchild raised his eyebrows and tapped the table with a forefinger. 'Strawberries without champagne?' he asked.

His wife put a hand on the back of his neck. 'The expense account has limits,' she said.

'Champagne,' Rothchild said peremptorily.

Maria stroked his neck. 'Otto, the wine is making your veins throb. . . .'

Rothchild exploded, rising to his feet, screaming, his face swelling, blood inflating the skin. He shouted at his wife in French, as if Christopher, sitting quietly across the table, could not understand that language. The tantrum lasted for five minutes. When Maria left to get the champagne, Rothchild followed her; Christopher could hear his shrill voice at the other end of the apartment.

When Rothchild came back to the table, he resumed his monologue as if nothing had happened. With eagerness he spoke the names of famous men he had known as boys, and who now did him invaluable favours, never asking for whom he worked. 'It takes a lifetime to build up this kind of trust and friendship, and then the lifetime is over, or nearly so.' He touched his pill bottles with his dessert spoon. 'This is the revenge my body takes on me for putting it in hazard for forty years. The Russian Revolution, the Nazis in the streets of Berlin, the civil war in Spain, Madrid with the shells falling like rain, France with the Marquis and the OSS. Never a wound, but it seems I am not immortal after all.'

He put his arm around Maria's hips when she came back with the champagne and poured it into his glass. 'Kiss your husband,' he said. Maria drew away; Rothchild held her against him, smiling upward into her eyes. She kissed him and he released her. Her face was flushed and for the remainder of the meal she ate in silence and avoided Christopher's eyes. Rothchild ignored her.

Maria, when she let Christopher out, looked over her shoulder at Rothchild's straight figure, still seated at the table in the sunlight. She took Christopher's hand and went into the outer hall with him. She rang for the elevator and while it lumbered noisily up the shaft she spoke to Christopher. The blush came back to her face.

'Paul, Otto is in a bad way physically. He doesn't know what his illness does to his personality.'

'You're very good with him.'

Maria dropped Christopher's hand. '*Good* with him? I'm not his case officer any longer,' she said. 'You don't handle someone you love.'

Christopher nodded and turned to go. Maria caught his sleeve.

'Paul, all those stories of Otto's are true, you know.'

'Yes, I know.'

'All his closest friends are world famous. He made them that way, and even they forget it. It's hell to be a great man in secret.

He's sick, it's hypertension, high blood pressure. The wine makes it worse.'

Her face was controlled. 'You see what it is, don't you?' she said. 'He thinks he's going to lose everything. It happened in Spain, it may have been my fault for being so much younger. I couldn't make him see I loved him better than I could ever love a boy. He just woke up in Seville twenty years after his friends lost the Civil War and knew that he was old.'

Finally, Rothchild had an operation at a clinic in Zürich to relieve his high blood pressure. The surgeons performed a sympathectomy, severing the ganglia of the nerves down the length of his spine. Afterwards he had greater control of his emotions. But he could not walk without collapsing, or read more than five pages of type without exhaustion, or drink wine or stand the cold.

'His mind is exactly what it was,' Maria told Christopher, after the surgery, 'but it's perched on a column of dead nerves. He can't feel his own flesh.'

4

Patchen and Christopher left the Tuileries and walked along the Seine.

'The ghost from Otto's past, in this case, was a Russian named Kiril Kamensky,' Patchen said. 'We've been hearing about him for years. He's supposed to be the new Tolstoy.'

'It's his manuscript Horst brought out of East Germany?'

'Yes. The only copy. Kamensky's friends in the literary underground carried it across Russia and Poland. We wanted to break the bucket brigade in East Germany, so that the destination of the package could not be known by our friends in Moscow.'

'That seems not to have worked out,' Christopher said.

'We'll see.'

'They killed Bülow.'

Patchen stopped walking and tugged his grey scarf higher on his throat. 'Paul, I know your man is dead and I'm sure it was a bad thing to witness. But you've told me about it. Once is enough. We have to go on to the next thing.'

Patchen coughed, a gloved hand over his mouth, one eye streaming tears and the other, paralysed by his war wound, open and dry and alert. 'Let's get you something to drink,' Christopher said. They had just crossed the Pont des Arts.

'The Deux Magots?' Patchen said.

'No, Cathy's waiting for me there.'

'Singing in the rain?'

It amused Patchen to pretend that Christopher's wife had danced out of a musical movie. He had not imagined that his friend would marry a girl who looked so much like a starlet. A Japanese grenade had scarred Patchen and crippled him. Believing himself ugly, he was embarrassed by beauty. In Cathy's presence he talked intently to Christopher about music, or about men they had known at Harvard who had gone into Wall Street. He ignored Cathy, as if she were a girl who, knowing no one, had been foolish enough to come to a house party of lifelong friends.

Christopher led Patchen into a small bar in the rue Jacob and ordered a toddy. Patchen sipped it and his cough quietened. The place was deserted, so they sat at a table in the corner and went on talking.

'Kiril Kamensky and Otto are old friends,' Patchen said. 'One day, just after Christmas, comes this letter, postmarked in Helsinki, telling Otto that Kamensky wants to entrust him with the novel he's been writing for the last twenty years.'

'Just like that? Through the open mails?'

'Yes.'

'Kamensky must be a simple fellow.'

'Very Tolstoyan, I'm told. He was a Bolshevik as a young idealist. You've read his early stuff, I know. It was published in Paris after the war, stories and poems. You brought it into the room at Harvard.'

'Yes, but I thought he was dead.'

'So did a lot of people. In the thirties' purges he was denounced and tried and sent to a camp. The KGB erased his work. It hasn't been in print in the Soviet Union for years. I don't know how long he was in prison, but evidently he kept writing.'

'Writing? In a labour camp?'

'In his head, according to Otto. It's the way he kept from going crazy. When he got out last year, he only had to copy it down.'

'And he made only one copy?'

'Yes. I suppose he figured he could always write out another. We'll make a photocopy or two.'

French workmen began to drift into the bar for a noontime glass. Patchen and Christopher went out the side door. Patchen, with his ruined face and his limp, attracted some notice, as he always did. He showed signs of nervousness; in his own country, at Headquarters where everyone was used to him, he forgot his wounds. Foreigners made him remember. Besides, he wasn't used to talking outside an office where he was absolutely certain there were no listening devices.

'Why did Kamensky pick Otto?'

'Who knows? Otto doesn't feel he has to explain everything. Besides, who else did Kamensky know in the West? He wants his work preserved.'

'He doesn't know what Otto has become.'

'I should think so. I don't imagine Kamensky would want us as literary agents.'

'How does Otto feel about that?'

'Well, Otto pretty well feels we're a great force for good in the world.'

'That's not the view of the K G B, and Kamensky is inside the Soviet Union.'

'Yes. I believe he has children in Russia from an old marriage, and he's taken up with a young woman since they let him out. He and Otto have that in common.'

Patchen had begun to cough again. Christopher waited for him to finish.

'I should think Otto would be worried about his friend,' Christopher said.

'As far as I can see, Otto is happy just to be busy again. Getting the manuscript out gave him an interest in life.'

Patchen looked at his watch. 'I have a lunch date,' he said. 'Is there a taxi stand nearby?'

'Across the street. What about Kamensky's manuscript?'

'The manuscript,' Patchen said. 'Yes. Well, now that we have it, we will read it. Maybe it's the masterpiece Otto keeps telling me it is. The people in S R have had reports from Russia, gossip of the literati. The novel is supposed to rip the black heart right out of the Soviet system. If it's a work of art as well, all our trouble will be justified.'

'And Kamensky's trip back to Siberia, too?'

'That presents a problem. In his letter to Otto, he asks that Otto put the book away until after Kamensky's death.'

'Then we'll have to do that.'

'Otto's not so sure that's a good idea.'

'He wants to *publish*?'

'He hasn't said that,' Patchen said. 'He wants you, and only you, to handle the outside work. Otto wants to sit in his bedroom with the shades drawn, and send you out under radio control.'

'Does he?'

'You're the logical one. If we go ahead.'

Christopher and Patchen, standing in the Place de Saint Germain des Prés, looked without expression into each other's faces. Patchen broke off his gaze.

'Look,' he said. 'Do you suffer from jealousy?'

Cathy was sitting next to the glass wall of the covered terrace of the Deux Magots, a tumbler of mineral water in front of her. A man was smiling down at her, talking animatedly. As they watched, she sent him away. She put the fingertips of both hands lightly against her drink and watched her own gesture with an intent smile. Her blonde hair touched her cheek; her profile was perfect. Christopher and Patchen stood only a few feet away from her, but Christopher knew there was little chance she would notice them. When Cathy was alone, she looked into space or watched parts of her own body. It was not her way to pass the time by reading, or by studying the faces of strangers. She wore the dreaming look of one who is amused by a memory.

Patchen touched Christopher's arm. 'Forget about Otto and Kamensky for a while, forget about Berlin,' he said, nodding at Cathy beyond the glass. 'Go wake her with a kiss.'

Patchen walked away. Christopher went into the Deux Magots. Holding his wife in his arms, he watched Patchen get into a taxi across the street, grimacing as he lifted his long stiff leg into the rear seat of the undersized car.

Two

I

They lay together in the narrow lower berth of a first-class compartment of the Blue Train to Rome. Though they had completed the act of love, Cathy continued to press her tense body against Christopher's, her fingertips digging into his back, as if pleasure would escape if she relaxed her grip upon his flesh. The compartment was overheated and they perspired. An empty champagne bottle rolled over the floor. Cathy pressed her lips against Christopher's chest and murmured wordlessly. He looked down at her body, rosy even in the dim light of the reading lamp at the head of the berth. She lifted her face. He closed his eyes.

'Where are you?' Cathy asked.

'Somewhere in France.'

'Don't joke, Paul. I mean in your mind. You're not with me.'

He tapped her temple with his forefinger and smiled.

'But you're not with me,' Cathy said. 'You almost never are. I can't hold on to you at all.'

They passed another train. Speech was impossible while the two fast trains ran side by side. Cathy lifted herself on to her elbow and gazed into Christopher's face, her vivid eyes unblinking. She stroked his chest and stomach and smiled brilliantly, then put both palms over his ears to shield him from the noise. Cathy knew how beautiful she was. She had told Christopher that she had fallen in love with him because he made her forget this fact about herself. When they were together, she stared at him for minutes on end.

'It's fascinating to look at you,' she said. '*You're* beautiful.' It gave her pleasure to speak these words, which she had heard repeated endlessly in her own ear since childhood.

The trains passed. Cathy took her hands away from Christopher's ears and ran her thumbs over his cheekbones, the ridge of his jaw.

'Tell me what's in your mind right now, at this exact moment of the present,' she said.

Christopher closed his eyes. Cathy said, 'Don't escape.' She rolled back his eyelid and put her own eye close to his. She continued to stare into his face. Christopher passed his hand between her eyes and his; her glance did not shift but she began to smile again.

'Cathy, look out the window for a while, will you?'

'I want to look at you.'

It didn't trouble Cathy that her behaviour annoyed Christopher. She chose to understand everything he did as a sign of love. 'You don't give me very many signs,' she told him, 'so I have to make up for what you leave out, for what you won't say. Why should I stop what I'm doing just because you don't like it? I like everything you do, Paul. I want you to learn to like everything *I* do. I'm searching for you.'

'You're training me.'

'Ah, you're beginning to understand.'

Christopher, whose work was a game, hated games. Cathy loved them: 'Let's pretend this. We're from different planets, but we're almost, not quite but almost, the same species. We've been asleep in our two space ships and everyone we ever loved on our two planets has been dead for thousands of years. We meet in space and want to make love but we aren't sure if we can. We *look* like people on earth and on the other world, but what will happen if we try? We have to make up a language. We're very intelligent and still as young as ever we were though we've been asleep through most of the history of our planets. We have to find a way to *ask* one another. We'd be like kids, Paul, filled with desire, unable to make the first move. Let's. You make up the first word of our new language. You have to make me understand. We're suspicious, like human lovers at the beginning. We don't touch. . . .'

But Cathy wanted to touch Christopher. All her life she had been stroked, kissed, dressed in clothes so expensive that they were like another skin against her own. She believed that the sense of touch was the key to all the other senses, and she was interested only in sensation. Like the astronauts of her fantasy, she needed speech only to arrange for the opening of the flesh to pleasure. As she lived in her body, Christopher lived in his mind. She knew it. 'I have to know your thoughts,' she told him again and again. 'Whether you want me to or not, I am going to become you,' she said.

On the train, Christopher's body stiffened and he uttered a curse before he could control himself. He had been at the edge of sleep. He had not slept for thirty-six hours, not since before the death of Horst Bülow. It was the memory of Bülow dying that woke him. 'What's the matter?' Cathy whispered.

'Nothing.'

'Did I hurt you?' Cathy had not wanted him to sleep; a moment before he cried out she had bitten him gently. Perhaps the small pain had caused him to remember.

'It's not you,' he said.

Christopher pushed his wife's head away and turned his back. He was trembling. He put his hand over his nose and mouth and turned off the light with his other hand. The train was passing through a station, and there was wind at the window of the compartment and a strip of fitful yellow light around the edge of the drawn shade. Cathy rose to her knees and climbed over him. She crouched on the floor of the compartment, trying to pull his hands away from his face. She was not strong enough and her fingers lost their grip and slipped away. She kept trying, speaking to him.

'Paul, what did I do?'

He shook his head. He wanted to think of something besides Bülow, bleeding into the rainwater, but he could not think about Cathy. The murder repeated itself in his memory; he saw it, detail isolated from detail. Fewer than eighteen hours had passed since the instant of Bülow's death. In that time he had been able to speak to other people calmly, in German, French, and English. He had been able to joke, to buy Cathy a dress, even to perform the sexual act, though his mind did not empty along with the seminal sac. Reporting Bülow's death, he had smiled when Patchen made a joke of it.

Now, as Cathy clawed at his hands, he cursed again. He uncovered his face. There was just enough light to perceive Cathy's form, kneeling before him. She let her arms fall helplessly to her sides. Her breasts, perfectly formed, did not change shape as they moved with the swaying of the train. Cathy kissed his face, gently, moving her lips across his cheek so as to cover every bit of skin with the pressure of her lips.

'Cathy, stop,' Christopher said.

'Something is happening, Paul.'

'Yes, but leave me alone for a minute. I'll be all right.'

Cathy knew what he did for a living. She longed for details but he would give her none; the secrets of his work were like lovers in his past, alive in his mind but invisible to Cathy. Each time he returned from an operation he found her in a state of jealousy. Christopher did not know what she imagined him doing when he went away from her. She worried only about other women; his death, to her, was a smaller danger than that he might go to bed with some unknown girl. She demanded that he not remember ever having made love before they met. She told him that she was without experience, that she had never even felt desire for another man. She wanted him to say that he believed that she had no sexual past. He smiled at her.

She sat with her back against the wall of the compartment, her legs crossed, her feet in her hands. She kept her eyes on Christopher's face. He rose, opened the doors of the washstand, and wiped the sweat from his chest and back with a towel.

'Do you want a drink?' Cathy asked.

'No.'

'I can have the porter bring something.'

'No.'

'What happened?'

'I remembered something.'

'About us?'

'Cathy, sometimes I think of other things.'

'I never do. I don't see how *you* can. Everything that happens has to do with the two of us.'

Christopher, standing, leaned across her and opened the

25

window. She placed both hands around him and drew him gently towards her. He pulled away.

'This is nothing you have to know about,' he said.

'Your mysterious damned work.'

'It's what I do.'

'You ought to write poems again, about yourself if you like. You'd be writing about me if you did that. You'd be happier, Paul.'

Cathy stayed where she was. He could see the effort it caused her. The train was running through a snowstorm. It was very dark, and a stream of cold air blew through the sweltering compartment. Even the fresh air had a burnt smell. Christopher remembered another detail: a shower of blue sparks and the smell of sulphur as the tram, approaching Bülow, crossed a set of points.

Cathy said, 'I've never known before this moment how much I hate what you do. It takes you away all the time, and . . .'

Christopher waited.

'And,' Cathy said, 'it makes you cry out. You won't do that for me.'

Cathy went to sleep at last. Christopher covered her with the sheet and climbed into the upper berth. So long as he was awake, he was able to control what he remembered. When he slept, he dreamt of the murder. In his dream he felt fear for himself and pity for Horst Bülow. Christopher dreamed of himself screaming. On the street in Berlin, Christopher had felt nothing as he watched Bülow die. He could not bring his feelings back to life even in the arms of his wife. The condition could not be explained to Cathy, or to any outsider. They had not lived Christopher's life. It was the only sort of life he wanted to live.

2

Christopher had been back in Rome for a day when the man from the local station phoned. They met an hour later in the Borghese Gardens.

'It isn't often we see you,' the man said. 'We are aware of you,

26

though, as you pass through town on your busy rounds. You covert action types are regular Scarlet Pimpernels.'

'I'm sure you play a useful role, too, at your desk in the Embassy,' Christopher said. 'What can I do for you?'

'For me, nothing. For Security, you can get on a plane and go to Frankfurt. We've had a priority cable for you.'

'Can I see it?'

'Some cables we take out of the Embassy. We're not that fussy about regulations. Cables from Security we read and swallow immediately. They want you to go up tonight and call this number when you get in.' He gave Christopher a slip of paper.

'You're to say you're a friend of Horst's.'

'And they'll say?'

'They'll say Horst is out of town for one day, or two days, or some such. The number corresponds to the time they'll pick you up, in front of the opera house, in a blue BMW with Wiesbaden plates. So if they say he's out of town for three days, you be there at three o'clock. Got it?'

Christopher nodded.

'Have a good trip,' the man said. 'They're *such* nice chaps.'

3

Christopher had left Cathy asleep. She would sleep until he wakened her. Cathy could not wake herself up. She had never had to do so; it was one of the things that others were glad to do for her. She had never properly learned a foreign language, or memorized the streets of the towns in which she lived. She often forgot to carry money. She never wrote letters or made telephone calls. Her beauty made everything possible; others had always given her, unasked, anything that she needed in return for the gift of her appearance.

'I dreamed of us in St Anton,' Cathy said. 'Do you remember the Mooserkreuz? There were flowers painted on the doors of the bedrooms. You were with that black-haired English girl all the time. It's a good thing she had to go back to London when she did. She wouldn't have lived a day longer.'

Cathy had had the head waiter seat her at Christopher's table as soon as he was alone. 'I've heard you speaking German,' she said to him, 'so I know you can get me something to eat. What I want is something *light*, not fried or cooked in lard.'

'You're in the wrong country.'

Cathy found it strange that Christopher asked her no questions. 'Don't you want to know anything about me?' she asked. 'Men are always grilling me from the minute we meet. Do I like Mozart? What kind of skis do I use? Have I tried the local drink? Do I mind cigar smoke? Why do they do that?'

'They're afraid of you,' Christopher said.

'*Afraid* of me!' Cathy cried. 'Why?'

'Because you're beautiful. That frightens men.'

She watched him, wide-eyed and intent, as if she were learning some secret ritual, as he drank from a glass of wine.

'But not you.'

'Maybe when I know you better.'

When she knew more about Christopher she could not understand why they hadn't met sooner. Their mothers had been in the same class at Bryn Mawr, their fathers used the same law firm in New York, Christopher had played baseball and lacrosse against her cousins in school and in college. She was sure they had been aboard the *Queen Mary* at least twice on the same voyages.

'I'm ten years older than you,' Christopher said.

'That's no excuse. You should have fallen in love with me when I was ten, and waited for me to burst into flower.'

Now, a year later in their apartment in Rome, Cathy recited their first conversation. 'I asked you what made you think you were going to know me better, and you said, "Because I'm going to pursue you to the ends of the earth",' Cathy said. She drew a sweater over her head and began to brush her hair. 'Do you remember that?'

'No,' Christopher said. 'I never spoke a line like that in my life.'

'Yes you did,' Cathy said. 'To me. But I'm the one who does all the pursuing. I chase you to Paris, to London. You never stay put.'

Christopher said, 'No, I don't. I have to go somewhere tonight.'

Cathy stopped brushing, her hands still at her hair. 'Where?' she asked.

'To Germany.'

'You've just *been* to Germany.'

'I have to go back.'

'Oh, Paul, Jesus Christ! We've only had about three waking hours together.'

'Cathy, I was only gone overnight the last time.'

'And this time?'

'I don't know. A few days, maybe only a day or two.'

Cathy went to the window. The sun was going down and the lights had been turned on in the streets. The room was in darkness. She opened the sash and the sound of traffic came in with the wet smell of the March night. Christopher saw the Ponte Sant'Angelo with its rows of statues silhouetted in the last of the light, and the battlements of the round castle on the other side of the river. Cathy closed the window and turned round, her head back against the glass, her eyes closed.

'Take me with you,' she said.

'I can't, this time.'

'Paul, I don't like to be alone. I've never been alone before. Never, in my whole life.'

Christopher didn't answer.

Cathy put on her rain coat and tied a scarf under her chin. 'Do we have time to go out for dinner before you go?'

'Yes. We can go to Da Mario if you want to. The game season is almost over.'

She loved this dark restaurant, filled with the aroma of cooking, where pheasants and partridges, boar and deer, hung in the rafters. But she showed no pleasure.

'And afterwards you'll put me in a taxi.'

'Unless you want the car.'

'I want the car.'

Christopher stood up. He gave Cathy a handful of money, large soiled ten-thousand-lira notes. She put them into the pocket of her raincoat without looking at them.

'I want to tell you something, Paul,' she said. 'Lately, sometimes, I've hated being in love with you.'

Three

I

'I hope you don't mind our doing this in a military installation,' the man from Security said. 'It's just more convenient all around.'

Christopher handed the man his wet raincoat. They were in a room on the Army base at Frankfurt.

'I know that Patchen doesn't like you to go inside US installations,' the man said, 'but it's secure here and you'll be all right as long as you keep your head down and look like an American.'

The room was furnished like the sitting room of a hotel suite in a small American city. There were no windows. An electric percolator, on a small table by the wall, deposited a film of steam on the plaster.

The man from Security, after hanging the coats in the closet, strode across the carpet and smiled, offering his hand to Christopher. 'My name is Bud Wilson,' he said. In the car, he hadn't introduced himself or spoken at all after he and Christopher had exchanged greetings. During the ride they had listened to the American Forces Network on the radio, popular music and sports scores. Approaching the gates of the base, Wilson had handed Christopher a wallet containing identification papers for an Army civilian employee named Peter A. Carmichael. Christopher's photograph had been attached to the AGO card and the driver's licence. 'Just in case,' Wilson said. 'Sometimes the MP asks for ID when you come through the gate in a car with German plates.' But the MP had merely given them a snappy salute and waved them through.

Christopher shook hands. Wilson offered Christopher a paper cup filled with coffee and a sandwich wrapped in transparent plastic.

'Tuna,' he said. Christopher ate. He was unused to American food; it tasted odd, not quite as he remembered it. The coffee, sweetened with saccharine, was bitter. Christopher pushed it away. Wilson drank his coffee at a gulp.

'This room is swept regularly,' Wilson said, 'and it's absolutely secure. It's miked but the tape will not be running unless I tell you it is. I'm going to take some notes as we go along. My report will go to the chief of my division, to Patchen as chief of your division, and to the Director's files. No one else will have access. You've done this before, I know, but I want to remind you of the ground rules, okay?'

Wilson had removed his jacket and tie and rolled up the sleeves of his white shirt. He opened his attaché case after working the combination lock, and put a stack of lined file cards on the table between them.

'I also want you to know,' Wilson said, 'that I've read your file. I'm aware of your rank and your record. I'm not here to be disrespectful, but I think you'll agree it'd be a waste of time for the both of us if I called you sir.'

'You can go ahead any time you want.'

'All right. At 02.30 on 25 March 1960 you contacted your asset Q. K. BOWSTRING, true name Horst Heinrich Bülow, on a street called the Wannseebad Weg in West Berlin. You were in a rented car and he was walking. You made a secure contact and, as far as you knew, held a secure meeting in the car lasting until 06.12, at which time the agent got out of your car in Kant Strasse, in sight of the Zoo station of the S-Bahn. At that point, Bülow was struck by a black Opel sedan with West Berlin plates. You drove away after making the assumption that Bülow was dead, parked the rented car near the Hilton, took a taxi to the Tempelhof Airport, and flew out.'

'That's essentially accurate. Between 02.40 and maybe 03.30,

Bülow and I were out of the car, walking on the beach of the Wannsee, about a kilometre from where I picked him up.'

'Why did you do that?'

'Bülow was jumpy. He'd just come from Dresden on the train carrying something incriminating. He wanted to walk, he needed to cool off. Also, I had a rented car and I couldn't be sure it was secure. I knew he'd be more comfortable talking in the open air. Horst was a fellow who worried about bugs.'

'What was the weather?'

'Wind and rain.'

'And you stayed out in that for fifty minutes?'

'Yes.'

'Why didn't you use a safe house?'

'I didn't have access to one.'

'Did you contact the Berlin base about one?'

'They didn't know I was in town. Bülow was our asset, not theirs.'

'What's your procedure for contacting the Berlin base?'

'I don't contact local stations in Europe. It's insecure.'

'Insecure? Because you're a singleton, or what?'

Christopher explained, although Wilson knew the reasons. Christopher and the men in the stations belonged to different parts of the espionage service. The others operated in one country, gathering information. Christopher went everywhere in the world, looking for men who were capable of acting, and making it possible for them to act. Like Rothchild before him, he invented the politics, wrote the propaganda, calmed the fears of men who sometimes rose to lead parties and nations. Like Rothchild, he worked with his mind and his personality; he formed secret friendships. Bribery, coercion, threats were of no use to him; he wanted agents whom he could liberate, through his expertise and his government's money, to be themselves. He was alone, a singleton in the jargon, living under deep cover, with an ordinary passport and no protection from his government. He had been told when he began his work that he would get no credit if he succeeded and no help if he failed. The men in the stations belonged to another breed; they lived within the bureaucracy, they gathered facts, they seldom loved their agents. They defended their territory. They looked on men like Christopher, who had permission to change facts by meddling with history, with suspicion.

'In Berlin, for example,' Christopher said, 'every German policeman above the rank of sergeant knows Barney Wolkowicz is chief of the base. It's best if I don't go out to dinner with him.'

'And no one knows you?'

'Not by true name, the way they know Barney.'

So far, Wilson had written nothing on his file cards. He sat with his elbows on the table, his eyes on his coffee cup, speaking in a flat tone. There were inflections in his voice that made Christopher think that Wilson might once have been in the FBI. He sounded like a policeman.

'How did you schedule meetings with Bülow?'

'There was a standing arrangement. The first Tuesday and the second Thursday of alternating months. Always in Berlin, always in a park – the Grunewald or the Jungfernheide at alternate meetings.'

'The 25th was the last Friday of March.'

'Yes, this was a special meeting. It made Horst very nervous.'

'Why?'

'Horst was nervous by nature,' Christopher said. 'He didn't like meeting a stranger in Dresden and finding an excuse to travel again only fifteen days after he'd been out for his routine meeting. The trip made him sweat. He'd been doing this work for a long time.'

'Did you think he was breaking down?'

'Yes. I was going to recommend that he be terminated, defected to West Germany. We could have found some job for him.'

'What was his cover in the DDR?'

'Horst was an official of their state broadcasting secretariat.'

'Was that his target?'

'Yes, but not for itself, primarily. His job put him in contact with a lot of people from third countries – Bloc types and, lately, Asians and Africans who come to the DDR as visitors. We used him as a spotter. He put us on to some people who turned out to be recruitable and useful.'

'That sounds pretty low risk for him.'

'It was. He'd give us a name and we'd assess the man and make a recruitment five thousand miles away, a year later. Horst had just run out of breath. It makes people nervous, living in a police state.'

Wilson smiled for the first time. 'Your man sounds like a normal agent,' he said. 'What was the handle on him?'

'Horst would have said idealism. He didn't like the Communists; he was annoyed at them for making his life squalid. He carried a lunch in his briefcase still, and he knew that no West German in his position had to do that in 1960. The Occupation was still on in the DDR. That exasperated him. He liked the money. He liked, passionately, the idea of himself as a spy. Horst had a perversion for tradecraft. He couldn't cross the street without looking suspicious.'

Wilson listened impassively to Christopher's replies. The Security man had a habit of shutting his eyes before he asked a question; he was remembering and going over details that had been included in Christopher's written report. He raised each point in the order in which Christopher had typed it on the page. Christopher supposed that Wilson wanted him to realize that he had memorized the report.

Wilson, in a long string of questions, established that Horst Bülow had lived in East Berlin. He traced Bülow's movements, as Bülow had explained them to Christopher, on the night that he had gone from Berlin to Dresden to pick up the Kamensky manuscript. Wilson did not refer to the manuscript by its name; he called it 'the item'.

'Who did Bülow meet in Dresden – who handed him the item?' Wilson asked. He opened his eyes to ask the question and stared at his blank file cards; he had not yet met Christopher's eyes.

'A Soviet, an Army captain named Kalmyk. He was on a short mission to Dresden from his post in Warsaw. He brought the package with him.'

'You exposed your agent to a Soviet Army captain?'

'It was supposed to be a dead-drop – Kalmyk was told to leave the package on the luggage rack of Bülow's compartment in the train. Horst was supposed to swap it for another, identical package. But Captain Kalmyk found himself alone in the compartment with Horst. He saw that Horst had a package identical to his own all ready for the exchange, so he decided to say hello. Kalmyk said he wanted to make sure the package got into the right hands because it was so precious.'

'What did Bülow do?'

Christopher smiled: Jumped out of his skin, he wanted to say, but he held his tongue. He had begun to be wary of Wilson's digressions.

'Horst took the package, said thank you, and got off at Dresden. According to him, he sauntered across to the other platform and took the Berlin express in the opposite direction five minutes later.'

'What was in the package?'

Christopher did not reply.

Wilson didn't repeat the question. 'Do you know?' he asked.

'Yes.'

'Who else knows? Did Bülow know?'

'He may have looked at it, but that wouldn't have told him much. I don't know what Captain Kalmyk told him. He doesn't seem to have been very careful about what he said.'

Wilson wrote on a file card for the first time – the name 'Kalmyk'.

'Now,' he said. 'Bülow was under discipline. But not Kalmyk or anyone else who brought the Kamensky manuscript out of the Soviet Union. Is that right?'

Christopher waited, a long moment, until Wilson lifted his eyes. 'That's correct,' Christopher said.

Wilson wrote on a file card.

2

Wilson rubbed his face, massaging the sockets of his eyes. His pallid skin was shiny from recent shaving. He emitted a faint odour that Christopher, searching his memory and catching the scent of his grandfather, braces hanging as he shaved, identified as bay rum. The fingers of Wilson's right hand had been broken, the forefinger so often that the nail was twisted almost at right angles to the knuckle.

'Did you play baseball in school?' Christopher asked.

Wilson lifted his damaged hand. 'I played all my life. I caught Class C ball, the Canadian–American League, when I was studying law.' He paused. 'I couldn't hit the curve above Class C,' he said. 'That's why I'm here, instead of batting .350 for the Red Sox.'

When Wilson was not asking questions he lapsed into a kind of street speech. He made deliberate mistakes in English, hardened his consonants. He said 'ch' for 'g' and 'd' for 'th'. He wore a light green gabardine suit that was too large in the shoulders and too wide in the lapels, and brown shoes and ankle socks; his

35

muscular bare calves showed when he crossed his legs. On his left hand he wore a wide golden wedding band; he had set out, on the table beside the sofa bed, a photograph in a leather frame of his wife with two babies on her lap and three older children posed around her. Wilson insisted on semaphoring what had made him: a double house on a street in a factory town, parochial school, Legion baseball, Boston College, the infantry, law school at night, marriage, the FBI, and now the Security Division. Christopher thought that Wilson must find it hard to deal with men from Christopher's side of the outfit, with whom he could not sympathize at all.

'I don't understand why you're so reticent about this book that Bülow carried to Berlin for you,' Wilson said.

'It's a sensitive operation.'

'You didn't think I'd have a need to know?'

'Yes, but telling you would be Patchen's decision, not mine.'

'Berlin doesn't know?'

'Once again, no. It's a covert action project.'

'Do you guys tell anybody anything?'

'Wilson, that's a frivolous question. We both know what the rules are and what compartmentization is. We both know what the resentments are. The stations don't like us because we operate on their territory and take the credit, and incidentally the blame, for the results. If you want to talk about the conflict between the CA mission and the collection of intelligence, we can. But it's off the subject.'

Wilson listened without expression. 'And you,' he said, 'are a busy man.'

'I'm a man who doesn't like to lose agents.'

Wilson, lost in thought, tapped the table with his blunt fingers, a quick march rhythm. Christopher wondered if one of Wilson's pretty female children, back home in some Virginia suburb, might be a majorette.

'I'll tell you, Paul,' Wilson said, using Christopher's given name for the first time, 'so far it makes no sense to me at all. Why kill Bülow? He was a low-grade asset. He would have talked if they'd snatched him. They could have had him peaceably when he went back to East Berlin. He'd already made the delivery. It was a stupid risk. You know all this as well as I do.'

'Yes.'

'Then why? What do you think?'

'You'd have to know who did it. If it was the Russians, and they knew what Horst had collected from Kalmyk, then it would be a warning. They'd be saying don't go any farther if you don't want your principal damaged.'

'The accepted Headquarters theory is that the Russians don't indulge in wet work the way they used to,' Wilson said. 'The thinkers back home have decided that the Soviets are hungry for respectability. They want to be like us – too great a power to stoop to violence.'

'I know.'

'Do you believe it?'

'Sure. They have the Czechs and the Poles and the East Germans if they need them.'

Wilson's manner warmed. The methods of the opposition, murder and blackmail and kidnapping, were his specialty; he was a scholar, speaking to another scholar.

'You think it might have been one of the satellite services?'

'It's possible. The East Germans could have thought it was a way to upset our stomachs. Horst could easily have blown himself to them.'

'You didn't have much respect for him, did you?'

'I knew his weaknesses. If they watched him, they would have suspected what he was doing just by the way he sneaked around.'

'Couldn't you train that out of him?'

'By the time I got him he was set in his ways. He was a born amateur.'

'But you liked him.'

Again, Christopher waited until Wilson lifted his eyes. 'I was responsible for him,' he said.

'You still are,' Wilson said.

3

Hours later, Wilson came back into the room with more coffee and sandwiches. 'Are you tired?' he asked.

'Not yet.'

'It's practically morning. Without windows, you don't notice.' Wilson unwrapped a sandwich and ate it.

Wilson took a file folder from his attaché case and slid it across the table to Christopher. 'Photographs,' he said. A child's crayon drawing lay on top of the material inside the file; Wilson took it back with an apologetic smile. He chewed, licking mustard from his fingers, as Christopher looked at the police photographs of Bülow's corpse, lying in the street in its long stained overcoat, then naked on a slab in the morgue. The skin was white as talcum under the strong light, and Horst's broken spine gave his body the emaciated look of a corpse in a death camp, thrown contemptuously into a corner, the first of a great heap.

'What does all that tell us?' Christopher asked, giving back the photographs.

Wilson put his fingertips against his heart. 'That you can go from this to that in less than a second. You watched it happen.'

They had been talking for almost ten hours. Wilson had gone over the details again and again, covering his file cards with one crabbed notation after another. He wiped his mouth with a crumpled paper napkin, yawned and stretched.

'Now the real work begins,' he said. 'I hate to think of the hours this is going to cost.'

Wilson took another sandwich and chewed it eagerly, as if the long hours of concentration had drained his body of nourishment. He cast his eyes downward again. Christopher wondered why a man with Wilson's specialty should be so embarrassed to ask direct questions. Wilson wiped his lips with a Kleenex, cleared his throat.

'One last aspect we have to cover, a very, very remote thing,' he said.

Christopher didn't help Wilson. There was a silence.

'Your wife,' Wilson said.

Christopher thought of Cathy for the first time since he left her in Rome.

'She was in Paris while you were in Berlin?' Wilson asked.

Christopher nodded.

'She knows people there?' Wilson asked.

'She's lived there, off and on, most of her life. You have all that on the file.'

'Untrained people like your wife think they have to explain everything. Would she mention where you were, that you were in Berlin, to an outsider?'

'She might,' Christopher said. 'I'll ask her.'

'Do that.'

Wilson had drawn his chair closer to Christopher's for this exchange. When he looked up and smiled, parting his tight lips over his teeth, his eyes came into focus. He seemed to be seeing Christopher for the first time, as if his status as Cathy's husband had made him visible.

'I *hate* it when families get mixed up with the work,' Wilson said.

Wilson put his papers back into his attaché case, and locked the case itself in a safe concealed in the night stand where the picture of his family stood. He straightened the frame, smiled at the photograph.

'Someone wanted to do poor old Horst harm,' Wilson said. 'Who knew him? On our side, you knew him, Patchen knew of him. The Berlin base knew of him. Otto Rothchild knew of him.'

'That's your short list of suspects?'

Wilson remained as he was, on his knees by the safe. He worked the combination again and put the photograph of his family inside.

'That's the list of people who might have been careless,' he said. 'Once I had a job where I arrested people for murder or filed charges against 'em for being accessories before the fact. But I wasn't chasing Harvard boys in those days. The worst you guys can do is to be found guilty of a security violation.'

'And if nobody is guilty of that?'

Wilson looked at his damp palms, wiped them on the carpet. 'Somebody will be. Those guys in the black Opel had to know where Bülow would be, and at exactly what time. They had to find out somehow.'

Wilson handed Christopher his raincoat. He had looked at the label when he hung it up, hours before. Now he ran his eye over Christopher's standing figure, the English shoes, the Brooks Brother's suit, the plain tie. He was amused. He touched his own stomach. Wilson was as tall as Christopher but not so muscular; his brawn was already going to fat, though he was, like Christopher, still in his thirties.

'Are you guys going to run this operation anyway, to see what happens?' Wilson asked.

'Ask Patchen.'

'Of course you're going to, Paul. You think there's a cheat in the officers' club, don't you?'

Wilson went to get his own coat; he did not expect an answer. Finally he unlocked the door and led Christopher out of the building, into a cold rain that glistened in the rays of the mercury lights that still burned in the parking lot at seven in the morning.

4

After they had passed through the gates of the Army post and were back on German territory, Wilson held out his right hand while he steered with his left. Christopher gave him back the wallet containing the false documentation. Wilson, shifting his eyes from the road, flipped the plastic windows to make certain that all the papers were still in the wallet. He switched on the radio and moved the dial until he had the early news on the American station; he turned the volume high. He sat squarely in the driver's seat, shifting and steering with great sureness, like a fine rider on a horse that trusts the man in the saddle.

'It's harder than you think, killing a man with a vehicle,' he said. 'It's got to be done just right.'

They were passing through the outlying streets of the town, past grey buildings, under rows of young plane trees pruned for the winter so that they looked like cactus growing in the wrong country. Wilson asked, again, for the details of Bülow's death. Christopher remembered no noise at all; the Opel had lifted Bülow, almost gently, out of the place where he had been alive and put him down in the place where he was dead.

'That was because they hit him square, with the bumper and the radiator,' Wilson said. 'Probably there was a thud, but you wouldn't have heard it in your car with the windows closed. He hit solid metal. There must have been very little damage to the Opel. In the old days, the opposition used to like to crush the victim into a wall. Fly-swatting, it was called. It's surer, but sometimes they'd bang the car up so bad they'd have to leave it, boiling water running out of the radiator all over the corpse, and leg it out of there through the ruins.'

'But they've changed technique.'

Wilson nodded. 'We wondered why. We had a defector, one of their case officers from Berlin, and we asked him. He said they'd gotten a lot of static from their finance about the cost of smashing up cars. That was post-war, when they had captured a whole bunch of German vehicles whose owners could not, shall we say, be traced. So they were killing people with nice old Mercedeses and BMW's that were state property. They had to retrain the drivers.'

Wilson cleared his throat. 'Q. K. BOWSTRING met a professional,' he said.

Now that they had left the secure environment of the Army base, Wilson had ceased using true names. He would speak of Patchen as your friend back home; Bülow as Q. K. BOWSTRING, Rothchild as the fellow who had the operation.

'I'm not telling you anything you don't know,' Wilson said abruptly. 'There are only two ways to go. We talk to everyone at our end. Probably that will produce nothing. You, for example, don't seem to make mistakes.'

'What about the other end?'

'Well, that's a little trickier. Maybe we can put the daisy chain together – find out who carried the package and where to. Then do name checks on everyone. We can watch the fellow your man talked to on the train and see what happens to him.'

'What's your guess?'

Wilson looked steadily into the rear-view mirror. A car in the street behind them made a right turn. Wilson, too, turned right, and arrived at the intersection of the next parallel street in time to watch the other automobile park in the driveway of a house. A woman wearing a belted coat got out of the car and walked quickly into the house. Wilson grunted and drove on.

'Guessing is a waste of time. We'll see. That chain of couriers may go off like a string of firecrackers. If so, that's the end of your friend the scribbler at the other end. It would be logical to expect that.'

'Not so logical. If they make a martyr of him, that would be good from our point of view. They'd want to avoid unfavourable propaganda.'

'They could leave him alone, and still blow up all the post offices. They wouldn't want all those guys hanging around waiting for the next masterpiece to come into the pipeline.'

'Yes, they could do that.'

'Let's see if they do. We'll look for blood on the snow.'

Wilson pointed at the sky to the west. A silver aeroplane dropped into a bank of ground fog on the approach to the airport. They heard its engines fade, then resume power. The same plane rose out of the fog and made a steep climbing turn. 'I've been watching them do that for the last five miles,' Wilson said. 'You may not get out on the early flight.'

'I can have breakfast and read the paper.'

'Don't talk about this to the fellow who had the operation,' Wilson said. 'I want to make my own contact with him.'

'All right.'

'We go back to the war, the old days. He and I knew each other. We were worlds apart then, of course.'

'He hasn't changed, except for his illness.'

'I'm not surprised,' Wilson said.

In the airport parking lot, Wilson pulled the car into a space in a long rank of empty vehicles. He turned in the seat, using the steering wheel to help shift his bulky body in the small passenger compartment. He shook hands. The gesture surprised Christopher.

'There's one thing,' Wilson said. 'I know how you are, because I've read everything we have on you. You have this reputation for never giving up, for going after things. Don't do it this time.'

'Why?'

Wilson drummed a parade rhythm on the steering wheel. 'Just don't go looking for them. Just leave it alone,' he said. 'You're out in the open, like your friend was when he was waiting for the tram. Somebody knew about him, somebody knew where he'd be. That's all it takes.'

Wilson turned his head and Christopher saw him full face for the first time. The overheated passenger compartment of the BMW smelled, as the room on the Army base had smelled, of bay rum, Brylcreem, tuna sandwiches, American coffee, American cigarettes. Christopher wondered if he smelled, to Wilson, like a member of another race. Wilson winked at him.

Four

I

Otto Rothchild refused the costume and the manners of the invalid. He wore a grey tweed jacket and an open shirt with a silk scarf at his neck. Maria had crossed his right leg over his left, and the perfect crease in his flannel trousers had been arranged so that four inches of dark blue stocking showed between the cuff and the top of his suede shoes. He sat in a high-backed chair, with his head pressed against the upholstery and his hands clasped. Before the surgeon had severed his nerves, Rothchild had trembled in moments of excitement. Afterwards, his body lost the power of involuntary movement. He sat very still, moving his lips only. The loss of his gestures was very strange; the Rothchild who confronted Christopher was like an impersonator who had not got things quite right: the telling characteristics were missing. Still, Christopher thought, the man had not changed in any important way. He had lost energy, not intelligence. The surgery had given him back the use of his mind; he could control his thoughts again, now that the blood no longer pumped itself without warning into his brain. From his chair, alert and wary, he watched Christopher.

Christopher said, 'Have you had a chance to read Kamensky's book?'

'Some of it,' Otto Rothchild replied. 'It's very long. Kamensky has tried to put fifty years of Russia, everything about it and everything about himself, into one novel. No one will ever be able to comprehend it all.'

'What do you think?'

Rothchild began to speak. Midway through a sentence his throat dried; a healthy man would have cleared it or coughed. Rothchild unaware of what was happening, went on speaking, his lips moving silently as bits of his sentence disappeared.

'. . . . work of genius,' he said. 'Of course Kamensky has always had it in him, no Russian of my generation had such gifts . . . curious old-fashioned quality to it, not just the language but the attitudes. Paul, he writes like Tolstoy or like Lawrence in English . . . clumsy language, a kind of invincible stupidity so that everything they observe, though it's worn and familiar to a normal man, is an incredible surprise to them. They make us see life through the eyes of a fool, so we see it as it really is. Only the greatest writers have that gift.'

Rothchild closed his eyes; a smile came on to his face. Maria looked at him without anxiety.

'Otto has read almost all of it,' she said. 'It's terribly exciting for him. He reads himself unconscious, day after day.'

'Unconscious?'

'Yes. When he does too much, has too much excitement, he just drops off. He's done it now. It was scary at first, but I've learned he'll come out of it and go right on with what he was doing.'

'Isn't it bad for him, the excitement?'

'Being turned into a wreck by that operation was bad for him. He's happy again. I turn the pages for him. He reads like the wind. "Turn, Maria, turn!" he says. His eyes gallop down the page. It's as if he expects to find something; it's like a chase.'

Christopher glanced at Rothchild's figure, collapsed in the chair, the smile still on his lips.

'What do you think Otto's looking for in Kamensky's book?' he asked.

'Himself,' Maria said. 'What else could it be?'

'The amazing thing is,' Maria said, 'Otto's mind is better than it's ever been. He can only stay conscious for ten minutes or so, if he's working with his brain, but he's so lucid in those periods that it's practically supernatural. He's been relieved of his anger. To that extent, the operation accomplished what the doctors promised.'

Rothchild opened his eyes. 'This novel,' he said, 'if we handle it correctly, will shake the world. It's a matter of designing the right operation, Paul. You and David and I can do it. Headquarters must be kept out of it as much as possible. Those people are bulls in the china shop. They don't understand the world. They don't have to live with what is done.'

'David is at Headquarters.'

'Yes, but he has the power to put Headquarters's trust in you and me.'

Rothchild's eyes moved from Christopher's face to Maria's. He tapped his thigh with the reading glasses he held in his hand. Maria poured Elvian water into a crystal wine glass and held it to her husband's lips. Rothchild made little noises as he drank. She masked his face with her body, but Christopher saw that she was holding a napkin under Rothchild's chin, and wiping away the drops of water that ran from the corners of his mouth.

'The first translation,' Rothchild said, 'must not be into English. Do you agree?'

Christopher said, 'If we publish.'

Maria sat beside Christopher on the sofa. He felt her body stiffen as he spoke. She threw Rothchild a glance, but he ignored her.

'*If* we publish?' Rothchild said. 'We will publish.'

'What are Kamensky's wishes?'

'Kamensky? What does Kamensky know? When he came back from Spain they locked him up for twenty-two years. Politically, he's a deaf man. He always was.'

'So are a lot of artists, Otto. But this is his book. It's not ours.'

Rothchild's voice vanished and Maria gave him more water.

'A book such as this is not anyone's property,' Rothchild said. 'It's a work of art. Or will be. Now it is merely the seedbed of a work of art.'

'Meaning what?'

Rothchild moved, very slightly, inclining his body towards Christopher.

'Kamensky has done his work, Paul. He's covered a thousand pages with his handwriting. Wonderful work, all of the Russian horror is there. But to be completed, it must be read. Any novel is a collaboration between the writer and the public. The author is the camera, his work is the film. It must be developed in other human brains, over and over again. Only a fool would say we won't publish.'

'A fool,' Christopher said, 'or someone who thought that we had a duty to protect Kamensky.'

'Protect him?'

'He's still behind the Curtain. Otto, he's only been out of prison for a year. He was in the camps from 1937.'

Rothchild took a moment to compose himself. What right had Christopher, an American, to speak of the camps? Rothchild said, 'Yes, and knowing the worst, having lived through it, he sent me his novel. Why do you think he did that?'

'For safekeeping, as David understood it.'

'Maybe that was what Kamensky told himself. Very possibly that's what he told himself, if I remember Kamensky.'

Rothchild's voice was neutral; he was assessing Kamensky as an asset, not expressing contempt for a friend. He kept friendship and professional behaviour in separate compartments.

'What exactly did he tell you, in his letter?' Christopher asked.

Rothchild closed his eyes. They sat in silence in the elegant room. Rothchild's narrow brown shoe lay on the Kerman Ravar carpet. Books, written by his friends but unsigned, bound in leather, lined the shelves. 'Men like you and me cannot keep photographs,' Rothchild had once told Christopher, 'every one of these objects suggests a friend.' Behind him on the wall hung a sketch with which Picasso had paid the bill in a restaurant owned by one of Rothchild's friends; the artist had scribbled the line of a cheek, an empty human eye, the movement of a gull, on the back of the bill, and the column of addition on the front had begun to show through the drawing.

Rothchild's lips moved. 'Kamensky asked me to put the book away until he dies,' he said.

'You don't think he meant it?'

46

'I don't know what he meant, Paul. I'd like to get a message to him.'

'Saying what?'

Rothchild smiled. His eyes were open, but they were looking into the past.

'Saying "Choose fame",' he said.

'And what would Kamensky reply?'

Rothchild stirred.

'*Yes.* That's what Kamensky would say, Paul. Like Molly Bloom, he would whisper, "*Yes, oh yes yes.*" When he was young, when I knew him better than anyone, he was a devourer of life. Yes was always his answer.'

Maria watched anxiously as Rothchild's body slumped in the chair. His head fell slightly to one side. She went to him, touched his forehead, lifted his leg from his other knee and placed both of his feet on the floor.

'This time he's asleep,' she said. 'I'll cover him. He may doze for hours.'

Maria adjusted the blanket, tucking it around Rothchild's lax frame, and removed the shoes from his bony feet.

3

'You're right, Otto is not what he was,' Patchen said. 'Since the surgery, I have the feeling that he's in the spirit world and I'm talking to him on the telephone.'

Christopher had met Patchen in a safe house a few blocks from the Embassy. One of the station's secretaries lived in the apartment. Patchen had gone through each room like a cat, observing everything. On a stiff forefinger, he lifted the girl's quilted dressing gown from a hook on the bathroom door, and looked at the faint line of dirt on the collar without expression. 'No sex life, obviously,' he said.

In the living room Patchen opened a cabinet and removed a bottle of Scotch whisky. 'Ours, I presume,' he said. He went into kitchen. Christopher heard the sound of ice being broken out of the metal compartments of a freezer tray. Patchen returned with two glasses of Scotch.

'Otto has given me a complete operational proposal,' he said. 'It would work. Otto's proposals always work. Or almost always.'

'What does he tell you he wants?'

'What he always wants. Humiliation for the opposition, secret satisfaction for us. Otto and you and I will create a world best-seller, maybe even an immortal classic. And no one will know we did it. Another prank. The three of us tittering after lights out.'

'And Kamensky in his grave,' Christopher said.

Patchen waved the sentence away. 'That probably wouldn't happen. Anyway, it's not an operational consideration.'

Christopher began to speak before Patchen finished; he had known what the words would be without hearing them. Patchen listened to Christopher with even less surprise.

Christopher said, 'It's an important operational consideration. If the KGB kills Kamensky, or locks him up, we'd love it. You couldn't buy the publicity that would create. He'd be a martyr.'

'Yes. It would be nice to have world opinion on Kamensky's side.'

'Wouldn't it be on his side anyway?'

Patchen jerked his head, as if calling Christopher's attention to the world outside curtained windows of the safe house.

'You haven't read the book,' he said. 'Kamensky eviscerates the Soviet, from the days of the old Bolsheviks down to Khrush-chev. Every Communist saint is in the book, with blood on his chin. He has Beria shitting his pants from overeating at a feast with Stalin during the war when the Russian people were starving in the snow. It's the most vicious thing I've ever read, and it rings with truth. Kamensky has impeccable credentials. He was one of the first members of the Party. He was there. And he's a great writer. Everyone knows those things about him.'

'I see.'

'Yes. I wonder if we can get away with publishing it. I think the whole intellectual establishment in the West will come down on Kamensky like a ton of bricks.' Patchen wanted no interruptions. 'Otto thinks the intellectuals can be handled,' he said. 'He wants to find a way to make them read Kamensky's book as something other than what it is. In fact, it is an act of treason to their illusions. If the book is published cold, they'll want to hang Kamensky for it in the press. They're just getting over their embarrassment about Hungary. They want to believe

48

that Khrushchev is the man who'll make the future work. The Mechanic-Messiah.'

'What does Otto suggest?'

'He's still turning it over in his mind. Actually, he's turning it over in his intestines. Otto has always been an instinctive operator. He *feels* results before they come about.' Patchen coughed into his handkerchief. 'That's why he likes to work with you,' he said. 'You're just like him.'

Patchen held out his glass to Christopher. He would not have asked another subordinate to wait on him. Christopher had been his friend since the war; he knew what pain it cost Patchen to rise from a chair. The two of them lived for secrets, but this was the only personal secret between them. Christopher made Patchen's drink; the whisky melted the tiny French ice cubes before Patchen could lift the glass to his lips.

Patchen drank and laughed. 'You know,' he said, 'visiting Otto the other day it crossed my mind what a trio we make. You're his intellectual heir, he thinks. And he and I are heirs to the misfortunes of the flesh.'

'I'm not quite Otto's spiritual double.'

'I know that. But Otto thinks he's trained you up to be a paragon of operational skill and virtue. Otto, if you listen to him talk, is always betraying his belief that people are born on the day they meet him.'

'Yes, and die when he sees the last of them.'

Patchen lifted his glass again. When he spoke, he still had whisky in his throat, and the distortion made him sound as if he were speaking through a chuckle.

'You're describing the perfect secret agent,' he said.

4

Patchen had been in Paris for a week. He could stay away from Headquarters no longer. Rothchild had made him uncomfortable. 'Otto's ego has been reborn,' he told Christopher, 'he's full of ideas again. He takes it for granted we'll do things his way.' Twice, Rothchild had asked to see Patchen alone. On both occasions he had discussed Christopher as if Christopher were the agent and Rothchild the case officer. 'He's using everything on me – the past,

49

his illness, what he calls his friendship for Kamensky,' Patchen said. 'He told me, "Paul is a wonderful boy, everyone admires him, but he's timid about risking agents, and he doesn't understand the Russian mind."' Rothchild had a legitimate claim on the operation: he had brought Kamensky and his manuscript into the house, after all, and he had conceived the plan. But he wanted it too much, and that was reason enough for Patchen to deny it to him.

'You've got to run it,' Patchen told Christopher. 'Otto can't, he's lost too much of what he used to be.' Patchen smiled affectionately. 'He hasn't lost so much, Paul, that he won't try to take it away from you.'

'Do you think we can stop him doing that?'

'We can limit what he does without telling us. After all, he's not Jack-Be-Nimble any longer.'

'He has Maria.'

'Maria is under disipline.'

'Still?'

'She hasn't lost the habit of trusting us.'

'She's Otto's wife.'

'She's one of us. Whom do *you* trust more, Cathy or the outfit?'

Rothchild, Christopher thought, does not understand the American mind. To Patchen he said, 'In the Tuileries, the other day, you used the word ghosts.'

'Did I?'

'Yes. You were talking about Otto's assets. You realize that Kamensky is just that to Otto – a ghost? He thinks of him as having been dead for twenty years, or however long it's been since he saw him last. He knows he'll never see Kamensky again.'

'That would be like Otto. Does Kamensky have some greater reality for you?'

'No. Not yet.'

'But you expect to be seized by fellow-feeling before all this is over?'

'Maybe not before it's over. Afterwards. So will you, David.'

Patchen put on his coat and hat and prepared to go. 'There's no point in planning just now,' he said. 'I wish you'd think quietly about this, away from Otto, for a week or two. Read the Russian manuscript. I'll get a translation to you as soon as I can, maybe in a couple of weeks if I can put a team on it. I'd like you to do the final polish.'

'What about the planning?'

'I won't brief Paris or Rome just yet. I guess Berlin will know pretty much what's going on, with that fellow Wilson plodding around.'

'Yes. He doesn't like covert action ops.'

'I know. He doesn't like F I ops, either. Whether it's us or the stations, we cause him trouble.'

'I wonder how he'll get along with Otto.'

Patchen hesitated. 'So do I,' he said. 'He discovered something in the file. Otto, in all these years, has never been fluttered.'

'That's impossible.'

'I would have thought so, but it's true. Otto has always been a contract agent, it seems, and regulations don't require the box for that category of employee unless it's requested for security reasons. I suppose no one ever wanted to offend Otto. So he escaped the ordeal.'

'That must bother Security.'

'That's a mild way to describe it,' Patchen said. 'Otto was born a Russian, he spent his whole youth fooling around with every leftist cause in Europe, he drank schnapps in Berlin with members of the Red Orchestra.'

'What are they going to do?'

'Flutter Otto. How can we possibly know if he's told us the truth about *anything* if we haven't buckled a lie detector on him and asked him whether he's ever had a blow job or taken money from the opposition?'

'You'll approve that?'

Patchen shrugged. 'Security is a law unto itself. What would I say? That Otto is a dying man? They'd reply that in that case they'd better hurry.'

5

Maria Rothchild was waiting in the open door of the apartment when Christopher reached the top of the stairs. She wore a white pleated skirt; she had the smooth legs of a tennis player, still faintly sunburnt even in winter. Christopher did not think of her as a member of the opposite sex. They had known one another always as fellow professionals. What they had in common was their work, and a way of thinking that grew out of their work. When Maria had first come to Europe and begun to work with Christopher, the wife of a station officer had tried to make a match of them. She had invited them both for a weekend at a rented country house, and Christopher remembered how startled he had been by a rush of sexual feeling when he had encountered her, skin gleaming with oil in the noonday sun, beside the swimming pool. She had a lovely body, and he had seen amusement in her eyes when she observed his surprise on finding it stretched out in a bikini. The idea of seduction had passed in and out of Christopher's mind in a moment, but he and Maria had, without regret, remained colleagues.

'I didn't want you to ring,' Maria said now. 'Otto is up. I want to talk to you before you see him.'

They went inside. Maria closed the huge oak door softly and led Christopher into the kitchen. She closed another door behind them, and turned on the radio.

'Speak softly,' she said. 'It's odd, but he hears much better than he did before. One sense compensating for the loss of another, I suppose.'

She pointed at a tray of liquor bottles and raised her eyebrows in inquiry. Christopher shook his head. Maria gave herself a glass of vodka.

'We've had a visit from Security,' Maria said. 'A man who told Otto his name was Bud Watson. David told us to expect somebody named Wilson. He's an apelike creature in a Robert Hall suit. He massages his face when he's confused and can't look anyone in the eye.'

'Watson?'

'Yes. These Headquarters types can never remember what cover name they're supposed to use. I used to see him in the halls back home when I carried files from one temporary building to another. His name is not Wilson *or* Watson.'

'Wharton,' Christopher said. 'His true name is Wharton. When I saw him, he had a crayon drawing by one of his children in his briefcase. It was signed Debbie Wharton, love to Daddy.'

'What does he want?'

'What did he ask you for?'

'That's the problem. Nothing, really. He just chatted to Otto about how they knew each other after the war. He hinted that he'd run the security check on Otto before he was recruited. Otto doesn't remember him.'

'I thought Otto never forgot anyone.'

Maria had been standing, buttocks against the kitchen sink, with her arms crossed. She unfolded them and, hiding a smile, gave Christopher a cool, level look. Something in Christopher's tone had awakened her training, taken her back into their professional style. She was an agent even before she was a member of her sex. Christopher was the same. She treated him as another woman might treat an old lover, encountered by chance in a place where they had been together years before. A remark, a touch of the hand, a smile turns the eye towards the past, upon scenes that only the two of them know. Friendship becomes passion again. She goes matter-of-factly to bed with him, and then returns home, guiltless, to make supper for her children and her husband.

'Total recall is one of Otto's conceits,' Maria said. 'In fact he only remembers people who gratify him. Otto's not one to store the memory of a man who never did anything important.'

'How did the two of them get on?'

'All right. Otto condescended to him, because of the appearance Wilson-Watson-Wharton made in his cheap clothes. The man liked that. The contempt of others gives him an edge.'

Maria, bright-eyed, watched the smile of admiration form on Christopher's lips; they saw the same things in other people, and liked each other for it. She touched Christopher, a fingertip on his arm.

'What's going on?' she asked.

'David told you nothing?'

'Nothing.'

Christopher fixed his eyes on Maria's. 'Horst Bülow brought the manuscript out of the DDR. He was killed after he delivered the package to me.'

Maria frowned, compressed her lips. She closed her eyes tightly for an instant, as if she remembered, or foresaw, something. She knew Bülow – not as a person, Christopher thought, but as a man in the files. She knew him better, having read his reports, and the reports about him, than she would know her own child, if she ever had one.

'Am I to tell Otto about this?' she asked.

'Use your own judgement. Is the Security type coming back?'

'Yes, tomorrow. Otto can only take him for about twenty minutes at a time. He'll have to return several times, unless he takes a night course in coming to the point.'

'*He'll* have to tell Otto eventually. That's what the investigation is about.'

Maria, without asking Christopher if he wanted it, made him a drink, and another for herself. They stood face to face in the dim kitchen. In their silences, the motor of the old refrigerator laboured noisily.

'There's no way to spare Otto any of this?' Maria said.

It was not a question, and Christopher did not answer. Maria finished her drink quickly, dumped the ice cubes into the sink, rinsed her glass.

'Is the investigation about anything else, besides the murder of the asset?' Maria asked.

Christopher said, 'Maria, come on.'

'It's about everything,' she said. 'Of course it is. Otto's last operation. What a way to end a career like his, being required to remember everything for a man in a forty-dollar suit.'

Five

I

In Rome the winter rains were over. Christopher, riding into town from the airport, rolled down the window of the taxi. Even at four in the morning, the air was balmy and he could smell the earth of the farmlands along the Via Ostiense. He looked out the rear window of the speeding taxi and saw that the long straight road behind him, with the moon at the end of it going down into the sea, was empty. He had slept and eaten too little and drunk too much, and was left with a bitter taste in his mouth and a ringing in his ears. The operation, like the imagined form of a child not yet born, passed through his mind, a series of pictures: Kamensky's tattered manuscript, Rothchild in his tall chair, Maria Rothchild with tradecraft bringing the light of passion back into her face, Patchen's cold even voice. And beyond that the future, with Christopher himself moving from place to place, talking, acting out the patterns of deceit that only he could execute because he possessed the talent that Otto Rothchild had once had, the gift of inspiring trust in others. Saying goodbye before he went to Zürich for his surgery, Rothchild had been especially garrulous, telling tales of agents he had had to sacrifice. 'Betrayal is an act of strength, Paul,' he had told Christopher; 'a man with your gifts

55

will learn, in time, to disguise it as an act of love, and you'll be astonished to find how much more you'll be loved, afterwards, by the person you betray. Human beings are perverse creatures.' Maria, seated on the floor beside Rothchild's chair, traced the pattern in the carpet as her husband spoke; Rothchild stroked her hair. Her cheeks burned. In the hall, as Christopher left, she told him that Rothchild, though he had never said so even to her, believed that he was going to die in Zürich. 'I know,' Maria had said, 'because he talks about all the times he's almost died in the past, and mentions the things he's ashamed of in his life. Betrayals, Paul, and failures.' Christopher had touched her eyelids gently with his knuckle; when she spoke to him of Rothchild, she had a way of closing her eyes.

Now, Christopher saw Bülow die again, and knew that he would see this picture once an hour, awake and asleep, until the Kamensky operation was over. Afterwards, he would see it only when he was very tired, or when he glimpsed a man in the street who had one of Horst's foolish mannerisms. All the images he had just seen began to flash through his mind again, in slightly different order. Christopher stopped them running and cleared his head.

By the time the taxi passed through the wall of the city at Porta San Pãolo there was a light in the east. The streetlights were still burning; the city smelled of coffee and flowers and crowds. 'You said Lungotevere,' the driver said. 'Where on the Lungotevere?' Christopher gave him an address ten blocks from his own apartment.

Christopher, alone, strolled along the Tiber. His bones ached. Years before he had been shot in the knee and when he was tired the wound throbbed; compared to Patchen's injuries, the bad knee was nothing, but the pain reminded him that he had a body. From childhood, Christopher had had a tendency to forget that he existed in physical form; he came out of his mind only for brief periods, as an animal will come out of its burrow, in order to eat or make love. He felt pleasure with great intensity but he did not desire pleasure all the time, as Cathy did. He thought of it only when he was in the midst of it.

The light increased; he walked on to a bridge, the Ponte Sisto, and watched the domes of the city out of the shadows, taking on mass at first, and then, gradually as the sun rose, colour. The sun's heat could not yet be felt on the skin, but it was stirring the mist

56

on the Tiber. Pigeons, roosting on the bridge and almost the colour of its stones, stirred and began to murmur. In the limpid light, which lasted only for moments before the full sunrise, each building, each line of roof became distinct. Church and palace and house drifted apart, as a couple asleep in the same bed will drift into dreams, and become what each really is until they wake. The sun rose above the horizon; Rome flowed together again, hues of rose and terra cotta. Christopher began to hear the sounds of traffic, music from radios, dishes clattering.

He walked away from the river to a coffee bar near the Piazza Navona that he knew to be open early. He was the first customer. The sleepy fat girl at the cash register took his money and gave him the printed stub from the machine. At the bar, he drank a double *caffè latte* and ate a bun. When he went back outside, the day had begun. The narrow street was filled with people, and the cool new air, which had been so still only half an hour before, quivered with the sound of their voices.

2

The bed in Christopher's apartment was empty. It was neatly made, as the maid had left it the day before. Cathy's clothes, the ones she had worn during the day, were scattered across the bedroom floor. She had left the bathroom light on, and a brush filled with her hair lay on the sink. She wore no make-up, used no hairpins, so she left little trace of herself, except for a trail of clothes, and dishes and glasses still half-filled with the food and drink she had thought she wanted but could almost never finish. There was no note. Christopher, remembering her angry mood when he had left her two nights before, opened her closet. Her clothes and shoes were where they had been, her suitcases were stored on the shelf. She had left her jewellery, as she always did, scattered on her dressing table; she often tried on every ring, every necklace, every bracelet that she owned before finding the ones she wanted to wear. She left the rejected pieces – pearls and rubies from Cartier that had belonged to her grandmother, a dead aunt's great diamond engagement ring – where she had dropped them, as though she would never want to wear them again. Cathy had been raised in a house where it was taken for granted that the rich were too much admired to be robbed.

Christopher took the phone off the hook and undressed. Naked, he carried Cathy's damp towels and his own soiled linen from the bathroom to the clothes hamper in the kitchen. He took a shower and got into bed. He thought, with great concentration, of a baseball game in which he had played as a schoolboy. The bat stung his hands; he saw a fly ball, hit to him in centre field twenty years before, descend slowly out of the dull sky into his glove, felt the loss of breath like broken glass in his lungs as he ran the bases. He went to sleep.

What woke him was not Cathy's weight in the bed, or the touch of her body, or his awareness, as he might be aware of another presence in a dark room, that she was staring into his sleeping face. It was the scent. Her face, lowering towards his own, was cold, and in her hair was the smell of the city. Cathy drove, night and day, with the top down on the convertible. There was a trace of perfume on her skin, all that was left of what she had worn when she went out the night before; it was almost too faint to be apprehended. Overwhelming all these aromas was another, rising from within her body, that Christopher knew. She had been making love.

Christopher, wide awake, saw through closed eyelids that the room was flooded with sunlight. He was lying on his side with his back to Cathy. She grasped his shoulders and moved him on to his back. He felt her watching him intently, 'Don't wake up,' she whispered. He didn't know whether she really believed him to be asleep, or if she was playing dolls with him. She lay on her back beside him. Lifting his inert hand, she placed it between her thighs. She was still wet from the stranger she had left. Christopher moved his hand away. Cathy whispered again, 'Don't wake up.' She moved lightly over the bed. He felt her lips on his body.

'No,' he said.

Cathy went on trying to arouse him. She lifted her head and said, in a firm voice, crouching with her whole body flinching and rigid, 'Please!' She wept, and put her eyes against his body so that her tears, warmer than her tongue had been, wet his skin.

Christopher lifted her and turned her rigid body towards him.

58

He kissed her. Her lips moved against his. 'Oh, Paul, Jesus, I can't bear to be alone and I can't bear what I've done,' she said. She trembled violently in his arms. 'I couldn't finish,' she said. 'It went on for hours and I couldn't. Couldn't. Help me, Paul.'

Cathy lay absolutely still beneath him, accepting his body. She reached orgasm, as she always did, with her eyes open and staring into his. A long cry escaped her, growing louder and louder. Christopher put his hand over her mouth; she snatched it away and went on uttering the hysterical sound. She seized his hair so that he would look at her eyes. He realized that she was making an accusation. She was repeating the word 'love' over and over again, as if they were, indeed, from different galaxies and life depended on making him understand the meaning of this monosyllable in her language.

3

Christopher woke when the late afternoon sun came through the west windows of their bedroom. Cathy did not stir. She lay on her back, her limbs composed, her hair framing her face. Not even sleep could blur her beauty; she was as perfect unconscious as awake. No trace of her tears remained; the only mark on her body was a faint blue bruise on her neck where she had been bitten by her lover. Christopher looked at his watch; they had been asleep for ten hours. He went into the bathroom and shaved, and took another shower.

When he emerged, he found Cathy rushing through the bedroom. Her hair was still uncombed, but she was fully dressed except for the shoes she carried in her hand. At the sight of him, she paused in mid-flight, tottering for a moment on one stockinged foot. Finally she completed the step and staggered with hand outstretched for the support of the wall. Then she stood there, in silence, with both high-heeled shoes clutched to her stomach. Her eyes widened as Christopher approached her. He kissed her softly on both cheeks, his hands resting on her shoulders; she wore a soft woollen sweater, blue-grey like her eyes. Cathy did not move; it was the first time he had ever touched her without feeling a response.

'I'm going now,' she said. The sentence began in a whisper and ended in a sob. She shook her head violently, as if to drive away a voice, and lifted first one foot and then the other putting, on her shoes.

Christopher sat on the disordered bed. His hair was still wet and he rubbed it with a towel. Cathy's head was turned away; she bit her lower lip. Christopher saw that she was watching Christopher's face and her own in the mirror. He caught her eye in the glass.

'Stay until I get dressed,' he said. He put nothing into his voice. Cathy was waiting for a sign. Her face turned towards Christopher's as if an invisible hand had grasped her chin and forced her to look at him.

'We're going out together,' she said, 'is that it?'

'Yes.'

'And that's all?'

Christopher moved her away from the dresser; she misunderstood the reason why he put his hands on her, and resisted. 'I want a clean shirt,' he said. Cathy clenched her fists and tightened her eyes. 'I want to tell you things,' she said. 'Paul, listen to me.'

'No. Cathy, I think we'll both feel better if we do normal things for a while – walk, have a drink, have some dinner. Then you can say anything you like to me.'

In a breaking voice, she said, '*Nothing* touches you.' As she spoke, she watched in the mirror. Christopher's eyes changed and he turned away. Still watching herself (Christopher could feel her behind him, facing the glass) she said, 'It was Franco Moroni. You ought to be willing to hear the man's name.'

'Later,' Christopher said. 'Not now.'

Cathy was trembling. 'His body is covered with black hair,' she said. 'It was no good. In the end, he wanted me to lie to him about it. Do you know what I said to him, Paul? I said, "It's not really adultery if the man can't give you a climax." He slapped me and threw my clothes at me and told me to get out. He takes pills, pep pills, handfuls of them.'

Christopher waited for her to stop speaking. 'Do you feel changed?' he asked. 'Are you different than you were before this happened?'

Cathy put both palms flat against her stomach. 'I don't know,' she said.

She shuddered. 'Nothing touches you,' she said again. 'Nothing.'

She undressed quickly, pulling the sweater over her head,

kicking off her shoes, turning her skirt and slip inside out as she pulled them off by the hems. She saw the look in Christopher's eyes and laughed.

'No,' she said, 'not that. Don't worry. I need a shower.'

In the bathroom door she paused and looked over her shoulder at Christopher. The smile gave him was a smile of forgiveness; he had not given Cathy the anger and jealousy she wanted, but she was ready to pretend that all was once again as it used to be.

'Make us a drink,' Cathy said, in her lightest tone. 'We'll have it in the living room and watch the sunset. The sky is beginning to be nice again in the evening.'

4

Cathy wanted to dine in Trastevere. Christopher knew that she thought she would be safe there from Franco Moroni, who spent his evenings on the Via Veneto. There he could be seen by motion picture people and by foreign girls who wanted to be in his films. He had begun as an actor. Discovering politics, he went on to make movies about revolutions in which the creatures he loathed – American millionaires, American spies, American girls – died screaming for mercy. 'In Franco's films,' a Communist journalist called Piero Cremona had told Christopher, 'only Arabs have virtue. A view of the human race that is unique to Moroni.'

It was warm enough to eat outdoors, and Cathy and Christopher sat at a table in the Piazza Santa Maria in Trastevere. Cathy finished all of her *fettucine* and most of her *scampi*. She drank no wine in Italy. She had a sensitive mouth and could taste each ingredient in even the most complicated dishes. 'I haven't really eaten anything since you left,' Cathy said, 'you take my appetite with you when you go.' Then she put down her fork and stared at her hand, palm upturned on the tablecloth, as if she had lost the right to say such things to Christopher. A group of strolling musicians came to their table and the singer, an ugly youth with a true tenor voice, gave Cathy a rose after he had sung to her.

Christopher paid the bill and they walked back to the river, then northwards along its banks with the mass of the Janiculum Hill, lights on its face like droplets of rain on a window-pane, rising to their left. Cathy walked a step ahead of Christopher. She didn't know the streets, and she gave a little gasp of surprise when she found that she had led them into St Peter's Square. It was deserted. She went on walking, with Christopher following after, until they were among the tall columns under Bernini's colonnade. Cathy put her hand on one of the columns, as high as she could reach, and stood in that position, motionless. With her back to Christopher, she said, 'May I speak?'

Christopher made no gesture. Cathy, sighing, turned round and held out her hand to him. He took it, and she pulled him towards her. The light from the street was yellowish and weak, and the mass of the basilica absorbed most of it, so that Cathy and Christopher, under the colonnade, stood in darkness.

'You'll have to put your arms around me,' Cathy said. 'Otherwise I can't do it.' He did as she asked, and she slid her arms around his waist. She took her hair away from her face so that their cheeks would touch, and with her lips against his skin she began to speak. Christopher moved a step to the right so that they could lean against a column; Cathy's whole weight hung in his arms. She stumbled when he moved, then righted herself and again found the position she wanted.

'Ever since I've known you, Paul,' Cathy said, 'I've known that you don't like the things between us to be said out loud. Maybe everyone is that way if you love them. I don't know. I've never loved anyone else. I know you don't believe that. But with you, Paul, I feel like a person who wants life desperately, but knows she's dying. That's how you make me feel, it's nothing you do or intend, but all the time I'm with you, I'm frightened, terrified, because I believe that no one can feel what I feel for you and go on living. I think I'm dying. All the time.'

Her voice was a murmur. Christopher could barely hear her. 'You think no one can know anything about you,' she said, 'but I can read your body. I know, and I've known ever since we went to Cannes together and made love for the first time, that you think I'm a clumsy lover. And selfish. Isn't that true?'

Christopher said, 'Yes.'

'Still you want me a lot, really want me, don't you?'

'Yes.'

'But I disappoint you in bed every time, no matter what I do or try to do for you, because I don't know how to make you happy.'

62

'That's not true, Cathy. You lose yourself, I think. I've never seen anyone like you.'

'You've had better girls than me.'

'Cathy, I've never had a girl I wanted as much as I want you.'

She hung in his arms, fragrant, breathing softly; he felt the twin streams of breath from her nostrils against his neck. Christopher shifted his own weight.

'Don't move,' Cathy said, 'please don't move. I think there was, at some time in the past, a girl.' Her voice broke. 'Don't move. I'm not going to cry. One girl out of all the ones you've had. I think you loved her the way I love you, Paul. I think she spoiled you for me. She poisoned you. You wrote those poems to her, and now you never write poems.'

'Cathy, there was no such person.'

'Paul, I can't believe that, it's a lie.'

Christopher tried to push her away so that he could look at her but she resisted. He put his hand on her face and spoke into her hair.

'Cathy, I don't lie in our part of life. I tell you the truth, and only the truth.'

Cathy uttered one harsh sob. As if the sound had released her, she stepped back out of Christopher's arms.

'But if it's not a lie you're telling me, if there was no girl, then what does that make me?' she asked.

5

Someone in Paris, Christopher never discovered who, had given Cathy the book of his poems. After reading them, she had flown to Rome; he found her waiting in his apartment when he returned, exhausted, after a long operation in Africa. Cathy had persuaded the *portière* to let her in; she had only to smile at him, she said, and give him five thousand lire.

'How much is that in real money?' she asked Christopher. He told her; he didn't like the phrase, but it was one of Cathy's favourites. 'It expresses exactly what I mean,' she said, 'dollars are real money – if I were an Italian I wouldn't *accept* that funny-looking stuff.'

Christopher's poems had excited Cathy. When she first read

63

them, a month or two after they met at St Anton, she and Christopher were not yet lovers. A few weeks before, he had called her in Paris and taken her to dinner. She told him she was perfecting her French and studying the piano. She lived with a maid and a cook in an apartment owned by her parents in Auteuil. Her father liked to be in Paris for the racing season; he bred thoroughbreds in America and his friends were horsemen too. 'Papa likes to know what a man is going to say to him before he starts to talk,' Cathy told Christopher. 'If there's no horse in the first sentence he knows he's in the wrong company.'

Cathy invited Christopher to lunch in the apartment. He expected to find other guests, but they were alone. Facing each other across the centre of the table, they ate fresh salmon in mid-winter. The maid, a bony woman in uniform, clucked over Cathy, urging her to finish the food on her plate. The dining room had an enormous north window, and Cathy sat facing this source of light. There were no shadows on her face, and her eyes, which changed from grey to blue according to her mood as the pupils enlarged or shrank, were fixed on Christopher's face. She wore a blue frock and a scarf at her neck. Behind her was another window, and its white frame enclosed her like a figure in a painting, with the city in its winter mist brushed into the background. It seemed impossible that she could be a living woman: Botticelli might have imagined her colour, Gainsborough her bones. Cathy, watching Christopher's amusement, asked him, for the first time, 'What are you thinking?' For the first time, Christopher refused to respond.

They kissed lightly when he left. His hands were on her waist. She moved her body inside her clothes, and with this small gesture she wakened him sexually. In the street below her apartment he laughed aloud at the strength of the desire he felt for her; he had never felt such heat for a woman, or known so surely that it was returned.

While Christopher was in the field, and actually operating, he had no sexual thoughts. Cathy did not change that in the weeks that followed, but when he found her waiting for him in Rome he told her, truthfully, that he had been thinking about her and about nothing else during the long plane ride from Leopoldville. 'I know, I think of nothing but you, and I've been sending out messages to you,' Cathy said. 'Reading your poems told me what I guess I already knew. I love you. I want us to make love, and afterwards I want to watch us making love in the poems you'll write about us.' Christopher explained that he had stopped writing poems. Cathy paid no attention. She did not at that time doubt the power of her beauty. 'We mustn't become lovers in a city where we know anyone,' she said. 'We have to be alone. Let's go to Cannes, now.' They took the five o'clock plane.

In the hotel room, unclothed, Cathy changed. She lost her lighthearted way of speaking, her smile, her grace of movement. She ceased flirting. Giving Christopher her body was the most serious act she had ever carried out. She tried to say so. 'When I look at you,' she told Christopher, 'I see only you, I don't see myself. That's never happened to me before.' She asked Christopher if she had made him happy. He didn't reply.

Next morning, at breakfast, Christopher watched Cathy peel an orange. She turned the fruit against the knife so that the skin came off in one long unbroken spiral. He wondered how she could do everything else with such effortless skill and be so blundering a lover. She told him that she was a virgin. He thought that she would learn the technique. She came around the breakfast table with her mouth filled with food and kissed him and led him back to the bed. They spent a week together on the Côte d'Azur. At the end of it he handed in her name to Headquarters for clearance. A month later they were married.

He told Patchen, his best man, that he had spent less time and thought in taking a wife than he had ever done in recruiting an agent. 'With the agents,' Patchen had said in his uninflected voice, 'you were doing the seducing.'

6

Beneath the colonnade of St Peter's, Cathy came back into Christopher's arms. They swayed slightly, like a couple waiting on a dance floor for the next song to begin.

When she spoke again her voice was stronger. 'I thought I could swap Franco for that girl in your past,' she said. 'Hurt for hurt was my idea. I wanted to make an exchange, the way you do with captured spies, on a bridge between the free world and the beastly world.'

Cathy did not speak for a long time. 'It was the loneliness,' she said at last.

Christopher waited. He knew well enough what she was going to say, and what she meant.

'You never take me with you into yourself, and that's the only place I want to go,' Cathy said. 'You never understand what I mean when we talk about this.'

Christopher sighed; Cathy put her fingers on his lips, hiding his displeasure for him, as if she knew he would not want her to see it.

'I'm lonely even when we make love, Paul,' Cathy said. 'I know you don't know what wanting someone you love can be like. I know because I love you. You *can't* love, can you?'

'Yes,' Christopher said, 'I can.'

'Then you can't show it, you can't let go. I feel it in you. It's that God-dammed work you do. Paul, what *happens* when you go away?'

'Mostly nothing happens, Cathy. It's a question of control. I try to control circumstances. That's what I'm trained to do.'

Cathy stepped away from him again. 'When does the control stop?' she asked.

Christopher made no effort to touch her. 'I'm going to tell you something,' he said. 'I don't know if you can understand. I doubt if anyone can who hasn't lived the life. Cathy, I use people. I make them trust me, sometimes they even love me, and I betray them. I make traitors of them. I give them money and advice and they sign for it with their thumbprint, their actual thumbprint. That way, if they get out of line, we have incontrovertible proof that they've taken money to commit treason. We can mail the evidence to their secret police. They know they're agreeing to blackmail in advance. Sometimes they're ruined, sometimes they go to their deaths. I make these things happen. I couldn't do it if I felt anything while I was doing it. To stay sane, if that's what I am, I've learned to put my emotions somewhere else while I'm committing an act with another human being.'

Cathy stared at him, nodding, as he spoke. 'What do you think of these people, these agents, that you're manipulating?' she asked.

Christopher said, 'In my way, I love them. I love secrets, we all do. That's why we do the work. While we're working, we're together in a region of experience where very few humans have ever gone.'

'*Love* them? You just said you feel nothing while you're with them.'

'No. I said that I put my emotions aside. Because what I feel is so strong that I couldn't do the job if I let myself go free.'

'And you're telling me that this – what do you call it? – this *technique* spills over into our lives and into our bed?'

'Yes.'

'I understand,' Cathy said. 'Then there's no difference. Absolutely no difference.'

'In what?'

'In loving you, Paul, and in lying down and letting Franco Moroni masturbate in me.'

Six

I

'There's too much of the Sybarite in you,' Patchen said, as a plate of *quenelles* was set before Christopher. Patchen had ordered raw spring vegetables as his first course. Rich food annoyed him in the way that cigarettes annoy a non-smoker. Patchen himself had made this comparison. Years before, when he and Christopher had been undergraduates, Patchen had come back to their room after buying a Radcliffe girl an expensive meal in Boston. 'She smelled of food all through the theatre and all the way home,' Patchen had said. 'Like a full ashtray the morning after a party.' In the end he had married another Radcliffe girl, one as thin as he and almost as still. Christopher had dined with the Patchens in Washington a dozen times, and had never been given anything but rare roast beef, green salad, and Stilton cheese that Patchen bought in England to set off the clarets he had shipped to him from France.

'What did you think of Kamensky's book?' Patchen asked.

He had given the rough English translation to Christopher the night before, at midnight. It did not occur to him that Christopher might not have read all seven hundred typed pages in the twelve hours since.

'It's a pedantic translation, but you can see what the novel must be. I want to read the Russian.'

'Yes,' Patchen said, 'but can it play the guitar?'

This was a joke between them from their first days in secret life; they had been trained by a man who had once run, or had invented for their education, an agent inside Nazi Germany who had gained entry into the highest circles of the regime because he could play the guitar and was always welcome at parties. 'Always ask yourself,' their trainer would tell them, 'whether your asset can play the guitar.'

Christopher said, 'Of course it can play the guitar. Otto said so when he read it in Russian.'

'But?'

'But how to do it. *Whether* to do it, David. What's the news from the author?'

'Kamensky is just as he was, rolling about in bed with his young Bohemian girl in his *dacha*.'

'No one has bothered him?'

'Not a whisper, not a hand raised in anger.'

'You speak as if you're completely sure.'

'I am,' Patchen said. 'We have certain . . . technical resources inside the *dacha*.' He rolled his eye. Patchen held the gadgetry of espionage in amused contempt, in the way that an old-fashioned mountain climber might despise pitons hammered into virgin rock. He whispered the next word: '*Microphones*.'

There was nothing for Christopher to say. The risk to Kamensky, and to their operation, was appalling.

'The Moscow station is very proud of those wires,' Patchen said. 'They've got hours of Kamensky reciting poetry to his mistress, sounds of dishes being washed, tea kettles bubbling. The real stuff.'

'Why?'

'Why what? Bug the *dacha*? Because it was there. They didn't know Kamensky was a CA target.'

'Do they know now?'

'I'm afraid so,' Patchen said. 'CA ops inside the Soviet Union! It makes their blood run cold.'

Patchen explained. The report of Bülow's death had been circulated within Headquarters to the head of the Soviet Russia Division, a man called Dick Sutherland. 'Dick came to see me,' Patchen said. 'He loves being chief of SR, he has a keen sense of ownership. He was not pleased that Kalmyk, a captain in the Red Army, had been part of the picture. "You're putting another Turd in my soup," Dick said to me.'

'That was his expression?'

'Yes. He calls CA agents Turds. He calls our division the Turd Shop. I want you to know where we stand.'

'I know where we stand.'

'You do? Well, Dick is one of those wastebasket cleaners who'd rather lose the Cold War than accept help from covert action to win it. Someday this inner tension in the outfit is going to cause an explosion and we're going to be spattered, Turds and Sutherlands together, all over the scenery. But not today. I want to go on with this, because it's something you have to know.'

Before Patchen spoke again, he cut all the lamb on his plate into pieces and ate it. When the watchful waiter started towards the table to serve him more, Patchen held up a palm to keep him away.

'Sutherland told me that Kamensky's mistress is in the employ of the KGB,' Patchen said.

'What a surprise.'

'Ah, but there *is* a surprise. She is also in Sutherland's employ. She was a KGB party girl. Her employers sent her to Stockholm last year to perform disgusting acts with an American colonel for their cameras, and Sutherland set her up. He got pictures of her enjoying a Swedish girl when she should have been munching on the colonel, doubled her, and sent her back to Moscow. When the KGB assigned her to make friends with old Kamensky, Sutherland thought *he'd* get first look at any manuscripts, and all the credit.'

'And now he knows we got in before him?'

'Yes. It appears there are some things Kamensky doesn't tell young Masha, or whatever her name is. No doubt he learned caution the hard way.'

'Or else there are things Masha doesn't tell Sutherland, but does tell the KGB.'

'Dick says no. Evidently he has a control of some kind on her reporting to the Russians.'

'So the KGB doesn't know we have the book?'

'If it was the KGB that killed Bülow, then they know. We simply don't know what they know.'

Christopher asked for more wine. Patchen put a finger on the rim of his glass to stop the *sommelier* from pouring claret into it.

'We seldom *know* anything,' Christopher said. 'What are we assuming?'

'Dick Sutherland talks about something called gaming. It's what used to be called the scenario. The way Dick games it, the opposition knows everything, the opposition is responsible for the event in Berlin.'

'Therefore?'

'Therefore publishing *The Little Death* will protect Kamensky rather than put him in hazard because, if they kill him as a punishment for being a genius who wrote the truth, they will have to kill him in full view of the world public.'

'That's assuming a great deal.'

'Yes, but don't we always?'

What Patchen said was true. For the most part men like him had nothing to go on but assumptions. They guessed at the truth, seizing facts as a pack of hunting animals will rip mouthfuls of meat from a large beast they have surrounded in the dark. They assumed that everyone was an enemy and a liar. They believed nothing, especially not a concrete fact. Concrete, Patchen was fond of saying, could be poured in any shape. He and his colleagues never knew anything for certain. They had a dangerous weakness, and Christopher spoke of it now.

'I have an eerie feeling that I've been here before,' he said. 'Headquarters wants this operation. Therefore they are making the only assumption that makes the operation inevitable.'

'You really don't have to go on, Paul. I know how angry our frailties make you.'

'Men die. You gamesters are always a long way away when that happens.'

Patchen pointed at Christopher's untouched food. Christopher didn't pick up his silverware. They were almost alone in the restaurant, and the sound of traffic came into the room.

'Aren't you going to tell me that we're making the precise assumption that Otto wants us to make?' Patchen asked.

'Otto usually pushes the right buttons.'

'Sometimes he's right, Paul. He's an old hand.'

'If he's wrong this time, we'll have killed Kiril Kamensky,'

Christopher said. 'I don't give a shit what Dick Sutherland wants to believe.'

Patchen stretched and put a hand on the small of his back. He sat straighter in his chair, watching impassively while Christopher ate the food that had gone cold on his plate.

At last, he said, 'The significant fact is that the smuggling operation was airtight until it got to Berlin and Horst Bülow.'

'Yes. Don't you find it curious that the Soviet service would let the manuscript get that far if they knew what it was? Doesn't Dick find it odd?'

'It's Dick's job to blame everything on the Russians,' Patchen said. He broke off some bread and put it into his mouth and chewed while he spoke; the crudity of the act suggested Sutherland, as it was supposed to do. 'The KGB makes Dick possible, after all,' Patchen said.

A young black dressed as a Moorish servant brought coffee. Patchen drank his at a gulp. He tapped his watch; they were due at the Rothchilds' in twenty minutes, and Christopher knew that he wanted to discuss ways of stimulating Rothchild to speak of his feelings about the Kamensky operation. There was time enough to do that on the walk to the Île Saint-Louis. Patchen called for the bill.

'There is,' Christopher said, 'another possibility, of course. That Horst was set up by somebody from our side.'

'Yes,' Patchen said, counting out bright French banknotes on to the tablecloth. 'I'd thought of that.'

2

A bell system had been installed in the Rothchilds' apartment so that Otto could summon Maria, or the maid, when he needed something. Now, as he pressed his foot on the concealed button, he explained apologetically to Patchen that he did not like the idea of having uninspected wires of any kind in his house, but the bells were a necessity because he could no longer speak loudly enough to be heard from room to room. Maria came in, and he said, 'Give David and Paul to drink.' There were small lapses in Otto's flowing English, as in his French. He spoke both languages with a faint

German accent, because German had been the first foreign language he had learned.

Rothchild was alert, almost nervous. Christopher thought that he must scent something in the way Patchen was treating him. Patchen was more aloof than usual, less interested in Rothchild's small talk. Rothchild was wary of small changes in men. He watched Patchen and Christopher, his head at one side as if he could hear, very faintly, the dying sounds of the words they had spoken to each other about him as they approached the apartment. Patchen was looking at a painting. Rothchild spoke his name sharply; Patchen turned.

'Time is going by, David,' Rothchild said. 'Why aren't we moving faster?'

'There are always delays, Otto. The bureaucracy worries about taking risks.'

'There will be *risk*,' Rothchild said, 'any way we do it. If you don't take risks you don't get anything done.'

Patchen turned his eye from Rothchild to Christopher. 'Otto's Law,' he said.

'I am trying to teach you,' Rothchild said. He closed his eyes. Patchen went on talking to him; he had discovered that Rothchild heard what was said to him even when he seemed to be unconscious.

'It's Christopher who'll be taking the risks,' Patchen said. 'You and I will stay inside while he does all the work. It's his skin, and I want him to control the temperature of the operation.'

Rothchild awakened. With a weak movement of his head he invited Christopher to speak to him.

'Otto,' Christopher said, 'I have to tell you that I have misgivings about this project.'

'We'd all be astonished if you did not, Paul,' Rothchild said. 'What bothers you?'

'Security. We've had a man killed. Usually we take that as a sign that something is wrong.'

Rothchild glared at Christopher. It was evident, whatever Maria thought, that the surgeons had not got all the anger out of him.

'Paul,' he said, 'I'm tired of hearing about Horst Bülow being run over in Berlin. The idiot from Security has been here half a dozen times, asking this, asking that, gnawing the bones of this

73

dead German. The incident is irrelevant. Horst Bülow was irrelevant. He always was.'

'You knew him?'

Patchen, who had gone back to the bar, waited with an empty glass in his hand for Rothchild's answer.

Rothchild lifted a trembling hand, the shadow of his old fierce gesture of impatience. 'Of course I knew him,' he said. 'I recruited him. He was a prisoner in the French Zone and he thought they would shoot him if they found out about his Abwehr connection. It's all in the file. I keep telling that person from Security that simple fact – everything is in the file.'

He began to cough. Maria strode across the room and held a glass of water to his lips.

'This is very upsetting to Otto,' she said. 'Do you have to talk about this particular subject?'

'Yes,' Patchen said.

'Bülow's death doesn't seem irrelevant to me,' Christopher said. 'If it was the opposition . . .'

'Who else would it be?' Rothchild asked. 'A careless driver?'

'If it was the opposition,' Christopher continued, 'then we have to assume they knew what Bülow was carrying, and that they'll take reprisals if we publish.'

'Reprisals? Against whom – Kamensky?'

'Yes, and his friends who took the risk of getting the manuscript out for him.'

'You keep forgetting. It was Kamensky who initiated this situation. He sent me the book. I didn't ask him to do so.'

'So you've said before. But, Otto, he instructed you not to publish while he was still alive.'

'We can't let ourselves be controlled by any such sentimentality as that.'

Rothchild slumped in his chair again. His mouth was open, and he ran his pale tongue over his lips. Maria gave him another drink of water. Christopher sat back in his own chair and crossed his legs. He looked at Patchen, but as usual could read nothing on his friend's deadened face.

'What do you mean, Otto, by sentimentality?' Patchen asked.

'I've told Paul before. Kamensky *wants* to be martyrized for this great work of art he has sent to me. That's why he sent it.'

'That's not what he said in his letter.'

'No Russian, and in particular not Kamensky, ever says what he means. I used to be a Russian, David, Paul – trust me.'

'Kamensky trusted you,' Patchen said with his crooked smile, 'and look what it's getting him.'

3

Patchen chose to keep silent as he rode the Métro the two stops to the Place de l'Odéon, and then walked to the Luxembourg Gardens. He and Christopher strolled side by side through the gardens, crowded because of the fine weather with mothers and children and with students from the university. Christopher removed his coat and slung it over his shoulder; Patchen in his black suit walked with his hands clasped in the small of his back.

'Why did the French put so many statues in this park?' Patchen asked. 'It doubles the crowd, having all these stone poets and politicians standing around.'

They were passing the marionette theatre. Patchen had a weakness for the art, and he stopped to read the posters. Christopher watched the broad walk behind them: baby carriages, young mothers, a couple lying together on the lawn; the girl was as blonde as Cathy and she gazed as intently into her lover's face. He saw, striding through the crowd, the person he and Patchen had come to meet.

Maria Rothchild joined them, as Patchen had asked, by the Medici Fountain. Otto had returned to his bed, she said, exhausted.

'He thought Paul was taunting him,' Maria said. 'He doesn't like your way of playing dumb, Paul. After all, he knows you're not stupid.' She smiled. 'Otto doesn't even believe in your bleeding heart.'

'Bleeding heart?' Christopher said. 'I was telling him the truth. I don't understand the way he's rationalizing what he wants us to do to Kamensky.'

'*Do* to Kamensky? He loves Kamensky. He wants to give him to the world.'

'Oh. I thought he wanted to sacrifice him. I don't see why. Doing it for sound operational reasons would be bad enough, but that at least would be professional. But Kamensky is not under

75

discipline, he hasn't accepted the risks, he isn't being paid. He doesn't know who he's dealing with.'

'He's dealing with Otto, his friend.'

'He's dealing with an agent of US intelligence. Our Otto is not Kamensky's Otto. Kamensky isn't an agent, Maria. He's an outsider.'

Maria gave a giddy laugh, a sign that she was annoyed. Patchen stepped between them, smiling, and put a finger on his lips. He led them to the back of the fountain, where the crowd was thinner, and pointed at the carving of Leda and the Swan. 'I've always thought that this Leda rather favoured you, Maria,' he said. She gave him a cold look. 'I won't pursue the analogy,' Patchen said.

'Good,' Maria said. 'Let's say what we have to say. Otto doesn't sleep long. He frets if I'm not there when he wakes up. Especially when you're in town, David.'

'I wouldn't want to put a strain on your marriage. I want to ask you how you think Otto is doing, under the tension of work.'

'I'd say he's thriving on it.'

'I thought so. Some of the bastard showed through today. It was like old times seeing Otto behave that way.'

'It's not good for him, losing his temper. I hope you can have calmer meetings with him from now on.'

'Yes,' Patchen said. 'I'm hoping the same. It's delicate, you know, because Otto can't really run this operation. Paul has to do it, and we all have to save Otto's feelings.'

'Is that my assignment?'

'It's already your vocation, Maria.'

Maria filled her lungs with air and exhaled in exasperation; it was one of Otto's lost mannerisms, and Christopher wondered if she knew it.

'Otto has been very ill,' Maria said. 'The surgery changed a lot of things.' Patchen returned his attention to the fountain. The rush of water nearly drowned their low voices, and Christopher moved a step closer to his companions.

'I was surprised to learn that Otto knew Horst Bülow so well,' Christopher said. 'He never mentioned it to me before.'

'Did you ever mention Bülow's name to *him*?' Maria asked.

'No.'

'Then the question wouldn't arise, would it? I've learned not to

76

be surprised when Otto turns out to have known someone. He knows everyone.'

'Did you know he knew Horst?'

'No. Even when I was Otto's case officer, we spent very little time bandying names. He only talks about the people who are in play at the moment. He's an activist, not a raconteur.'

'I wonder why he kept telling me how irrelevant Horst and his death were,' Christopher said.

Maria made an abrupt movement with her hand, slapping the empty air sharply; it was another of Otto's gestures, and Christopher saw that Patchen noticed, too. Maria turned her back; Christopher tapped her on the shoulder and she spun on her heel and faced him.

'Because the murder of Bülow is not irrelevant at all,' he said. 'Otto of all people must realize that.'

The tone of Christopher's voice had drawn Maria into a silence. She was too well trained to show hostility. She was trying to show nothing. Patchen watched her intently.

'There's only one way for Headquarters to read Bülow's being killed as he handed me Kamensky's manuscript,' Christopher said. 'That the opposition killed Horst. That the opposition knows we have the book.'

'All right, Paul,' Maria said. 'I see your point.'

Christopher smiled at her; she moved back slightly, like a woman discouraging a kiss.

'If the opposition *knows*,' he said, 'then every reason for protecting Kamensky is removed. We have to assume they'll kill him, no matter what we do. Why didn't Otto see that, when it's so plain to all the rest of us?'

Maria gave Christopher a defiant look, but when he took her hand and led her to an empty bench, she went with him unresisting.

'David wants to talk to you,' Christopher said.

4

Patchen and Maria sat on the bench, with Christopher on the grass beside them, facing the other way so that he could watch for listeners behind them. Patchen turned his calm face towards Otto Rothchild's wife.

77

'What I want you to understand,' he said, 'is that I wish Otto to have his last success. We all do. But this is going to be a sensitive, difficult operation. Otto hasn't the powers he used to have.'

'He does, you know.'

'No, Maria, he doesn't. He's lost his bodily functions and some of his mental functions, and it scares him. He's not the man he was.'

'Still,' Maria said, 'he's better than almost anyone.'

'Granted. Otto is adaptable. He's survived a lot in his life. As he's always telling us, he's lost things before – his money, his country, his politics. He's changed when he had to, always.'

'David, you're contradicting yourself.'

'I'm describing Otto, so contradictions are bound to creep in,' Patchen said. 'What I believe, what makes me anxious, is that Otto is adapting. He's developing new powers.'

Christopher saw a remark occur to Maria; it was reflected in her eyes, she parted her lips to speak, but kept silent.

'Otto has set things in motion,' Patchen said. 'He's created an operation. I've never seen him want anything as much as he wants this. I'm going to give it to him because the target is irresistible. But I am not going to let him control it.'

'Otto knows that.'

'Yes, he does. And that's why he's struggling with me. I want you to help me to do him the kindness of letting him believe that he's running things.'

'You want me to report on him.'

Another man, having been Maria Rothchild's friend for years, might have put a hand on her arm. Patchen did not even raise his voice. 'Yes,' he said.

'And it's for Otto's own good?'

Maria's voice was weary. She crossed her ankles and put her head on the back of the bench. She had not expected an answer from Patchen. She watched the clouds, tinted red by the setting sun. After a time she sat upright again. She spoke now as Patchen and Christopher had been speaking, without emotion.

'Otto's idea,' she said, 'is to wait a few more days for you to act. If you don't, he's going to take the Russian manuscript to a French publisher.'

'Where is he going to get a copy? I took the one I loaned him back to Washington after he'd read it.'

78

'I photographed it for him. Otto thinks ahead.

Patchen, for the first time, smiled. Rothchild's cunning had awakened his admiration for the agent. Christopher, watching Maria, saw no response.

Patchen said, 'What else does Otto have in mind?'

'Claude de Cerutti,' Maria said.

'Kamensky's discoverer. We'd thought of him, too. Otto knows him, of course.'

'Of course. He comes every Wednesday and brings champagne. Cerutti used to be silent partner in a restaurant where Picasso went and paid his bills with a sketch. That's where Otto got the one in the sitting room. They go back a long way.'

'All the way to Kamensky?' Christopher asked.

Maria lifted her glance. She made a thoughtful face, holding Christopher's eyes. 'That I don't know,' she said.

Only that morning, Christopher had read the file on Cerutti; Patchen had brought it with him from Washington. Cerutti was a Frenchman, a disillusioned Communist who had left the Party even before the Purges. It was he who had first published Kamensky's work in the West – a volume of poems, a book of stories, a novel. It wasn't known how the work had come into Cerutti's hands; Kamensky was already in the camps when the books appeared in Paris, after the war.

'What Otto's planning to do,' Patchen said, 'is pretty much what we would have done anyway.'

'Otto couldn't know that. Paul has reservations, and everyone knows you listen to Paul.'

'Not always,' Patchen said. 'Will Cerutti accept a proposal?'

'Otto is sure he will. So am I. He hasn't had a real success in publishing since the last time he brought out a book by Kamensky. He'd leap at the chance to do it again.'

'On what basis?'

'For money, for respectability,' Maria said. 'Cerutti is recruitable. Otto has used him in small ways. He knows what's happening, all right, but he wants to wake up in the morning clean as a whistle. He insists on being unwitting.'

Patchen nodded. He let a few moments pass. Maria showed no signs of nervousness. Guilt had come into her face only once, when she had confessed to photographing Kamensky's manuscript, a secret document belonging to the Agency.

'Can you bring Cerutti and Paul together?' Patchen asked.

'Yes. He's coming to see Otto at four o'clock next Wednesday.'

'Is that the day Otto plans to hit him with the manuscript?'

Maria shook her head. 'Otto is giving you a little more time than that.'

'How much more?'

'I don't know. He's waiting to get the feel of what you're doing. You know how he is.'

Maria lit a cigarette, a Gauloise, and deeply inhaled its rank smoke. Patchen coughed and she put it out.

'Why is Otto in such a rush about this?' Patchen asked her. 'Have you any idea?'

'No. He's been in a mood since Paul brought the manuscript out. If it were anyone but Otto I'd call it apprehension. He has no reason to be impatient.'

'His health?'

Maria gave a sudden brilliant smile. 'Otto knows that he's not going to die,' she said. 'The doctors gave him a choice before the operation – death in the near future, or what he is now for twenty years. He made his choice.'

'Not much of a choice for you, Maria,' Patchen said. He touched her gloved hand. Christopher saw that she was startled by Patchen's sympathy; he saw something else, deep in Maria's disciplined face, that he hadn't seen there before – a flash of mockery. Patchen had made a mistake with her, tried to come too close.

Maria walked away without a goodbye, her heels clicking vigorously on the paving stones, her skirt swinging. The near wall of the Luxembourg Palace lay in shadow as Maria approached it, and the westering sun, behind it, left a strip of light around its edges.

'A good officer,' Patchen said. 'She always was.'

'Do you think we can contain Otto?'

'Maybe, if Maria is the key.'

'What if he redoubles her?'

'Unlikely,' Patchen said. 'Otto may have no scruples. But Maria has no illusions.'

Seven

I

Christopher took the Métro across the river. At the PTT on the
Champs-Élysées he placed a telephone call to Cathy in Rome, and,
reading the Somerset Maugham novel he carried in his pocket,
waited for it to go through. At the end of an hour the telephonist
sent him into one of the booths. He closed the door behind him,
and was enveloped by the odours of old sweat and stale Caporals.
The telephone rang a dozen times on the crackling line; at last the
operator in Rome told him that there was no reply.

He walked up the Champs through the evening crowds. A man
in an open car, a Lancia like Christopher's, kissed the girl in the
seat beside him as he waited for the light to change. Christopher
bought *Le Monde* at a kiosk and glanced down the wide street; it
was impossible to spot surveillance in such a throng, but he looked
from face to face in the approaching crowd, so as to remember any
that he might see in an emptier street. He sat at a table on the
pavement at Fouquet's and drank a glass of beer. Then he walked
on, turning down the rue Marbeuf, and took the long way around
through quiet streets to the avenue George V. There was no one
behind him. He had not expected that there would be.

On the stone wall of the American Cathedral, Christopher

looked for the yellow chalk mark he had been told he would see. Patchen apologized for it. 'These fellows from Security are great believers in elementary tradecraft,' he told Christopher. 'You'll just have to be patient, they like to play spy when they go overseas.' Christopher went inside the church. Wilson was seated in the corner of the last pew, the bridge of his nose gripped between his thumb and forefinger. Christopher sat down beside him. Wilson's eyes, the whites shining in the dim light, swivelled towards him.

'I apologize for this meeting place,' Wilson said. 'No safe house was available at this hour, and your tall friend with the war wounds wouldn't hear of your coming into the Embassy.'

Wilson, after a pause, began to speak again, then fell silent as a robed man padded down the aisle and nodded to them with a cordial American smile. He knelt, on one knee, in front of the altar and prayed in a whisper. The acoustics were excellent. Wilson, too, changed to a whisper, and his sibilants mixed with those of the priest in the vault of the nave.

'I wanted to give you a little report,' Wilson said, speaking behind hands clasped for prayer. 'I'm puzzled by the way things are going.'

The clergyman finished his prayers. Wilson went on whispering.

'I've got nothing definitive,' he told Christopher. 'You and your tall friend ran this thing so close to the vest that no one on our side *could* have known where Bülow was going to be when he was zapped. Even you didn't know until almost the moment before he was hit, isn't that right?'

'Yes. We've been over that.'

'I don't want to go over it again. I just want to know if you agree with something. If no one knew except Bülow where Bülow was going to be at 06.12 on the morning in question, then nobody but Bülow himself could possibly have told the killers where he was going to be.'

'Unless there was surveillance and I missed it.'

'At that hour of the morning? Is that possible?'

'No.'

'You're absolutely certain that no one except Patchen knew you were meeting the asset.'

'Yes, and Patchen didn't know the place or time.'

Christopher spoke Patchen's name aloud. Wilson flinched. He had been using true names, but he mouthed the syllables rather than whispering them. Wilson, Christopher thought, must believe that he is safe in church from lip readers, if not from microphones.

'That's all I wanted to confirm,' Wilson said. 'Thanks. I'll go first. I'm going to turn towards the Champs when I go out, so maybe you should head down the other way.'

Wilson started to rise. Christopher gripped his forearm and he sat down again.

'What are you on to?' Christopher asked in a normal voice. He knew that its tone would carry less well than a whisper in the stone building. Wilson hesitated, lips pursed. Christopher insisted.

'Are you thinking that Horst was turned around?' he asked.

'Horst,' Wilson replied, 'or somebody. Most likely Horst.'

'Doubled by whom? He was fluttered six months ago and nothing showed up.'

'Six months can be a long time in a life like Horst's.'

'You've got something new on him.'

Wilson sighed. 'You always paid him in cash. West German marks in a sterile envelope, sterile receipt. Right?'

Christopher nodded.

'Horst had some extra money,' Wilson said. He took a breath before he spoke again, in a flat tone. 'We have a sort of arrangement with a little German unit in West Berlin, and this unit took an interest in Horst,' he said. 'They wanted to run him themselves, and the Berlin base had a time flagging them off. Of course they knew why we were fidgety so they kept an eye on Bülow from time to time to see which American was handling him – professional curiosity. They never picked him up with you, your meetings were too secure. But a few weeks before he died they saw him in the Tiergarten with a woman. They talked, Horst and the female, for fifteen minutes, Horst nodding all the time. An envelope passed between them. It was morning, eight o'clock. Horst went to the nearest branch of the Berliner Bank and deposited the money to an account in the name of Heinrich Beichermann. One thousand Deutschmarks. The file says that Heinrich Beichermann was a cover name Horst used during the war, when he was an amateur spy with the Abwehr. The bank says someone from Zürich opened the account for Horst, through the mail.'

'Are there photographs of the woman?'

'Our Germans say not.'

'Description?'

'Youngish, prettyish. It was winter. She was all bundled up.'

'What language did she and Horst speak?'

'Russian.'

Wilson cleared his throat.

'Where did they go after the meeting?'

'Horst left the bank and got on the S-Bahn and went back to work in East Berlin,' he said. 'The lady took a walk down the K-damm, then made a right turn into the American Consulate.'

Wilson smiled.

'Did she come back out?' Christopher asked.

'They don't know. The kid following her got cold and figured she must be an Ami who'd stay inside till nightfall, so he went somewhere for a cup of coffee.'

'Didn't he think it was curious that someone speaking Russian to an East Berliner would go straight into the American Consulate?'

'He wasn't paid to think. You don't have to be an American to get past the Marine guards at the door.'

The priest reappeared through the chancel door. He had removed his gown. He put his hand on a switch. 'Gentlemen,' he said, in a hearty voice, 'if you've finished your devotions, my wife will be wondering where I am.' He smiled across the ranks of the pews, and, buttoning his jacket, gave them a small ironic bow.

Wilson left as the clergyman came down the aisle, still smiling urbanely, but too far away to see Wilson's face clearly. Christopher smiled back and walked out the door less quickly than Wilson, had done. Christopher heard the lock turn and saw that Wilson, on the way out, had taken time to wipe away his chalk mark. Christopher watched the burly figure of the security man as he sauntered up the avenue. Christopher turned in the opposite direction, towards the Seine.

There were few pedestrians this far away from the Champs-Élysées, and Christopher heard the hurrying footsteps behind him when they were still some distance away. He put himself close to the wall and turned the sharp corner, almost reversing his direction, into the avenue Marceau. Once round the corner, he stepped into a deep doorway and waited. The footsteps, running now, turned the corner behind him.

Wilson reached the doorway, went by. Christopher heard him stop. He came back and peered into the shadows. He was panting slightly and his flowered necktie had worked its way out of his coat. He handed Christopher an envelope. 'Almost forgot,' he said. He touched his forehead and went back the way he had come, still panting.

Inside the envelope was a typed note, unsigned. 'Your wife called,' it read. 'She's in Paris, and will meet you in the bar of the Ritz at 5.00 this evening.'

Christopher's watch read 5.10. He got into a taxi as it let a passenger out. He rested his head on the back of the seat and closed his eyes. Cathy, when he had left her in Rome, was asleep and frowning as she dreamt. She had always insisted that she had no dream life.

2

Even before he became a spy, Christopher had disliked being recognized by headwaiters and bartenders. As a youth he had never exchanged a word with the New York Irishmen who tended bar at P. J. Clarke's or the Frenchmen behind the zinc bar at the Dôme, though others seemed to attach importance to being known by name to these contemptuous men. Now, as a matter of professional caution, he booked table reservations in a false name, and made certain that he did not eat at the same restaurant, or drink at the same bar, more often than two or three times a year. He broke these rules in Rome because he lived in that city, and never operated there; it was important to his cover to live as much like a normal man as possible when he was at home.

Cathy made caution difficult when she travelled with him. She had favourite bars, favourite drinks, favourite restaurants and dishes. She refused to give them up. In the Ritz bar, when Christopher entered, he did not see her. A waiter approached.

'Madame has gone into the foyer for a moment,' he said.

He took Christopher to the table; Cathy's purse hung by its strap over the back of the chair, and a bottle of champagne stood in a bucket with two glasses chilling in the ice. Cathy had been drinking Perrier water as usual, and bubbles still rose in her half-empty glass. Christopher saw the men at the bar watch her come into the room behind him. A moment later she put a hand on the back of his head and kissed him softly on the cheek. The waiter was at her chair back, smiling. He filled their glasses. It was the most expensive champagne sold by the Ritz; Cathy told Christo-

85

pher, as she did each time they met there, 'This is the very first wine my father let me drink, when I was fourteen, here in this bar. "Cathy, my dear, let Dom Perignon be your standard," he said.' She was a fine mimic, and Christopher grinned at the deep voice and the scowl of affection that for an instant turned her face into her father's.

'What made you think of coming to Paris?' Christopher asked.

'Thinking of you. I took the next plane after you left. We can have the weekend together.'

Cathy ran a wetted finger around the rim of her champagne glass and it gave off a musical note. She listened, drank a bit of wine, and did it again, producing a slightly different tone. 'I played the piano today,' she said. 'I haven't played in months but I'm really not bad, Paul. I feel the music more. I had a teacher who used to tell me that I'd never have anything except technique until I'd suffered. *She'd* suffered, from the look of her, but still she couldn't play worth a nickel.'

'The difference between talent and genius,' Christopher said.

'No, the difference between being alone and being with you. When I woke up and saw that you were gone the heart fell right out of me.'

She put both of her hands on the table, asking for Christopher's. Tears rose in her eyes; they ran over her cheeks to the corners of her unpainted upper lip. Cathy licked them away, tongue as quick as a cat's.

For dinner, Cathy had duck in orange. She and the *sommelier* had a running joke at Christopher's expense; the wine waiter believed that white wine should be drunk with duck in orange, but Christopher would have nothing except red Bordeaux. Cathy would take a half-bottle of Sancerre and remark, each time the *sommelier* refilled her glass, how remarkably it cleared the palate and intensified the sweet flavour of the duck. She would tell him that he must convince Christopher. 'Monsieur is a man of principle,' the *sommelier* would reply, and leave him to pour his own wine.

When they were alone, Cathy had little to say. They walked along the river. She led him up the steps to a café near the Beaux-Arts, and there they drank coffee and Cathy ordered Cointreau. 'I can't get enough of the taste of orange tonight,' she said. They crossed to the right bank and went down to the Seine again and walked in the dark, past men sleeping under the bridges and lovers embracing against the rough stones of the embankment. The electric glow of the city made the stars invisible, but there was a moon behind dark cirrus clouds on the horizon. Cathy walked with her eyes on her feet, as if the white shoes that she wore came into her circle of vision one after the other by some force independent of her body. They climbed back to the street at the Grand Palais, and walked on to the Pont Alexandre III. Midway across the bridge, Cathy stopped and looked over the railing. She placed Christopher's hands on her breasts. Turning, she kissed him, and the taste and scent of orange passed from her mouth into his own. 'I love you,' she whispered. Christopher tightened his arms around her. 'Can't you answer?' Cathy asked.

Cathy's parents were using their apartment. They had come over for the race meeting that began on Palm Sunday at Auteuil; they had a horse running in the President of the Republic Stakes. 'Papa would like to have an American horse win that particular race while de Gaulle is President of France,' Cathy had said in the Ritz Bar. 'He plans to show the General his shrapnel scars from Château-Thierry and ask him if *he* was ever wounded for France.'

Christopher and Cathy slept at the Ritz. They had not made love since the night she had come to Christopher from Franco Moroni. Wine had left Cathy peaceful; she lay in the broad hotel bed, her face in shadow and then in the lamplight that came into the window from the Place Vendôme, and accepted pleasure quietly. But afterwards she moved to the edge of the bed and shuddered, as Christopher had done on the train when he remembered the death of Bülow. He touched the skin of her hip. 'Paul, don't talk,' she said. She lay in silence, and when she spoke again her voice was under control. 'I used to watch you remember things and I could never understand why you wanted to keep secrets that caused you so much pain,' she said. Christopher stroked her hair.

'Jesus,' she whispered, 'I wish I didn't understand now.'

3

While they were having breakfast the next morning, the telephone rang. Cathy answered, made no reply into the instrument, and handed it to Christopher.

'Sorry to disturb you at the Ritz,' Bud Wilson said, 'I hope it's all right.'

'It's no disturbance.'

'That's good. I heard you were there with your wife and I remembered that we had a loose end with her. You never got back to me with the answer to that question. You know, about her circle of friends in Paris.'

'Yes, I remember,' Christopher said. 'I haven't had a chance to ask her.'

'Can you do it now?'

Christopher put his hand over the mouthpiece. 'Cathy,' he said. She turned a page of her newspaper and looked up.

'When we met in Paris and went home on the train,' he said. 'Did you tell anyone you saw here that I was in Germany?'

She frowned. 'Why would I?'

'You didn't talk to any outsider about me, about where I was?'

'No. I know I'm not supposed to say, unless it's someone with the Company I'm talking to.'

'And you didn't see anyone else?'

'I saw you. I saw David walking with you in St Germain des Prés. People like that, in passing. I'm more observant than you think. But I didn't tell any secrets to any outsiders. Okay?'

Christopher spoke into the telephone. 'The answer is no,' he said.

'Good. That makes things easier.'

'Tell me,' Christopher said. 'How did you happen to know to call me here?'

Wilson laughed 'Elementary, my dear Watson,' he said with his heavy jocularity. 'The Ritz is your kind of place, right?'

While Cathy bathed, Christopher went out to a café, bought some *jetons*, and used the pay telephone to call the Embassy. 'There's not much news,' the self-conscious girl at the other end told him. 'Martha Riley went through a red light and she wants to know if you can fix the ticket.'

He put another token in the telephone and dialled the Rothchilds' number. Maria answered on the first ring. Christopher did not identify himself; Maria knew his voice. Her own voice was controlled.

'I'm glad you called,' she said. 'I wonder if you'd be free to make a fourth at bridge today.'

'Yes, I'd like that. What time?'

'The usual time. I promise you a good tea.'

'Fine. I'll look forward to it.'

Christopher hung up and waited for a moment before putting his last *jeton* into the telephone. A man waiting to use the instrument rapped loudly on the glass door of the booth. While Christopher dialled, the stranger opened the door and said in French, with exaggerated politeness, 'It's very kind of you to make all these calls while others are waiting.' Christopher pulled the door shut; the man went on gesticulating beyond the glass.

Cathy came on the line after the phone had rung many times.

'Something has come up,' Christopher said. 'It shouldn't take long.'

'Paul, it's Saturday. My mother has asked us to lunch with them. Papa wants to show us his horse.'

'That's all right. You go on ahead and I'll be there in time for lunch.'

'Paul, come with me now. I don't want to show up alone. I can't *explain* to them. They don't understand.'

Christopher waited. He could hear Cathy's breathing. Disappointment caused her to pant, as if she were running.

'One hour,' Christopher said.

Cathy broke the connection.

4

Maria Rothchild was waiting in the open door, as she had been on his earlier visit. She wore a dressing gown, and a scarf covered her hair. Christopher had never before seen her dishevelled. She led him into the kitchen and turned on the radio.

'Where is David?' she asked.

'He flew home yesterday, after we saw him.'

She lit a Gauloise and inhaled deeply, the cigarette trembling in her lips. She crushed it in the sink. Maria, though she disposed of a whole package of Gauloises every day, never took more than one puff from a cigarette before putting it out. Christopher had never asked why.

'Come with me,' Maria said.

She led Christopher into the sitting room where Otto Rothchild received visitors. Rothchild, fully dressed and awake, sat in his chair. Bud Wilson sat in another chair. Behind Rothchild, on a card table, a lie detector had been set up, and a third man stood by the equipment.

Rothchild lifted his head, as if he were much taller than Christopher, and must speak down to him.

'Explain this,' he said.

'Mr Rothchild,' Wilson said, 'Paul here is not involved in this procedure in any way.'

Rothchild ignored him. 'Maria,' he said, 'has Paul explained this to you?'

'Furthermore,' Wilson said, 'your calling him here is a breach of security.'

'Answer,' Rothchild said.

'No,' Maria replied. 'I didn't discuss it with him. David is in Washington.'

'Did David authorize this?' Rothchild asked.

'His authorization is not required,' Wilson said. 'This is a security investigation and the chief of my division approved the decision.'

'Paul,' Rothchild said, 'were you aware that this was going to be done?'

'The possibility was mentioned to me,' Christopher said.

'What was your reaction, please?'

'Surprise that it had never been done before. And I thought you'd react to it pretty much the way you seem to be doing.'

Christopher crossed the room and looked at the machine. He touched the blood pressure cuff, the chest band that measured respiration, the device that recorded the amount of sweat on the palm of the subject's hand. 'It's the standard box,' the technician said. 'You've seen them before.' The paper tapes were blank. Christopher went back and faced Rothchild.

'What do you want me to do, Otto?' he asked.

'Tell these people to take their machine and go.'

'You can tell them that yourself. They'll leave.'

'But you won't do it?'

'I haven't the authority.'

'Haven't the authority? You're a supergrade staff agent, and you're my case officer. How can they flutter your asset without your authorization?'

Rothchild's voice wavered. Christopher had never heard him refer to himself as an asset. Maria moved to her husband's chair and sat on the arm.

Wilson, one hand dangling over the arm of his own chair, cleared his throat. 'Christopher seems to understand the situation,' he said. 'I'll explain it to you again, Mr Rothchild. This is a routine flutter. It happens to be taking place in the midst of a security investigation, but that doesn't mean that we think you've been lying to us. It's just a matter of making the file complete.'

'The file is complete,' Rothchild said. 'You should read it. I've been in the employ of this organization since before it had a name. No one has ever questioned my integrity in all those years.'

'No one is questioning your integrity now,' Wilson said. 'Every person in this room – Christopher, your wife when she was an officer, myself, Charlie the tech over there – all of us from the Director on down have taken the polygraph. It's required of everyone. We regard it as an essential security tool.'

Christopher said, 'Wilson, can I have a word with you?' They went into the kitchen together. Wilson did not wait for Christopher to speak.

'The answer is, yes, it really is necessary,' Wilson said. 'However, he can refuse.'

'And be fired.'

'That's the usual procedure. For all I know he's a special case, but if he is, he'll be the first.'

Wilson's feet were planted firmly; he faced Christopher in the narrow kitchen as though he had been ordered to defend the room.

'Otto has always been a special case,' Christopher said. 'I don't know why he's never been fluttered. It must seem very strange to you.'

'Unbelievable. How did you guys let it happen? Jesus, Paul – he knows *everyone*. He could blow the whole outfit.'

Christopher saw that there was no hope of explaining this lapse to Wilson. Rothchild was too valuable to lose; no one had wanted to take the consequences of offending him. He insisted on being trusted absolutely, and so far as anyone knew he had always been absolutely trustworthy. Patchen had given Rothchild what no other employee of the Agency had, his privacy.

'All right,' Christopher said to Wilson, 'get your tech out of the room and I'll see what I can do.'

'Look,' Wilson said. 'It's just going to be a routine flutter. Is he queer, is he doubled, does he steal money? It'll take thirty minutes, tops, if he loosens up.'

Christopher sent Maria out of the room with the technician. Rothchild slumped in his chair as the door closed behind her. His eyes remained open and fixed on a point in space between himself and Christopher's standing figure.

'Otto,' Christopher said, 'I'm sorry this is so upsetting to you. But it's no worse than an electrocardiogram. You've had it done a hundred times to other men.'

'Yes, and I suspected every one of them of playing me false.'

'If you don't agree, you'll be terminated. No one will be able to prevent it. It's a bad way to go out, after all you've done and all you've been.'

'It's an insult.'

'That's ridiculous.'

'What can it possibly mean at this of all times except that suddenly I am not trusted?'

Rothchild's eyes were still turned away. Christopher snapped his fingers. Rothchild, startled, looked into his face.

'Otto,' Christopher said, 'if I had known that you'd never been on the box, *I* wouldn't have trusted you. Nor would any of us.'

'That's wonderful to hear. First I give up my health. Now my reputation goes.'

Christopher made no acknowledgement that he had heard. He stared coldly at Rothchild; something moved in the agent's eyes. Rothchild tugged his slack body, inch by inch like a very old man putting on a heavy garment, until he sat upright again. He gazed out the window. At last he nodded.

Christopher called the technician back into the room. Maria returned and stood by with Christopher while the machine was connected to Rothchild. They removed his tweed jacket and lifted his arms while the tube was strapped around his chest. Christopher saw how wasted the muscles had become. Rothchild paid no attention to what was being done. The technician smeared a substance on the palm of Rothchild's hand before attaching the device that measured perspiration. 'The others can leave now,' the technician said. 'We can make this very fast if you can relax, Mr R.'

To Maria, Rothchild said, 'Uncross my legs, please.' Maria lifted the leg, holding it at the knee and the ankle, and placed the foot beside the other. Christopher watched impassively from the doorway.

In the kitchen Wilson suggested a game of gin rummy. He told Christopher, as he dealt the cards, that he always carried a deck in his pocket. Maria Rothchild watched the cards fall for a moment, and then, uttering an unbelieving laugh, left the room.

Wilson won the first two hands. He played with intense concentration and his broken fingers handled the cards with great delicacy. Christopher was reminded of a fat girl he had known in school who was a graceful dancer; she had had a habit of singing as she waltzed, and Wilson, too, hummed a tune as he chose cards and discarded.

Only a few minutes passed before the technician came into the kitchen and took Wilson away with him. Christopher heard the shower running on the other side of the wall, and Maria's sharp smoker's cough as the water was turned off. She returned to the kitchen dressed in one of her pleated skirts, a cardigan around her shoulders. Wilson returned, putting on his coat. He gave Christopher and Maria a quizzical look.

'Charlie put *me* on the box,' he said. 'He wanted to test it. He thought it might be out of commission.'

'Is it all right?' Christopher asked. 'I don't think this ought to be prolonged.'

'On me, the machine works all right,' Wilson said. 'Maria, what kind of operation, exactly, did your husband have?'

'It's called a sympathectomy,' she said. Her eyes widened and she put a flat hand over her mouth. 'Now that's really funny,' she said, and began to laugh.

'They severed the nerves along the spine, and some in the neck, too,' Christopher said. 'It controls his high blood pressure.'

A smile spread over Wilson's face. 'Scared the hell out of Charlie,' he said. 'He thought Rothchild had died on him. Nothing on the box registered except a little bit of respiration. He's got no readable blood pressure, he doesn't sweat. Nothing happens.'

Maria's eyes danced as she listened. 'Of course nothing happens,' she said. 'The nerves that control sweating were cut by the surgeon, and when Otto goes unconscious he has no blood pressure. It really is too funny for words. All this pomposity, with Paul

93

of all people having to pull rank, and then Otto's body turns out to be an unbreakable code.'

In the sitting room Rothchild had been rearranged in his chair by the technician. Christopher went in to say goodbye to him, and together they heard Maria's strident laughter pealing in another part of the house.

With his arched nose and his bottomless eyes, Rothchild looked like the mummy of an Inca, skin turned to parchment by the icy air of a mountain tomb. He laughed aloud, a dozen sharp bursts of breath. A tear of merriment ran crookedly through the hatchwork of wrinkles on his cheek.

Eight

I

The early sun began to warm the earth, and a gusting wind blew streams of ground mist, like the breath of an animal in winter, over the green lawns of the racecourse. Cathy stood by the rail with her hands in her pockets and a long red scarf down the back of her coat. She had been awake for less than half an hour but her eyes were clear and her skin was touched with colour; after sleep or passion or grief, her face at once regained its perfection, showing no traces of the changes that had passed over it.

'They're going to breeze him now,' she said. Her father's thoroughbred, moving on to the track at the opposite side of the infield, was invisible, cloaked in mist to the stirrups. The horse was a bright bay, and seemed to carry its rider, an exercise boy wearing a yellow sweater and a cloth cap turned backwards, through a cloud. Proof that the horse was not in fact flying came to them in a moment, as they first felt the vibration and then heard the sound of its hoofbeats on the turf. Cathy hugged Christopher's arm in both of hers. 'Oh, come on!' she whispered, and the young stallion burst out of the mist and bore down on them with clods of earth flying from his shoes. They smelled the animal, sweat and breath, as he flashed by. Cathy watched him until the boy turned him off the track and the grooms led him back to the stables.

She and Christopher walked toward the gates. 'I like horses better in the morning, when you're in private with them, than when they're racing,' Cathy said. 'Once, at home, when I was little, Papa and I watched a grey colt breezing. He held me up so I could see. It was a perfect morning, sunburnt, the way it can be in Kentucky in the springtime. Watching the colt run – he'd named him Owen Laster after a friend – my father had tears in his eyes. He said, "Catherine, a blooded horse is the only thing in the world lovelier in my sight than you." I've never forgotten those words. It's strange how you don't get the things you want most. I always wanted Papa to name a horse for me and he never did. Just as you won't write a poem about me, Paul.'

Back at the Ritz, they ate breakfast in their room. Cathy kept silent; she had spoken very little since the day before. Christopher found her eyes on him.

'Paul,' she said, 'where did you go yesterday?'

Christopher refolded the newspaper he had been reading and dropped it on the floor. 'I had to go see a man who's sick.'

Cathy said, coldly, 'You had to sit up with a sick spy.' She bit into a croissant. 'Just as you went out the door yesterday,' she said, 'you had a phone call. It was a female.'

'Females make up half the human race, Cathy. If you answer the phone, you've got a fifty-fifty chance of hearing a woman's voice on the line.'

Cathy gave him a tight smile. She did not like his way of treating her jealousy lightly. In Cathy, it was a force, like the flow of blood to the brain, that was in play all the time. When Christopher looked at another woman in the street, Cathy would strike him; once, in the Grand Vefour, she had diverted his attention from a slender French girl at another table by pouring most of a bottle of Pommard into his lap. If he sang a love song she demanded to know what woman from an earlier life he was thinking about. 'To be the way you are,' she told him, 'not to feel jealousy at all, to be that heartless, is a form of madness.'

'I knew the voice of this female,' Cathy said. 'It was Maria Custer. We were at Farmington together. She was three years

96

ahead of me. I thought I knew her voice. I said, "Maria, isn't that you?" And she said, "Who's this?" "Paul's wife, Catherine Kirkpatrick Christopher," I replied. Maria went dead silent and then she said, as if I didn't exist, as if only she and you existed, she said, "Tell Paul I called." That was the whole conversation.'

Cathy was sitting with her back to the tall window, her hair gathering the light.

'I knew that you had been at school at the same time,' Christopher said. 'Maria remembers you.'

'I'm not surprised. She was famous as a field hockey player, and she used to knock me down in practice every chance she got.'

Cathy spread jam on a bit of croissant, then placed it uneaten on her plate.

'Is Maria married?' she asked. 'Does she have children?'

Christopher answered the questions. Cathy asked how long he had know Maria.

'Five years, more or less.'

'And you never thought it would interest me that you and my old schoolmate were friends? Paul, why did she call? Why did you go see her yesterday?'

Christopher returned Cathy's steady look. At last she broke her stare and let her hands fall helplessely into her lap.

'Don't tell me,' she said. 'Maria is a lady spy.'

Christopher did not respond.

Cathy turned her profile towards him. She tossed her head as if to throw back a lock of hair; it was a gesture she seldom made, and one of the few false ones she used.

'Maria,' Cathy said, 'is married to an older man, a White Russian who looks like someone in a silent movie. His name is Otto Rothchild. They live in a place on the Île Saint-Louis that costs four thousand francs a month if it costs a penny, and he's had a stroke or something so that he's partially paralysed.' She paused. 'That's just so you'll realize you don't know everything.'

Christopher laughed at Cathy's animation. She snatched the croissant from her plate and ate it, and drank greedily from her coffee cup.

'How did you find out about Maria being married to Otto?' Christopher asked.

Cathy grinned. 'I have my ways.'

'Seriously, Cathy.'

97

She licked her fingertips. 'Well, I don't exactly live in a vacuum, you know. I'd heard from some of the girls that Maria had married an old man. And I knew she was in Paris because people had seen her, to say hello.'

'So you hunted her down remorselessly.'

'No. I was shopping one day in the Fauborg St Honore, looking for a scarf for me and those nice gloves I got for you, and when I turned around in a shop there was Maria. We were eye to eye. She looked like she wanted to jump through the window for a minute, and then she smiled. We chatted away and then she said it was four o'clock and why didn't we trot down to Queenie's for some tea. Trot down to Queenie's is how she put it. These muscular women are always so arch. So we trotted. We told each other all our news. I said I'd married this delicious man named Paul Christopher and got out all my pictures of you. She said *hmmmm* when she saw you, but she never let on that she knew you. Not a hint.'

'And Maria showed you her pictures of Otto in his wheelchair?'

Cathy shook her head. 'No. After a couple of hours in Queenie's Maria said she was having so much fun talking to me after all those years she wondered if I was free to have dinner at her house. She said she wanted me to meet her husband and they were having something that the cook could stretch for three, and would I come as I was. I had nothing to do except wait for you, so I said sure. The Rothchilds have a very good cook. He, Otto Rothchild that is, did his best to be hospitable. But he really was ill, poor man. He kept lapsing into a stupour, and coming out of it. It was sad. I don't want to go back there.'

Christopher gave himself another cup of coffee. 'When was this?' he asked.

'When you were in Germany,' Cathy replied.

2

On Palm Sunday, Cathy's father's horse fell early in the race. The family stayed late at the American Hospital with the injured jockey, and missed the party they had hoped to attend as victors. 'Your father is positively grateful to Fernando for having broken his leg and rescued us from the Bourbon de Blamonts' soirée,'

Cathy's mother said. 'He says the French are a young man's vice. He likes them less and less as he grows older and older. He doesn't understand why they think they're flattering him when they insult his nationality. Eleazer Kirkpatrick does not take it as a compliment to be told that he is, *heureusement*, not like the other Americans. I have to bind him hand and foot to get him to go inside a French house.'

Cathy and Christopher dined at home with the Kirkpatricks and afterwards watched the older couple play cribbage. Cathy's father broke his silence only to count his cards and peg his score on the board. Her mother had the Southern belle's gift of releasing butterflies of wit each time she spoke. Her name was Letitia, and she and her husband were both called Lee. They were cousins, and even before they were married they were named Lee Kirkpatrick and Lee Kirkpatrick. The male parent seldom spoke. On first meeting he had established that he and Christopher had been in the same regiment of Marines in different wars and in the same house at Harvard; he had never asked Christopher another question. 'He knows everything about you, knowing those two things, that he needs to know,' Cathy said.

Letitia Kirkpatrick was a storyteller. 'Aunt Elizabeth came to stay the week before Ash Wednesday,' she said of an aged relative. 'She likes to be with us before Lent begins, so that she can drink Maker's Mark for her winter ailments without giving offence to the Lord.' She gave an exclamation when she saw the cards her husband had dealt her. 'Eleazer is going to be *skunked*!' she cried. 'Aunt Elizabeth kept fondling your wedding photograph, Cathy, and one night, finally, she said, "Oh my, Lee, what a pity that you did not require Catherine to have a white wedding as every one of our other brides has done since dear dead Ambrose Kirkpatrick came to these lands from Virginia before the Revolution. Dear Catherine looks so much like dear beautiful cousin Eugénie.' Cathy's father knocked peremptorily on the table and his wife counted her score, moving her peg to the last hole.

'My husband is a hateful man,' said Cathy's mother, 'who doubts the genealogy of our family. He believes in the bloodlines of horses because there are witnesses to their acts of procreation, but he is convinced that humans lie about their sex lives. However, and what luck it is for us, Aunt Elizabeth has the family tree by heart. Eugénie *was* our cousin through her Southern mother, and

99

even after she married the Emperor of France she never ceased to long for us. "I have been saving a dozen of Eugénie's crystal goblets," Aunt Elizabeth told me, "dear Eugénie entrusted some of her lovely things into our care after Napoleon lost everything and she had to move to England and didn't entertain nearly so much as she had in Paris. I wanted to give them to Catherine, but of course I had thought she would marry one of us, and I don't know if that Northern boy she ran away with would understand." Understand what? I asked. "That his lips were touchin' the goblet that had been kissed by dear cousin Eugénie," she explained. I said if Cathy was anything like the rest of *my* branch of the Kirk-patricks she would not want a necrophile for a husband, and poor Aunt Elizabeth packed her bags on the instant. She ran wild-haired and weeping down the drive, and I thought we'd have to send the dogs to bring her back. But she came by herself after sitting on her valise for a while under the willow tree.'

Cathy's accent, never entirely subdued in Northern schools, returned to her when she was with her family. As her mother talked, Cathy's eyes shone with the recollection of a childhood in a great creaking house, with packs of dogs in the dooryard and mad cheerful relations in the remodelled slave quarters in the back garden. When her father finished his game of cribbage, she sat on a sofa with her head on his shoulder, asking for more family stories. An amiable ghost called General Wellington Kirkpatrick, Letitia said, lived in the Kirkpatricks' stables. He had fallen from a horse and broken his neck while recuperating from wounds received at the Battle of the Wilderness. Each year, on the night before the Kentucky Derby, the ghost went into the paddocks and frightened the horses at midnight. 'It's one of the sights of the countryside, and relatives come from miles around on the first Friday in May to hang on the fence and watch the horses flying around,' said Cathy's mother. 'Of course, the General is invisible.'

Cathy, fighting tears, said goodbye to her parents. They were packed to fly back to America the next morning. Christopher held her face in his hands as they descended in the elevator. Her eyes had turned a deep bruised blue. Loneliness was, as she had always tried to tell him, a knife in her heart.

They moved from the Ritz to a flat in Montmartre that was used as a safe house. Christopher rose at dawn, and went each day to a different meeting place where Kamensky's novel, a photographic copy of the original and a typescript of the rough English translation, was handed to him by a messenger from the Paris station. At the end of the day he went out again, and gave the pages back to the messenger so that they could be locked overnight in the station's safe.

While Cathy slept, Christopher worked on the book. He read Kamensky's manuscript, and read it again. The Russian language flooded back into his consciousness. At the end of a week he was able to read Kamensky's sentences almost as fluently as he read English, and to feel the rhythm of the language.

The translation into English was the work of technicians and it had come from several hands. Christopher worked on it, as Patchen had ordered him to do, with a red pencil, restoring as best he could Kamensky's original meanings. The beauty of the writing could not be transposed from the Russian to the English. Reading Kamensky, re-creating his echoing sentences, Christopher grew to love him.

Cathy wakened just before noon each day and went out to the market. She would come back with *charcuterie* and cheese and bread and fruit. She bought wine for herself and beer for Christopher. She arranged the food on white plates, folding the cold meats, having bought them as much for colour as for taste, into the shapes of flowers and animals. She liked to see Christopher's amusement. 'What I miss, away from home, is the laughter,' she said. 'You and I laugh all the time, or used to. But no one over here seems to find things funny. I feel impolite when I laugh in public in Europe.'

The weather had turned cold again, and in the afternoons, Cathy wrapped herself in a blanket and curled her legs beneath her in a chair. The dome of Sacré Cœur rose just outside the windows of the apartment, and Cathy gazed at it for hours on end through the blurring rain. She played the piano, softly, at the other end of the long room where Christopher worked. In Kamensky's book was a girl who played the piano. She was blonde like Cathy, and melancholy. Christopher was startled to find Kamensky's girl speaking in Russian to her lover a phrase that Cathy had spoken in English to Christopher. The Russians in the novel were walking in a forest, while Christopher and Cathy in life had been standing on a beach, but the words were almost exactly the same. 'What do you want?' the real girl and the imaginary one had been asked. Both had replied, 'Not what other girls want. No children, no career. I want a perfect union with a man.'

Cathy found the mechanics of secret life ridiculous. Christopher would not let her use the telephone in the flat, or leave letters that came to her parents' apartment lying about in the safe house, or have deliveries made from shops. One night the messenger had been ill, and Christopher had carried Kamensky's heavy manuscripts with him in a briefcase to a restaurant and the theatre and had gone to sleep with them on the bedside table.

'Really, Paul, it's like Tom Sawyer and Huck Finn swearing oaths in the haunted house.'

'Yes. It's asinine. The whole idea of secret life is asinine, but if you don't live it by these rules you make mistakes. Others are involved, and to them it's no joke.'

'More and more it seems to me it's a mistake to live it at all. You can live any life you want to, Paul. You can, you know.'

'This is the life I want, not any other.'

'If this is what it is, sitting around in a shabby apartment watching it rain, I don't see why you love it so.'

'It's not always so tranquil.'

Christopher had finished his work for the day. Cathy crossed the room, bringing her blanket, and sat on his lap; she covered them both with the rough woollen robe. 'My papa used to tell me that my bones were filled with air, and that I was no heavier than a hummingbird when I sat on his lap,' she said. 'Did he lie?' Christopher nodded. 'Southern men are perfect,' Cathy said.

The happy days with her mother and father, the long quiet hours in the apartment, the simple pattern of work and music, eating in plain restaurants, going to the movies, had begun to take Cathy back to what she had been before she had gone to bed with Franco Moroni. Christopher did not speak to her of her adultery, and after a few days Cathy stopped talking about it as well. She made love more shyly now, she waited for Christopher to move towards her in bed. He asked her why.

'I've lost the right to ask you for love,' she said.

'You're wrong.'

'You keep on saying it's all right, Paul, that I'm the same. But I'm not. You can't really think that I am.'

They were lying in the dark. The bedroom in the safe house had no windows; some earlier owner had torn out the whole interior of the apartment in order to make an enormous salon and dining room, but he had left only one small dark corner in which to sleep and another for a kitchen.

'Cathy, you think of that night you spent with him as a mutilation.'

'You are so right.'

'What do you need to be healed?'

'Paul, the only thing I need is for you to care that it happened.'

'I care.'

Sentences formed in Christopher's mind: It's your body, you can do anything you like with it. I don't own your flesh or your mind because I love you. He didn't speak; Cathy would never abide such thoughts.

'I know you care,' Cathy said. 'But for me, not for yourself. If you did to me what I've done to you, I'd kill you in your sleep.'

Christopher gathered her body into his arms. She lay inert for an instant before she responded. In daylight, now, she sometimes looked away when she spoke to him.

'I wish I had another life, the way you do, Paul,' she said. 'Maybe I could stay inside it, as cold as you, and learn the secret you told me when I told you about Franco.'

'The secret?'

'Of how to love, and feel nothing.'

4

Christopher finished his work on the Kamensky manuscript and gave it to the Paris station to be retyped.

Christopher, meanwhile, waited for an agent to come from Dakar for a meeting in Paris. The man had been instructed to meet him on the last Wednesday in April at noon, by the tomb of the unknown soldier beneath the Arch of Triumph. If the meeting failed, he was to come to the same place again at ninety-minute intervals until he made contact with Christopher. The African was six hours late. Christopher watched his tall figure, swathed in a heavy overcoat, as it dodged through the traffic of the Place de l'Étoile. Tyres shrieked, horns sounded in violation of the law.

'I assure you,' the African said, 'that I was not followed for the last hundred metres of my journey.' He offered no explanation for being late and Christopher asked for none. He led the agent into the underground passage, then into the crowded Métro. When he was satisfied that they were alone he took the man into a brasserie and ordered dinner. The man's name was Iboudou; he sent his steak back to be cooked again; he had the horror of the *civilisé* for rare meat.

The debriefing took a long time, as it usually did with blacks. The man was a rising politician. Christopher had given him money and technical assistance to found a party newspaper. He had financed trips abroad for the politician's supporters, and arranged scholarships for promising young men. The politician had gradually, with Christopher's secret funds and Christopher's secret advice, built up a base of support. Christopher had recruited him because he was intelligent and self-interested, qualities he had derived from a European education. Also, he was from a minor tribe that was acceptable to the two large ones which contended, sometimes bloodily, for control of their new nation. It was thought that Christopher's agent might even, if a compromise became necessary to avert civil war, be made prime minister. He was already in the government.

In Iboudou's country, Christopher had seen one man mounted on a writhing woman while a second waited to cut her throat, and yet another man, his white robe spotted with blood and his face dazed as if by a powerful drug, walking down a dusty road with the severed heads of children swinging from either hand. When all the members of the rival tribe had been hunted through the streets and killed in this village, Christopher had seen a grave containing a hundred bodies. All the young girls, and many of the women, had been disembowelled. There had been no reason for the massacre, no spark that could be said to have set off the carnival of rape and murder; it had just happened, as it happened again a week later, with the tribes changing places as victims and murderers, in a village at the other end of the country. Iboudou was the alternative to slaughter. That was the policy conceived in the brain of the American government. Christopher, executing policy deep in its body, had lost his trust in ideas. In a *pissoir* he gave Iboudou the money he was owed, and required him to sign the receipt with a thumbprint. 'Do you,' asked Iboudou, 'use invisible ink for white men?'

5

The safe house in Montmartre was at the top of a flight of stone stairs, and Christopher mounted them slowly, so as to remain behind the pair of policemen who climbed ahead of him. There was no light in the windows of the flat on the top floor. Christopher entered the darkened hallway. The concierge, a grey bony woman who seemed never to sleep, came out of her lodge and switched on the motor of the elevator. Christopher thanked her, and exchanged a word with her about the cold rain while he waited for the lift to descend; she told him that the weather made her joints ache. Cathy, accustomed to her parents' concierge who had been made servile by large tips, was disconcerted by this suspicious female, and after the first few days in the safe house had ceased speaking to her. Christopher, going up in the cage of the elevator, watched the concierge below, shivering in the night air. When she heard him close the gates at the top she brought the lift back down and turned off its motor again.

The flat was empty. Cathy's music, sheets that she had bought in a neighbourhood shop, was still on the rack of the piano, and the plate she had used for lunch was on the table with the remains of her food drying on the surface of the china.

Her clothes were gone, and her suitcase. Christopher looked for a note, but found none. He went over the apartment foot by foot. There was no sign that Cathy had come to any harm.

Downstairs, he found the concierge still loitering in the hall. She pressed the light switch; the dim bulb was on a timer, designed to give the tenants time enough, and no more, to pass from the outer door to the lift. As she and Christopher spoke, the light went on and off repeatedly. The bulb, when it was burning, buzzed like an insect trapped between the panes of a double window.

'Mademoiselle departed at about five o'clock,' said the concierge. 'She had a large bag, and there was no one to help her with it. It took her quite a long time to go down the steps. She found a taxi at the bottom.'

'She left no envelope for me?'

The concierge gave Christopher a sardonic look and shook her head.

'We were expecting a visitor,' Christopher said. 'Did any one come?'

'Male or female?'

'One of each, madame, a man and his wife.'

'Evidently the wife remained at home. The gentleman came at noon, only minutes after you yourself had left. He remained for two hours, perhaps longer. No doubt Mademoiselle invited him to lunch.'

Christopher nodded. 'I'll be leaving myself in the morning,' he said, 'and I wanted to thank you for your kindness to us.' He gave the concierge a fifty-franc note. Without looking at it, she crumpled it in her fist like an unwelcome letter.

'The gentleman who came,' Christopher said. 'Describe him.'

'American, not handsome, middle-aged. His clothes did not fit. He was evidently a strong man. He went up the stairs instead of using the lift. He ran all the way up.'

From a telephone in a bar, Christopher called the Kirkpatricks' apartment, and asked the maid, in French, for himself. Then he asked for Mme Christopher.

'Neither Monsieur nor Miss Catherine is here.'

'May I leave a message?'

'But they are in Rome, monsieur. I don't know when they will be back, it may be weeks.'

Christopher dialled the home number of the chief of the Paris station. He identified himself, and, using Wilson's telephone name, asked where he was staying.

'I don't know.'

'I want to see him now.'

There was a silence. 'All right. Inside, in an hour.'

The crowd of French police lounging outside the American Embassy watched Christopher idly as he walked through the front door. The duty officer was waiting for him by the Marine guard's desk. Upstairs, in an empty corridor, he stopped and faced Christopher. 'The French may have taken your picture,' he said. 'We gave t hem some infra-red equipment, and it would be like them to try it out on us. Was the police van parked where it usually is?'

'Yes, down the avenue Gabriel.'

'Too far away, then. But we'll sneak you out the back. Bud is here, working late. He awaits. Call me when you're ready to go.'

Wilson was using an office in which the entire ceiling was covered with fluorescent light fixtures. He sat with his feet on a green steel desk, covered with file folders with secret labels on them. The burn basket, a transparent plastic tube, was half filled with fragments of torn paper. Wilson pushed his reading glasses on to his forehead and reached inside his shirt to scratch his chest. He wore no tie and a thick tuft of greying hair curled at his unbuttoned collar.

'It's two o'clock in the morning,' Wilson said. 'Don't you ever go to bed?'

Christopher sat down and moved the burn basket to one side in order to have an unobstructed view of Wilson.

'You called on my wife this afternoon,' Christopher said.

Wilson nodded.

'You didn't think it was necessary to tell me beforehand?'

'I assumed you'd be there. When you weren't, I thought I'd come to the point anyway.'

'Which was?'

Wilson laced his hands behind his head and examined the canopy of light on the ceiling. In the absence of shadows, he looked older, more pallid. His beard showed patches of white.

'I ask you,' Christopher said, 'because I found her gone and I don't know where she is.'

Wilson put his feet on the floor and looked at the burn basket.

'I'm sorry,' Wilson said. 'She was uspet. Sometimes you touch a nerve you don't expect to.'

Christopher moved the burn basket again, putting it out of sight on the floor. He watched Wilson.

'Putting pieces of paper together,' Wilson said, 'I saw that she and Maria Rothchild had once known each other. I asked her about that.'

'And that upset her?'

'No, it was the other connection.'

Wilson picked up a cardboard coffee cup and turned it between his fingers, delicately, as he had handled the cards at gin rummy.

'I'm telling you what I'm telling you as an officer, not as a husband,' he said. 'You and your wife know an Italian named Franco Moroni. He's a film-maker in Rome. He calls himself a Communist. A romantic. I had a piece of paper from Rome. The station there is running a German girl who likes to screw Communists and movie producers, sometimes both at the same time.'

'Come on,' Christopher said.

'The German kid has been doing it for Moroni, with us paying her the fee. We want to know where he gets the money for his movies, and so on. To make it as short as I can, the German asset reports that Moroni is boasting that he's sleeping with the wife of a prominent American journalist named Paul Christopher.'

Christopher did not move. 'You asked Cathy about that?'

'Not directly. I asked how well she knew Moroni, and if she had ever discussed your whereabouts with him when you were out of town.'

'Why?'

'You know why. I'm trying to find the blown fuse. Maybe if Moroni knew you were in Berlin, he told somebody like our German girl and the word got passed to Moscow or somewhere. If they've got him on the string, they've got someone talking to him.'

'What did Cathy reply?'

'She didn't. She just ran into the other room.'

'You were there for two hours.'

'Your wife gave me a nice lunch, and played the piano. We talked about you. She acted like a woman who really loves her husband. It was only in the last five minutes that we discussed Moroni.'

'What's your conclusion?'

Wilson put down the empty coffee container. 'I don't know. I told her it wasn't you who had told us about Moroni. I had to shout through the closed door. She wouldn't open up. I don't know if she believed me.'

Nine

I

Christopher telephoned Cathy at six in the morning. She must still have been awake because she answered on the second ring. He heard music, tape recordings of Cathy's own performance of Schumann, playing in another room of the Rome apartment. When she heard his voice she hung up the phone. Christopher told the telephonist that he had been cut off. But Cathy did not answer when the call went through again, and in the days that followed he heard the busy signal again and again, and knew that she had taken the telephone off the hook.

Christopher met an agent in Casablanca and walked with the man through the dark shuttered city which might have been, except for the smell of dust and the deathly night-time silence, a French town in the provinces. The Arab held Christopher's arm like a petty French functionary imparting a confidence, and murmured his report as they strode with measured step back and forth for an hour in the same narrow street. Christopher listened, and responded, with the surface of his mind. In its depths he listened to Cathy and heard himself reply. He glimpsed her in his imagination as she knelt in a bed and lifted her breast towards the lips of a stranger.

Christopher stopped in Rome on his way back to Paris. Cathy wasn't in the apartment on the Lungotevere, though her jewels were scattered on the dressing table and there were other signs of her presence. Christopher looked for her on the Via Veneto and in Trastevere. The car was gone, and he supposed that she was driving around the city with the top down in the mild night. He went back to the apartment and left a letter for her. At first he laid it on her pillow; then he moved it to the dressing table.

In Paris, Wilson sought him out. His voice was strained and he had more trouble than ever meeting Christopher's eyes.

'I want you to know,' he said, 'that we had our German girl plant a transmitter in Moroni's apartment.'

'Do you really think that's going to produce anything?'

'Somebody had to blow your meeting with Bülow. If you've got a better candidate than Moroni I'll be glad to hear about it.'

Christopher ceased replying. Wilson, at length, shook his head, looked at the floor, and clumsily squeezed Christopher's shoulder. '*She's* not a suspect,' he said.

'Her voice is on the tapes?'

Wilson yawned; Christopher had never observed in one man so many signs of embarrassment.

'I'm the only one that recognizes her voice,' Wilson said. 'Moroni doesn't call her by name, he calls her Bella.'

'Small "b",' Christopher said, '*bella*. Beautiful.'

2

Patchen was more comfortable in Paris now that it was May and his conversations with Christopher could take place without discomfort in the open air. On the day of his return to Paris, they met at the café in the Pré Catelan in the Bois de Boulogne. Patchen arrived first but ordered nothing until Christopher joined him; he read French perfectly, but he let Christopher speak for him to the French; to be misunderstood was, to Patchen, humiliation. With a vermouth cassis before him, he began to talk; it was too early for the luncheon crowd and he and Christopher were all but alone.

'We've got a crypt for the Kamensky operation,' he said. 'It will be called Tuning Fork.'

'Then there will be an operation.'

'Yes. Beginning now.'

'I'll point out for the last time that we're risking Kamensky's life.'

'You do insist on that point, don't you?' Patchen said. 'You'll be glad to know that I've got the Tuning Fork Working Group to act on your scruple.'

Patchen's voice had no timbre; one had to infer his tone from his choice of words, and he was never more sarcastic than when he had done a favour. It's no wonder, Christopher thought, that you have enemies. Patchen continued, fingering his untouched drink.

'We're going to try to get Kamensky out. It was decided, even Dick Sutherland agreed, to give them something for him, something important.'

'What?'

'I don't know. Trade goods. Sutherland is looking in his cupboard.'

Christopher said, 'What if the opposition doesn't buy it?'

Patchen watched a woman and a child as they fed a flock of birds. He kept his eyes on them when he spoke to Christopher again.

'Then we'll have done our best. We'll publish and Kamensky will be left behind.'

'We'll execute Otto's plan, in short.'

'Yes. I circulated it. It reinforced what the whole working group wanted to do. Otto foresaw that, of course. No one in Washington really wanted to make the case for publication of the novel, on the record. It might look bad if, after all, the KGB killed Kamensky. Otto has always been hailed as an unimpeachable expert on the Russian mind. Maybe he is. In any case, he gave them the rationale to do what they wanted to do, and if anything goes wrong it will be Otto who looks bad. And that doesn't matter.'

'How will you and I look?'

'Like fools. As you might suspect, there's an element of hope back home that that's the way we *will* look. The area divisions are with us in case we win. If we lose, and Kamensky is murdered and the KGB can find a way to prove we had a hand in causing them to do it, then our allies at Headquarters will have to say, as they have said before, that covert action operations really ought to be given to the real pros. Themselves.'

Patchen put money on the table and stood up. He and Christopher walked through the Shakespeare Garden. Patchen was amused by the idea of making a garden of all the trees, plants, and herbs mentioned in the works of the Bard. 'Where,' he asked, 'does the wild thyme grow? Some Frenchman must have known God's own amount about Shakespeare's botany. Another expert in the trivial.' Patchen strolled on. 'Isn't there a place to rent rowboats here?' he asked. 'Let's have a ride on the water before lunch.'

From the lake, the huge studio windows of the Kirkpatricks' apartment could be seen, like mirrors in the midday sun. Patchen sat errect in the stern of the rowboat. Christopher shipped the oars.

'I'll give you the scenario,' Patchen said. 'It isn't exactly what you'll want, but, then, it never is. You're free to modify it, within reason, in the light of conditions in the field.'

Christopher's eye was drawn to the Kirkpatricks' windows. He envisioned the room beyond them glowing in sunlight that magnified the objects within and intensified their colours. He uttered Cathy's name. Patchen raised his eyebrows. Christopher told him to go on with what he was saying.

'It has been decided,' Patchen said, 'to use this Frenchman, Claude de Cerutti. He is, after all, Kamensky's discoverer. He's in a bad financial position. Otto knows him. Otto will introduce you to him under a cover name. You'll be an innocent young man, just back from Russia. This manuscript has fallen into your hands by means you cannot, as a matter of honour, describe. You will be jumpy about the whole transaction. You will give Cerutti the notion that he, not you, is the old hand at international intrigue. So far, it sounds just like you, doesn't it?'

'Yes. You're quoting my operational proposal.'

'I know. You are going to give Cerutti world rights to this book and let him peddle it in other countries in other languages.'

'World rights? They might be worth millions.'

'A thought that will, I'm sure, occur to Cerutti. But you'll have a secret agreement with him, that one quarter of all profits will be paid into a numbered Swiss account. Ostensibly, that will be your share of the take.'

'What if he doesn't pay?'

Patchen put a hand in the murky water of the lake, and snapped the moisture from his fingers on to the bottom of the boat.

'People pay,' he said. 'Cerutti is not, according to Otto, a cretin. In the end, he'll certainly figure you for what you are, and I think he'll surmise that it's a matter of sound business practice to play it straight with you.'

'What happens to the money in Switzerland?'

'Another point for you, Paul. We deduct operational expenses and hold the rest for Kamensky or his heirs. Sooner or later he or his kids will get out of Russia. When they do, they'll be rich. It's a little gift from us to them, in addition to the regular royalties that will be put into a blocked account for Kamensky.'

'Why did Headquarters agree to that?'

'It was something you said to me. I paraphrased it, of course. You said Kamensky wasn't an agent, so we had no right to sacrifice him. Of course, he *is* an agent – unwitting, yes, but an agent from the moment we got our hands on his book. That's the way the KGB would look at it. Kamensky's spent twenty years in prison camps. If one of our fellows is captured and put away, we give him his back pay when he gets out, no matter how long he's locked up. Same principle for Kamensky. At first the concept baffled every-one back home, but then they saw it as a way of congratulating themselves on their instinctive human decency. And, of course, it cost the treasury nothing. So they approved.'

'Very nice,' Christopher said. 'Worthy of Otto.'

'I'm glad you approve. I want you to seduce this Cerutti before the end of the month. Put all your other ops aside, cancel all your agent meetings. Stay in Paris. I don't want any paper on you in true name anywhere for at least two weeks. I have a Canadian passport for you and other black ID. Move into a hotel. Don't give Cerutti a moment's rest until you've got him. I want this book printed, bound, and ready to go, if we have to go, in sixty days.'

'How is Cerutti going to pay for all this?'

'An angel is going to appear with a black bag. That's how Claude will know that God is on his side. You can remind him that He's a jealous God.'

Christopher put the oars back in the oarlocks.

'Pull for the island,' Patchen said. 'Isn't there a restaurant there?'

Maria Rothchild brought tea on a silver tray. Patchen, who had the full use of only one hand, refused a pastry. So did Christopher, who did not like sweets. Maria ate a *mille feuilles*. 'I do this in the intervals when Otto's eyes are closed,' she said. 'He thinks I'm reckless about my figure.'

Patchen walked with his teacup around the four walls of the sitting room. He looked intently at each picture. 'Otto, you've collected wisely,' he said. Rothchild gave Maria a look: what does this bureaucrat know?

'Have you had this place swept, as I asked?' Patchen asked.

'Yes. Wilson-Watson-Wharton had his technician do it. No enemy is listening.'

'Is Wilson still coming around?'

'Every day, practically,' Maria said. 'It's not as bad as all that really, but he does come often. You heard about the great polygraph adventure?'

'Yes. Evidently those Swiss surgeons disconnected your conscience, Otto. You ought to tell Paul the cost of the operation. I think we could justify it as an operational expense in his case.'

Without preamble, Patchen told Rothchild that the Kamensky manuscript would be published.

'Tomorrow,' he said, 'I want you to introduce your pal Claude de Cerutti to your young Canadian friend, Paul Cowan, here.'

'Paul will handle the seduction?'

'Yes, and all the leg work. He'll keep you posted.'

'I am to know nothing of what is going on between Paul and Cerutti, so far as Cerutti knows?'

'Nothing. You just bring them together.'

'I've known Cerutti for twenty-five years. He will know.'

'No, Otto, he will not *know*. He'll suspect. We know how to live with that.'

Rothchild whistled through his bloodless lips. Patchen refused to believe in Rothchild's boredom.

'I'm going to speak plainly to you, Otto,' Patchen said. 'This is your operation. You conceived it. But in its execution, you are in the background. You must not show up on anybody's screen. If there was some other way of putting Paul and Cerutti together, I'd do it.'

'Then let Paul walk in on him cold.'

There was a sound of breathing in the quiet room. Maria, her lips and her fists clenched, was staring fixedly at the pattern in the carpet.

'David,' she said, 'what, exactly, is the point of treating Otto like some GS-8 just off the farm? I don't understand you.'

'Then I must make myself plainer. The security of this operation was compromised at the beginning. I don't want it compromised again, not in the smallest way. Not through ego, not through mistakes.'

Rothchild glanced from face to face, as if he were chairman of the meeting. 'If there's no more to be said on this subject,' he said, 'I suggest we discuss more pressing questions.'

Patchen described to Rothchild the outlines of the operation. Rothchild said, 'You've changed very little of what I recommended. The money arrangement is good. Cerutti will be dazzled by it. He'll have too much to lose to compromise us.'

'That's the idea.'

'You haven't said what language you intend to publish in.'

'We're using a French publisher.'

'A French publisher,' Rothchild said, emphasizing each word, 'who was once the leading publisher of Russian language books in Europe.'

Maria, as Rothchild spoke this last sentence, stirred on the sofa beside Christopher.

'Paul has read the Russian original,' Rothchild said. 'What does he think of it?'

'I've told you, Otto,' Christopher said. 'It's a great novel.'

'Could you do it justice in your attempts to fix up the English translation?'

'You know the answer. Kamensky's writing can't be translated. It's still very powerful in English, but it hasn't the heat of his Russian.'

'Exactly. If you cannot do it in English, and you're a man with a mind and a poetic gift very like Kamensky's, Paul – if not in English, which is the closest language to Russian in its depth and its resonance, what will happen in French?'

'French isn't *big* enough,' Maria said. 'French is too limited a

115

language to encompass such a vast work of art as *The Little Death*.'

'French managed to contain Voltaire and Flaubert and Baudelaire,' Christopher said.

'And Victor Hugo, *hélas*,' replied Maria.

Patchen avoided Christopher's eyes. 'I thought I understood you wanted this book published first in French, Otto. Did I miss something?'

'No, David, *I* missed something. Incessantly, you and Paul talk about Kamensky, Kamensky, Kamensky. Well, what about him?'

No one replied. Rothchild waited until he had their full attention.

'What Kamensky wants is for his work to be published in Russian,' Rothchild said. 'Cerutti has the printer to do it. He can bring it out in French and in Russian on the same day.'

'It's brilliant,' Maria said. She went to Rothchild and put her hands on the back of his chair, caressing the fabric as if it were part of his body.

Patchen now looked full at Christopher. 'Yes,' he said. 'It is brilliant. Dick Sutherland will love it. Russian émigrés will be smuggling copies into the Soviet Union like girls into Arabia.'

'That may happen,' said Rothchild. He stirred in his chair. 'It might even make a nice little secondary op for Sutherland's shop, to keep him happy. But the main thing is Kiril Alekseivich Kamensky. We've decided to give his work to the world. Let's give it to the world whole, as he made it.'

As he spoke, Rothchild actually leaned forward in his chair, panting with effort, pointing a trembling forefinger at them.

It was dusk when Patchen and Christopher left the Rothchilds. They walked over the Pont Sully and along the boulevard towards the Bastille. Patchen was limping badly. They found a café and Christopher ordered beer for them both.

'You said nothing to Otto about getting Kamensky out.'

'No,' Patchen replied. 'I don't think Otto needs to know about that.'

Christopher said, 'David.' Patchen kept his eyes on the passing traffic.

'David,' Christopher said, 'you do see that Otto is trying to kill Kamensky, don't you?'

Patchen snapped his tongue against his teeth, softly.

'So it seems,' he said. 'It must be his illness.'

'You think Otto doesn't see what he's doing?'

Patchen was weary. 'I don't know. Why would he want Kamensky to die?'

'Printing his novel in Russian will guarantee it,' Christopher said.

'Perhaps.'

'No, David, not perhaps. It's a death warrant. Are you going to do it?'

Patchen turned to Christopher and this time there was emotion in his voice. 'Am *I* going to do it?' he said. He spoke Christopher's false name, the one by which he was known inside the Agency. 'Not alone. If we do it, *we* are going to print Kamensky's book in Russian – you, me, Otto, Sutherland, Horst Bülow's ghost, all of us. And if it kills him, we'll accept that and do the same thing another day. We are the apparatus, and that's the kind of thing we do.'

Ten

I

Claude de Cerutti wore the rosette of the Resistance in the button-hole of his sober blue suit. He was a short round man with a rubicund face and a halo of grey curls around his bald skull.

'In the Resistance,' Otto told Christopher, 'one of Cerutti's cover names was *Le Frère Éméché*, the Tipsy Friar.'

'What was Otto's?'

'That's still a secret,' Rothchild said.

'Jaguar,' said Cerutti. 'He was head of counter-intelligence in our *réseau*. A stealthy night-living animal, much feared by those who had reason to be afraid.'

Cerutti, when he was introduced to Christopher, stood back and examined his face, a puzzled look in his bright eyes. Maria had forewarned Christopher that it was one of Cerutti's poses to pretend that he had previously met everyone to whom he was introduced, but could not quite remember the new person. He asked Christopher where in the United States he came from.

'I'm a Canadian, from Toronto.'

'Surely not? You don't speak French like a Canadian.'

'French is not spoken in Toronto.'

Cerutti, when he spoke to Otto Rothchild or made a remark

Rothchild was meant to overhear, had a way of raising his voice. 'It's extraordinary,' he said in a piercing tone, 'how all the North Americans I meet at the Rothchilds' talk French like natives. No Frenchman will believe it. They say I am the only man in France who has ever met a comprehensible American.'

Cerutti had brought a bottle of champagne, carrying it from his car in a silver ice bucket, and he rose from his chair to give more wine to Maria and Christopher. He brushed Maria's hand as he filled her glass.

'It was that touch of Maria's skin for which I travelled all the way from the avenue Foch,' he said. 'Otto thinks I am performing a corporal act of charity, visiting him each Wednesday as I do. The truth is more corporeal. I hope to persuade Otto's wife to come away with me to the South Sea islands. I am mad for American girls, a Neanderthal entranced by a female of the Cro-Magnons. Such exquisitely cruel beauty; they are the first examples of another stage of mankind.'

Cerutti, standing above Christopher's seated figure, asked him a series of questions about himself. He spoke still in the light tone of voice that he had used when flirting with Maria, but with the faint hostility of a European speaking to a foreigner whom he cannot define by the standards of his own circle. Christopher answered easily with his cover story: his name was Paul Cowan, he was the orphaned son of a banker from Toronto, he was unmarried, he had gone to McGill University, he was hoping to write.

'One must not *hope* to write,' said Cerutti. 'One must write. It is necessary to wring an apology from Gide.'

'I'm not aiming to be Proust. I think it's better to get out of the cork-lined room, to travel. Even to catch cold. I've just been to Russia.'

Cerutti's interest was aroused. 'And what is Russia like? I haven't been there since I was younger than you. As Otto was coming out, a dispossessed aristocrat, I was going in, a young firebrand who thought he'd inherited the future. Ah, the Russian Revolution! All my friends died of it.'

'Not quite all,' Rothchild said.

'No, Otto, there's you, but ex-Social Democrats hardly count. I speak of the Red heroes. You were a pink hero – the only one ever, so far as I know.'

Cerutti returned his attention to Christopher. 'Tell me about your trip,' he said. 'Was it one of the Intourist things where you see no one and look at all those pictures of boys and girls on tractors?'

'Mostly. I tried to get off the beaten track a little. You can slip away if you're not too obvious. I talked to some of the ordinary Russians.'

'Talked to them? You speak Russian?'

'A little. I had a Russian mother.'

The real Paul Cowan, who had died at Dieppe, had in fact been the son of a woman who had been brought out of Petrograd in 1917.

Cerutti's eyes, shining but opaque, never wavered. 'What sort of people did you speak Russian to in Moscow?' he asked Christopher.

'All sorts. Of course everyone thought I was an American, it's the bane of Canadian nationality. The Russians seem to feel about Americans as you do about American women, that they are one stage ahead of everyone else in the evolutionary process.'

'Do you agree with that view?'

'Not quite. I come from the most anti-American country on earth.'

'Canada? Ah, no. *America* is the most anti-American country on earth. When you speak of public opinion, my dear young man, you speak of the opinions of the intellectuals because they are the only ones who publish and broadcast. The masses *are* dumb. Intellectuals always hate their own country, but the United States has produced an intelligentsia that is positively bloodthirsty.'

'You see America as a benevolent force?'

'What does it matter what it *is*?' Cerutti asked. 'It's what it symbolizes. Food, clothes, cars, dancing. Money. These are the things mankind lusts for. If one country shows that these things are available to the comman man, all others will have to become like it, or fall.'

Otto Rothchild cleared his throat. 'This is the young Communist who fought the Whites in Russia, Franco in Spain, the Gestapo in the streets of Paris,' he said.

'Yes,' Cerutti said, raising both short arms above his head, 'with these little fists. One day I unclenched my hands and wondered why I had not preferred the itching palm all my life.'

Cerutti resumed his questions. Christopher told him that he

had tried to meet other writers and artists. There was, he had found, a considerable underground. Stories, poems, even whole novels were passed from hand to hand. Their readers copied them on typewriters so that extra copies could be circulated.

'They confided this to you, a foreigner? Showed you the manuscripts?'

'There's not much to confide. It's well known that this goes on. The Russians, the literary sort of Russians anyway, are dying to speak to the rest of the world. Their country is a huge cloister, intellectually speaking, with everyone in involuntary celibacy.'

'And you got in the window, among the novices?'

Christopher grinned. 'I hadn't thought of it in quite that way. We talked, drank, stayed up all night. It was like being back at the university.'

'Surely it was very dangerous for these young Russians?'

'We were careful.'

'Careful? You're very innocent. Probably one in five of your young rebels was a KGB informer.'

'That I doubt.'

Cerutti shrugged. 'Good luck to your friends, then.'

Descending in the lift Cerutti clasped his silver champagne bucket, elaborately chased and decorated like a coarse enlargement of a Cellini miniature, to his chest. His chatter had ceased as the door of the Rothchilds' apartment closed behind him.

For two hours, Cerutti had barely interrupted himself. He had flirted with Maria, told stories of Russia and Spain during their civil wars – he had fought for the Communists in both conflicts. He spoke of his ancestry: he was descended on one side from a Jesuit philosopher of the French Revolution, on the other from the chef de cuisine Catherine de Medici had brought to Paris when she married Henri II. 'How can one be descended from a Jesuit?' Maria asked. 'Don't ask rude questions,' Cerutti replied; 'my ancestors introduced cooking and even the fork to France, and, having civilized this country in the sixteenth century, radicalized it in the eighteenth.' In the lift with Christopher, however, Cerutti was quiet.

'You've known Otto a long time, I gather,' Christopher said.

'During two wars.'

'Don't tell me you met in the First World War as well as the Second?'

'No. In Spain in 1936 and then during the last war with the Germans.'

They were very close together in the tiny cage. Christopher smiled, reflecting how little Patchen, who had arranged this situation, would have enjoyed feeling the heat of Cerutti's body, smelling the wine on the Frenchman's breath and the cologne beneath his sweaty clothes. Cerutti stood back and permitted Christopher to struggle with the doors of the lift after it had groaned to a stop. The two men shifted their bodies to make room for the inner doors to swing into the cabin with them; Cerutti held his silver bucket aloft to protect it.

'How do you happen to know Rothchild?' he asked. 'Of course, he knows everyone.'

'My mother. Russian émigrés all know one another.'

'Was she, too, a member of the old nobility?'

'Weren't they all?'

Cerutti pursed his lips; he was beginning to look upon Christopher with interest.

'Otto is quite genuine, a descendant of Demetrius Donskoy, who defeated the Golden Horde on the Kulikovo Plain in 1380,' he said. 'Much better than being a Romanov. For years I doubted Otto's lineage. His behaviour was all wrong for a displaced boyar.'

Christopher, with a change of expression, asked for the completion of the joke.

'He never borrowed money,' Cerutti said.

In the street, they shook hands. Christopher hesitated for a moment, then asked Cerutti if he would care to have dinner with him one night that week. Cerutti handed him the ice bucket and took a date book from an inner pocket. He studied it, holding it at arm's length.

'Tomorrow,' he said. 'I have no other free night this week.'

Christopher agreed. Cerutti uncapped a large fountain pen. 'It's Paul what?' he asked.

'Cowan.' Christopher spelled the name. 'Hotel Vendôme.'

Hearing the name of this hotel, Cerutti showed new signs of alertness.

'What restaurant do you prefer, and what time? You're my guest, of course.'

'Something simple,' Cerutti replied. 'Lasserre, for example.'
'Fine. Eight o'clock.'

Cerutti disappeared around the corner. Christopher, walking more slowly in the same direction, saw him drive away in a battered Simca.

2

As they rose in the elevator at Lasserre, an even smaller cage than the one at the Rothchilds', Cerutti ran a fingertip over its walls lined with red and gold cut velvet. 'The perfect place in which to ravish a virgin, I've always thought,' he said. 'But when to do it – going up with all the senses undulled, or going down, with all appetites satisfied except the sexual one?'

Cerutti was known to the head waiter; Christopher, as usual, was not recognized. They were moved from the small table that had been reserved for an unknown named Cowan to a more favourable location. Cerutti, tonight wearing the Legion of Honour in his buttonhole, ordered the dinner and the wines; he explained to Christopher how each dish was made, and instructed him to search for the taste of the ingredients. He told him anecdotes about the wine they were drinking. In the war, he said, he had watched from a hiding place while German troops with flame-throwers destroyed a whole field of vines at a château famous for the white wine they were now drinking. The German commander posted a notice explaining that the chatelaine had given food to the Maquis. 'In fact, she had been the German colonel's mistress, and they had quarrelled,' Cerutti said. 'I thought I'd never drink this wine again.'

Christopher listened. He had done what he was doing a hundred times before. Cerutti was an intelligent man, and according to the files he had been a brave one. As he talked, observing Christopher for signs of admiration, making himself a familiar of the waiter, Christopher began to see his weakness. It could not be called vanity; it was worse. Cerutti was a man who had had to settle for the mere forms of recognition. He knew that he was more than the head waiter in Lasserre or the Minister who had done him the offhand favour of putting him up for medals realized. Cerutti was too small, too funny, too reckless in showing his intelligence. It had cost him his place as a man among serious men. The fault was so evident that Christopher, reviewing in his mind all that he had read and heard about Cerutti, felt a pang of anxiety. It seemed impossible that this man had not already been ensnared by another intelligence service. It made no difference; Christopher, often enough, had found use for men that others had believed worn out. It was thought that Cerutti had not been part of a network since the Resistance disbanded. But a lifetime was not long enough to kill the taste for secret life; no one who had ever lived it believed that he could lose his skills.

'You say you're a writer,' Cerutti said. 'You are, I take it, as yet unpublished?'

'I'm afraid so.'

Cerutti drew a circle in the air above his head, to encompass the voluptuous décor. 'You are not a starving artist, evidently. This is the most orgiastic restaurant in Paris.'

Christopher gave Cerutti no more information about himself.

'Did you describe this debauchee's life to your underground friends in Moscow?' Cerutti asked.

'They only asked about Hemingway, and the movies.'

Cerutti spoke earnestly to the head waiter about dessert, then turned back to Christopher.

'I have a professional interest in what you've done,' he said. 'I don't know if Otto mentioned that I own a small publishing house.'

'I knew that you discovered Kiril Kamensky and published his work.'

'Ah. Then you know I used to publish a lot of Russian books. At one time my imprint was quite famous in that regard. But there's no money in it.'

Cerutti, touching his lips with a napkin, watched Christopher begin to say something, then change his mind. His eyes shone, for an instant, with curiosity. Then he spoke of other things.

Christopher paid the enormous bill. Cerutti suggested they walk to the Crazy Horse Saloon; inside the door there, he gave money to the greeter to get them a table near the stage. There was a new act: a very tall German girl who began her striptease in a Wehrmacht helmet and ended it with a swastika on her G-string.

They drank Scotch whisky. Finally Cerutti, his speech faintly slurred began to ask questions again.

'Otto says you really found your way to interesting people in Russia. The luck of the innocent, was it?'

'As I said, I just met people, and they introduced me to other people. It's the same the world over.'

'For the young and beautiful, perhaps.'

The music had begun again, and the master of ceremonies introduced another girl. Cerutti called the waiter and watched him make his way among the tables, putting his hands on the customers to move them aside because their attention was fixed on the girl. Cerutti's face, like the flesh of the dancer, went from pink to blue to green to stark white as the filters were changed on the spotlight.

'Otto was hinting to me,' he said, his voice straining to penetrate the throbbing music, 'that you got through to someone very interesting in Russia. One of the great lost writers. Otto was very mysterious.'

Christopher smiled, as if in the din he could not hear what Cerutti was saying.

'Did you? Who was it?'

Cerutti made a megaphone of his hands and asked his insistent question again.

Christopher ceased smiling. 'There are some things,' he shouted into Cerutti's ear, 'that you just don't ask. I'm sorry I said anything to Otto.'

Cerutti shrugged, but he held Christopher's glance for a long moment before he turned his chair around in order to have a better view of the girl, now almost naked, who danced in the changing colours of the limelight.

3

Maria Rothchild met Christopher in the bar of the Hotel Scribe. Christopher heard her brisk unmistakable footsteps as she came down the corridor. She wore a tartan skirt and before she sat down at his table she spread its pleats and made a curtsy. 'I forgot that this bar is upholstered in the Campbell plaid, or whatever,' Maria said. 'It wasn't my intention to match my costume to the room.

She ordered a Bloody Mary and then brought the waiter back with a crooked finger. 'Make it two, both for me,' she said. 'Otto had a spell last night,' Maria said, 'and after I put him to bed I was so bloody depressed I sat up till three drinking gin and listening to Vivaldi. I'm turning into a housebound alcoholic.'

'What sort of spell did Otto have?'

'Petulance. It's hard to be an invalid. He resents my youth and my glowing good health. Life is getting to be like a novelette in a Hearst magazine.'

'Or the Brontë sisters.'

'Same thing,' Maria said. 'Everything in nature, if I may quote you in the long ago, Paul, is the same unless it's touched by genius.'

'I wonder what I meant by that?'

Maria, eagerly consuming her second Bloody Mary, did not reply. She had a reputation, as Christopher did, for remembering with great exactness everything that was said to her. Unlike Christopher, she liked to quote sentences back to the people who had spoken them; sometimes Maria waited years for the opportunity.

She finished drinking and sat back with a hand on her stomach. 'I can feel it consuming the evil humours,' she said. 'God bless the discoverer of alcohol.' She took a Gauloise from a blue package, lit it, and inhaled her one long drag with such force that Christopher could hear the paper burning. Then she snuffed out the cigarette, three-fourths of it unsmoked.

'Your small friend, the descendant of the Jesuit philosopher, enjoyed his dinner at Lasserre,' she said. 'He wanted to know where you got all that money. We said we thought you had inherited young. Cowan *was* an only child, wasn't he? David left that detail out.'

'Yes. Tell me the rest.'

'About Claude? He brought you into the conversation very casually. Slyly, I'd call it. Otto thought that that was quite telling; so do I. Evidently you gave him just enough to make him want more.'

'I found a message from him at the hotel today. He wants to meet for a drink tomorrow afternoon.'

'Only a drink?'

'It's his turn to pay. I'll stretch the evening out, somehow.'

'He's not bad company,' Maria said, 'but of course it's business. God the pain of eating rich food with poor fools. When I resigned from the Company I promised myself I'd never again have a meal with someone I didn't really like. It hasn't turned out that way, living with Otto. The agents still come for lunch. Maybe when he retires.'

'Give me the rest on Claude,' Christopher said.

Cerutti, Maria reported, had said very little when he came by with his weekly bottle of champagne, but he had come two days early. Cerutti had wanted to know, in detail, who Paul Cowan's Russian mother had been.

'Otto was vague. Like a lot of reformed revolutionaries, Cerutti is an awful snob – where the "de" came from in his name is a mystery to all – so he thinks it's natural that Otto wouldn't have taken notice of anyone who had a Russian title granted after the reign of Peter the Great.'

'What else?' Christopher asked. It was unlike Maria to chat instead of reporting.

'He mentioned several times what a dish you are. I asked Otto if Claude was maybe a little bit queer, but he says no. It's not a tendency Otto admires. He's brutal to fairies, always has been.'

'Otto's brutal to a lot of people.'

'So they say,' Maria replied, 'but especially to fools and queers. Claude, believe me, is neither or they wouldn't have stayed in touch, when there was nothing in it for Otto, for all these years.'

Maria's habit of putting a finger on her husband's flaws interested Christopher; she spoke to him of Rothchild as a liberal in America might speak to another liberal about the fecklessness of Negroes, knowing that his credentials were too good for him to be mistaken for a bigot. Christopher seldom knew what to say in return.

'The important thing,' Maria said, 'is that Claude believes, or is beginning to believe, that there may be something for Cerutti in Paul Cowan, the Canadian. He's keen to know what you know about the new Russian writers. He made some money out of those books in Russian he used to publish, including Kamensky's. He's sniffing the air for the scent of easy money again.'

Christopher let her drink. While the glass was still at her lips he said, 'Sniffing the air, Maria? According to Claude, Otto has already let him smell the bone.'

Maria put the glass back on the table, dabbed at her lips with a paper napkin.

'Otto *did* tell Cerutti that I had met one of the great Russian writers,' Christopher said, 'or was Cerutti just putting a little blood in the water?'

'Yes, Otto told him that.'

'Why? David told him not to interfere, not to show his hand.'

Maria Rothchild began putting things back into her purse.

'Because, Paul, my husband does things his way. Not David's way or your way or my way.'

'I've noticed.'

'And done nothing.'

'So far,' Christopher said.

Maria closed the snap on her purse.

'Is that a message?' she asked.

Christopher helped her with her chair and walked with her in silence out of the bar and up the stairs. Outside, Maria studied the façade of the Opera House.

'You know,' she said, 'before you ever met Otto, David came around to describe you. Otto asked how good you were. "Better than you, Otto," David said, "because he has the power of honesty." What a remark. What an error in handling. Otto has never forgotten.'

She kissed Christopher's cheek and left him.

4

Christopher was alone when he wasn't with agents. He woke at dawn, and went out of the hotel for breakfast. He liked the backstreet cafés that catered to the gruff early-morning trade. Often, near the Madeleine in the morning, he would be stopped by smiling young women, as fresh as Cathy, who would ask him if he wanted them. He refused; he felt not even the ghost of desire.

Waiting for Cerutti, Christopher sat alone in his high white room in the Hôtel Vendome and tried, for the first time in years, to write poetry. The lines came to his pen as easily as ever, but they were about flowers, trees, the sky, streets; he wrote a sonnet that described the hill at Pontoise as Pissarro had painted it. He could not make verses about anything that had a voice or warm flesh.

He wrote to Cathy. He could send nothing through the mail that might give someone who intercepted the letter insight or advantage. He didn't think that Cathy would believe in a love letter. He made up a long joke about a woman who would not answer her telephone and woke up one morning to find, as Kafka's hero had found himself turned into a cockroach, that she had been transformed into a telephone. Strangers shouted into her ear and listened at her mouth and punched her nostrils and eyes with dialling fingers.

He mailed the letter at the post office in the sixth arrondissement and asked at the window if *poste restante* had anything in his name. He was given an envelope addressed in Cathy's round hand-writing.

> I've heard the phone and knew it was you but I don't know what we'd say if I picked up the receiver. I'm terrified to think of you but I'm trying to get over that. I've been asked to go away to Capri for the weekend, and I may. Wherever I am, I'll be with you. I do believe you see me in everything I do. If you haven't the sight, then what is the explanation? What I must do is to become like you. I'm making a project of it and Christ it can be painful. When you come back, come on the late flight. Wire me. I'll meet you at the airport. Don't be anxious about how I'll be. I'm all through talking. I know it's a fool's way of speaking love.

5

Cerutti had suggested meeting in the bar of the Crillon at five o'clock, an hour when it was frequented by English-speaking journalists. Some of them, hanging together in an atmosphere of sad gossip, knew Christopher in his own name as the correspondent of a great American magazine. Christopher avoided them when he could, and when he could not, he bought them drinks with his own money. It was against regulations to spend secret funds on the American press.

He asked Cerutti to meet him instead at the Brasserie Lipp, on the other side of the Seine. They had to wait, standing up, for a table. Cerutti made no attempt to cover his annoyance. When at last he and Christopher sat down, Cerutti looked contemptuously at the clientele. 'Tourists,' he said. He mopped his face with a handkerchief and drank off half of his tall glass of Munich beer at a swallow.

Christopher had brought the English translation of the Kamensky manuscript with him, wrapped in cheap paper and tied with string. Cerutti eyed it as it lay on the table, but said nothing about it. He described an encounter he had had that day with an American film director who was interested in one of the novels on the backlist of Cerutti's publishing house. 'It's about the Spanish Civil War,' Cerutti said. 'I asked him how he expected to get money from American bankers to make a film on that subject. "No problem," he said, "I'm on the Hollywood black list. That makes me a hero in Europe and I can get money over here, *pour épater les États-Unis*".'

'Is it a good book? You said you were in the Spanish war.'

Cerutti grunted. 'There were no good books about that war. Too much idealogy. Even the best writers were scared of losing their friends; they had to write what was expected of them, not what they saw and felt.'

'Did you know Otto in Spain?'

'Very slightly. I was in a fighting unit, the XI International Brigade, in Madrid in '36. Otto was a journalist, living at the Gran Via Hotel. He always had Martel cognac, I don't know where he got it all, so we were glad to be interviewed by him.'

'Did you tell Otto what you saw and felt?'

'I told him true stories about the valour of the Spanish workers. Otto in those days was one of the deluded; he professed to believe in the Popular Front.'

'You didn't?'

Cerutti gave Christopher a sharp look; up till now, it had been he who had asked all the questions, chosen the shades of meaning.

'I was a Communist, and one who had fought with the Reds in Russia. I understood what fun it was going to be shooting Otto and all the other Social Democrats and Socialists after the war.'

'But you lost the war.'

'Yes, and my faith. I'm a defrocked zealot. Franco did the job for us – he shot a lot of Otto's kind.'

'What did Otto lose?'

Cerutti made a kissing noise. 'Ask Otto. The odd thing was, all the Spaniards thought Otto was a Frenchman and I was a Russian. The Madrileños thought every armed foreigner was a Russian. They used to shout at all of us in the streets, ¡*Viva Rusia*! It was the slogan of the war that winter – in Spain the Germans tested aerial bombing tactics, the Soviets propaganda. You see who won in the end. In 1945 there was no more Luftwaffe. No one has yet found a way to shoot down the illusions of the Left.'

'Or of the Right?'

'The Right doesn't need illusions; it has factories and mines and banks.'

'You're still part Communist, my friend.'

Cerutti showed his yellowing teeth. 'A very small part, withered like an old man's penis,' he said. 'It was once the seat of pleasure, but that was a long time ago.'

Cerutti lapsed into a mood. Christopher did not disturb him. The waiter brought more beer and a plate of cold sausages.

'Were you in battle in the last war?' Cerutti asked.

'Yes.'

'Then you know it's bad enough to see your friends fall, and know that they are dead. It's worse when they go back to the country they were fighting for, Soviet Russia in this case, and die or perhaps do not die, there. You don't know. They are swallowed up by the earth. You hear rifle shots in your sleep.'

'I thought the purges came later.'

'They began in '37, in Russia. Practically everyone who had been in Spain was shot when he got back to the Soviet Union. The comrades went from one abattoir to another.'

Cerutti lifted a piece of sausage from the plate, then put it back. He pushed the plate away.

'We all lost friends,' he said. 'Even Otto lost friends.'

'Otto had the same friends as you?'

'One or two. Otto, even then, was ubiquitous. He knew everyone in Madrid. Once, even, I found him talking to Konev – Paulito, he was called in Spain – who was in charge of training Spanish terrorists. And Otto and a young Russian, also a journalist but a Soviet citizen and a Communist, were close. I suppose the fellow died for it along with all the rest, when he got home.'

Christopher asked no more questions. Cerutti blinked his eyes and gave a little laugh.

'That Hollywood director took me back,' he said. 'The black-list. He thinks it's *chic* to play around with politics. "*Épater les États-Unis*". He thought he was speaking my language. He'd have done better to study Esperanto.'

They went on to dinner at the Coupole. The walk through Montparnasse cheered Cerutti, and in the noisy brasserie with its throng of garrulous people, he took off his coat and loosened his tie. 'After all,' he said, 'this is a better ambience than Lasserre. One has to prefer soap to perfume.' He ordered carafe after carafe of rough wine, and ate the simple food with appetite. He seemed to have a different set of manners for every situation. Christopher felt affection begin to stir within him. He was glad to have this sign. He had never been able to seduce anyone, a woman for her body or an agent for his fantasies, with a cold heart.

Finally, drunk, Cerutti tapped the package Christopher had left between them on the table. It was a question.

'It's a manuscript,' Christopher said.

'And you think I ought to read it.'

'If you read English.'

Cerutti put on his glasses and ripped open the package. He read the opening paragraph aloud. His English was accented but perfect, and to demonstrate something to Christopher he translated what he had read back into French, at sight. Then, quickly, he read the first five or six pages of the typescript. There was no title page and no author's name. Cerutti said nothing about this.

'Not bad,' he said in English. He looked at the number on the last page of the manuscript and raised his eyebrows. 'But if I'm going to read seven hundred pages in English, my friend, you are going to pay for dinner.'

At the taxi rank outside, he borrowed another fifty francs. He didn't give the driver his destination while Christopher was still in earshot.

6

When it happened it happened quickly, as it always did. Christopher waited in his hotel room, leaving only to eat, and once to meet a man from the Embassy. On the third morning Cerutti phoned from the reception desk. Christopher told him to come upstairs.

Cerutti laid the bulky manuscript on the table, but he kept the palm of his hand pressed upon it, as though he wished to prevent its being put back into hiding.

'This is a translation,' he said. 'Where is the original?'

'I have it.'

'Who is the author?'

Christopher said, 'It's a nice morning. Let's go outside.'

Cerutti, with the manuscript clutched to his breast, followed him down the stairs. Christopher took him to the Seine embankment, and they walked along the river in the gentle spring sunlight.

Under the Pont de la Concorde, Cerutti stopped. Traffic soughed and thudded above them; the pylon of the great bridge quivered like a wooden stake driven into the ground by a sledgehammer.

'Who?' Cerutti said.

'Kiril Kamensky.'

Agents are seized, at the moment of submission, with a certain emotion. The transaction, the decision to give up resistance, causes the face to twist with something like humour, and the eyes to look back, as Christopher sometimes thought, upon an earlier, more innocent person than the one the agent has just become. Now this happened to Cerutti.

'Kamensky is alive?' he said.

'Yes.'

'And he wants to publish this novel in the West?'

Christopher, unresponsive, watched Cerutti's eyes as a hunter will watch a covert, waiting for an animal to give way to fright and break into the open. Cerutti walked past Christopher to the water's edge. He gazed for a moment into the discoloured river.

'Have you the Russian original?'

'Yes,' Christopher said.

'There's no question of authenticity?'

'It's in his own handwriting.'

Cerutti spat into the moving water, turned around. He knew what Christopher was.

'What are you offering me?' he asked.

'World rights. You'd get three-fourths of all profits, according to whatever arrangements you make with publishers in other countries. One-quarter goes into a Swiss account.'

'How quickly must we publish?'

'Quite soon. You'll be told. You must be able to print at once, if necessary.'

'In French? Is there a translation?'

'No, you'll have to do that. You must publish it in Russian at the same time. Even a little before the French, if it seems that that's better.'

'In *Russian*?'

Christopher did not repeat himself.

'Do you know what that could mean for Kamensky?' Cerutti asked.

'I've described the situation.'

Cerutti had been standing with his heels on the edge of the embankment, the Seine at his back. There was no one in sight on either side of the river. He was a much smaller man that Christopher; he was almost an old man. He moved away from the water before he spoke again.

'I'll need capital,' Cerutti said. 'For the printers, the binders, the distributors. You must leave everything about the technical side in my hands.'

'All right.'

'And the publicity?'

'It's best that you do everything. You know better than anyone how to arrange things in France.'

'You want no control?'

'I didn't say that. Someone will come to you with contracts and the money you'll need.'

'Evidently I'll be a rich man before I know it.' Cerutti let himself be himself for an instant. 'In memories as well,' he said, in a voice filled with scorn.

A pair of young gendarmes walked by, arguing about the Tour de France. The newspapers were full of advance stories on the great bicycle race.

'There's one question before we part,' Christopher said. 'Who was the Russian journalist in Madrid? The young fellow Otto was so friendly with?'

Cerutti held the manuscript more loosely now. He looked away, in thought.

'Everyone in those days had a *nom de guerre*,' he said. 'This fellow called himself Kolka Zhigalko. Ask Otto, they were always together. Zhigalko used to go wild on cognac. He was a poet. He'd shout out his poems in Russian during a Fascist bombardment, stand on the roof of the hotel and do it, as if he were firing back at the enemy batteries.'

134

'Who else knew him?'

'Everyone, but they're all dead. There was a Spaniard who hung around them a lot. He was some kind of lackey for Comrade Mediña, the Comintern instructor in Spain.'

'Name?'

'Carlos. He was a high-bred fellow, like Otto. Zhigalko called them the duke and the marquis. Zhigalko had learned to put his face in his plate and make noises like a dog when he ate, he was a real member of the proletariat. It was while observing Otto and Carlos watch Zhigalko at table that I saw they were both fallen aristocrats. They were excited by their disgust.'

'You don't know what became of Carlos?'

Cerutti said again, 'Ask Otto.'

Christopher took a fifty-franc note from his pocket, tore it in half, and gave one portion of it to Cerutti.

'Tomorrow, at nine in the morning,' Christopher said, 'by the columns in the Parc Monceau. The man will give you the other half of this. And a copy of the Russian manuscript.'

'And the money.'

'Some of it.'

'How will I keep in touch?'

'The man will tell you all that.'

'Have you any last recommendation?'

'Be silent. Wait. Act openly, once Kamensky's book is in the open.'

Cerutti fingered the torn money, shifted his grip on the manuscript.

'It's wonderful, dealing with a professional,' he said. 'You took me by surprise. I'd forgotten what a mistake it is to think another man is stupid.'

7

Christopher was out of the Hôtel Vendôme in half an hour. He took his suitcase to the Aérogare des Invalides and left it in the baggage room. At noon he met Wilson in the safe house where Christopher and Patchen, weeks before, had first spoken of the possibility of Kamensky's death. The secretary's gown, smudged at the collar, still hung on the bathroom door.

Wilson took back Christopher's false Canadian passport and the other identification describing Paul Cowan. He gave him back his own passport and wallet in a sealed envelope.

'Did you make Cerutti this morning?' Christopher asked.

'I watched the two of you saunter through the Luxembourg Gardens. I'll know him.'

Wilson drew the blinds and turned on a reading lamp. He handed Christopher a plain file folder; inside it were Agency forms with the headings clipped off. The material dealt with the death of Horst Bülow.

'You read,' Wilson said, 'I'll wait.'

Christopher went through the pages rapidly. The material was terse. For the most part it was raw, but at the head of a page, sometimes, were numerals and letters of the alphabet that signified the degree of reliability the analysts had assigned to the source, and the degree of truthfulness they assumed for the material itself. No symbol existed to denote absolute reliability or absolute truth.

Christopher read the material twice over, then looked up at Wilson, who was peering at a stain on the ceiling.

'What do you make of it?' Wilson asked.

'It's interesting. But it's all hearsay, all speculation.'

'Sure it is. But the times and places fit. Contact breeds contact.'

Christopher asked another question. Wilson answered. In Christopher's ear their voices sounded thin, because of what they were discussing.

'Do you think,' Christopher asked, 'that I can talk to this German in Berlin, the one who saw Horst with the woman in the Tiergarten?'

Wilson, stolid, said, 'I don't know. It's bad procedure. You'd have to let him see you. Why can't I ask for you?'

'Because the fault was mine, for not foreseeing the problem. Because I know so much better than you do what the patterns of behaviour would have been. I'd pick up on things you might not.'

Wilson drummed on the cover of his attaché case.

'Besides, I have another idea, something from a long time ago,' Christopher said. 'I'll give you that.'

Wilson didn't ask what it was. He had no more desire than Christopher to go on talking about what the two of them suspected.

'I'll try to fix you up with Berlin,' Wilson said. 'Let's meet here again, same time, next Friday. I think we ought to move slow, Paul.'

'Yes. But not so slowly that it happens again.'

Wilson gathered up the papers and put them back into his attaché case. He made a tour of the apartment to make sure nothing had been left behind. He washed the glasses they had used. Christopher left first; Wilson locked up.

From the PTT on the Champs-Élysées, Christopher wired Cathy that he would be home the following night, on the late flight. The telegram said nothing of flights or times; any phrase containing the word "love", she understood, meant that he would land in Rome on the flight that arrived from Paris at one o'clock in the morning.

Next day, back in the safe house, Wilson showed Christopher the contracts Cerutti had signed.

'He's hard-nosed,' Wilson said. 'He wanted the handwritten Russian manuscript. Our fellow let him look at it, but not take it away. It's got more fingerprints on it than a whore's backside.'

Christopher read the contracts. He hadn't seen them before, but they obligated Cerutti to deposit the moneys for Kamensky in a small bank in Lucerne. It was all laid out as Patchen had described.

Wilson put a receipt for twenty thousand dollars, in hundred-dollar bills with the serial number noted, in front of Christopher. There was a thumbprint, Cerutti's, at the bottom of the page.

'He's not going to remain unwitting for very long,' Christopher said, 'if you have him signing for money with a thumbprint.'

'I cleared the procedure with Patchen. Cerutti's better off realizing from the start that this is real life.'

'Patchen thought it was all right to blow me?'

Wilson was rummaging in his briefcase. 'Cerutti knew what you were before he ever put his thumb in the ink,' he said. 'He'll never know who you are, and that's what matters.'

Wilson found what he was looking for – a cheap French envelope from a *bureau de tabac*. He handed it, still sealed, to Christopher. 'From Cerutti,' he said.

Inside, on a sheet of paper, was typed a name. Christopher looked away, then read the name again. He didn't know how well he was controlling his face; had the man himself burst into the room he would have been all right, but the name, lying alone on the page, had taken him unawares. Cathy was infecting him.

Christopher showed the name to Wilson. The Security man copied it on to a file card, and spoke the name aloud. 'Jorge de Rodegas. Who's that?' he said.

'Someone from the past, maybe a connection. Someone Cerutti knew in Madrid, when he knew Otto.' Wilson massaged his face and when he raised it he looked like a man tired to the bone.

'Pretty soon,' he said, 'you and I are going to have to tell someone else about all this.'

Christopher rose to leave. He coughed on Wilson's cigarette smoke.

'When you run the name check on Rodegas,' he said, 'you'll find that he's my wife's godfather.'

'You know him?'

'Cathy will introduce us,' Christopher said.

Eleven

I

On the flight from Paris to Rome, Christopher was alone in the first-class compartment; the stewardess gave him a drink and a foil package of nuts and retreated to the lounge behind the cockpit. He left the whisky and slept a little. Dreams woke him, as they always did at the end of an operation, again and again.

Cathy was waiting, unsmiling, beyond the Customs barrier. She wore a raincoat, with pearls showing at the open neck and sandals on her bare feet. When Christopher came closer he saw that she had painted her eyelids. He had never seen make-up on her face. She didn't move towards him or speak, but waited passively for him to kiss her. As they left the terminal, Cathy walked a little ahead of him, as she had done on the night she had led him through Trastevere and into St Peter's Square. In the parking lot she handed him the keys to the car. It had been raining and the top was up; Cathy put it down at the exit while Christopher paid the parking fee. When they entered the Via Ostiense she put her foot on top of Christopher's on the gas pedal. 'Go fast,' she said. She increased the pressure until the speedometer needle passed 150 k.m.h. The wind took her hair. She moved back to her side of the car and lay back, knees parted, her painted eyes turned towards Christopher. The road was empty, and he kept the speed she wanted. 'Slow down now,' Cathy said. They were passing the ruins of Ostia Antica, and inside the low walls they could see the broken columns and the fallen brick.

'From here you have to do everything I ask,' Cathy said, 'or you'll spoil what I want to do.'

Christopher took his foot off the accelerator and the compression of the engine slowed the car.

'Park,' Cathy said. 'I want to go inside.'

Christopher parked the car close to the wall, in a dark patch of ground between two trees.

'You go over first,' Cathy said. 'We can just climb up from the car.'

Christopher went over the wall. Standing on the grass inside, he watched Cathy climb after him, balancing and swinging one leg up and then the other, like a rider mounting a horse. She stood erect on top of the wall and removed her raincoat. He had already seen that she wore nothing else. She rolled up the coat and threw it down into the seat of the car. She leaped, naked except for the pearls around her throat, on to the grass. She moved close to Christopher. When he reached for her she leaped back, turned and ran. He waited for a moment, then followed her into the ruins. She waited for him by a wall, then hid again. She appeared, disappeared, reappeared. At last she came up behind him, he heard her breath and the fall of her bare feet. She seized him and pulled him to the damp earth. It had begun to rain again, the warm rain of June in Italy. Their hair was soaked, Cathy's bare legs were splashed with mud. She lay unresponsive through the act, the rain washing the eye shadow over her cheeks like black tears. But she would not let him stop and finally she was turned back into herself again, clasping Christopher and crying out to him.

In the car, wearing her raincoat again, she put her head in his lap. He thought she was asleep. Then she stirred and said to him, in a steady clear voice, 'I'll learn not to cry out, Paul. You're still the only one I can't help it with.'

The next day was bright and warm. 'The sun has come out to apologize for the rain,' said Cathy. She wanted to eat at midday at Da Necci, a restaurant they liked in the Piazza Oratorio. One entered this tiny square through a passageway whose high walls were covered with faded frescoes; the Trevi Fountain was a few steps away but owing to some trick of acoustics the rush of its waters could only be heard halfway into the frescoed passage; Cathy liked to step back and forth across an imaginary line, listening to the fountain on one side of it, hearing nothing on the other.

Cathy spoke, with her musical Southern good humour, to the owners of the restaurant, and to the boy who brought them coffee at the end of the meal from the bar next door. But she and Christopher said nothing to one another. When they had finished she turned her face, masked by enormous sunglasses, towards his.

'I've got something to show you,' she said.

Cathy led Christopher across the piazza and into a building. He followed her up the narrow unlighted stairway to the second floor. She took a key from her purse and opened the only door on that floor.

They were in a small flat. Cathy stood in the centre of the sitting room, holding the ends of the silk scarf that she had draped around her neck. She lifted a hand in invitation. Christopher opened a door and saw a bedroom and a bath beyond. The walls were covered with enormous photographs of Cathy's face. The pictures were new; they were like publicity stills for a film star. She opened a closet; it was filled with clothes, plainly Cathy's from the colour and style, that he hadn't seen before. The flat was shuttered, chilly and damp like a summer place rented from strangers. Christopher caught the afterscent of marijuana.

Cathy went to the door, waiting for him to open it for her. Then, before Christopher could move, she flung it open herself and walked into the hall.

'You've seen it,' she said, beckoning him to follow. 'I don't want to talk to you about it inside it.'

They walked the few steps to the Galleria Colonna and ordered more coffee. The orchestra was playing, so they could not speak above its noise; Cathy listened to the waltzes in the echoing stone gallery for a moment, then covered her ears and, making a sign that she would be back, walked away into the crowd.

When she returned, the orchestra had gone. She opened her hand; in her palm was a gold wedding ring. 'I know you don't like rings and wouldn't have one when we were married,' she said, 'but I bought you this just now. I think it will fit.' She slid it on to Christopher's finger. He took his hand away, and she did not resist; a month before she would have struggled with him.

'I said in my letter that I was done with talking about love,' Cathy said, 'but there's quite a lot I have to say to you. I want to explain what's happening, or what I'm trying to make happen, so that there'll be as little confusion between us as possible. So will you let me talk this one last time about you and me before I let it alone for ever?'

Christopher nodded. 'Start with the place we just saw,' he said.

'All right. I was going to, anyway. You remember, when I came down here to tell you I loved you and we went to Cannes, what it was you did, directly after we'd been to bed?'

Christopher was not likely to have forgotten. In Cannes he told her what he had not told his mother or his brother, or any person outside the Agency – that he was a spy, a secret agent. The words, spoken aloud, sounded ridiculous. They were seated at the break-fast table. Cathy had pushed the table on to the tiny balcony because the sun was shining, but it was cold and they wore their winter coats over their naked bodies. Cathy, a mink collar turned up around her face, greeted the news with a laugh of delight, then turned serious as he told her more. Even now she could not under-stand what a proof of love Christopher's confession had been; even loving her, it had made him ill, caused him to tremble and sweat, to speak the inmost truth about himself to an outsider.

'I had no idea what you were saying to me,' Cathy said now. 'I was so dazed with love and desire. You said you'd never told anyone else, but you told me, and later you told me more. "That's where I live," you said to me.'

Cathy had removed her sunglasses. Her glance was inward as she spoke; she might have been reading off a page. Her slim body was as straight as that of a young girl at a recital; she sat on the café chair as if it were a piano bench.

'You just showed me the rooms, though, not what was hidden in them,' Cathy said 'That's what I thought at the time, and have thought ever since – your life, this secret existence you lead when you're not with me – is like a darkened house. I'd say a haunted house, but you'd make one of your faces, Paul. You do so hate for me to dramatize.'

Cathy, as she spoke, turned her own wedding ring round and round on her finger. She wore no other jewellery.

'My life with you is like living on some planet that has a year of night for every hour of daylight, Paul. When you're gone, I'm in the dark. I try to go with you in my mind, in my heart, but I can't make the journey because you can't tell me where you are or what you're doing. You just vanish, and sometimes you have dreams about where you've been after you come back, but you won't tell me what they are, so I know they must be true memories of what's happened to you. You shut the doors on me. For all I know you kill and torture; I don't believe you do, but I don't know. If I asked you now those two simple questions: do you kill, do you torture, would you answer?'

'Yes, I'd answer. I don't do either of those things.'

'But *would* you, if there was no other way to do what you do?'

A man they knew went by; he waved and called out a greeting in Italian.

'Yes,' Christopher said.

'I thought so. There must be a reason. You're such a sweet and gentle lover, Paul, I've never known a man who wants so much not to *hurt*. You've never hurt me with your body. Never.'

Cathy uttered a long sigh, caught up Christopher's hand, fondled the ring she had just given him between her thumb and forefinger. She lifted his hand to kiss it, then stopped herself. Before she spoke again, she let go of him.

'I've decided to take the rights you say I can have, Paul,' she said. 'I've rented that place you just saw for myself. To use for my own purposes, to vanish, to go black – isn't that the word you use when you become someone else?'

She shook his hand again and leaned across the table. Christopher saw the shape of his own face, his movement of surprise, on the glistening surface of her eyes.

'You can never come back to my place,' Cathy said; she touched his face, smiled. 'It has nothing to do with you and me. What I do

143

there is secret. You can't touch it, see it, know about it. I have different clothes I wear there. I'll speak a different language. I'll bring nothing from one life to another. Like you, I'll never lie in our part of life. In the other part I'll do what I want, according to rules others and I will make. You can't know the rules.'

Christopher's life had taught him that it was no use to ask questions. There was nothing to ask Cathy; he understood what she wanted. It was what he had always wanted – to make it impossible for him to banish her from his mind even for an instant.

'You'll dream of me now the way I've dreamt of you,' Cathy said. 'If you feared anything, Paul, if you were capable of it, you'd be afraid. I've had my share of being terrified for your sake.'

'Will what you're doing cure you of that?'

'So far it hasn't even made me forget, not for an instant. No matter what's happening to me.'

Cathy's dry hand, a musician's hand, long-boned and muscular, lay in Christopher's open palm. He imagined it, a frozen detail like the focus of a painting, stroking another man's body. Emotion kindled within him for an instant that lasted no longer than the glimpse of Cathy's flesh, and then his mind extinguished his feelings.

'You're doing something dangerous,' Christopher said.

'Then save me from it.'

'You'll do what you want to do.'

'You say that about everyone, Paul. It's one of your sayings.'

'It's true of everyone.'

'People do what they have to do,' Cathy said. 'There's a difference.'

Cathy's face was shaped, for a moment, by an expression of wisdom. Everything that she felt registered on her flesh; it was as much a screen as Christopher's mind. The changeful face and voice, the body that danced or collapsed as her moods changed were the things that he loved in Cathy and remembered in her absence. He felt sexual desire for her only when he was with her, and all the time he was with her. He had never had a sexual dream about her.

'Paul, you won't ask me why I'm doing this to us, will you?'

Christopher took his hand away and called for the bill.

'Because I thought that the love I felt for you was a force that would bring you to me, make you choose me, over anything,'

Cathy said. 'I told you from the start – I thought I could make you become me.'

The waiter was at the table. His eyes were on Cathy, and she spoke quickly while her voice was still in control.

'I'm doing what I'm doing, Paul, to see if I can become you. If I can, surely you'll understand love and I'll understand you.'

When they rose from the table, Cathy took a step towards Christopher, halted, then put her arms around his waist. He held her against his body, increasing the strength of his embrace as she tightened her arms. Her face was crushed against his chest.

'*Bella*!' cried a stranger, passing by.

3

Cathy wanted to leave Rome for a while. She and Christopher, having a drink on the pavement at Doney's, a day after his return, had met Franco Moroni. The Italian, tailored and barbered, sat down with them and spoke about his new movie; he was going to film it in Spain, with Spaniards playing a band of terrorists who kidnap an American President's daughter. 'Cathy would be perfect for the girl, she'd only have to be herself with that glorious American face that has no memory of passion and no idea of pain,' Moroni said. 'But she won't agree to take the part.' Cathy watched Moroni with mocking eyes. 'What happens to the girl in the end?' Christopher asked. 'She's killed by the CIA; my films are true to life,' Moroni answered. He called the waiter over and paid the bill before he left, and while he spoke to Cathy, asking her again to be in his movie, he gripped the back of Christopher's neck with warm damp fingers, as though touching her flesh at second-hand.

The next morning they left the city. Cathy wanted to be near the sea. They drove through the mountains straight across Italy to Pescara on the Adriatic. They found a hotel by itself on a long sand beach. It was too early for tourists and the weather turned windy; danger flags flew all along the shore, keeping swimmers out of the water. They walked on the sand for hours; Cathy stopped sleeping so much and rose at dawn with Christopher. 'I don't know why I gave up the early morning for so long, I used to love being up and out at sunrise with my papa on the farm,' Cathy said. 'I love this, too, it really is the sweetest time of the day, anywhere in the world.'

Cathy teased Christopher and laughed. There was no great change in her, or in the times they had together. She bought a lot of cheap jewellery made of shells from an old man who overcharged her for it. 'I love to let him cheat me, he's such a transparent villain,' she said. 'Eight thousand lire – how much is that in real money?'

Christopher asked her, driving back to Rome, what Maria Rothchild had been like as a girl.

'Strange and alone,' Cathy said. 'Maria was a funny combination of things. She was a super athlete, but she was clumsy off the playing field – she bumped into things. She was an honours student, but she didn't know things everyone else knew, like who was in what movie. No trivia for Maria. The main thing about her, though, was that she could only have one friend at a time. She'd be all tooth and claw about someone and absolutely wear the person out, and then she'd find another and do the same. But never did she have two human beings in her life at any one time.'

'Girls, you mean.'

'Well, Miss Porter's is a girls' school. Maria was not exactly fixated on the opposite sex. I couldn't have been less surprised when I found her nursing that wrinkled old Russian in Paris, and married to him. Why, Paul, he looks like somebody who died for the love of Bette Davis and was stuffed, and Maria found him in a cute little shop on the Left Bank near the Pont des Arts.'

Cathy was bouncing in her seat, loving every syllable of this wicked gossip about a woman she had never liked.

'Otto wouldn't be amused to hear you say that,' Christopher said. 'He's led an adventurous life.'

'Yes, he told me. Maria says the blood of Ivan the Terrible runs in his veins. All he talked about the night I met him, in the periods when he would come back to the world of the living, was Oriental carpets. Shah Abbas and Kashan and Beluchi prayer rugs. He does know the subject. And Berlin between the wars. All the colourful decadence and politics of it, it sounded like Fayette County. It was carpets, carpets, carpets, and Berlin, Berlin,

Berlin. I tried to mention other things, like you, and what an expert *you* were on Berlin, which was where you were at that very moment. But they just went on as if they didn't know you. What actors you spies become. Maria's husband kept reeling off the names of people he knew in Berlin before they went to Buchenwald. It was like a telephone book of the dead.'

'You mentioned that I was in Berlin?'

'I expect so – it was the subject of the hour,' Cathy said. She was eager to go on with her gossip.

In Rome, Cathy was quiet again. She sat with Christopher while he wrote or read a book. Looking up from his work, he would find her eyes on him sometimes; but sometimes, now, she looked elsewhere – out the window at the city as its colours changed in the light of the strengthening sun, or at herself. She would spend long periods turning her hand or her bare leg, studying the flow of the muscles and tendons under the skin, the articulation of the joints. She had read in a novel of a girl, also from the South, who, when she wished to do so, could visualize the interior of her body – heart, lungs, the miles and miles of veins and arteries and blood vessels, the brain filled with tiny leaping charges of electricity.

'I wish I had that gift,' Cathy said. 'In the old days I used sometimes to begin to see *your* flesh melt away, Paul, and I'd get a look at the shadow inside.' They had been married a year; she spoke of the time before her adultery as the old days. 'In the old days,' she told Christopher, 'I was trying to write my life on the pages of your absence, like a bride in wartime would keep a diary while her husband was off somewhere with the cavalry.'

On the anniversary of their marriage, on the night before Christopher had to leave again, they had dinner at Dal Bolognese, sitting outside so as to inspect the Piazza del Popolo again; Cathy, each time she saw this square, discovered some object of beauty that had escaped her notice until then. She believed that one could spend one night a week for a lifetime in the Piazza del Popolo and still not notice everything that artists and architectural pranksters had done, century after century, to make it more beautiful. Christopher agreed.

When they finished eating the shops were still open, and they strolled down the Corso. In the via Condotti, Christopher saw a

147

bracelet in the window of a shop and took Cathy inside and put it on her wrist. Cathy asked, seeing the row of figures on the check that Christopher wrote, how much it was in real money. Christopher put a hand over her mouth and she seized it and kissed the palm.

Cathy, paying no attention to the little cars that darted through the narrow street, walked along with her wrist before her eyes, turning the bracelet so that it caught the light; the gold was not very different in hue and texture from the skin of her arm. Christopher put his arms around her, turned her body, and kissed her.

Farther on, they found a pet shop. Cathy went inside. She asked the clerk to open a cage and let her hold one of the Siamese cats inside. 'It's a risk, signorina, these cats don't like strangers,' said the clerk. But the Siamese lay in Cathy's arm, purring, and rubbed its head against her hand.

Christopher bought it for her. Cathy unclasped the bracelet and put it around the cat's neck like a collar. 'Look, Paul, the stones match her eyes. The colour's brilliant, but the stones have more depth in them. And more warmth.' She touched Christopher under one blue eye, then under the other.

There was a second cat in the cage. Cathy bought it. She hadn't enough money with her to pay for it, and wouldn't take any from Christopher. She left ten thousand lire as a deposit and said that she'd be back the following afternoon. Christopher, by that time, would be in Paris.

'I need two of almost everything now, one for our place, one for the other place,' Cathy said.

She put the bracelet back on her wrist. She carried Christopher's cat home in her arms, refusing the cardboard box the shop offered.

Cathy wore her new bracelet all night. But in the morning, at the airport, he saw her take it off and put it into her pocket as she walked away after kissing him goodbye.

Twelve

I

Wilson had been to Zürich, and he carried the data he had gathered there on an index card in an inside pocket. Christopher noticed changes in the security man; he spoke more gently, he had begun to look Christopher in the eye. As he collected information, he abandoned mannerisms. He believed now that he was close to the truth.

'The dates fit,' he said. 'The phoney passport Bülow had on him when he died could have been made in Zürich. There's a fellow there, a former Abwehr forger, who does similar work.'

'What about the airlines, the hotel, car rentals?'

'Zero. I'd have used phoney paper, wouldn't you?'

'Yes, but the hotel clerk might have remembered a night's absence.'

Wilson shook his head in bewilderment. 'It's hard. We have this liason thing with the Swiss, that we won't operate on their territory. Bern takes it seriously. They wouldn't let me talk to the hotel fellow without informing the Swiss. I wanted to send him some money in an envelope and have him meet me in Germany. Bern said that that would transgress the parameters of liason proprieties.'

'What about the money? It went from Zürich to Berlin.'

Christopher had no hope that Wilson or anyone else could breach the Security of the Swiss banking system. But Wilson smiled broadly. Years before, he said, when he was in the FBI, he had found an embezzler that the Swiss had wanted, and the man had been brought back to Zürich, money and all, in the most discreet possible way.

'Embezzlement, to the Swiss, is what arson is to the Japanese,' Wilson said. 'Cops have a kind of freemasonry – catch a crook, make a friend. The embezzler I caught made me a true friend of one particular Swiss. I had supper with my friend. He was able to help, because there is *nothing* in Switzerland that the Swiss police don't know. It makes you envious. The money, Paul, went to Berlin from a numbered account in the Swiss Credit Bank. This is a photo of the transfer order, with one of the authorized signatures. It's a funny name, of course, but do you know the handwriting?'

Christopher looked at the card. He felt no anger, no surprise. It was what he had expected. His talent, the gift of the operative, was to separate from years of talk the one phrase that betrayed the truth, and from miles of action the single deed that revealed the person.

'Yes,' he said, 'I know the handwriting.'

Wilson took the photocopy back. He looked at Christopher with undisguised sympathy. When he spoke there was tenderness, almost a caress, in his hoarse voice.

'What now?' he asked.

'You'll have to put it in the mill. But knowing who had Bülow killed is no good to us. *Why?* I'd want to know that before I swept them up.'

'So would I. I think we ought to let it run. Maybe even make something happen.'

'I want to talk to Patchen.'

Wilson took a cable out of his briefcase and handed it to Christopher.

'He wants to talk to you,' Wilson said. 'But it can't be about this. I haven't put anything on this subject into the traffic.'

The cable told Christopher that Patchen would be in Paris in the morning; it set up a meeting for ten o'clock in the zoo in the Bois de Vincennes.

'Can you brief me afterwards?' Wilson asked. 'I think you and I had better move together on this as much as we can.'

'All right. I'll phone when Patchen is through with me.'

Wilson held up the photograph of the bank form he had brought back from Zürich.

'Do you want to show him this? I think you ought to tell him what we know, instead of my doing it. After all, I'm a stranger to you two, and I guess you'd have to say this is a private grief.'

Christopher shook his head. 'David can look at it when he gets back to the Embassy,' he said. 'I wonder if he'll want to.'

2

When Christopher arrived on the dot of ten, Patchen was waiting by the great artificial rock in the centre of the zoo, watching the mountain goats. It was summer, and Patchen had changed from his black chalk-stripe suit to blue seersucker; he had Brooks Brothers send him one of each in September and May, and every other year he bought a tweed jacket for winter weekends and a linen blazer for summer. Christopher, who had been his roommate in a military hospital and later at their university, had seen him sometimes without a necktie. Few others had done so. 'David undresses in the dark,' Patchen's gaunt wife had told Christopher one evening after too much to drink; 'it's his wounds, you know – he thinks being disfigured makes him unattractive sexually.' Laura Patchen was an intellectual woman. 'I've wondered,' she added, 'if some race memory isn't involved – there *is* a biological alarm system that warns one not to mate with defectives. But war wounds've never bothered the ladies – tell him that, Paul, will you?'

In the zoo, Patchen caught sight of Christopher and clasped his hands behind his back, the signal that he had seen no surveillance and it was safe to approach. Christopher smiled, his signal. Patchen thought these precautions foolish but he took them automatically. He knew that Christopher, failing to see a signal, would break the contact and make him wait for an hour and go to another place to meet him.

Patchen waved a hand at the jagged concrete alp with goats clinging to its side; no verbal joke was necessary. They walked on. It was not too early in the day for crowds; the paths of the zoo were filled with children, being herded from species to caged species by scolding adults. Patchen and Christopher went back outside the gates, and walked down a wooded path until they found a bench where they could talk undisturbed.

'I'm afraid I have some unhappy news for you,' Patchen said. 'Two things have happened about Tuning Fork since we talked, and neither is going to make things easier for you.'

'I'm listening.'

'First, the swap for Kamensky. We can't do it. We had a heavyweight of theirs and they had a collection of small fry, ours and the Brits', and we were going to work up a package. We were going to say, as sort of an afterthought, "Oh, by the by, we have something else to sweeten the pot. Why don't you make yourselves some propaganda hay by letting some of your unhappy intellectuals out? We'll even pump a little applause into the Free World's press. No question of defection, you understand; you just give them exit visas and say how *anyone* can travel to the outside world from the great Soviet Union. Like, uh, Blank and Blank — and what's that fellow's name? Kamensky".'

'You thought that would work?'

'Dick Sutherland did. They want their master spy back. But then, last week, the Soviets snatched one of ours. One of Sutherland's. If they publicize it, it's sure going to look like we've been meddling in the internal affairs of the USSR because this fellow they've got in Lubianka has been giving us everything except the time and duration of Krushchev's erections.'

'He's a Russian?'

'He is indeed. But one of their fellows in Delhi, of all places, has come to our man out there and told him that just as soon as they wring out our agent they'd be quite glad to deliver him to us on neutral ground in exchange for their fellow, who's languishing in prison.'

'I see.'

'Yes. Dick Sutherland may have faults, but leaving one of his assets in the hands of the KGB's interrogators is not among them. He went for the deal like a hungry muskellunge — the swap will take place before I can get back home, probably.'

'There's nothing else he could do.'

'No. And the other thing is, the Tuning Fork Working Group, taking into account the possibility, the probability even, of a lot of bad press because of the arrest of Sutherland's agent, wants to publish Kamensky's book as quickly as possible. Yesterday, for example.'

'To show what a hero our spy was, to try to kill the Soviet system?'

'By indirection, yes,' Patchen said. 'It's not fully appreciated outside our little profession that it's sometimes an honourable act to commit treason.'

In the shade where they were sitting it was many degrees colder than it had been in the sunlit zoo. Patchen shivered in his thin suit and stood up, ready to walk again.

'What word would you use to describe the act we're about to carry out against Kamensky?' Christopher asked.

Patchen walked away.

Christopher followed. Patchen asked for a report on the Rothchilds, and Christopher told him of his conversation with Maria.

'Did I say such a thing?' Patchen asked. 'Place you, place anyone, above Otto?'

'It sounds like you, and Maria never misquotes.'

Christopher led Patchen through the maze of footpaths. They went on talking about the Rothchilds. Christopher told him Cathy's story about her evening with them, and Patchen stopped in his tracks to guffaw at the idea of Otto in a Bette Davis film. 'You know,' he said, 'Maria looks a little *like* Bette Davis, the bangs and the eyes. I wonder if she knows it.'

Christopher didn't laugh. He let a silence collect, and then, on a bench in the sun, he told Patchen in a few sentences what Wilson had found in Zürich, what they both suspected. Patchen's body jerked as though he had taken a physical blow. Then he listened coldly. When he had heard it all, he made his perfunctory protest. It was a last word of loyalty to people who had betrayed him.

'There doesn't need to be a connection,' he said. 'It's an indication, Paul. It's not proof.'

'That's true. David, do you think I want to believe it?'

Patchen shook his head, looked at nothing for a time, shook his head again. Nothing astonished him. What Cathy believed she must develop occult powers to achieve, Patchen did every day with paper and money and radio transmissions – saw the shadow inside the flesh.

'Cuckolds never want to believe it,' he said to Christopher now.

'We have to know, David.'

'What does Wilson want to do?'

153

'Let them run. Maybe feed the baby and watch it grow.'

'What do you want to do?'

'I'm going to Berlin myself to check as much of it out as I can. I may make a second trip, to Spain, with Cathy. But I think Wilson's right. We have to set up a reaction, and read it.'

'All right. But I suppose you want to keep it in the family. You're closest to it.'

'Until we're sure, yes. Then it will have to be handled however these things are handled. I insist on the consequences. No rescues, David.'

He told Patchen what action he wanted to set in motion. Patchen listened, nodding; at one point he smiled at the cruel humour of what Christopher was doing to himself in the name of something that he held to be more real than he.

'All right,' Patchen said, and in addressing Christopher he used his secret name again. 'I'd like to ask you this: is there any limit on what you'd pay for the truth?'

Christopher turned his back.

'I don't know why it surprises me,' he told his friend, 'but it always does, when you decide to show what a cold-blooded son of a bitch you are.'

3

Otto Rothchild permitted Christopher and Patchen to see him walk. They heard his wheezing breath in the hall and the slow shuffling tread of his shoes on the carpet before they saw him. He leaned on two canes with his elbows locked, the weight of his body pushing the bones against the stretched flesh of his shoulders. He nodded to them as he entered the sitting room. Patchen, whom Christopher had watched in the hospital as he learned to walk again after the war, ran his eyes up and down Rothchild's ruined body. Emotion flickered in Patchen's deadened face – kindred feeling, the memory of disgust; Christopher heard again, like a shout coming into a house from the street, Patchen's cries of loathing for his own body, fifteen years before, when it would fail to obey the commands of his brain.

Rothchild sat in his chair, arranged his clothes. He was breathing rapidly, shallow inhalations, strong exhalations through the nose – an athlete after a run. His eyes did not close. While he waited for his voice to return he rested his eyes on the small Klee that was the pride of his collection.

'The canes,' he said to Maria, 'are not good for the rugs. You must get some of those rubber tips.'

Rothchild turned his gaze towards Patchen.

'You seem to be making progress, Otto. Everyone will be glad to hear that.'

'Yes, David. Part by part I am hauling my body out of the grave. What brings you here? You're commuting from Washington these days.'

'The Kamensky business.'

Rothchild lifted a glass of water, using both hands, and wet his mouth.

'Paul is handling it extremely well,' he said. 'He has Cerutti under contract, if not under discipline. It's all going according to the scenario.'

'That part, yes. But more and more, Otto, I worry about the effect on Kamensky. So do the others at home.'

Maria, seated with ankles crossed, did not bother to watch Patchen as he spoke; his face showed nothing. She had her eyes on Christopher, who was listening passively as usual, and when Christopher caught her glance she gave him a smile, a crinkling of the skin around the eyes, a widening of the full lips; it was the grin a sister might give to a favourite brother.

'Each time we meet, David, this subject arises,' Rothchild said. 'But it never advances. We are worried; we see what the consequences for Kiril Kamensky may be – probably will be. What, my dear David, can we do about it?'

'We had a plan, Otto. We thought we could get him out.'

'Get him out? How? Send in parachutists and kidnap him? Really, David.'

'Trade goods, Otto.' Patchen named the captured Russian spy that Headquarters had been willing to exchange for Kamensky. Rothchild flinched in surprise. Then, preparing a reply, he looked from face to face. When he spoke, he was gazing at none of them but at his Klee: a flower, a stick figure, a line of colour like a cancellation; it was a picture with no depth, it suggested nothing but its surface. Christopher wondered why Rothchild, of all people, loved it so.

'I can't believe it,' Rothchild said. 'Exchange a man of that stature for a writer, a forgotten writer? It would never have worked.'

'There were permutations. It would have worked.'

'Do I understand that the plan has been abandoned?'

'Yes.' Patchen explained what had happened, as he had explained it to Christopher.

'Then it's a dead issue. Is that what you're telling me?'

'Not at all. We're afraid that Kamensky, if he comes to a bad end, would be an operational liability. One way or another, we have to save him.'

'You've just said that's gone by the boards,' Maria said.

Rothchild lifted a hand, forbidding another interruption. He nodded to Patchen.

'There are two things we can do, it seems to me,' Patchen continued. 'We can postpone publication of the novel. We can orchestrate the world intelligentsia in a campaign to release Kamensky. It would take a long time, maybe, but in the end I think we could get him out that way, by hard-nosed public pressure. Paul has a head of state on the string in Africa who'd put Kamensky's name in for the Nobel Prize. That's Option One. What do you think?'

Rothchild put his head back and lapsed into one of his stillnesses. Maria cocked her head, examined her husband. She asked Patchen and Christopher if they wanted tea. They refused.

'I think it's possible, David,' Rothchild said, opening his eyes. 'But the time element is a strong, strong negative. It might take ten years. Kamensky could die in the meantime. Also, and I know you've considered this, it would certainly arouse the suspicions of the Soviet security apparatus. Why, they would ask, why? So you might put Kamensky in greater hazard. Besides, I don't know if we could keep up the campaign long enough. Intellectuals are like children; they're passionate about the interest of the moment, but they're easily diverted. They wouldn't stay with it.'

'So you think this is not a viable option?'

'No. Because of all I've said, and because of another, much more important element.'

'Yes,' Maria said in her hard-edged voice, and gave a knowing smile. 'The fatal flaw is pretty obvious.' Rothchild waited, with his new patience, for her intrusion to end.

'Kamensky wouldn't come,' he said. 'He would never consent to

156

leave Mother Russia. Bone and blood, brain and flesh, Kiril Kamensky is a Russian. He'd rather be in a prison camp in Siberia or in Lubianka than to wear silk and eat caviar with foreign earth under his feet.'

Rothchild, having finished this speech, looked again from Patchen to Christopher to Maria, his eyes glinting with amusement, as if he had told them some delicious joke. Patchen, unresponsive, broke Rothchild's pose with a question.

'What would induce him to break this mystical bond with Holy Russia?'

'Nothing.'

'Come on, Otto. Fame. I got the idea you thought he hungered for it.'

'He does. But fame among Russians. He cares about no one else.'

'A woman?'

'At his age?'

Patchen moved his head towards Maria. She bit her lips and flushed; pushed back a strand of hair.

'Let me ask you this,' Patchen said. 'If we found a secure way to communicate with Kamensky, would you, as his friend, plead with him to come out? A letter.'

'Of course,' Rothchild said. 'I'm under discipline. I've done many silly, futile things for that reason. David, it would not work.'

Patchen stood up abruptly. 'Excuse us a moment,' he said. He took Christopher by the arm – Christopher saw that Maria was as astonished as he that Patchen should touch another man – and led him to the far corner of the sitting room. There, Patchen, with his eyes fixed on a tiny fragment of old carpet in a heavy gold frame, whispered at length in Christopher's ear. They returned to the sofa and sat down.

'What's that scrap of rug you have framed, Otto?' Patchen asked.

Rothchild closed his eyes again. Maria answered for him. 'It's supposed to be a bit of a seventh-century carpet called the Springtime of Chosros. The Arabs cut it into sixty thousand pieces as booty when they sacked Ctesiphon. It belonged to Otto's family. He brought it out with him in 1917.'

'A piece of the True Cross, in carpet-worshipper's terms,'

Rothchild said. 'If you have faith that it's what you think it is, it's priceless.'

Christopher said, 'Otto.'

Rothchild opened his eyes. The light of interest had gone out; fatigue whitened his face.

'Otto, everything you've said makes sense,' Christopher said. 'David agrees.'

'David is letting you speak for him?'

'Still we're worried. I don't like the atmosphere of this operation. I have a feeling, just a feeling, that something is going to go really wrong. I'm not thinking about Kamensky, I'm thinking about ourselves.'

'I'm growing very tired, Paul.'

'This won't take long. Option Two is to print Kamensky's book under a pseudonym. No one except those of us inside, and Cerutti outside, will know who wrote the book.'

Rothchild's lax body stiffened. He stared first at Christopher, then at Patchen. He started to speak, coughed, covered his mouth. Maria rushed across the room and gave him water. He pushed her body aside as if it were an object of furniture between him and the two intelligence officers.

'That's monstrous,' he said. 'It's theft from Kamensky. You're proposing his lifework, give him nothing, take everything for our dirty little purposes. This novel is a work of art.'

Christopher crossed the room, knelt at Rothchild's feet, took his hand.

'Otto, I'm trying to save his life,' he said.

Rothchild extricated his hand which had lain, boneless as a glove, for a moment in Christopher's. In a man who had any strength left in him, Rothchild's gesture would have been a brutal one.

'His life?' Rothchild said. 'Kamensky's life is in his book. What other life has he had, first as a fool of the revolution, then as its prisoner? And you, Christopher – you want to throw him into an unmarked grave.'

Rothchild again moved his eyes from Patchen's face to Christopher's. The irises were hidden and then revealed by Rothchild's blinking lids, as though a camera lay behind them in Rothchild's skull and he was recording their features on film.

'From the first day,' Patchen said, 'Paul has been trying to keep

Kamensky out of the grave. I think he's found a way. The book won't be signed with Kamensky's name. I won't kill this man. Otto, accept it.'

Rothchild turned to Maria and spoke to her, peremptorily, in Russian. She helped him from the room.

Christopher went to the window, open to the warm breeze, and stood between the billowing curtains, looking down on the Seine. Once again he had the illusion of sailing in this building on the prow of the island.

Maria returned. She went to the bar and filled three glasses with ice cubes and poured Scotch over them. She handed out the drinks.

'Permit me to offer you the hospitality of Otto's house,' she said.

'He's gone back to bed?'

'Yes. I gave him a pill to make him sleep.'

They were standing, like a conversational group at a cocktail party, in a little circle in the centre of the room.

'How do you explain Otto being so angry?' Patchen asked.

Maria finished her drink, rattled the ice in the empty glass, went back to the bar and poured herself more Scotch.

'After all,' Patchen went on, 'it's not such an irrational thing to do, to protect Kamensky. And the book will exist. Sooner or later, as soon as it's safe, we'll let the author's name out. I should think it would intensify his fame, to have this work of art, as Otto calls it, wrapped in mystery for a while.'

Maria finished her second whisky, looked quizzically at the empty glass, and resolutely put it down on a table.

'I don't know exactly what goes on inside Otto,' Maria said. 'But he really feels that the book ought to be Kamensky's monument. Kamensky was a friend of his youth. Evidently he genuinely loved him. You two, of all people, ought to be able to understand the nature of friendship between males. It's a mystery to my sex, but *voilà*.'

'When and where were they such friends?' Patchen asked. 'I've never been clear on that point.'

Maria made one of her husband's gestures. 'Otto doesn't speak of times and places any more than you do, David. It's training. They were young, I know that.'

'It doesn't matter. Go on.'

'The rest is obvious. Otto saw that you were, finally and irre-vocably, taking all control of this operation away from him. He feared that. You knew he feared it. Frankly, I don't see what it would have cost you to keep up the illusion. It's a mistake, David, hurting a man like Otto for no good reason.'

Patchen made no effort to fill the silence that followed Maria's last sentence. Thinking that she wouldn't speak again if no one replied, Christopher said, 'There was no intent to injure him, Maria. We thought he'd be glad of a way to save Kamensky.'

'You have some indication that Kamensky's in danger? Now, at this moment?'

Christopher answered easily. The exchange of information, the low unhurried voices of the two men had soothed Maria. Patchen watched her fixedly, as he had watched Rothchild. Each time one of them looked up it was to look into Patchen's opaque eyes. Christopher didn't like Patchen's unveiled watchfulness; he liked nothing that was obvious.

'No, that's just it,' he said to Maria. 'Horst was killed. But the whole string of couriers that brought the manuscript out, from that Red Army captain, Kalmyk, who handed Bülow the baby in Dresden on March 24, all the way back to Kamensky himself, has been left untouched by the KGB.'

Maria was keeping a careful hand on her emotions, and she let it show in the hard-eyed way she was receiving Christopher's information.

'And what does that say to you, Paul?' she asked.

'That they don't know who the couriers are, or what was in the package. If we publish the book under a pen name, it will have just as much impact in the West. We'll accomplish our objective and also keep Kamensky alive. Or at least increase his chances of staying alive.'

Maria nodded. 'That's what I thought. Otto sees it too – intellectually. But his emotions are involved in this operation.'

'Otto's not the only one,' Christopher said. 'Everyone wanted this operation too much from the start. We jumped to conclusions, we went too fast.'

Patchen made a sound of disgust. He began to speak to Christo-pher, then turned away.

'Even David,' Christopher said. 'Everyone believed as soon as Horst Bülow was killed that the opposition had done it. Therefore we could go ahead, Kamensky was already a target for the Soviets.'

Patchen faced them. 'Paul doesn't believe the Russians killed Bülow,' he said. 'He never has.'

Maria glanced at the closed door of the sitting room, listening for sounds of Rothchild beyond it. She said, 'What's your opinion, David?'

Patchen had stopped watching her, and she had to move across the room in order to look into his face.

'I think,' Patchen said, 'that it's very odd that the Soviets would kill Bülow and just let it go at that. Why not this Kalmyk? Why not the other couriers? Why not Paul, for that matter?'

'Have you thought that from the start, or has it been just Paul, alone again?'

'I haven't Paul's instincts.'

'Very few people have, even Otto says so. He almost thinks Paul is a reincarnation of himself. But I don't have to tell you two about that – you use Otto's weakness well enough.'

She took the empty glasses out of their hands.

'Every time David wants to do something brutal,' she said, 'he has Paul do it. That kneeling on the carpet at Otto's feet was a lovely touch. Otto should have laid a hand on your golden head, Christopher – the "verray parfit gentle knight . . . he was as fressh as is the month of May". As if Otto doesn't know, as if *I* don't know, what Paul is capable of.'

4

An hour later, waiting in the safe house for Wilson, Patchen passed the time by discussing marriage. 'It's analagous to trade-craft, you know – there's that helpless love of the other partner, as of an agent,' he said, 'and still either of the two will deceive, betray, revile the other with a third party. Take Maria as an example. Or my own Laura. Bitterness runs like an underground river in women. Laura had an aunt whose husband lost every penny of her inheritance in the stock market; she went out within the month and got some other man to father a baby on her. Never told her husband – just watched him love the child to distraction for thirty years. The sweetest moment of her life, she told Laura, was *not* revealing the secret to him on his death bed.'

'Interesting blood in Laura.'
'In all of us.'

Wilson was five minutes late. He let himself in with a key. 'I'm sorry about the time,' he said. 'The secretary who housekeeps this place was out. I waited, so I could send her to the movies. It must be hell, living in a safe house and being sent out to play all the time; these girls earn the rent.'

Patchen said. 'Christopher has briefed me on your conversations in Zürich. I'll let him tell you what's happened since then on our side.'

Christopher recounted their meeting with Rothchild.

'You think he accepts the decision?'

'Even Otto has to accept Headquarters decisions,' Christopher said.

Wilson nodded. In Patchen's presence, he was making no notes on his file cards.

'We've finished the wiring on Cerutti,' Wilson said. 'There's a twenty-four-hour audio surveillance – phones, office, apartment, car. We had to rig a tape recorder in the car because of all the interference from mobile transmitters; you just can't read anything from a moving vehicle in a city this size. We've glued a bleeper on the car, too, in case we want to follow.'

'What have you picked up so far?'

'Routine. He's been talking to the woman who's translating the novel from Russian into French. She's gaga over the book, wants to know who the author is. Cerutti won't answer. He's not what you'd call pally with people who work for him.'

'Nothing else?'

'Everyday life. Of course we'll always be twelve to twenty-four hours behind. It takes time to listen to the tapes, pick out the significant segments, transcribe. It takes manpower, and manpower I don't really have.'

'Audio surveillance is not enough,' Patchen said. 'He has to be covered, surveilled by a team, twenty-four hours a day.'

'That's impossible. There aren't that many men in the whole Paris station who have the expertise.'

Patchen for the second time that day, put a hand on Christopher. 'Paul will watch him at least half the time.'

'Alone?'

'He'll just be *with* him. They can hole up somewhere and talk and talk and talk about this publishing project. Paul can give him some more money, take him to some more three-star restaurants.'

'When is Christopher going to tell him about publishing under a pen name?'

'Right away,' Christopher said. 'He's not going to be any happier about it than Otto was.'

'We don't think he's going to do anything tricky while Christopher's with him, is that it?' Wilson asked.

'That's it. But when they part, you and whoever you can rustle from the Paris gumshoe stable will have to keep an eye on him.'

Wilson nodded. 'He'll not be alone.'

Christopher spoke for a moment, reminding them what the objective of the surveillance was.

'If something develops in Berlin, I'll go,' he said. 'Someone else will have to baby-sit Cerutti.'

Wilson nodded. Patchen, immobile, asked if any additional men were needed in Rome.

'No,' Wilson said, 'Franco Moroni is no Cerutti. We have the German girl on him, and audio surveillance. It's enough. Besides, we know his Soviet case officer – a friend of yours, Paul, that Tass man called Klimenko. We have the Russian covered all the time.'

'Paul shouldn't have anything to do with the Rome part of it. He lives there; he has to stay clean.'

Wilson showed nothing. 'Agreed. I've already accepted Christopher's reasons for not wanting to get involved down there.'

Patchen asked Wilson to leave the room. He went into the secretary's bedroom and closed the door behind him, but they heard the clasps of his attaché case snap open.

'All that remains, I guess, is to spring the news on Cerutti,' Patchen said.

'And wait for the mousetrap to spring.'

'Your mouse, Paul, and your trap. You're looking a little haggard. It's a costly business, curiosity.'

Thirteen

I

Christopher met Cerutti in the children's garden in the Pré Catelan on a Wednesday, the afternoon of Cerutti's regular visit to Otto Rothchild. Cerutti recited history. 'The Pré Catelan is named for a court minstrel, murdered here in the fourteenth century,' he said. 'One pays in the end for making jokes about the king.'

Now that the recruitment had been completed, there was no need for Christopher to be amused by his agent's jokes. He walked on, looking for a quiet place to talk. Young mothers, speaking in the sweet tone that Frenchwomen use in public, scolded and warned their children. (Christopher, when in later years he dreamt of this operation, would dream of it mixed up with nursemaids and young mothers and prams; Patchen and Maria in the Luxembourg Gardens and Patchen at the Zoo; Cerutti affixing his thumbprint to a receipt in the Parc Monceau; now Cerutti again among toddlers in the Bois de Boulogne.) They found an empty bench, and Christopher told Cerutti what he had to tell him.

'This is not what we agreed.'

'The agreement is being changed,' Christopher said. 'There are excellent reasons.'

'Ah, yes. I am but a small part of the whole, and if I only knew the entire picture, I'd see that what appears to me to be stupid is in fact a vital piece of a jigsaw puzzle designed by a genius. How many times in the past have I heard that said!'

'I haven't said it. What I will say is this: it's a measure designed to protect Kamensky's life. Surely you don't object to that.'

'Not at all. I'm somewhat surprised, perhaps, that a man of your profession would take Kamensky's life into account.'

Cerutti turned his back, walked a few paces over the gravel. Christopher waited where he was for the agent to come back to him. He asked Cerutti the state of the French translation.

'One-third completed. It will be done, in rough form, in a month.'

'Two weeks.'

'Impossible.'

'Hire two more translators; let them work as a team. You and I will do the final polishing, together. For when have you reserved the presses?'

'For the first week in September.'

'For the French, make it the last week in July.'

'Impossible. August is the holiday month in France. No one works. You want to publish in *August*?'

'I want every reviewer, every editor, every prominent intellectual in France to take proofs with him on vacation.'

'Such a thing has never been done.'

'Then it will be something new. You'll go round to all of them, saying that you have a major manuscript by a major Russian author. You will not reveal his name. You'll say you know his name, that the book came to you out of the underground, that you can authenticate its authorship – but only after the author dies. Your background is known, it's just slipped everyone's mind. Let the journalists interview *you*. Speak of how you fought with the Reds before Petrograd in 1918 against the Whites under Yudenich. Speak of yourself in Madrid in '36. Renew your credentials.'

Cerutti turned his back again. He squatted – his round belly made stooping difficult for him – and tied a shoelace. He picked up three stones, and, with his back still turned, juggled them. A small boy, standing some yards away, pointed and laughed; Christopher supposed that Cerutti's performance, from that distance, would look like a pantomime because the flying pebbles were too small to be seen. Cerutti dropped a stone, made a frantic grab for it to amuse the child, and turned back to Christopher.

'It's not a bad plan,' he said. 'But I've never spoken publicly about these things before. Once one begins . . .'

'It's time you did. There will be suspicion – they will ask why you are doing this.'

'*Suspicion*, my friend? Hostility. I'll be called a turncoat. The Communists have access to the press in this country.'

'In every country.'

'But in certain countries, including France, they can awaken true passion. We make our bread of old political resentments. Here, believers are respected by the general public simply because they are believers.'

What Cerutti said was true enough, and his fear for his reputation was realistic. He needed a push. Christopher disliked revealing to an agent that he knew a secret about him; it reduced the anxiety that an operative must feel in order to keep alive the fear of loss, and the greater fear of injury to his idea of himself. Yet he had prepared himself with Cerutti's secrets, or as many of them as were recorded in the files Wilson had given him to read.

'If I were you, Claude,' Christopher said, and watched Cerutti stiffen, for Christopher had never before called him by his Christian name, nor *tu-toyéd* him. 'If I were you, I'd leak the story of why you left the Party, feed it to a sympathetic journalist. Better, have someone else do it. Perhaps we could arrange that for you.'

'It was a long, boring process.'

'Was it?' Christopher spoke a Russian name. He supposed that Cerutti had not heard it said aloud for forty years.

Cerutti neither answered nor moved. Like Rothchild's the day before, his eyes became lenses, and Christopher wondered how many brains stored these photographs of his face, taken as if a camera had been snapped in an instinctive action of self-defence at the moment a pistol was fired at the photographer. The bullet was frozen in mid-air, but only on the film.

'In 1920,' Christopher said, 'this man, your case officer in the Soviet intelligence service, instructed you to penetrate the French military staff that General Weygand had taken to Warsaw to run the Polish army in its war against the Russian Bolsheviks. You refused. You told him you wouldn't spy on France. Reveal that and the French, even the intelligentsia, ought to forgive you anything.'

Cerutti had recovered himself as Christopher spoke. He answered calmly.

'Yes. But who will vouch for it?'

'Not everyone was killed by Stalin in the thirties.'

'This man lived? You know who he is, where he is, now? He would reveal himself, speak out?'

'Yes.'

'Then he must owe you people a great deal,' Cerutti said. 'All right, it's agreed. What else?'

Christopher told him as if it were an afterthought:

'We want the Russian text to go to press immediately. Publish before the first of August. It will reinforce the French version, create the mystery.'

'The first card out of the shoe,' Cerutti said. 'Now you expect me to say I'll need more money.'

'I have it in my pocket,' Christopher replied.

2

Wilson took a clinical interest in facial expressions, tones of voice, gestures. He observed and recorded them as a physician, seeking signs of diabetes, will note the odour of acetone in a patient's breath, his thirst, his fits of irritability when deprived of food. In a new safe house, Wilson recorded on one of his file cards Christopher's description of Cerutti in the children's garden of the Pré Catelan.

He's pretty tough,' Wilson said. 'It takes a man to keep his head after he's told that a forty-year-old secret is still alive, that the fuse has been burning all those years.'

'Who have you got on him now?'

'I've got a young couple. They're good. I'm hoping she can get Cerutti into bed. That would give us twelve hours of control every night. The expense of this surveillance, if we lay it on the way Patchen wants to, makes my head spin.'

'Yes. But we have to have someone on Cerutti, and on Moroni, all the time. Otherwise, we can't be sure.'

'How long do you think it'll take?'

Christopher shrugged. 'Not long. We have to catch the move when the target makes it. Then listen. The way the KGB goes after things like this, I'd say two or three weeks, maybe less, to the day of reckoning. What do you think?'

'The same. If our target moves. That may not happen. It may not be as important to the target as you think.'

'We'll see,' Christopher said.

Wilson's throat was dry. He went into the kitchen of the apartment and Christopher heard him open and close the refrigerator door and punch holes in the tops of two beer cans. He returned with the beer, Schlitz from the PX, and gave Christopher a can. 'There's a messier girl living here than in the other place,' he said. 'Dishes for two still in the sink, bed unmade. Only one glass has lipstick on it.'

He described to Christopher the state of his negotiations with the Berlin base. There were difficulties about bringing Christopher together with the German stringer who had observed Horst Bülow's meeting with the Russian-speaking woman in the Tiergarten.

'The Germans are Wolkowicz's assets,' Wilson said. 'He doesn't like your shop. He keeps saying *you* killed Bülow on *his* territory. He gave me a general cursing-out about CA operations. He thinks you guys spend too much money on agents. But he sort of likes you personally; he says you pick up information sometimes, so you're not a total loss to the Company.'

'Yes, but will he help?'

'He has to. He'll cover the phones and the mail in Berlin. He'll let you talk to the German asset, in Berlin, if the Berlin base controls the contact one hundred per cent.'

'Meaning what?'

'Their safe house, their time, they get a tape of the conversation and a contact report from you.' Wilson grinned. 'One thing more. Wolkowicz wants you to wear a disguise. He's a great one for wigs and stuff. In this case, it's not a bad idea.'

Wilson's smile enveloped his face and infected Christopher. Wilson had read Christopher's file with care and he knew about Wolkowicz and disguises: Years before, when Wolkowicz worked in an Asian station, Christopher had asked him to deliver some money to a local agent. Wolkowicz, known to the agent as Mr Walters, a visa officer in the American Consulate, had thought it prudent to wear a blond wig and beard and to speak to the agent in a heavy Teutonic accent. He had reported all this and been admired by desk men in Headquarters for his cunning. A month later, the Asian had seen Christopher again. 'Paul, it was most curious the way your money came to me,' he said. 'Mr Walters brought it, but he had on a yellow wig and he's grown a beard. He spoke in such a strange way that I thought he had injured his tongue, and it was quite ten minutes before I recognized him.'

'Nevertheless,' Wilson said, sobering, 'I went through some of Berlin base's bio files – old stuff from the Nazi archives. The German political police watched everyone in the twenties and thirties, and I thought maybe something would jump off the page.'

Wilson opened his briefcase and gave Christopher a short report, a photostat of a photostat of the original handwriting of a secret police informer who had operated in Berlin twenty-five years before, when Horst Bülow had been living the happiest years of his life. Christopher read it. Wilson showed him another scrap of paper. Both were copies of Gestapo reports.

'Did Bülow ever mention these places to you – Peltzer's Bar and the Jockey? They were the intellectuals' hangouts in the thirties.'

'No,' Christopher said. 'He talked about dance halls, summer restaurants by the Wannsee, places where he picked up girls. What Horst remembered for my benefit was the life of the body.'

Wilson put away the reports, glancing again at the prim subordinate's German in which they had been written by the informers who had been watching Bülow in 1931.

'Evidently there was more to him than that,' Wilson said. 'There usually is.'

3

One of the extra translators hired by Cerutti was the young woman Wilson had assigned to surveille him. She had grown up in Montparnasse, the child of a French woman and an American painter who could not paint. 'She wants to be as much unlike her layabout folks as possible,' Wilson said. 'Good material. Her boy friend is a tech, a simple fellow like most of them, and *notre petite Joëlle* runs the team.' The girl worked all day with Cerutti in his tiny office; soon she was with him most nights as well. Her friend, parked outside in a car or following if they drove, recorded their conversations. The surveillance reports were routine: Cerutti carried out Christopher's instructions to the letter. When he used a public phone it was to call Christopher and arrange a meeting. His mail was clean. Wilson kept watch all the same; every other day he debriefed Joëlle. She kept a shorthand log of every minute of Cerutti's day. To this charcoal sketch of her target's life she added, in her verbal reports, the colour – Cerutti's jokes, his tempers, his manner towards the men and women he was contacting, his anecdotes. His behaviour in bed, she said, was entirely normal for a man at his time of life.

Her efficiency freed Christopher. Cerutti brought him each chapter of Kamensky's novel as it was translated into French. It had been transformed from a tapestry into a sheet of lace. Rothchild had been correct; no language except the original could contain the vitality of Kamensky's writing. Christopher, sometimes arguing heatedly with Cerutti, changed a sentence here, a phrase there. Neither man was satisfied with the result. 'Reading this in translation is like making love to one woman while imaging another,' Cerutti said.

He had given a copy of the Russian typescript to the printer. The type was being set. He had paid an enormous surcharge, using money bought with his thumbprint, to obtain such rapid service from the printer. Each afternoon he sent Joëlle to collect the typescript from the printer; she took it back to the print shop every morning. 'One doesn't want to take chances,' Cerutti said. 'A leak at this point would not be good.' Christopher asked Cerutti if he thought the girl was trustworthy. 'Trust? What's that?' Cerutti replied. 'One hopes for the best.'

4

Maria Rothchild, when she met Christopher on the steps of the Madeleine, told him that Cerutti, who had come to see Rothchild as usual on four Wednesday afternoons since his recruitment, had never mentioned Christopher or Kamensky's novel.

'He brings the champagne, he gets a little buzzed, he amuses Otto with stories about the old days,' Maria said. 'He and Otto, between them, know more about the European Left, all its fevers and perversions and its incredible web of connections, than Proust knew about the French upper class.'

'How is Otto?'

'Seething. How did you think he'd be?'

'Should I come to see him?'

'Not yet. I don't know when.'

Christopher persisted. 'I can cover for him for a while, but if he wants his pay he'll have to submit to a weekly contact while this operation is running.'

'I'll see what I can do,' Maria said. 'Do you want to come shopping with me?'

Christopher went with her to Hédiard while she bought tropical fruits. 'It's here I got the strawberries in autumn, the first day you came to meet Otto,' she said. 'It seems an age has gone by since then.' Nearby, at Fauchon, she found some Russian caviar and a small jar of *foie gras*. 'It's a constant struggle, tempting Otto's appetite,' she said. 'He's going back to his boyhood, he wants to eat the way he ate when his family was rich, in old Russia. More and more, Paul, that's what he talks about – Russia before the Revolution. He's gluing that life back together, piece by piece, like a smashed cup.'

'He did the smashing, or helped.'

'Yes, but that was when he was, politically, a child. He doesn't see why anyone would hold him responsible, now that he understands the value of what he broke.'

'You make him sound like a man who's losing his wits.'

'Otto? Not bloody likely. But he has his fantasies. Don't we all?'

In the street again, Christopher asked Maria to follow him; they crossed to the other side to escape the stream of customers entering and leaving the fancy grocery. Maria handed him her packages and began to go through her large purse, the picture of a woman who had misplaced something. Christopher admired her professional reflexes and had always done so. The natural appearance is the goal of tradecraft; not many operatives had Maria's gift for covering criminal behaviour with the wasted motions of everyday life.

'I wanted to keep you posted, even though Otto's mad at us,' Christopher said.

He told her about his arrangements with Cerutti, the printing schedule, the plans to exploit Cerutti's past as a means of certifying the authorship of an anonymous book. Maria asked the names of the printing houses – named the obvious ones, and Christopher

171

confirmed that these were the ones that were being used. Maria buckled her purse and took her packages back.

'Thanks, Paul,' she said. 'It makes me feel better when we're open with one another. It's hell to love Otto and also be loyal to the outfit in a situation like this.'

'Are we always so open?'

'I am. But I'm just a weak and foolish female.'

She started to walk, but Christopher did not follow. She turned around, waiting, and tapped her foot in pantomimed impatience.

'It's teatime,' Christopher said. 'Let's trot down to Queenie's and have a cup.'

Maria frowned, paused. The memory registered. She laughed again.

'Ah, Paul,' she said, 'you should have been on the stage, pulling things out of a hat. How perfect Cathy would be as your assistant, with those glorious legs and that glorious blonde hair and her glorious torso in a spangled bathing suit.'

But they went to Queenie's and had tea. Maria had several glasses of Dry Sack as well. 'I drink sweetish sherry when I'm out of Otto's sight,' she said. 'At home I'm allowed nothing but manzanilla.'

Maria offered no explanation as to why she had never mentioned her meeting with Cathy. 'I assumed she'd told you, why shouldn't she? She was not part of the picture with you and me and Otto. If I hadn't drunk so much sherry, being so glad to see an old schoolmate, I'd never have taken her home for dinner.'

'Didn't Otto think it was a mistake?'

'Otto tolerates my mistakes when I bring someone who looks like your wife into the house. He longed for her throughout the evening. Everyone has always longed for Cathy.'

Christopher let the subject go. Maria went upstairs and was gone for a long time. When she returned, they talked for another half-hour, the gossip of their trade – what old friend was chief of station in Tokyo, who was next in line as DDP, would the Director remain if the other party won the next elections? Maria was happy, lost in the secret world she had left for Otto Rothchild as he himself, if Maria was to be believed, was lost in memories of his noble family that went back to Alexander Nevsky and beyond.

'I'm more like Otto than I know,' Maria said at length. 'Russia is his whole subconscious, no other place is beautiful enough or interesting enough. I'm the same about the Company – it's my Russia. No one outside of it is real to me. Are they to you, Paul?'

'If they aren't, Maria, what use is the Company?'

She shook her head, took his hand, smiled at him as she had done many times before – an older sister remembering mischief, moments of pride, gruff boyish signs of love in a small brother, now grown up. Christopher was older than she, but since her marriage Maria behaved as if she had taken on her husband's age along with his name.

'You really do try to hold on to what you started out to be, don't you?' she said.

Christopher was annoyed; he let it show. Maria let go of his hand. She made up her face, peering into a hand mirror, while he paid the bill. Gathering her packages, she left before him. He watched through the window as she swung away into the afternoon crowds in the Place de la Madeleine, her head turning left and right, bobbed hair swinging, as alert as a doe.

Christopher remained at his table for a long time, watching the crowds. He did not think. All that was going to happen in his mind had happened; the sequence of intuition, suspicion, evidence had been completed. He was waiting for final proof. The soft light of evening faded from pink to grey. He wondered if Cathy – who never read, never wrote, never (as she insisted) *thought* as a conscious act – felt, as he did now, that she could not live another hour with dread.

Christopher knew that what he was making happen would happen; he hated the scenes he had invented for himself and others to live through. A week before, by the château at Vincennes, he had said so to Patchen.

'No one is responsible for suicide except the man who commits it,' Patchen had replied.

5

In less than a week, Cerutti phoned Christopher, and, using the code for urgency, asked for a meeting. Under the Pont de la Concorde, where, a few weeks before, the seduction had been completed, Cerutti told Christopher that a set of Russian proofs of the completed novel had been stolen from the printer.

'Vanished, vanished,' Cerutti said. 'They were supposed to be kept locked up at night.'

'Were they taken in the night?'

'The printer doesn't know. He just stuffed the package into his cabinet before he went home at the end of the day; the proof-reader brings them in to him at five o'clock.'

'Where is the proof-reader?'

'Still there, proof-reading. An old émigré. One can't make it seem too serious, questioning him. Anyway, what does he care?'

Christopher put his hands on Cerutti. 'No one knows the author's name? You're absolutely certain.'

'Absolutely.'

Wilson, giving Christopher the same news two hours earlier, had made the same assurance. Wilson's eyes were red-rimmed from reading – transcripts, reports, old files. He carried everything that had any significance written on his little stack of file cards in his briefcase during his waking hours; when he slept, he locked the locked case in a safe at the Embassy.

'Paul, if Cerutti's gotten word to anyone, he's done it by carrier pigeon while Joëlle was asleep. The tapes, everything, leave him absolutely clean.'

'Has Moroni had any contact with Klimenko?'

'No, the Russian is out of Rome, futzing around in Tanganyika,' Wilson said. 'Moroni is working on his next movie. He spends a lot of time in a new place, not his own apartment. But we have that wired.'

Wilson held Christopher's eyes. The radio, volume turned high to drown their voices, was at Wilson's elbow; as the news came on, he turned the sound even louder, and listened intently to the first few bulletins.

'We can assume something will break in a few days now,' Christopher said. 'As soon as it does, I want that meeting in Berlin.'

'I'll fix it up with Wolkowicz,' Wilson said. He hesitated, one hand lifted to give notice that he intended to say something. He dropped the hand, and his eyes, and gathered up his briefcase. But at the door, he put a hand on Christopher's shoulder. Christopher said, 'I know about the apartment in the Piazza Oratorio. You don't have to apologize for doing your job.'

'At this point, Paul,' Wilson said, 'anything you want from me, you've got.'

6

Christopher, alone in a hotel room, had photographs and sanitized files brought to him, and books from the Embassy library. He read all day, histories and geographies of Russia and Germany and Spain, old agents' reports, operational summaries, the crude ore of espionage. He was trying to understand Kamensky and his novel, trying to understand Cerutti and Rothchild and Bülow, attempting to put himself into their skins and into their time. He belonged to a different century, a different class, a different emotional style. He memorized a place name from Russian history, a date from a wartime OSS report on a Maquis network in Pau, a fact from a transcript of university grades. He wrote nothing down. At the end of each day he put the papers back into a Manilla envelope, sealed it, carried it back to a rendezvous, and gave it for safekeeping to a young officer from the Paris station. At night he worked with Cerutti on the translation.

When he left the agent, late, he walked the streets; in this city, in the past fifteen years, he had played out the best and the worst moments of his life. Here, talking quietly to men who had travelled thousands of miles to meet him, he had walked under the trees in the darkness and discussed their wish to murder the governments under which they lived; they spoke always in terms of a birth of liberty because they were talking to an American, but the violent death of their rivals was what they had in mind. Under the same trees, he had taken girls, one after the other, into his arms, overcome by the sweetness he saw in all women; and when he could still put lines on paper he had left poems all over this city, scribbled on napkins and tablecloths, and once, on the skin of a girl's arm. 'You do with your poems what a gambler in cowboy films does with banknotes, lights his cigar,' the girl had told him; 'one day it will be gone, *mon amour*, and you'll never get it back.' Christopher, remembering her ten years afterwards – every detail, the ink on her tan skin under the fine sun-bleached hairs, the brown eyes sharp with intelligence, the strong slightly crooked teeth that were the key to her sexuality – laughed again at her solemnity. The gift for poetry still seemed to him a trivial thing to lose; there was nothing he wanted to describe in rhyme and image. He had learned to see things as they were and to keep quiet.

On the fourth night after the theft of the Russian proofs, Christopher returned to his hotel at two o'clock in the morning. The directional signals of a car parked across the street blinked three times. Christopher crossed the deserted boulevard and got into the back seat. Wilson, alone, was at the wheel. He drove away without speaking, and circled through the streets, his eyes on the mirror, before he parked again, on a dead-quiet side street in Neuilly, where the diplomatic plates on his Citroën would draw the least attention from police patrols. Christopher got into the front seat.

'Not quite what we expected,' Wilson said.

He handed Christopher an envelope, a large bright yellow one of the kind that is manufactured only in Switzerland; it was rumpled and torn by its passage through the mail; it bore United Nations stamps and the postmark of the Palais des Nations in Geneva. It had been addressed with a typewriter to a radio station in Germany that broadcast propaganda in Russian into the Soviet Union. The radio was an Agency operation. The envelope was addressed to the head of the Russian section of the radio station.

'It came through the open mail yesterday,' Wilson said. 'The Russian proofs were inside, and this letter.'

The letter was in English, perfect but stilted – the sort of English Christopher might write if he wished the reader to believe it had been composed by a foreigner. The letter gave a synopsis of Kamensky's novel. It described without detail the plan to publish it in the West. It identified Kamensky as the author. It pointed out that no copyright had been applied for, and that the reading of the text over the air, in Russian, if it were done quickly, would infringe no legal contracts.

'No fingerprints, of course,' Wilson said, 'except the proof-reader's and the printer's. I think we can eliminate them as suspects.'

'No sighting in Geneva?'

'No, but we weren't covering Geneva for this target. I don't know why not – it's the obvious place, crawling with KGB, safe mail facilities. Using the UN post office was very picturesque, it eliminates a mail intercept by the Swiss liaison altogether.'

'What do the radio people want to do?'

'They await instructions.'

'Yes. But what do they want to do?'

'They want to read it on the air. The case officer says that his Russian wants to run the whole novel, take over the entire broadcasting schedule.'

'When?'

'Like tomorrow. They figure they can surprise the Russian jammers, get some of it through. Then they'll switch frequencies and slip in a chapter in the middle of a music programme from time to time – drive the Soviets crazy.'

'Identifying Kamensky?'

Wilson took the envelope and the letter out of Christopher's hands, and locked them away in his briefcase again.

'That's the whole idea, isn't it?'

'Yes.'

Wilson, for once, didn't have the radio playing; he knew that this car was secure.

'We have no match on the typewriter, of course. It's a Hermes portable – probably they bought it in Geneva and threw it in the lake after one use. I can't match this Russian at the radio station with the target. He says he has no idea who'd send him such a thing; his case officer believes it.'

'Will the guys from the radio project go along?'

'Oh, sure. They don't even think they have to cable Headquarters. Just put it on the air and watch Khrushchev dance.'

'Have you cabled?'

'Yes. Flash to Patchen.' He used Patchen's cryptonym; Wilson used everyone's cryptonym and so did Christopher; their speech, like their written communications to Washington, was in cipher.

'Has he got back to you?'

'Yes. Three words: "Christopher's judgement applies".'

'What's the time factor for the radio?'

'They can go on the air instantaneously. The case officer is here in Paris on a TDY. He says the best hour of the day is early morning. Evidently the Russian audience gets up early for the real goodies.'

Christopher didn't really want this information; he wanted a moment to calm himself. The target had wakened his emotions.

Hearing what he had heard, recognizing the profile of the operative, something had broken through the surface of his mind, a sensation in which anger and humour were intermixed. Even in trapping his enemy he had been, in a way, outwitted, because the target had acted in a way he hadn't expected. Wilson nodded, divining Christopher's thoughts.

'It's really and truly admirable, isn't it?' he said. 'What a picture book that son of a gun has been.'

'Still is. We haven't wrapped this up yet.'

'What about the broadcast? The case officer has to know pretty soon; he can lay it on by phone, but he has to call by three in the morning, because of the time difference. It's later in Russia.'

Christopher laid his face against the glass of the car window. His skin felt hot, as if he were drunk or sick. He'd had no alcohol for a week, had not touched the flesh of another human being since he had kissed Cathy goodbye in the airport at Rome. He'd thought of nothing – not of Cathy wounding herself in Italy, not of Kamensky and the long storm of the Russian's life, not even of this moment which he had planned. He had, for weeks, simply received data. Now he had more data. It was his function to act on it.

'Tell them to go ahead,' Christopher said. 'The fact that they broadcast will alert the target that we're running an operation against him. He knows we control what the radio does. But what difference does it make now?'

'He can run.'

'He won't.'

'You ought to know. But there's always that random factor – that's what he's lived on all his life. He sees it – the aberration, the hole, the flaw, a long way off.'

'Right. And what's the hole in him, Bud?'

Wilson waited; when Christopher didn't go on, he didn't urge him to do so. He started the engine. He put the car in gear, but waited, with the clutch out, for another instant.

'The hole in him,' Christopher said, 'is that, of all the people he's done this to, all through his life, we're the only ones who won't kill him for it. When he runs, he'll run to us.'

Fourteen

I

Christopher, before he went to Berlin, collected an express letter
from Cathy, and an old telegram, from *poste restante*. He had not
written to her or tried to telephone, and he had expected no word
from her. The telegram told him that she was going to Spain; the
letter was from Pamplona, written on the third day of the fiesta.

July 9th

Fireworks in the plaza, Pablo – I was just in time for them,
as you and I were last year. The clock striking midnight was
like my mind striking off the months of our marriage, and then
that great cheap explosion of coloured light in the sky, and
everyone singing and gasping. The Spaniards' festival clothes
were pure white when I got here and they were their good
selves, sober and nice and correct. Now they're drunk and
lewd and nasty in the same clothes, dirty and stained with wine.
Why don't *we* have a week in every year when it's all right to be
a beast? Far better than doing it a bit at a time. After three
days of this I'm not exactly squeaky clean myself. I'm going to
Madrid today, after the corrida. Paco Camino is fighting, and oh
so well. I saw him in Barcelona, in the rain, on the way down
here (I brought the car), and I longed to have you with me to

179

watch. Hemingway is *not* here again this year, and it's so comical. The crowd wants to believe he *is* here, and you hear them in El Choko and all over, saying to each other, "*Hemingway está aquí, Hemingway está aquí,*" and yesterday, some German movie actor who's burly like Hemingway arrived and everyone thinks Ernesto has shaved off his beard and *is* this German. So at the corrida, Chamaco (I think it was) spread his cape on the barrera in front of the German (I was sitting right behind him in the tendido) and dedicated his third bull to him, "A Usted, Don Ernesto," and a lot more flowery stuff. *He* thought he was killing the bull for Hemingway. It couldn't have been more funny if Mama had made up the story, the German was so thrilled at being recognized because *he* didn't know it was a case of mistaken identity, and his starlet catching the matador's hat. Oh, Paul, you would have thought it was so funny. I am feeling alone. I hope you are too. Will you come to Madrid? Will you wire me at the Palace Hotel? Will you please? Camino will be at the Plaza de Toros there. I *hate* seeing joy all around me. Is that all right? Do you see me at all in your mind these days? I believe you do. You knew I was here, I'll bet. (Yes, the room in Pamplona where I sleep has shutters at the foot of the bed and a pottery crucifix with a chalkwhite Jesus you can see in the mirror from any point on the bed; and, yes, I swam at the waterfall in the modest blue bathing suit. And yes, what's been said between us rings in my ears, and yes, I borrowed a guitar from a man in Las Pocholas at four in the morning and sang "La Paloma.") And yes, you're right, it's a beautiful song. And Paul if I don't have you soon in Madrid, with me in the places we've loved, I'm going to be worse off even than I am now.

Christopher, standing in the noisy foyer of the post office, read Cathy's letter and read it again. It was 12 July. He sent her a wire:

JOINING YOU MADRID JULY NINETEENTH MEANWHILE
I DO SEE YOU BETTER EVEN THAN YOU IMAGINE AND
SOMETIMES HEAR THE SONGS CATHY DONT SPEND ANY
REAL MONEY

Because they had made it into a code, he couldn't use the word 'love' in a telegram.

Barney Wolkowicz met Christopher at Tempelhof Airport, outside the customs barrier. Wolkowicz's presence was a calculated insult. Christopher walked by him as if he were invisible and went into the men's room. In a moment, Wolkowicz followed him. They stood side by side at the urinals, and waited for the cleaning woman to finish mopping and leave the room. Christopher and Wolkowicz had met first in East Africa, and when Wolkowicz spoke, he spoke in Swahili.

'Is this language secure enough for you?' he asked.

'You're good at languages, Barney,' Christopher replied, in the same tongue. 'It's a pity you like to let the chickens out of the hen house.'

'*Nataka kujua mahali utakapokuwapo,*' Wolkowicz said: I want to know where you are. 'Door to door, minute by minute,' he added in English.

Wolkowicz cared nothing about the security of covert action operations, and he lost no opportunity to show his contempt for them. He operated in Berlin, gathering information, under official cover; he was in daily contact with the police and the German security agencies. Meeting Christopher openly at the airport, where security operatives – eyes and cameras – were constantly on the watch, was as good as identifying him, in a liaison meeting as an agent of US intelligence. Wolkowicz was giving Christopher something – access to one of his agents. Exposing Christopher to embarrassment, if not to risk, was his way of exacting payment.

'*Niende sasa?*' Christopher asked – shall I go now? Wolkowicz began to speak, but Christopher cut in, speaking in English. 'Or shall I take out your dentures and throw them in the urinal?'

Wolkowicz showed his porcelain teeth. They were a sore point with him; a torturer had taken his own teeth during the last war after he had parachuted into Burma, into the middle of a Japanese patrol.

'Wait inside till you see me go by in a blue Mercedes with local plates, last two numbers 56, then take a cab,' Wolkowicz said. 'I'll stay ahead of the cab. Get off at Kempinsky's Hotel. Walk around

the block and I'll pick you up in front of the hotel when you re-
appear. If all's well, transfer your briefcase from your left hand to
your right.'

He walked out of the room. Christopher lingered, washed his
hands and face. He left a mark in the saucer for the old woman.
Wolkowicz, he saw, had tipped her ten pfennigs.

In the safe house, an actual house in Spandau rather than an
apartment, Wolkowicz drank beer from a bottle and watched while
a technician disguised Christopher. The technician fitted a dark
wig, salted with grey hair, over his head, and affixed matching
eyebrows with spirit gum. Christopher refused a beard. The
technician stepped back like a painter observing a brush stroke,
and changed one pair of window-pane eyeglasses for another,
tinted yellow. 'Your eyes are easy to remember, we'll just make it
a little harder,' he said. 'And your face is too lean; we can take
care of that.' He hooked a finger in the corner of Christopher's
mouth, slipped a thin sponge between his teeth and the inside of
his cheek, took it back out, trimmed it with his scissors. 'I think a
little pancake, don't you, Barney?' he said. 'And if we shadow
those eyes, they won't look so blue.'

Christopher said. 'I think we've gone far enough.'

'The sponges change his voice, they always do,' the technician
said. 'He'll be speaking German. Will the asset be able to tell he's
a foreigner?'

'No,' Wolkowicz said.

'Then he ought to have German clothes instead of that stuff he
has on. It has Brooks Brothers written all over it.'

'Too late. The fellow will be here in twenty minutes.'

'Then I'd better go,' the technician said. He walked around
Christopher slowly, shining a bright lamp on his head. 'You'll do,'
he said 'Just give the equipment back to Barney – and, oh, don't
drink anything with those sponges in your cheeks. It makes you
squirt when you talk. We almost drowned an asset once, spoiled
the whole effect.'

Wolkowicz let the technician out. When he came back and spoke
to Christopher his voice was friendly; the disguise, Christopher
supposed, had something to do with it.

'Now this asset is not the brightest kid in the world,' Wolkowicz said, 'so don't go too fast with him, and for Christ's sake don't let him get the idea that he's in on anything important. He's always after more money and I don't want him bringing you up as a justification. His name is Wolfram. I'll introduce you and leave. Actually I'll be down cellar on the earphones. We can't spare a tech for something like this. If you want me up here, say that you have a nephew in Munich.'

'Why would I want you up here?'

'Wolfram can be a little odd. He carries a gun, and I know you don't believe in violence.'

'You think he's going to stick me up, Barney?'

'Not for money. He may want your wig.'

3

Wolfram, though he could not have been older than twenty-five, was totally bald. When he removed his Tyrolean hat, after coming in out of the July sun, his skull shone with sweat. He shook hands with Christopher, then mopped his head with a handkerchief already damp from earlier use. The blinds were drawn in the room where he and Christopher sat in facing chairs; Wolkowicz, before he left, put two bottles of cold beer on the table between them. He gave Christopher a winking smile. The straps of Wolkowicz's shoulder holster were clearly visible under his summer jacket. He always went armed; the fact that this was obvious was, like having a disguise detected, one of the signs that Wolkowicz flashed to his agents that they were dealing with a real spy.

Christopher let Wolfram quench his thirst before he began to speak to him. The young German drank off most of his bottle of beer in one long pull. Wolkowicz had provided no glasses.

'Did you walk here in this heat?' Christopher asked.

'Almost a kilometre, from the S-Bahn station at Spandau-West. I was a little behind time, so I ran part of the way.'

'Surely that's not good security, to run in the streets?'

'Better than being late for a meeting with Krupp.'

'Krupp?'

Wolfram pointed a thumb over his shoulder and spoke the name by which he knew Wolkowicz. 'We call him Krupp because he loves his cannons so.'

The German settled back in his chair, his ankle thrown over his knee. He eyed Christopher's untouched bottle of beer; he had swallowed his own so quickly that his scalp was sweating again, and he wiped away the moisture with his sleeve. His shirt, under his woollen jacket, was soaked and transparent. Christopher uncapped the second bottle and gave it to Wolfram; the faint skunk-like aroma of German beer escaped from the neck of the bottle.

Christopher spread a half-dozen glossy photographs on the table under the strong light that the make-up technician had used. These were pictures of European men, some of them studio portraits, others candid shots of unwitting subjects. Wolfram leaned forward and moved aside with a stiff forefinger all but two photographs. One was a passport photo of Horst Bülow; the other showed Bülow in an overcoat and hat, crossing a Berlin street with a bombed wall in the background.

'I recognize this man,' Wolfram said. 'None of the others.'

'Tell me what you remember about him.'

Wolfram gave Christopher a complete physical description, an inventory of Bülow's mannerisms, the brand of cigarettes he smoked his drinking habits, a list of restaurants he frequented in West Berlin. 'He lived in East Berlin, in Christburger Strasse,' Wolfram said; he gave a music-hall smirk. 'That street is near some hospitals. The subject used to go out in the evenings and in the mornings and watch the nurses come and go when the work shifts changed. He liked to look at nurses, but he never approached one.'

'*Lived* in the Christburger Strasse? Past tense? Has he moved?'

'I don't know. I was assigned to surveille him for several weeks last winter, then I was put on to something else. I don't ask what I don't need to know.'

'What were the exact dates you were on him, please?'

'My superiors would have that.' Wolfram drank beer.

'So would you,' Christopher said. 'Your orders are to cooperate fully with me. If you haven't understood, I can contact your superiors and have them repeat your instructions in my presence.'

Christopher sat bolt upright, speaking in harsh German. There had been, on Wolfram's face, the beginnings of a smirk. As Christopher spoke, he cocked his head as if listening for an accent. Hearing none, his face cleared itself of all expression. He uncrossed his legs, sat up straight, put down his beer bottle. He took a note-book from an inside pocket and opened it.

'These are my field notes,' Wolfram said. 'I received the assignment to carry out a spot surveillance of this subject on 30 January. Surveillance commenced at 07.00 on 1 February, and continued, with one nine-day interruption, from 1 March to 10 March, until 24 March, at which time the assignment was terminated. I spent a total of 156 hours in actual surveillance of this subject.'

'In East Berlin as well as West?'

'Yes, sir. The nurses were from the Prenzlauer Berg Hospital, which is in the East. I went where he was, wherever he was, when I was on duty.'

'What about this subject was remarkable?'

Wolfram closed his notebook, marking the place with a finger, and made a show of collecting his thoughts.

'Number one, he was nervous, a regular alley cat, always looking around to make sure he wasn't being followed. Of course, he never spotted me.'

'How do you know that?'

'Because he never tried to lose me, and he never tried to lead me on wild-goose chases. When he went someplace, he always had something to do when he got there.'

'That could have been professionalism. Perhaps he knew you were on his back.'

Wolfram laughed. 'Never. You would have seen, if you had been behind him. This man was no professional. I followed him by myself, with no partners, alone, and never once lost him. That tells you something.'

'What did he do? What was his pattern?'

'To work every morning, right on time. Home every evening, right on time. He'd stop and have one beer on week nights, always at the same *stube*. He bought cold food and ate it alone in his room. He was very careful with money. But one night a week, Saturday, he'd cross into the West and have a tremendous big meal at a fancy restaurant; he'd find a whore first and take her with him to dinner, then go home with her for an hour, never more.'

'Different girls each time, or the same one?'

'Always different, always young. He'd *dance* with them – take them to places like the roof of the Hilton and buy them champagne cocktails. All week, evidently, he ate cold sausage alone in his room in order to have this night in West Berlin with a girl he had to pay for.'

'And this is what he always did, without fail, when he came into West Berlin?'

'So I thought for a while. I used to follow him to the girl's place, wait outside, take him home on the S-Bahn, see him into the door, and then go home myself. One night he made a lot of phone calls from public booths. I thought I'd wait around outside his place a little longer. It wasn't too cold.'

'And?'

'And at two o'clock in the morning, out he came, in his usual shabby clothes, with his briefcase, and walked across the zone frontier. He went the long way, up north, and through a bombed building instead of using a street.'

'What happened on the other side?'

'At 03.18, exactly, he was picked up in a car, in the Schiller Park.'

'Licence number?'

'I was too far behind – after all, we were practically the only two people on foot in Berlin at that hour and I had to stay out of sight. Also, the car had no lights on. It was a new car, an Opel.'

'Date?'

Wolfram opened his notebook and ran a finger down the page. 'Sunday morning, 7 February.'

'In the Schiller Park?'

'I've already said.'

'Did you follow up, go back to his place and wait?'

Wolfram laughed. 'My dear friend, it was almost dawn. It was starting to rain. I'd walked fifteen kilometres. The subject had gone somewhere in a car. I went home and went to bed.'

'Your unit didn't regard this target as high priority?'

'I don't know that. If they had, more than one man would have been used. I assumed we were spotting, assessing.'

'You had no back-up?'

'No, me alone. But I never lost him. He was slow, old.'

'You never saw him make another contact at night like that?'

'No.'

'Never saw the car again? It was an Opel?'

'It was a dark-coloured Opel Kapitän, and if I ever saw it again, this subject certainly was not inside it.'

Christopher had never met Bülow on a Sunday morning and

186

never in Schiller Park. He wasn't surprised that Horst, doubled, would stay in a pattern – early morning contact in a park – nor that he would sneak across the border, clambering through ruins like a commando, if left to his own devices. For Christopher's meetings he had been instructed to ride the S-Bahn, crossing in the rush hour, and to pass the evening in a cinema or a theatre, afterwards eating a simpler supper than the ones he had bought for his tarts, and to make secure contact in a secure location. But that had been Christopher's planning, not Horst's – and not that of the unknown people in the Opel.

'This period in February, from the 7th to the end,' Christopher said. 'What else did you observe?'

'Normal activity, except for one contact.'

'Describe it, please.'

Wolfram had been trained to speak when spoken to; Christopher knew it was no use waiting for him to volunteer information. He had to be activated, like a soldier in ranks, by voice commands.

'This contact took place at 08.18 exactly, on Monday, 15 February, in the English Garden in the Tiergarten,' Wolfram said. 'The contact was a woman. Clandestine signals were exchanged. The male subject removed his left glove; the female covered her mouth with her right hand and coughed. They walked together for a time, then sat down on a bench. The contact lasted fourteen minutes.'

Wolfram described the meeting between Bülow and the woman as Wilson had described it in the American Cathedral in Paris: the spoke Russian, an envelope passed, Bülow went to the bank, the woman went into the American Consulate.

'If there was only you on the surveillance, how do you know where both went?'

'That day there were two of us. I had an assistant. For him it was a training exercise. I put him on the man when they split; I took the woman.'

Christopher questioned Wolfram about the woman's appearance. He described her coat: green with a fur collar. She wore a fur hat; her hair wasn't visible. She held a scarf in front of her face; the day was windy and bitter, so it was a natural gesture. Christopher spread another set of photographs on the table. Wolfram could identify none of the women. Christopher went on to something else.

'On the last days of the surveillance, up through March 24, did you observe anything?'

Wolfram checked his notebook again. 'All routine until the 24th. Then, after work, he went home as usual, but went right back out again. He went to the station and took a train to Dresden – the 18.05. I didn't follow; I have no papers for the East Zone outside Berlin.'

'So at that point you saw the last of him?'

'Yes. But before he went to the station he took the S-Bahn into West Berlin and made a telephone call from a booth. I got the last three digits he dialed – two seven five. And the first two – eight four.'

'Did you hear anything?'

'He said, I have it down here, "Here is Heinz. Let's have an early breakfast tomorrow. Eighteen after the hour." Then he rang off, got back on the S-Bahn and took the Dresden train. Obviously he was setting up a clandestine meeting.'

'You didn't follow up?'

'Eighteen after *what* hour? Where?'

Christopher knew: Eighteen after the hour of eight on 25 March, by the Zoo. Bülow had been six minutes early for his own murder.

'Anyway, we ended the surveillance on that day, the 24th,' Wolfram said. 'I wasn't told why. I didn't ask.'

Christopher touched the photographs of the women one after the other, trying one last time to stir Wolfram's memory. But the German shook his head. 'She was wearing too many clothes,' he said. 'I never saw her face.'

'What about mannerisms? The voice.'

'Normal, a little harder than usual for a woman, but they were speaking low and I was twenty metres away. I had my young helper walk by to try to overhear, but all he could tell was that they were speaking Russian.'

'Nothing else? Nothing odd that sticks in your mind?'

Wolfram snapped his fingers.

'One thing only,' he said. 'It was the way she smoked. She would light a cigarette, take one very long inhalation – only one – and then throw the cigarette away. I thought that was very wasteful. Not like a Russian.'

4

Wolkowicz held out his hand and Christopher gave him the tinted eyeglasses he had been wearing and the salt-and-pepper wig. Wolkowicz, smiling, removed Christopher's false eyebrows with two quick motions. 'Like ripping band-aids off a kid,' he said, 'the faster you do it, the less they notice it.' Christopher went into the bathroom and washed his face; he used alcohol to remove the traces of glue above his eyes.

'That was a nice piece of handling you did on Wolfram,' Wolkowicz said. 'Of course, you sound like a high-class German, and look like one too with those thin lips and mean eyes.'

They were back in the sitting room. Dusk had fallen. Wolkowicz, while Christopher was out of the room, had taken away the bottles that he and Wolfram had handled, and washed and smashed them. The drapes were still drawn, and one dim light burned on a side table.

'What time did you tell Bud to come?' Christopher asked.

'Anytime now. I was just going to play his song.'

Wolkowicz put a recording of Mozart's 40th Symphony on the phonograph. Hearing it as he approached the door, Wilson would know that it was all right to enter.

Christopher and Wolkowicz did not speak to one another while they waited; Wolkowicz had heard everything that had passed between Christopher and Wolfram, and he would add anything he wished in Wilson's presence. Nor did he offer Christopher anything more to drink: he had already destroyed one set of fingerprints, smashing the beer bottles and wiping the furniture; the odour of American spray wax lingered in the unventilated room. Christopher sat in an upholstered chair, well away from the polished surface. Wolkowicz listened to the music with his hands cupped behind his ears; it was a trick Cathy had, she said it captured more sound. Christopher wondered if Wolkowicz was a musician. It was useless to ask; Wolkowicz answered all questions except official requests for information with sarcasm.

Wilson, when he arrived, asked Wolkowicz for an assessment of the young German Christopher had just interviewed.

'A good gumshoe,' Wolkowicz said. 'He's very good at simple jobs. Dogged, but no imagination. Just what you want.'

Wilson turned to Christopher. 'Anything?'

Christopher spoke the phrase, signalling success, that they had arranged between them, knowing that they would have to discuss this matter in Wolkowicz's presence. 'We went over all the details,' Christopher said. 'He added a dimension or two.'

Wolkowicz smiled; he knew a rehearsed phrase when he heard one.

'I suppose,' he said, 'that you fellows must want something else from us.'

'A thing or two, not much,' Wilson said.

'How about you, Graf von Kristofer und zu Grottlesex?'

'The telephone number,' Christopher said.

Wolkowicz made a face of exaggerated confusion.

'The digits Wolfram noted down when Horst was phoning on the night before he was killed.'

'Ah. Eight four blank blank two seven five. I checked that out before you got here, thinking you'd want to know. I have here a list of all Berlin numbers that begin and end thusly, and you're free to call them one by one.'

It was a long list, and it included three hotels and several public phone booths. They all knew there was no point in doing what Wolkowicz suggested.

'I might be able to narrow it down a little for you,' Wolkowicz said, 'but *I'd* like a thing or two, not much. I'd like a full briefing, in the next five minutes, Christopher, about what the hell is going on. You got a man killed on my territory. Your fucking operations cause me more trouble than the opposition. You and Patchen and the rest of his CA types think you can do whatever you like under that global charter you think you've got, come in and run ops under my protection and tell me nothing. So far, I've given you everything you asked for. I want my money, and I want it now.'

Wilson wasn't used to hearing one officer speak to another in this way. He said, 'Barney, Paul has been on the sidewalk as much as anyone.'

'I know twice as much about that subject as you do,' Wolkowicz said. 'I've seen Christopher work. There's nothing personal in this. Paul knows that.'

190

'I'm not authorized to share information with you on this,' Wilson said.

But Wolkowicz's full attention was turned to Christopher.

'Barney, turn off the tapes,' Christopher said.

Wolkowicz touched a switch under the rug with the sole of his shoe. Christopher told him what Wolfram's information had confirmed. Wolkowicz, stung, lurched forward in his chair.

'Jesus Christ, *why*?' he said.

'That's the question, isn't it? You see the obvious reason – we were supposed to see the opposition's hand in Bülow's death. That was supposed to make us reckless – and it did. But what's the real reason, the one in the guts? It must be something powerful, and black as hell. They really wanted the silence of the grave for all concerned.'

Wolkowicz walked around the room, excited by new secrets. He said, 'You have to admire the tradecraft, Paul. Meeting at eighteen after the hour, pickups in a blacked-out car, contacts in the open air, using the female Russian-speaker. The hit with the car. It's K G B technique right down the line.'

'Yes. And I'll bet you a gallon of *Bowle* that she spotted Wolfram and friend in the Tiergarten. That's why she went into the American Consulate. She'd have assumed Wolfram was on the other side, and that would double the hazard for Horst.'

'What the hell is *Bowle*?'

'It's something Horst used to drink, when he was young and happy,' Christopher said.

5

'This place would have made him happy, too,' Wolkowicz said.

He had taken them to a steam bath near the Schiller Park. Men and women, few of them beautiful, walked about naked in the hot mists, and plunged into bubbling pools of water dyed blue, red, and green. The three Americans sat, alone except for a stringy woman who stared fixedly at the bullet wounds on their bodies – the neat puncture and incision on Christopher's knee; the puckered shrapnel scars on Wilson's flanks; the row of red dots like surprised crayon mouths that had been left by the exit of small-calibre Japanese machine-gun rounds on Wolkowicz's rib cage.

'Are you a scar freak?' Wolkowicz asked her. 'My friend here has one of only three circumcisions remaining in Germany. Come closer if you like.'

The woman hugged herself and scurried out of the hot room.

Wolkowicz was in a cheerful mood. Learning a new secret always made him happy; over the years, Christopher had fed him many bits of information. Wolkowicz was an honest trader who gave value for value. A few hours before, almost as soon as he had heard the truth from Christopher, he had offered something in return.

'The phone number,' he had said earlier, when they were still in the safe house in Spandau. 'My guess would be it's the Schaefer Baths, in Wedding. It's on the list, under S. The fellow who runs it is a sort of universal dead-drop and antenna. We use him, just a little. The *polizei* think that the opposition uses him. They know that the Berlin criminal element uses him – he's an arranger. A public figure. Everyone tolerates him because everyone can tap in. And he has a nice little business in the baths. On Saturday night more fornication is arranged in those steam rooms than in the rest of the city combined. What you see is what you get.'

Wilson, his file cards out, had asked a number of background questions. During the war, Wolkowicz said, the owner of the Schaefer Baths had been an enlisted man in the SS, a clerk in the occupation of France; when the Abwehr was absorbed in 1944, the man had moved to the Hotel Lutetia on the boulevard Raspail to help collate Abwehr files with the general security files of Himmler's apparatus.

'Schaefer was one of the forgivables,' Wolkowicz said. 'After the war he was denazified, having coöperated like a prize student, and sent home to Berlin. He changed his name. Our side gave him genuine documentation as a member of the fighting SS named Karl Schaefer.'

'Where did he get the money for the baths?'

'I suppose he salted something away while he was in the SS; a lot of sergeants came out of that war rich.'

'What was he before the war?'

'He was an under head waiter at the old Jockey Restaurant in Berlin in the late twenties and thirties. Of course it was blown up by our brave aviators, so when peace returned he had to find some other way to fleece his betters.'

'When did he join the SS?'

'Openly, in '39. But he'd been a Gestapo informer for years. It, the Gestapo, existed as a secret police under the Weimar Republic, you know. The Nazis inherited it – and refined it, as you might say. Karl went way back. He was giving them bits and pieces while he was working at the Jockey. Waiters hear a lot of stuff.'

Wilson took his sensitive file out of his pocket and leafed through the little stack of file cards. He was confirming dates and names. Christopher had already made the connections, but Wilson was a researcher, not an artist.

'Okay,' Wilson said. 'Bülow was at the Hôtel Lutetia as a captain in the Abwehr's secret police, Section III F, from May 1943 until early August 1944. He and Schaefer met there, certainly. And, of course, at the Jockey before the war.'

'Along with a lot of other people.'

'It's just a matter of blowing the dust off,' Wilson said. 'The contacts are there. They're always there. You just have to find the cross-references.'

Wolkowicz had made a kissing sound.

Now, hours later, in the sauna room, Wolkowicz was talking in Swahili again.

'There are two ways to handle this,' he told Christopher. 'You can expose yourself to Schaefer and ask your own questions. Or you can let me shake the tree. I won't make a recommendation.'

Christopher realized that it was just a matter of confirmation now. He asked Wilson if he would remain behind for a few hours and bring Wolkowicz's information with him to Paris.

'You have to realize,' Wolkowicz said, 'that old Karl isn't going to tell us the identity of the driver of that black Opel that killed Bülow. He doesn't owe us *that* much.'

'All I want is the auspices – whether it was freelance or an organization. And how the killing was set up. I'd like the phone codes, the dates, the amount that was paid. If there was a sighting in this place – that, too.'

'That's a lot.'

'Pay him.'

Wolkowicz gave his dazzling smile.

'Yes,' Christopher said. 'You can use CA funds, and you can

put in a formal bill so that your hand shows in the file. It'll show in Bud's report anyway.'

Christopher stood up. Wolkowicz, reclining on the smooth wooden slats of the bench in the sauna room, raised himself on an elbow. He shook hands with Christopher. Their bodies glistened with sweat.

'Paul,' Wolkowicz said, 'for whatever it's worth, I don't take any pleasure in this. We have different philosophies and different methods and all that. But I don't like to see you kicked in the crotch.'

Christopher took a cold shower and dressed. His locker had not been disturbed, the marks he had left were untouched. The man at the desk, a battered middle-aged German with the manners of a clever servant, called a taxi. He paid no obvious attention to Christopher, who had come in fifteen minutes before Wolkowicz and Wilson, and was leaving while they remained. The man wore a white singlet with the name of the bath house printed across the chest. On the inside of his heavy bicep was the tattooed double lightning flash of the SS. Schaefer may have been rewarded with a new name, but he had kept the real marks of his identity.

Fifteen

I

'Let me amuse you before we get down to brass tacks,' said Patchen. They were outdoors again in Paris, by the aviary in the Jardin des Plantes. Rain, falling the night before while Patchen was airborne from Washington and Christopher from Berlin, had laid the dust and left a fresh smell in the air. The tropical birds tumbled inside their great cage in the sunshot morning, their colours brighter than usual, as though the rain had washed them, too.

'I had lunch with Hopkins from the British service last week,' Patchen said, 'and he remarked that I was looking rather peaked. "Been flying a lot, have you?" he said, "In and out of time zones, in and out of climates?" I was professionally non-committal, but you know the Brits. Hopkins is like all the rest, not shy about asking questions. "The jet aeroplane," he said, "really is the fatal weakness in American foreign policy. In *our* day, old boy, we went out to those godforsaken places in gunboats – gave us weeks to think up what we were going to do to the Wogs when we got there. But you poor chaps can get to the Guinea Coast or Vietnam or wherever in a matter of hours. No time to think. That's your dilemma. Like the birds you were given wings. You lost the need for ratiocination." I'd never heard that word used in conversation before.'

Patchen had shaved and he wore a fresh shirt, but his seersucker suit was rumpled after his night in the seat of an aeroplane. He was haggard, his eyes were bloodshot, and there remained on his breath the last faint odour of the alcohol he had drunk the night before. Christopher knew that Patchen must have something unpleasant to say if he would begin, as he had done, with small talk.

'I have come to tell you,' Patchen said, 'that what you predicted would happen has begun to happen. Captain V. I. Kalmyk was arrested by the KGB in Warsaw ten days ago, and taken to Moscow to the cellars at No. 2 Ulitza Dzherzhinskogo. He broke after forty straight hours of interrogation. We had a further report, during the night, that Kalmyk was shot late yesterday.'

'That must mean they've picked up the next link in the courier chain.'

'Yes, and broken that man, too. If we knew how long the chain was, we'd know how much time we have to play with. But we don't. Dick Sutherland says there may be only two or three roaches to step on – that's KGB lingo, I'm told.'

'The broadcasts began after they broke Kalmyk. They won't need to unravel the whole courier network in order to guess what Kalmyk gave to Horst.'

'No, but they don't like loose ends. They'll want to roll it up just to make things orderly.'

The Jardin des Plantes lay between the river and a railroad junction, and some of Patchen's words were smothered by the drone of morning traffic on the quais of the Seine and the squeal and clatter of trains entering and leaving the Gare d'Austerlitz. He sounded something like Otto Rothchild had sounded in the days after his operation in February, when words and phrases were snuffed out by the after-effects of what the surgeons had done for him in Zürich. 'Have you seen Cerutti since you got back from Berlin?' Patchen asked.

'No. There's no hurry about it now. Wilson will pull off the surveillance when he gets back this afternoon.'

'I suppose there's no point in going on with it.'

'None. It's served its purpose. But the girl may stay with him. She's a competent translator, and I think we'll need her. It's not a bad thing to have an ear inside the house.'

196

'Even when it's falling down,' Patchen said. 'Tell me about Berlin.'

This time it was Christopher who took Patchen's arm. Patchen flinched, almost imperceptibly; Christopher thought that it must be distaste, to have even the hand of his best friend laid upon him, because Patchen knew already what Christopher was going to tell him. The death of Kalmyk in the punishment cells of the KGB's centre in Moscow had forewarned him.

'We're not just speculating any longer,' Christopher said. 'We can see their faces now.'

Patchen listened. There was no need to ask questions; Christopher gave him the details, one after the other – dates, places, methods.

'Everything but motive,' Patchen said at the end of Christopher's report. 'It's quite a feat to do what you and Wilson have done, to work backward. Detectives are supposed to solve crimes by finding the motive.'

'I plan to go on a little longer.'

'Do that. I want to know. I don't understand wanting the death of others – a poor fool like Bülow is the worst. You were right about that from the beginning. What could be worth it?'

'I don't know. They'll never tell, of course. It's too deep. Barney, who ought to know, told me even torture can't get a human being to confess a personal act that's covered him with shame. Anything else, but not that.'

'You think that's what it is?'

'Yes.'

Two attendants carrying cleaning tools entered the aviary. Patchen and Christopher moved away, towards the elephant cage. Patchen had saved the foil packages of nuts that he'd been given on the plane. Taking them from his pocket, he handed one to Christopher and kept one for himself. They fed the fancy nuts to the elephants.

'You think you can find out why in Spain?' Patchen asked.

'Possibly.'

'Even with Cathy right there? It's not the ideal operational climate, is it? Bullfights and big luncheons and lazy afternoons in the hotel room?'

Patchen crumpled the empty package and threw it in a trash barrel. 'Why does something as small as a nut mean so much to something as large as an elephant?' he asked. 'I'm left with nothing to say except crap like that.'

'I'm meeting Cathy in Madrid day after tomorrow.'

'Because you can't live without her, or because she can introduce you to this man Jorge de Rodegas?'

Christopher answered half of Patchen's question. 'Cathy knows Rodegas very well. Not only is he her godfather, he breeds thoroughbreds. These horse people are worse than we are for living in each other's pockets.'

'Everyone's world is special,' Patchen said. 'It's funny, isn't it, how outsiders, unwitting damned dreamers, are usually the ones who drive the last nail for us?'

2

Wilson had not learned to relax with a man of Patchen's rank. He sat on the edge of his chair while he made his report. Patchen and Christopher had come first to the safe house, in the early evening, and they were drinking Scotch when Wilson arrived, straight from the airport. He refused whisky but got himself a can of beer.

'The fellow in the Turkish bath instantly made both photographs,' Wilson said. 'Bülow and the female target.'

'Her, too?' Christopher said.

'I thought that would surprise you. It seems she came to the Schaefer Baths as a customer, to make the first contact. Evidently she had bona fides that she had to present in person.'

'Which were?'

'Details of an old operation during the last war. Schaefer let somebody slip through the Gestapo's fingers in return for certain considerations – cash on the barrelhead and a good word for him in the right places after the war. This was in 1944 – even SS sergeants had figured out who was going to win by that time.'

'Can we cross-check?' Patchen asked.

Wilson hastily swallowed a mouthful of beer, almost choking on it. He nodded deferentially to Christopher.

'My suggestion would be to have Paul draw it out of Cerutti. He was involved. Schaefer remembered that cover name of his, *Frère Éméché*. He said he knew a literary type must be using it – no one has used a word like *éméché* in French since Rabelais.'

'I want to go back to something,' Christopher said. 'She came to the Schaefer Baths *as a customer*?'

Wilson was truly embarrassed. 'Yes, according to Schaefer. She walked in stark naked, sat on the edge of his desk, and laid it all out. Wolkowicz was amused. He asked a lot of questions.'

'What sort of questions?' Patchen asked.

'About her appearance. Schaefer was impressed. He said she was like a ripe peach. I guess he doesn't get many women in his establishment with bodies like hers.'

'I'm surprised she'd show it to Schaefer,' Christopher said.

'Technique,' said Patchen, once more the misogynist. 'Women are born with a sense of it.'

Wilson's file cards made a thick pile now, frayed at the edges. He slipped the heavy rubber band that held them together over his wrist and began to read. The woman had contacted Schaefer on 14 January, almost three weeks before Wolfram's surveillance had begun.

'Where was Christopher on that date?' Patchen asked.

'In the Congo,' Wilson said. He pointed a finger at Christopher. 'Did the target know that?'

'That I was not in Europe, yes.'

Wilson made another notation, nodding. He rubbed his eyes before he spoke again. 'The woman had two sets of photocopies – one to reassure Schaefer and let him know that her principal was his old pal from Occupied France,' Wilson said. 'The second were incriminating documents, signed by Bülow at the Hôtel Lutetia in '44. They were death warrants for a bunch of Resistance leaders.'

Wilson repeated Schaefer's description of the scene. The woman, naked, sat with her legs crossed, watching him at his desk as he read the photocopies that could send him to prison for twenty years. She asked him for a cigarette and then for a light. Schaefer thought she wanted to see if his hand trembled because she snuffed out the cigarette after one puff.

'Then she asked Schaefer if he knew anyone in Berlin who could kill with a car,' Wilson said. 'He told the gal he didn't know such people any longer. She wouldn't take no for an answer. After some special persuasion, as Schaefer called it, he gave her a phone number. He tried to suggest the special persuasion included sex – but, Paul, I don't believe that.'

'Have you a tape of this conversation?' Patchen asked.

'No. Schaefer will only converse with naked people. Barney made him strip, too. We talked in the outdoor swimming pool. I must say it's good protection for him.'

'Schaefer claims that was the end of the deal, on his side – giving her the phone number?'

'Tried to,' Wilson said, 'but Barney wouldn't buy it. Finally Schaefer said, okay, so I passed a little money for this woman. That's what he did – set up the kill, paid the killers. He was the broker. The target gave him the whole scenario.'

Wilson went on in his level tone of voice. His words were transformed in Christopher's mind into a running series of illuminations: Horst Bülow hearing from his old sergeant, his obsequious old under head waiter at the Jockey Restaurant. Horst coming to the baths, being brought together naked in a room with strangers, being told that his past in the Abwehr could be brought to the attention of the East Germans; perhaps even that his present position as an American spy could be exposed. Horst being given bait – money, the promise of a girl, the flattery of being the key to a big operation that would hurt no one, the lost pleasure of working in secret again with Germans instead of foreigners. Being given, finally, the phone number to call to set up his own murder.

'That's how it was,' Wilson said. 'Simplicity itself. The night before he went into East Germany to pick up the package, he phoned and set up a meeting at the Zoo at 06.18 the next morning. He thought they were going to ram your car, take the manuscript, and run with it.'

'Didn't he think they'd kill Paul?'

'Horst tried to protect Christopher, according to Schaefer. Horst said Paul was *his* agent, a mere courier. Bülow implied that he was pretty big stuff in the spy game still. Killing Christopher would be unprofessional, he kept saying.'

Patchen waited, to see if anything would be added. Wilson went through his cards, checking off the items he had covered.

'Who did Schaefer think the naked lady was?'

Wilson shook his head in admiration. 'He has no more idea than the man in the moon. She spoke French to him with a Russian accent. She turned him into a cut-out on the first night. He hired other cut-outs. There were three layers of soundproofing between the killers and this dame.'

'What did Schaefer think she was?'

'Dynamite. Scary. He figured her for the opposition right from the start. It was her cold-bloodedness.'

Wilson had arranged to have the surveillance logs for the past forty-eight hours brought to the safe house. He met the courier in the hall, and shut him up in there with a second radio playing at high volume.

It didn't take Wilson long to go through the material; he had been given synopses, not the minute-by-minute, word-for-word raw logs. Twice he got out a fresh file card and recorded new facts. He put the papers back in the envelope, sealed it, went into the hall, and saw the courier out the door before he spoke again to Patchen and Christopher.

'Two new items,' Wilson said, holding up the white cards one after the other. 'First, Moroni is in Spain, shooting his movie. The German girl says he did some crowd scenes in Pamplona during the fiesta, and then went on to Madrid.'

He cleared his throat and, quickly, sipped beer from his can of Schlitz.

'And, believe it or not, audio surveillance finally turned up something. The target, talking to her case officer. They've had a surprise, Paul. They're upset. But, Jesus, they're professional – they want to turn it back on us. On you. They don't miss a trick.'

Wilson didn't read aloud from this card, but handed it to Patchen, who read it and passed it to Christopher. Wilson took the card back and tapped it against his front teeth.

'We know she's a cold one,' Wilson said. 'But, Paul, will she really try to use this on you?'

Christopher was tired. His bones ached – ankles and shins and the reconstructed joint of his knee. He wanted to eat something and go to sleep.

'I guess I'll find out when I see her,' Christopher said.

3

Cerutti met Christopher at the mouth of the Métro station at Porte Dauphine. He carried all the morning papers under his arm, and his face was reddened by agitation. But he kept discipline and followed Christopher at a discreet ten paces into the Bois de Boulogne. When they were alone, on a bench beneath a plane tree, Cerutti threw the stack of newspapers on to the wooden seat between them.

'You've seen the wire service stories?'

'Yes.'

'Kamensky's novel is being read over the propaganda radio. They are broadcasting his name!'

'That's what the papers say.'

Cerutti pounded his small fist into his palm. There was ink from the fresh newsprint on his fingers, and it was smeared on his face as well.

'Who is responsible?'

'Whoever stole the proofs from the printer, I suppose,' Christopher said.

'But to know it was Kamensky's work? Who knew that?'

Christopher, who had been looking upward into the dappled interior of the spreading tree, slowly turned his head and gazed without expression into Cerutti's eyes. Cerutti recoiled.

'You're maddened by your trade if you think that of me,' he said.

'Am I?'

In one of his darting movements, Cerutti rose from the bench and crossed to the other side of the path. From there he stared at Christopher.

'Yes, crazy,' he said, 'like every one of you I've ever known since 1918. It doesn't matter where you come from, what government sends you out. You're nationality to yourselves, a species to yourselves. You think everyone is like you. Merely to be in the thoughts of men like you is an insult.'

Christopher neither moved nor spoke. Cerutti came back and sat down. He was breathing rapidly. He continued to hold Christopher's eyes. There really was no fear in him; if the file on his long life in an age of political panic showed anything, it showed that.

'It didn't occur to me to accuse you, Claude,' Christopher said. 'The harm is done. It has nothing to do with our arrangement. There's no point in chewing it over. We need each other. We'll go on with what we were doing.'

'But this changes everything.'

'It restores everything to what it was at the beginning. Put Kamensky's name back on the book.'

'And then?'

'Behave like a publisher. Obviously this situation is going to generate its own publicity. Act normally, as you would if all this were honest. If you need money, call. I won't advise you further on how to handle the book. Sell it to whoever wants it for whatever you can get for it. Just run with it.'

Cerutti, fingering the rosette in his lapel, went blank for a time.

'What a joke the past seems,' he said. 'When I saw what Kamensky had entitled this novel which says everything about the torment of my generation, I was angered. He had spat on our lives and on his own great work with such a title – how can you translate it? "Death, My Pet", "Deathikins"? But then I saw. Kamensky went down deeper into this age of idealism than any of us. Despair, anguish, betrayal, sacrifice – my God, Paul, some submitted to castration, the actual surgical removal of the testicles, and went on like steers, loving their masters, believing in the humanity of the Party. We thought it meant something to die for an idea. In the last moment, it's all a joke, the kiss of a whore.'

Bit by bit, as the morning passed, Cerutti told Christopher about the past.

'It's kind of you to get my mind off Kamensky, and what this is going to mean for him.'

'I'm interested,' Christopher said. He asked a question about the Hôtel Lutetia. He mentioned the name Schaefer had had when he was an SS sergeant. Cerutti was alert again.

'You know a great deal, don't you?' he said. 'We're pickled, all of us, in the ink of those secret clerks.'

Cerutti related the story. In 1944, before the invasion of Normandy, the German security apparatus was rolling up Maquis networks all over France. But Cerutti's network, with Otto Rothchild handling security, was untouched. Then, somehow, Otto had learned that the network had been penetrated. A woman, one of their best operatives, was working for the Germans. Otto confronted her. She made no attempt to resist his suspicions. Before the war, she had had a Jewish lover; her child belonged to the Jew, who was already cremated in Auschwitz. The Germans knew where the child was hidden in the countryside. She would kill the whole network to save the child.

'Otto came to me; I had a certain feeling for this girl,' Cerutti said. 'He asked me how to handle it – the only occasion in all our time together he ever asked advice. It was because I loved the girl. I had no ideas; I said I'd do anything to help. I thought of killing her myself, as a favour to a comrade. For the others who trusted her to find out what she was would be like leaving her wounded on the battlefield.'

Rothchild, as always, had had an idea. He decided to redouble the woman, play her back against the Germans. She was terrified for her child. Rothchild told her he would rescue the child at night from the farm where he was staying near Pau, and get him across the Pyrenees. The woman was terrified for herself. Rothchild guaranteed her life. A person detected in treason will believe anything of a man who shows no anger. Patiently questioning, putting details together, Rothchild identified the German officer who was handling her.

'This man was a Gestapo type,' Cerutti said. 'In early '44 he was still wearing Wehrmacht uniform and Abwehr badges, but he had the power of life and death over any non-German in France. He was in Abwehr Section III F at the Hôtel Lutetia, the section that killed Resistance fighters after suitable torture. But Otto had found a key. He had known this Abwehr officer in Berlin before the war.'

'He showed himself to this German?'

'No, Otto played him with the girl. Otto knew something about this German officer. I don't know what it was. A weakness.'

Rothchild found a way. He came back to Cerutti, reminding him that he had offered to do anything. Rothchild asked him to put himself, for one day, into the hands of the SS.

'What were Otto's words to you?'

'He said, "You may die. We both know that. But if you don't, we can save everything, and have more besides".'

At this period, vast sums of money were coming into France from Britain for the support of the Maquis. Rothchild was a handler of money. Here Cerutti hesitated.

'This is terribly difficult, even after all these years,' he said.

Christopher stopped walking. Cerutti halted as well, and spoke into the air, with face averted.

'Rothchild, by now known by the German to be the man beyond the girl, found out what networks were going to be rolled up by the Germans. He warned London about all but one – the one that was expecting a large shipment of funds on a certain day. He gave the German the date on which the money was coming in.'

'How could he have known?'

'I don't know. Perhaps he was the back-up in case the man who was supposed to receive it was lost. Perhaps someone in the doomed network just told him. Security was not always the best in the Resistance. Otto, even then, had lines out everywhere. On the night the money came, he gave me and the girl to the Germans – that is, to the Abwehr officer and the SS sergeant, who were splitting the money. It was a vast sum. They wanted a true hostage, me; they assumed that Otto didn't care what they did to the girl, after what she'd done to us.'

Cerutti, with the girl, spent the night with Schaefer in a Maquis safe house in a warehouse behind the Gare de Lyon. Schaefer, without removing his uniform, used the girl several times as they waited for the money to come.

'The idea of the money excited him, the girl could feel no more shame,' Cerutti said. 'You must remember, I'd loved this woman. It wasn't easy.'

All had gone according to Rothchild's plan. The Germans had got their money. They let Cerutti and the woman go, and even gave them papers to travel to the Pyrenees.

'I'm surprised they didn't kill you,' Christopher said. 'They had what they wanted, and you were witnesses.'

'I was amazed. I can only assume that Otto had promised them something else. The war was ending, the Germans were losing.'

Rothchild preserved his network. When the Americans came he put it at the disposal of their newborn intelligence service, as if the British and the Gaullists didn't exist. The Americans accepted, and Otto did invaluable things for them in France and later in Germany.

'What happened to the girl and her child?' Christopher asked.

'I took them myself through the mountains to the Spanish frontier,' Cerutti said. 'It was night and I was carrying the child on my back. The guide was ahead of me and the girl, Solange was her name, was behind. When we got to the frontier, I handed the child – it was hardly more than a baby and we'd given it cognac to make it sleep – to the man who met us, and turned around to say goodbye to Solange.'

The woman wasn't there. Cerutti went back down the path, feeling his way around rocks on the strange terrain, and at last he found her. She was lying in a patch of snow that hadn't yet been melted by the April sun, and she had cut her own throat with a razor blade.

'I went into Spain with the child,' Cerutti said. 'It couldn't be left alone.'

He remained in Spain until the end of that summer, crossing back into France when the Americans had cleared the German Army out of the south. He left the child with a Spanish family.

'Otto raged at me when he found that out,' Cerutti said. 'He hated Spain, the very dust and stones of it. I wanted him to cross the Pyrenees for safety's sake, after that business in Paris, but no. There had been too much shame and defeat in Spain for him ever to set foot in it again, he said. I've often wondered – what could have been so much worse that happened to him, and to all of us, in Spain, than what happened in France during the war?'

'Maybe it was winning in the end, the second time.'

Cerutti smiled, the first time he had done so since he and Christopher had met in the early morning.

'Very possibly,' he said. 'Victors are washed of their sins.'

4

Maria Rothchild, in another part of the Bois, had coaxed a squirrel to eat from her hand. Christopher stopped at the turning of the path, so as not to frighten the animal, where he caught sight of her. Maria wore a flowing summer dress, the skirt spreading around her in a perfect circle on the grass. She saw Christopher at once; her white teeth flashed in her tan face and she stood up in a swirl of pastels. The squirrel scampered away, scolding. Maria gave Christopher the second signal to approach; she lifted an arm and grinned again, the spontaneous gesture of a woman delighted by the sight of an old friend.

'You're getting quite a tan,' Christopher said. 'Have you been slipping away to the Côte d'Azur for weekends?'

'No, lunch on the terrace, and reading in the park on the afternoons when I can get Otto to take his pill and sleep.'

She appraised Christopher.

'*You* look like you need a vacation.'

'I'm going to take one,' he said. 'If you don't prevent it.'

'Me?'

'The message said you wanted an urgent meeting, Maria. Here I am.'

Slung on a strap over her shoulder, Maria carried an airline bag – Royal Thai Airlines; she was not immune, she said, to the *chic* of having flown to romantic destinations.

'Let's go a little way off the path,' she said.

Christopher followed her across the grass. She wore a sundress, and the bared skin of her back, with columns of muscle along the spine, was smooth and as brown as her face. She found a place that suited her, in a glen, and knelt on the grass. From the airline bag she took a light picnic blanket, shook out it's folds, and spread it.

'You've nothing better to do for lunch, I hope?' she said.

She laid two large ham sandwiches on the blanket, and some fruit and cheese. She handed Christopher a bottle of wine and a corkscrew and produced two wineglasses, wrapped in napkins.

'No paper cups,' she said. 'I remember all your foibles, Paul, quite as if we'd been more than friends once upon a time.'

She held up her wineglass to be filled, and lifted it to him. 'To ties that bind,' she said.

Holding the glass at arm's length so that it could not spill on her dress, Maria reached into her bosom, groped for a moment, biting her lip in embarrassment, and produced a soiled envelope, folded in three. She handed it to Christopher.

'Otto got this in the mail,' she said.

She held out her hand for Christopher's wineglass; there was no level place to set it down. Christopher opened the envelope. Inside, in the same tiny, nearly illegible hand in which he had written his novel, was a letter from Kiril Kamensky. Christopher turned his body until the sun, which fell only in spots in the glade where he and Maria were picnicking, shone fully on the flimsy page.

'You can translate at sight, can't you?' Maria asked.

'Yes, I'm used to his style now.'

The letter bore the date of the first broadcast of Kamensky's novel into the Soviet Union. He had noted the time at the top of the sheet: 6.30 in the morning. Kamensky opened with a description of the dawn: the birches marching into the eye as the light revealed them, the temperature of the air, the smell of the lumber dacha, the sounds of a woman rattling pots, snapping a sheet as she made the bed, throwing open windows, beginning a song and interrupting it for a new task. Then, on the back of the sheet, Kamensky wrote:

> As I love you, I know it cannot be you who betrayed me. I heard my life in the air an hour ago, or heard the end of it, as one hears thunder a long way off, and sees the flash long before lightning or shrapnel pierces the flesh. I had hoped to appear harmless, to have "last years," to be quiet, to be old, to be alone. Foolishness. I know the world too well to have dreamt as I did of playing at happiness. Don't torment yourself with what has been done. Don't imagine that my trust in you is broken. Don't imagine that I have forgotten anything, not the smallest detail of our province of the past; it is like a bar of music in the skull of a man long since deaf. No sense shouting poetry at the howitzers. No sense in any of it except the meeting of man with man. Stop them now if you can. Perhaps then I'll live a little longer. If you cannot, I forgive you. And the others, too. I brought my book to life; it sent me to my death. It was a long, long march. I took the first step of it before my murderers were born; they were waiting, invisible as ova, to be fertilized by the blind swimmers that gushed from the brutal ape that was our new age.

Christopher held the letter in his hand, a badly made sheet of foolscap that soaked up the ink of Kamensky's pen.

'Is this all?'

'*All?*' Maria said.

'I mean just this one sheet. There's no salutation, no signature.'

'His other letter was the same.'

'This came to your house? When? What postmark?'

'No, not to the house. To a *poste restante*, one of Otto's accommodation addresses. Day before yesterday. The postmark was Helsinki, like the other.'

'How did Kamensky get hold of an accommodation address?'

'I've no idea, nor has Otto. This mail drop was used strictly for non-sensitive material. Otto gave it to a lot of people. Anyone, travelling in Russia and meeting Kamensky, could have given it to him. You *knew* this.'

'No.'

'Then Wilson-Watson-Wharton did. I remember going over it, Otto going over it.'

Maria gave Christopher back his wineglass. She held her hand out, palm flat. 'Otto would like to keep the original,' she said. 'I've brought you film of it so you'll have all the copies you need.'

Christopher folded the letter, put it back into the envelope, and gave it to Maria. She tucked it back into the neck of her dress. 'This is a damn uncomfortable secret hiding place,' she said. 'I only own one bra, and only wear it when I'm smuggling super-sensitive stuff. So it's been years.'

Christopher drank a little of the wine and ate some cheese. Maria had been eating while he read. She wrapped the remnant of her chewed sandwich in its waxed paper and put it away. Then she turned her face to the sun as Christopher had turned Kamensky's letter, and, shaking back her hair, closed her eyes against the heat.

'What was Otto's reaction to this?' Christopher asked.

'Devastation. He didn't understand at first what Kamensky was saying. He didn't know the broadcasts had begun – didn't know there were going to *be* broadcasts. Who's responsible for that?'

'Not I.'

'I didn't suppose so, after that scene you played the last time you saw Otto.'

'What would Otto do, if he were still doing things?'

Maria opened her eyes and spun round on the blanket. She crossed her legs modestly under her full skirt.

'What anyone would do – nothing. The situation is irretrievable, isn't it?'

'I'd say so.'

'But you wouldn't say, would you – being the sort of chap you are – that you were right from the beginning, that there was nothing in this for Kamensky but death?'

Maria waited a moment, her eyes bright with the stony control she had learned in her years as a professional. When Christopher didn't answer, she said, 'You're not eating.'

'No.'

'Otto asks me to tell you this: You were right, he was wrong. He apologizes and wishes to see you soon.'

Christopher gave her back his wineglass, still half full. He stood up; Maria remained on the bright blanket, woven of the lightest wool, designed by an artist – like all the Rothchilds' possessions, it was a ceremonial object.

'My part of the message is this,' she said. 'I'm not quoting Otto but my intuition as a wife. Otto, for the first time, is feeling the sorrow of death. I've never seen him as he's been since that letter came.'

She paused. She drank Christopher's wine. She was not like herself; she went on talking, as if Christopher were a man for whom explanations had to be re-phrased.

'Do you feel what Otto's feeling – perhaps a little of it?'

'I don't think so,' Christopher said. 'I'm not a Russian, after all.'

Maria took what he said as a statement of fact, nothing more. Insult was not possible between them. She burrowed in her airline bag and brought out a zippered leather case of the kind that men use for toilet articles when travelling. She opened the zipper and showed Christopher what was inside – yellow spools of undeveloped film, each with a number pasted on it. 'My pictures of *The Little Death*,' Maria said, 'the ones I took for Otto. The film has never been developed.'

'What would I do with it?'

'Otto thought you might like to know it wasn't our copy of Kiril Alekseivich's novel that was sent to the radio operation.'

'Tell Otto I never thought it was,' Christopher said. 'I'll be around to see him in a week or so.'

Maria was on her knees again, packing the picnic back into the bag.

'Then you really are going to take some time off?'

'A few days.'

'Sunshine and Cathy?'

Christopher nodded.

'Who could ask for anything more?' Maria inquired.

Maria slung her airline bag over her shoulder. She lifted a hand, as if to touch his face; he wondered if the first signs of loss showed in him as new love was supposed to do. Why else was everyone moved to touch him? Maria didn't complete the gesture. She blew him a kiss, and swung away through the trees with her rippling athlete's stride.

Sixteen

I

Cathy had a plan for them to follow in Madrid. On the hotel telephone, when Christopher called her from the airport, she asked if he had any work to do while they were together. 'One thing only,' Christopher replied, 'but it will be so mixed up with fun that you won't know it's happening.'

The line went dead briefly, then Cathy said, 'I'm better at reading you than I used to be, Paul. You'll see.'

In their room, when he arrived, she refused to make love. 'Luncheon first, in the cellar of the Nacional Hotel,' she said. 'I've booked one of those wonderful booths with the high carved backs and fronts – do you remember? And we'll eat the entire menu, champagne throughout.'

As she named each of the five courses, she gave him a fluttering kiss. He stepped back, holding her hands, and laughed with the joy of seeing her again. Her eyes darkened with pleasure. Cathy considered Paris and Rome home ground, but when they met in another city they gave each other gifts. Christopher had brought her a heavy gold necklace, an antique. She looked at herself in the glass while Christopher clasped it around her throat. 'It's a necklace for a queen!' she cried. She gave him his present, a tiny drawing.

'My God, Cathy, it's a Goya – what did you have to spend for this?' he asked.

She watched his delight. 'In real money, I don't know,' she said. 'Lots and lots of pesetas, though. It would have been more, but my wonderful Don Jorge got it for me from some ruined nobleman.'

'That's Jorge de Rodegas?'

'Yes.'

'You've seen him?'

'I always see him. When I was sixteen I wanted to propose marriage to him, but Mama said it would be incest. "Incest?" I said. "He's no more than a twelfth cousin by marriage and you and Papa are first cousins once removed." She told me Don Jorge would go to Hell if he married his god-daughter. He'd already sentenced himself to purgatory by being godfather to an Episcopalian.'

'Maybe you should have asked Don Jorge his opinion.'

'Maybe,' Cathy said. 'He's more beautiful than you, Paul, and a whole lot richer, and he stays at home. He's gone to the mountains now, back to his *estancia*.'

At lunch, in the cool restaurant with its dark wood, its blue tiles, she spoke about her music. She had rented a suite at the Palace Hotel with a piano in the sitting room. While he was in Paris and Berlin, after she had come down from Pamplona, she had stayed in the suite, alone, playing through the long afternoons.

'Did you see me?' she asked Christopher. 'Did you hear the music?'

'I do now.'

'Tell, Paul – all the details.'

In fact he had imagined her seated at the instrument. The picture had come into his mind, along with those of Horst Bülow being lured to his death, when Wilson had come back from the Schaefer Baths with his report. He had caught a look of puzzlement in Wilson's face because he had grimaced suddenly, at the incongruity of the mental images, a diptych with Bülow's sagging corpse on one leaf and Cathy's luminous figure on the other.

'All right,' he said. 'The shutters were closed and there were bars of light falling on your figure and running across the music

213

rack. The bracelet I gave you in Rome, on the night we bought the cats, was lying on the little piece of wood at the treble end of the keyboard, and it picked up the light. You were wearing a yellow dress, with the skirt pulled up over your thighs. Your feet were bare, working the pedals. You were playing Bach and not getting it right; you played a passage from one of the Preludes over and over and after making mistake after mistake in the same bar you crashed your fist down on to the keyboard, then sucked your hand because you'd hurt it.'

As Christopher spoke, Cathy, her eyes intent, sipped champagne thirstily, as though the wine were a potion that drew these visions from him.

'That's absolutely accurate,' she said. 'Paul, it's no wonder I'm living under an enchantment. How do you *do* it? What else did you see?'

Christopher seized her face and kissed it. He said, 'I made it all up. Cathy, how many times have I watched you play the piano? It's a game, this business of the sight. I don't have it.'

'You *do*. What else did you see?'

A waiter took away their empty plates; the head waiter, drinking the sight of Cathy as avidly as she gulped wine, poured more champagne and brought another bottle.

'I saw you, often, when you weren't alone,' Christopher said.

Cathy returned his gaze without embarrassment.

'I know. You'd come into my mind. I couldn't turn the others into you though; you wouldn't let me, Paul.'

Cathy would not give up her belief in magic, telepathy, curses, second sight; she had grown up in a house filled with ghosts, hearing tales of witches and enchantments. As a child, she had seen fortunes told with cards and chicken bones, and the future foretold in the liver of a bird.

Christopher held up his hand; they stopped talking. Another course was brought. 'If we lived in Spain, Paul, we'd die of gluttony,' Cathy said. 'Why *don't* we live here for a while? You love it so.'

'Live here? All you'd need is an eye for beauty and a heart of stone. Italy is bad enough.'

'Every place is bad enough. Shall we talk about the downtrodden nigras and the white trash and Miss Catherine up in her big ol' white house on the hill? That's what they used to do a lot in school; your pal Maria Custer would invite me to bull sessions so she and the other guilty rich girls would have a Southerner to whip, just like I whipped the slaves back home.'

'You really don't like her, do you?'

Cathy smiled, a parody of Maria Rothchild's bold and sudden grin. 'I *hate* her,' she said. 'I always have.'

'Will you say why?'

'I don't want to talk about Maria, or anyone except you and me.'

Christopher shrugged. Cathy's smile had vanished. Her hand had been lying on his thigh, and she took it away.

'All right,' she said. 'Maria is a snob. She's rotten with pride – in her family, her brains, her wit, her looks, and now that old Russian husband. She makes you keep quiet while she boasts – she's like De Gaulle talking about France. Everyone sees that utter nonsense is being talked, but it's so embarrassing that you let it pass.'

'What harm is there in somebody else's self-delusion?'

'Try contradicting Maria or frustrating her or insulting her and you'll find out Paul. If you touch one hair of her silly, transparent, pretentious idea of herself, Maria will kill you if she can. Literally. She's an assassin.'

Christopher picked up Cathy's wineglass and put it into her hand. 'I think we'd better talk of indifferent things for the rest of this lunch,' he said.

Cathy told him that she wanted to control their time in Madrid – choose the things they did, select the foods and wines, the times they slept and were awake, the things they bought, even the clothes Christopher wore. 'I've imagined it all,' she said. 'In *Life on the Mississippi*, Mark Twain tells how the pilot of a riverboat had to have the whole length of the Mississippi in his mind, every detail in this mental river – sandbars and channels and villages on the banks – exactly as they were in the real river. That's what I've done with Madrid, made it into a place in my mind for you and me. I'm the pilot, you're the passenger.'

Christopher laughed aloud again; he thought that he had never loved her so much, taken such pleasure in the flight of her mind, the rise and fall of her voice.

'All right,' he said. 'But I'll have to get off the steamboat just once. There's something I want to do.'

'Not alone, Paul. With me, every day, every minute.'

'This is something I can't do without you, Cathy. You're the key to the door.'

'What door is that?'

He didn't tell her.

The enormous luncheon, not begun until mid-afternoon, lasted till after five o'clock. Christopher and Cathy walked hand in hand up the Paseo del Prado, under a sun that was still brilliant and hot. Coming out of the darkened restaurant, Cathy was stricken blind by the light and covered her eyes with her hands. Christopher led her inside the Prado Gallery, and in the long, dim galleries her sight returned. They looked at the El Grecos.

'Part of the cruise on the Mississippi is a trip to Toledo to see more of these,' Cathy said. 'El Greco does get to you, doesn't he? He used lunatics from an asylum for models, and they're all stretched out that way because El Greco had a bad astigmatism. That's what I learned at Bryn Mawr.'

'I thought all you did at Bryn Mawr was play the piano.'

'I had to do some reading, and there were weekends when I did a power of kissing.'

Cathy pulled Christopher's head down and kissed him, long and searchingly, on the lips. An elderly Spanish guard, shouting his outrage, hobbled across the room and pulled them apart. Cathy, in her Spanish that kept sliding into Italian, told him that they were married. She showed him their rings.

'It's all a lie,' Christopher said. 'See? The rings don't match. And besides, she's been insulting El Greco.'

The guard was stern; there was a ban, imposed by the archbishop, on the sexes touching one another in public. 'The lady must be more modest while she is visible to Spaniards,' he said.

'Let's go indoors, then,' said Cathy.

But in the hotel bed she lay rigid, and shuddered at Christopher's touch. He moved away. 'No,' she said, 'go on, Paul. It's nothing to do with you. I'll be all right.' He touched her but came no closer. She spoke the words she had spoken when she had come back to their bed and awakened him, weeks before, in Rome. 'Help me,' she said. They slept, woke in the dark with the sounds of evening coming in at the shutters, made love again. Cathy had changed; there was a difference in her body. Christopher, unable to see her face, and still confused by sleep, thought for an instant that he was with a strange woman. He pulled away from her spasmodically, so suddenly that her fingernails raked his back. He fumbled with the bedside lamp, turned it on, and, crouching, looked down into her face.

'Paul, my God – you've got murder in your eyes.'

He rolled away, on to his back. She followed him, pushed the hair back from his forehead. She asked no questions; six months before she would have insisted on knowing what had happened in his mind. Then, he would have put her off.

'I had a hallucination,' he said now. 'I must have been asleep when we started. I thought it wasn't you.'

'Why?'

'I don't know. You feel different to me. It panicked me, to think I might have lost control and had another woman against my will.'

'Panicked you why – because you lost control, or because you thought it was somebody else?'

'Both.'

Once more he saw the image of Cathy, lifting her breast towards a lover's lips; he saw the man's dark face. He told her what was in his mind.

'That happened in Capri,' she said. 'Can you go on, knowing that?'

Christopher touched her lips. And, as Cathy began to cry out, he said, 'I love you.'

2

Cathy was as silent about her lovers as Christopher about his spies. What had happened to him in bed, he thought, was not entirely a trick of the mind: Cathy had changed, or awakened in herself a second identity. He began to understand why she had been excited by his own hidden life. His desire for her, which had always been almost unbearable, became stronger. Now, sometimes, it was Cathy who smiled at his ardour. He had never felt sexual jealousy, and he did not feel it now. Cathy, nevertheless, re-assured him constantly, in silent ways, accomplishing what she wished as she had always done, with her flesh. But she was more graceful, more gentle, more aware of Christopher. The mystery had begun to run both ways. Finally, as they lay resting one afternoon, he asked her if she knew these things. For a long time she remained silent, one long leg lifted and flexed in the shaft of lemon-coloured light that traced a diagonal from the window to the bed.

'Yes,' she answered.

'What made you change?'

'The others,' Cathy said, gazing at the play of the sun on her calf. 'I know you don't believe it, but you really were my first lover. I wasn't prepared for anyone like you.'

Her leg fell of its own weight. She turned over, looked into his face, pushed back his hair, traced the line of his features: all the old gestures. Something was gathering in her brain; Cathy had been trained to be amusing and musical and elusive, never to be honest with a man. Christopher, withholding from her part of his own honesty, the portion that had to do with his agents, had caused her to thirst for the truth. She had come, after only a year with him, to the point where she would accept almost any pain to have the whole truth. She would even speak it herself.

'What these affairs have been, Paul, is like dancing lessons. Sleeping with these men, so clumsy and so selfish, has shown me the mistakes I made with you. The same thing happened when I took ballet – I couldn't dance until I saw someone else making the errors I'd been making. After that, I knew what *not* to do. Is that the secret of life?'

'It may be.'

'You're never going to ask me anything about the others, are you?'

'No.'

In the end, he knew, the others would ruin them. Cathy hadn't the equipment to go on submitting herself to them without sensuality, in order to intensify the taste and scent and the visions of their life together. She was too open to pleasure, too conscious of physical beauty, too new at living in secret. Sooner or later she would begin to love her new self, which was separate from Christopher, as much as the old; the two lives would spill into each other.

218

Christopher knew. He was trained, and experienced, and cold; but, with all that, he could not control the spillage.

Cathy, already trading information, wanted to ask him a question. Their lives had changed, something had happened to her mind as well as Christopher's, on the train between Paris and Rome. It was then, as she looked out the windows into a hypnotic whorl of snowflakes, that she had decided that she must commit, as she put it to him, some act of madness in order to break through to him. She wanted to know what had happened in Germany – why he was so shattered. 'I saw cruelty in you that night,' she said. 'Not just your old hard-heartedness. Cruelty.'

'An agent was killed.'

Cathy was neither surprised at the statement nor surprised that he would tell her; he had not told her other things that she had no need to know, in the beginning when she required signs that he trusted her as much as the men and women with whom he spent his real life, and whom she never saw.

'How? Did you kill him?'

'No, I didn't commit the murder. But I caused it. I was stupid about something. I made a mistake.'

'And while I've been doing all these things you'll never ask about, you've been trying to avenge your own mistake – is that it?'

Christopher didn't answer, and Cathy, with her new senses awake, drew back.

3

The next day, Christopher asked her to introduce him to Jorge de Rodegas.

They were seated together under the awnings of the café in the Plaza de Cibeles. Cathy liked to go there in the forenoon, to hear the great clock strike eleven and twelve, to watch the crowds, to observe Christopher's pleasure in the small glasses of cold draught beer that were served there; she liked the thick discs of brown felt on which the glasses were set – she liked all small things, such as precious metals and common rocks and cats, that had more weight, when held in the hand, than their mass suggested.

When she heard Christopher utter Rodegas's name she came out of a reverie – the clock had been striking eleven.

'Don Jorge de Rodegas?' she said. 'Why?'

As always when she was taken unawares, her accent thickened; she spoke several sentences in her natural drawl before the intonations she had been sent north to learn returned to her.

'I want to know him,' Christopher said.

Cathy put a finger on Christopher's arm. 'No one knows Don Jorge. He's worse than you for secrets.'

'Let's be spies, then,' Christopher said. 'Brief me about Rodegas.'

Cathy spun the story in the air between them. She was as amused and as animated as her mother, and loved a colourful character as much. She came from a society in which the language was still used to express wonder at the comedy of life. Of Rodegas, she said that he had come to the Kirkpatricks' farm just after the war, when she was still a young girl, to buy horses. Her father had asked him to stay with them; there were no decent hotels in the nearest town, and Don Jorge carried a letter of introduction from a man in France who was much liked by her father. The two men spoke about horses all day. It was Cathy's mother, of course, who drew Don Jorge's story from him at the dinner table. He was a grandee of Spain, the childless head of an ancient family, a man of such sureness that he never, for an instant, mimicked the manners of his hosts; he was what he was. 'He wore a coat and tie and never a hair was out of place from sun-up to bedtime,' Cathy said. 'He was, in those days, twelve years ago this spring, incredibly handsome with a high forehead and a great aquiline nose – not unlike Maria's husband in looks, if Otto were in perfect health and fifteen years younger.' Don Jorge knew all about the Kirkpatricks' connection to Eugénie; he, too, was related to the fallen Empress through the Spanish branch of her family, and considered the Americans cousins. 'And, my dear Paul, he is once a duke, four times a marquis, and I don't know how many times a count.' On Cathy's thirteenth birthday, she and her parents and Rodegas had gone riding to hounds. Cathy's horse, a birthday present, had fallen as he tried to take a limestone wall that was too high for him, and Cathy had broken her leg. They were miles from the nearest telephone. Rodegas had carried her in his arms, guiding his horse with his knees only, at such a smooth canter that she had felt virtually no pain. 'Had I been the last glass of wine in the world, Paul, Don Jorge wouldn't have spilled a drop of me,' Cathy said.

'He had arms like steel. If I'd've had any sense I would have given him my virginity at the end of the ride. Instead, I cried because they had to cut off my new boot. My father made me drink bourbon for the pain, and it gave me a terrible crying jag – I couldn't stop. Don Jorge brought me, in the hospital, *five dozen* white roses, and the most beautiful pair of boots I have ever owned – he had them made in London and flown over for me. That was in the days when I thought flying was something boys in the Air Corps did; everyone else took ships. It was too romantic.' No one knew why Don Jorge kept so much to himself; not even Cathy's mother had been able to draw the secret from him. He stayed in Spain, never leaving except to buy breeding stock in America and in Ireland. He visited no other countries; evidently he had no foreign friends except the Kirkpatricks and a family of horsemen in Kilmoganny. He raced his horses only in Spain. His name never appeared on the card as owner; he used one of his lesser titles instead. He was almost never seen in public.

Cathy was radiant with remembered affection and with the vitality of the anecdote. To her mind, stories were like living creatures with hearts pumping blood. To speak about an absent friend was to bring him into the company, living and breathing and as much *there*, Cathy said, as those who were present in body. Then her expression became colder.

'Why do want to meet Don Jorge?' she asked, again.

'First, can you arrange it? If you call, will he ask us to his house?'

'His *estancia*. Yes. But why?'

'He knows something I want to know.'

Cathy frowned. While she had been talking, the clocks on the post office had rung the half and three-quarter hours, and now she listened to the striking of noon. She toyed with the felt coasters.

'You told me you'd never involve me in your work,' she said at last. 'Why is this different?'

'Because there's no other way. No one knows Rodegas.'

'What does Don Jorge know, Paul? What do you think he knows?'

There was no one at the neighbouring tables. The waiters stood together by the bar, talking in brittle Madrid Spanish of the next day's soccer match. Christopher leaned towards Cathy, took her hands, told her parts of what he knew.

'They might kill *him*,' she replied, whispering.

'I don't think so. They think he's dead these twenty-five years. I'll find a way to conceal the source.'

'But you can't be sure, can you?'

'No,' Christopher said. 'You can never be sure.'

Cathy could not make the decision at once; she was frightened by Christopher's information, unsure of his purposes. She had never known murderers. And now murder seemed real, as she told Christopher, because she knew what she herself was capable of doing in cold blood. Had she been in truth an agent, he would not have told her about the chain of deaths in which he was involving her – it was an error in handling, it put in jeopardy his single chance to find the truth. Because he loved Cathy, he could not deceive her. He realized that he was, all the same, using her as he used agents. With them, too, it was fear of loss, and sometimes even love, that made the hideous risks they took seem worth the danger.

For the remainder of the day, they followed Cathy's plan; got back aboard the steamboat, as she said. She wanted to walk in the Retiro and go for a boat ride in the artificial lake. Christopher had had enough of parks, but he went with her. Gradually the light came back into her face, and she began to talk again. Everything she wished to do was something they had done before, and while they were reliving scenes she had loved she spoke of others: How, in Palma de Mallorca, they had found their way through silent, sun-scorched streets in the last minutes of the hour of siesta, and had come down a long flight of worn stairs as a clock somewhere had struck five; and, at that exact moment, as they stepped out of the sun and into the thick shade of the trees on the Borne, hundreds of birds had burst into song in the branches above their heads. And now she had recovered her childhood fear of sin, seeing jewelled rings on the chipped fingers of the wooden virgin in the cathedral at Palma; the offerings told her that this smiling city was filled with women – the rings had all belonged to women – who went in shame and in fear of death. She remembered meals, drinks, a certain line of surf as they had swum together in the sea. No event of their honeymoon, the spring and summer before, which could be recorded on the physical senses had escaped her memory: they had driven from city to city and from fiesta to fiesta, from San Isidro in Madrid in May to San Fermin in Pamplona in July, seeing bulls killed in the ring and idols and relics carried in the streets, and touching and speaking to no one but one another. It was then that Cathy had told Christopher, as they walked at sunrise on a beach near Valencia, having spent the whole night drinking manzanila, alone with a troupe of musicians and dancers in a flamenco bar, that she had achieved what she had always desired, perfect union with a man.

Now, a year later in Madrid, after they had eaten *tapas* in the warren of streets between the Puerta del Sol and the Plaza Santa Ana (mushrooms in one place that Cathy remembered, grilled shrimp in another, gazpacho in another, *pinchos morunos* in another; *vino tinto* in all), they sat together in a café among the sickly trees of the Plaza de España that seemed, at night, to be an enclosing forest, and drank glasses of weak Spanish cognac that a footsore waiter brought to them, pouring Cathy's glass half full and Christopher's to overflowing. Cathy had been sunk in a long silence. Then, in a small voice, she said, 'All right, Paul; I'll phone Don Jorge in the morning, or wire, or whatever is quickest.'

Rodegas invited them to his ranch for the weekend. That gave them two more days together. They had already had eight.

'Ten days alone is better than nothing,' Cathy said.

4

On the ninth day, Christopher received, through the open post, a telegram from Paris; it contained a code phrase that told him that Kiril Kamensky was dead. A day later, the news was in the papers. The Soviet authorities spoke of a heart attack. Claude de Cerutti, in Paris, used the word 'murder' in a press conference. Journalists who had never known that Kamensky was alive began to describe his genius as his novel came out in Russian, and as the French translation, circulated in proof by Cerutti, began – as Otto Rothchild had put it – the process of developing Kamensky's work in the darkroom of the public mind.

Seventeen

I

The *estancia* of Don Jorge de Rodegas lay many miles from
Madrid, and Christopher and Cathy left the city before first light.
They drove with the top down in the chill of the dawn, and then
northward into the kiln of the summer morning, through the scor-
ched, rising country of Old Castille. On the horizon were lines of
trees, bent by the shimmering heat as the spinnakers of a sailing
squadron are tilted by the wind. Nearer were the villages, cubes of
earthy masonry with their blind walls turned towards the road.
Cathy imagined twisted dwarfs in their streets and widows in
black, and a corrupt priest, also in black, commanding the parents
of beautiful virgins to marry them to the humpbacked sons of
rich fathers. Christopher tried to make her see in the bleached
sky and the bleak landscape and the severe peasant architecture
the colours and forms in the painting of Picasso and Juan Gris.
But Cathy preferred ghosts and monsters. Wrapped round her
head she wore a scarf of the same changing blue shades as her
elongated eyes; as the heat increased she took it off, knotted one
end to her new necklace, and her hair and the silk, gold and blue,
flew behind them like pennants. She had bought a guitar in Madrid,
and when she could no longer get music on the radio she played the

instrument and sang. Her small, true voice sounded, in the rushing open car filled with wind, like that of a person singing in a wood – muffled, and coming from no direction that could be identified. She could not bear the lunar silences of Spain's empty places; she had only recently begun to learn to bear silence at all.

There was a ringing silence when Christopher turned off the engine of the car in the flagged outer courtyard of the country house of Don Jorge de Rodegas. They were expected for the midday meal, and they had arrived at one o'clock, a polite hour. The great stone house, lying at the end of a pebble road in a deep valley, was shuttered. They had driven down an avenue of plane trees; there was a lake made from a dammed river below the house, and they had seen water spraying gardens beyond high green hedges, and smelled flowers growing. On the irrigated green hillsides, little herds of horses grazed in the shade of trees. Everywhere on this land trees had been planted for the comfort of the horses. Here, there was everything for the eye, but nothing for the ear. Christopher and Cathy heard no sound at all; even the horses, drugged by the heat, did not snort or stamp or whinny. A pair of large Scotch deerhounds loped around the corner of the house; they sat down side by side and looked at the humans, but did not bark. Cathy spoke to them. They didn't move or pant or wag their tails. Like hidalgos who never remove their coats, the dogs took no notice of the heat.

Christopher and Cathy got out of the car, and at that moment two young servants in livery, wearing white gloves, emerged from the house. They were followed by a grander servant in a tailcoat. 'Mendoza, the butler,' said Cathy. 'I thought the first time I came here and saw him in his buttons that if Don Jorge was a duke, then Mendoza must be the king.' Mendoza was very tall, with the blond hair and the light eyes of Navarre; they were on the borders of that province. He spoke gravely to Cathy, with a shading of familiarity: 'Señorita Caterina.' He had known her from a child. Cathy spoke to him in French; he understood all that she said, but answered him in Spanish. He made no sign when Christopher addressed him in Spanish that he had noticed that husband and wife were talking different languages. Don Jorge was in the pastures with the horses, but he would return for luncheon at three.

Mendoza led them through the door and into the inner courtyard, flagged and tiled, with loggias on all four sides and a high fountain playing in the centre; citrus trees grew within the walls, oranges, lemons and limes, filling the air with a scent so heavy that it was apprehended not so much in the nostrils as in the roof of the mouth. They followed Mendoza down a long dim corridor, over carpets that Otto Rothchild, Christopher imagined, would have bent to kiss. Except for the portraits that lined the walls, the house reminded Christopher of the palace of an amir where he had once stayed in the Sudan. It had the same stillness, the same sense that the house and everyone in it were suspended out of ordinary time and place. Each was ruled by a man whose absolute authority was never exerted because it was never questioned.

Their luggage somehow reached their rooms before they did and the maids were unpacking it as they came in; other maids were drawing baths. When they were alone, Cathy stood in the centre of the sitting room, surrounded by vases of cut flowers on all the tables, and smiled in triumph.

'How long have you been coming here?' Christopher asked.

'Every autumn, after the Paris racing season, since I was thirteen. Twelve years. I came down last October to be with Mama and Papa for a weekend while you were in Asia.'

'You didn't tell me.'

'I wrote. It was one of those letters that never found you, and it came back. You never opened it.'

There was a Velázquez on one wall, a Goya on another, portraits of Don Jorge's ancestors – females and children. Cathy drank a glass of mineral water. She peeled an orange and gave half of it to Christopher. The moist green leaves were still on the stem to show that it was freshly picked. While she ate her portion she wandered around the room, looking at the pictures and removing her clothes, as if she were in a hotel suite. Naked, squinting with the pleasure of biting into each sweet section of orange, she walked into the bathroom, and soon Christopher heard her settle with a sigh into the tub. He went into a separate bathroom and bathed himself. The absolute silence was broken by the voice of a woman, singing as she swept the flagstones below his window.

It was evident that Don Jorge de Rodegas loved Cathy. He shook hands gravely with Christopher and looked him in the eye without a flicker of expression. But his face, tanned like a fine hide by decades of exposure to the weathers of the Meseta, burst with joy when he turned to Cathy. He gathered her into his arms and kissed her on the forehead and both cheeks, then stood back from her, with his hands on her elbows, and examined her musing face.

'Perfect,' he said. 'My dear Christopher, you have married the only perfect woman who has lived on this earth since ancient times.'

He spoke English like an Englishman. Cathy had named his English public school and his college at Oxford.

Champagne was brought to them and they drank, standing. The room was lined from floor to ceiling with paintings by the Spanish masters; most of the men, conquerors, were painted full-length. They all looked like Don Jorge – thin figures in close-fitting black, like columns of smoke against the landscapes behind them, with cruelty sleeping in their immobile faces.

At luncheon Rodegas asked Christopher to excuse his rudeness while he asked Cathy a number of questions about her parents and about horses. He seemed to know by name every animal on the Kirkpatricks' farm. He and Cathy discussed bloodlines and speed, and Christopher had never seen her so much at ease. Nothing showed in Rodegas's face when, upon asking, he learned that Christopher could not ride.

'What luck for me,' Don Jorge said; 'I can ride in the morning alone with my cousin. With your permission.'

Rodegas told them that he had arranged nothing special for the weekend; there was not much suitable company nearby, and he had supposed that the usual country-house entertainment in Spain, the fighting of heifers and the shooting of game birds, wouldn't interest them.

'You are,' he said to Christopher, 'a poet?'

'He is,' said Cathy.

'Your mother-in-law was kind enough to send me a copy of one of your books. I liked the sonnets very much.' He quoted lines from two of them. 'I've had the volume bound; perhaps you'd sign it for me.'

Rodegas studied Christopher. Cathy took his attention away with a description of Paco Camino's fight, just before San Fermin, in the ring at Barcelona. The corrida had been held in the rain, Camino had been gored by the second bull, but not badly, and had continued, bleeding, and taking greater and greater chances, until even the Spaniards in the crowd were moved. One man, sitting beside Cathy at the barrera, had wept openly.

'There have been others like Camino,' Don Jorge said. 'I wonder if the old ones were as classical as they say?'

'Surely you've seen some of the famous ones of the last twenty or thirty years?'

'Most of them. They're not so wonderful in memory as they seemed at the time. I no longer go to bullfights.'

'You feel they've been corrupted?'

'They were always corrupt. Pablo Picasso is said to have remarked of some Germans who liked bullfights, "They would – they like bloodshed". Very Spanish, that – to believe that only Spaniards can understand Spanish things.'

Christopher smiled at him. 'You must not have seen much of other nationalities, here in the mountains.'

'Not recently,' said Don Jorge, dabbing moisture from his lips with a napkin.

'Tonight,' Cathy said. 'I have a wish. Will you two grant it?'

Rodegas turned his smile on her. 'I say yes, Catherine, without even asking what it is. Tell me at dinner what it is you want.'

'All right.'

'What *I* shall want,' Don Jorge said, 'is to hear you play, and it's my wish that you should wear a white dress, if you have one with you.'

After the dessert, Cathy left them; it was a Spanish house after all, she said. Rodegas smoked a cigar while he and Christopher drank coffee. He chose to speak of poetry; he believed that only two languages, English and Russian, were capable of producing great poetry. Christopher asked if he spoke Russian as well as English; Rodegas let the question go by, and pressed Christopher for his opinion on this idea.

'I've heard that said, often,' Christopher replied. 'Always, before this, by Englishmen or Americans or Russians.'

'Well, I'm a sort of Englishman, my mind was formed in England. It always seemed odd to me that Russian should be the other language of great poetry, when the Russians are, generally speaking, so contemptuous of self-control. Poetry ought to deal with what did *not* happen.'

After a polite half-hour, Rodegas led Christopher out of the dining room. In the great hall, he showed him a huge portrait of a young woman in ringlets; a large ruby glowed between her fine breasts. 'My father called this the sacred heart portrait,' Rodegas said. 'It's Eugénie, of course. My ancestress, and Catherine's. They do look rather alike, don't they? But Eugénie, poor woman, seems a bad copy of a masterpiece beside Catherine.'

That evening they strolled in the garden. It was a hodgepodge of the Moorish, French, and Italian styles, with avenues of trees, beds of flowers planted in elaborate designs, a maze, and many fountains. One of Don Jorge's ancestors had come back from Versailles in the eighteenth century and installed a number of water jokes – jets that sprayed upward from the paths into women's skirts, or outwards from the walls into the face and hair. Don Jorge, cautioning them to stand well back, sprang some of the traps. 'These devices to mock and shatter dignity were never a great success with Spaniards,' he said. 'My grandfather used to demonstrate them on foreign servants specially hired for the purpose. I remember him doing so when I was a child.'

Mendoza and two footmen brought them cocktails, dry martinis containing olives stuffed with almonds. They drank two very large ones each, seated on a bench in a grotto with cool water running down the walls and bubbling out of the floor everywhere but on the stone island where they sat. One of the footmen stood just outside the grotto; the other, returning to the house with Mendoza, sang as he went. Rodegas asked Cathy what her wish was.

'I want you to talk about yourself, for a whole evening, Don Jorge,' she said. 'Especially about your youth – love and war.'

The footman returned with more martinis, in fresh glasses and, another plate of canapes.

'You wouldn't be amused,' Rodegas said. 'There was no love and too much war.'

'I insist.'

'Then I surrender. But not tonight. You must first play for me. Tomorrow morning we'll ride. Then we'll see.' He turned to Christopher. 'Perhaps she'll forget by tomorrow.'

'She never forgets an appetite.'

'So she doesn't.'

At dinner, an elaborate meal with long pauses between the courses, Rodegas asked about their life together. Cathy spoke of the journeys they had taken, of their meetings in Paris and Madrid and London, and how once she had come to Nairobi and Christopher had taken her up into the hills to see the game, and read to her from Isak Dinesen's *Out of Africa* the account of the death of the author's lover. Rodegas nodded and quoted from the book: '"It was fit and proper that lions should come to Denys's grave and make him an African monument . . . Lord Nelson himself, I have reflected, in Trafalgar Square, has had his lions made only out of stone".' Cathy, wearing the long white gown that Don Jorge had asked to see her in, said that it was unbearable that Christopher and Rodegas, the two men she loved beyond reason, should both be in love with the ghost of this Danish girl who had lived in the Ngong Hills when the one was a schoolboy and the other a child.

'I should think *you* would find it unbearable, to be apart so much,' Rodegas said, 'and to live so much in public when you're together.'

'Those parts are no great fun,' Cathy said.

Rodegas studied her with great seriousness, but if he saw her unhappiness he said nothing about it.

'I didn't realize,' he said to Christopher with a smile, 'that poets travelled quite so much as you seem to do.'

'Most don't, I suppose,' Christopher said.

'And what is he looking for, Catherine, in Germany and in Africa and in Indochina, and following the bulls in Spain?'

'I don't know,' Cathy said. 'He has his reasons.'

Cathy began to play at midnight. Rodegas and Christopher, drinking French cognac, sat in deep chairs at the other end of the room, so that they could hear the full resonance of the piano. Rodegas had a taste, surprising in so arid a man, for Chopin and Schumann. These were easy exercises for Cathy; she played for hours. It rained, a sudden downpour, outside the open window behind her. She played on through the storm. The wind blew the music off the rack and she completed the piece without an error. Don Jorge applauded and a servant, responding to the handclaps, came in and collected the scattered sheets.

'That was a great deal more pleasant than memories of war,' Rodegas said.

'Nevertheless,' said Cathy, 'I demand a story tomorrow night.'

Their bedroom was at the end of the house, so that one set of windows opened on the courtyard with its fountain and the other looked out on the slope of the mountain, which was strewn with white boulders. There was a bright moon and for a while they watched the horses, some of them dozing and some grazing in its light.

In bed, Cathy said, 'Listen, Paul – the fountain on one side, dead silence on the other.'

Like the Trevi and the Piazza Oratorio, Christopher thought.

'That was a stupid thing to say,' Cathy said, as if he had thought aloud. 'I forget I can't be completely honest with you any more.'

Neither of them could sleep, they had had such a long siesta and eaten so much food. Cathy spoke to Christopher about her ride with Don Jorge the following morning. She knew they would talk about Christopher. She did not want to deceive him.

'Can't you tell him what you are, before I make him tell you what you want to know?'

'No. It's not done; I can't do it, literally cannot speak the words to an outsider. Anyway, I think Don Jorge already has a good idea of what I am. He himself has been something like me in the past.' Still, Cathy worried. It was wrong to trick a man in his own house, especially a man one knew and loved.

'Can't *I* tell him, while we're riding in the morning?' she asked. 'Believe me, nothing will make him betray you; you're married to me.'

'All right,' Christopher said; it was what he had wanted her to do.

3

At dinner, Cathy wanted Don Jorge to begin his confessions with the history of his loves.

'Why, for example,' she asked, 'do you and Paul pine for that Danish woman who wrote about Kenya?'

'Because of the beauty of her mind, because she accepted her womanhood, and in her books, at least, took no revenge on anyone for it,' Don Jorge said. 'Weren't *you* moved by what she wrote, Catherine, when Paul read it to you?'

'I wept. But I get so sick of that word *beauty*. It's a male word. Do you live for anything else, any of you?'

Rodegas gave her a serene look, as if the sight of her were answer enough to the question.

'That look!' Cathy said. 'All my life I've seen it. If it comes from someone I love, such as either of you, I don't mind; in fact I adore it. But others, all my life, have made me feel like an animal that has the power of speech. As a little girl, I was *called* by the names of animals – Pussycat, Bunny Rabbit. Papa called me Filly.'

Rodegas and Christopher waited for her to continue, but she drank champagne and ate her soufflé instead. Tonight she wore nothing that Christopher had ever given her, and indeed had not since they had arrived; in Rodegas's house she wore the jewels that had been passed down to her in her family: pearls, rubies, diamonds that had become hers as a bride.

After supper, Rodegas showed them pictures in room after room of the house; Mendoza went ahead of them, turning on the lights. Cathy cared little for painting. 'Tell Paul what the duchess said,' she asked.

'This woman has the greatest private collection in Spain, portraits of her ancestors,' Rodegas said. 'She was asked by a journalist if she was not filled with awe, to possess the works of all those dead geniuses. "Awe?" she replied, "Genius? Goya, Velázquez, Rembrandt were simply the people my family hired before the invention of photography".'

Cathy would not let Rodegas stray from his promise. She pulled him into a room where candles burned in an old chandelier.

'Begin somewhere interesting in the story of your life,' she said. 'You don't have to begin at the beginning. But, Don Jorge, *begin*.'

Rodegas took her hand. 'One of the reasons I was so affected by the writing of Karen Blixen, Isak Dinesen as she called herself – that Danish woman in Kenya,' he said, 'was the manner of her lover's death. Denys Finch-Hatton was killed in an aeroplane crash; he capsized with his machine, as the author put it. That happened to my own parents, you know, when I was a small child. My father was mad to be the first to fly from Barcelona to Constantinople. He and my mother crashed on the day they set out, in the *cordillera* between here and Barcelona. Capsized.'

It was because of that that Rodegas had been sent to England to be educated; his father, one of a type, weakened by strange enthusiasms, that appeared from time to time in the family, had ordered it in his will. Rodegas was sent to a preparatory school near London when he was eight, then to Eton, then to Oxford; he spent the long vacations at the *estancia*, but hardly ever went into Spanish society. One of his father's brothers was in a diplomatic post in London, another was a high officer in the Army, a third was an archbishop. They gave leave to seedy Englishmen to teach Don Jorge Latin and Greek. But in the summers, they made him into a Spaniard.

'That didn't include marriage and the production of an heir?' Cathy asked.

'I failed to find the woman I wanted. Karen Blixen was born too soon, and you, Catherine, too late.'

'Be serious.'

'I am perfectly serious. No woman I met was suitable. Spanish girls of my class were, in my day, unknowable, though I was engaged to one for a long time. The English were too rude – that is their good manners among themselves but it would not be understood in this country. Americans are too easily bored to live as I live.'

'Was it the Civil War in Spain that made marriage difficult for you?'

'I didn't fight in that war as a soldier.'

'But you were in it?'

'Yes. Everyone in Spain was in it – and, worse, thousands of foreigners. Civil wars are always very much worse, Catherine, when foreigners take an interest in them.'

Then he told the tale, in the third person, using the artificial names that the characters in his story had employed, but describing real places and real acts in a real time.

4

Carlos, the young hero of the story, was born in 1910, of noble parents, who soon left him an orphan. He was sent to England in 1919. His uncle, the diplomatist, had a Spaniard's abiding suspicion of the British espionage service; it seemed inevitable to him that the English would, sooner or later, attempt to make use of a Spanish noble who had been wholly educated in their country and who might, the force of nature being what it is in young men, even marry an Englishwoman. Therefore Carlos was registered at his schools, and later at the university, not under the name that his family used – the one that went with his dukedom – but under the name that belonged to one of the minor titles the family had acquired in antiquity through marriage. He had no need of credentials, such as diplomas, in his true name. His uncle sent a car for him every week while he was in school and had him brought to London for the weekend, to speak Spanish and to learn about Spain. In summer, he returned to Castille to the remote country house that was the seat of his family. Here he was visited by relatives and trained by servants, but he saw almost no one else. There was no time for it; he had only three or four months out of each year to live his true life as a member of the Spanish ruling class. The result was that, though Carlos knew a lot of people in England, none of them knew him by his real name; and though everyone in Spain knew his famous name, almost no one in that country knew him by sight.

Between Eton and Oxford, he performed his military service. His uncle the general arranged that this should be done in a remote post in Morocco. The idea was to show him blood. At that time there was war between the Spanish colonial forces and the desert tribesmen. Carlos, as a lieutenant of cavalry, killed five men in the course of a year and was himself wounded twice, once by a spear, once by a bullet. Spain was in political uproar. Carlos took no particular interest in the rise and fall of dictators, the rebellion of garrisons on the Peninsula. This had always gone on. The

Bourbon king abdicated. It had nothing to do with his family, or with the other ancient families connected to his family. His uncles believed that the real threat to Spain – and to Catholicism, which was the same thing in the mind of the archbishop and probably in the minds of the others as well – came from outside Spain. They were greatly afraid of Communism. Of Anarchism, too, and Socialism. All were the same thing in their eyes. Carlos's uncle the archbishop, then only a monsignor, had seen forty-eight churches burned in 1909 in Barcelona, and drunken workers dancing in the streets with the corpses of nuns they had taken from the catacombs.

'In that tragic week,' the archbishop would tell his brothers, and his nephew, 'I looked the Antichrist in the face.'

They were Spaniards, nobles and prelates. They decided that they needed an agent in the enemy camp. Carlos was engaged, by arrangement, to the daughter of another duke who was a party to the conspiracy, and sent to Oxford. He studied Arabic for his own pleasure, and Russian in preparation for his mission. He was instructed to ingratiate himself with the English Communist movement that was flourishing at Oxford in the 1930s. It was an easy job; many of the people the Communists were recruiting at the university were from the aristocracy or its fringes, class renegades. Outwardly, Carlos became like them. In 1934 he was introduced by one of his dons to a Russian, who recruited him as an agent of the Comintern. The resources of the NKVD were not sufficient to discover Carlos's real identity, much less his real purposes. The Russians knew that nations had intelligence services; they never suspected that a class, even the class they were hoping to destroy in Spain, should send secret agents against them.

Carlos went down from Oxford in that year. He spent the next months in Barcelona being trained as a terrorist; there he met many other Spaniards, all of them of a different class and all of them going under false names. He memorized all their faces. In 1935 he was sent away from Barcelona with a false English passport supplied by the Russians, with instructions to go to Madrid and wait. He did so. When the war broke out, in the summer of 1936, Carlos was in place.

That autumn, his fiancée, whom he had not seen for two years, decided to join him at the *estancia*. No one ever knew why she imagined he was there. ('She was a simple girl, Carlos hardly knew her,' Rodegas related. 'In order to get from where she was to the *estancia* she had to cross the front lines. She decided that she would certainly be safe, even from Communists and Anarchists, if she disguised herself as a nun. She had led, as you can see, a very cloistered life. She set out, walking, like a heroine of the Middle Ages. Of course she was raped and killed by the first Loyalist patrol she encountered; her maid, too.')

Carlos learned nothing of this until the war was over. He became a successful spy, and had many adventures.

('One in particular will, I think, satisfy Catherine's curiosity because it is, like the romantic death of Carlos's betrothed, a story that combines love and war,' said Rodegas.)

During the Siege of Madrid, in the autumn and early winter of 1936, Carlos was, at one and the same time, an important agent of the Comintern, and the leader of the Fascist Fifth Column in Madrid. Carlos met with Comrade Medina, the fat Italo-Argentine who was the Comintern's 'instructor' in Spain, and with Mediña's assistant, a Bulgarian named Stepanov; he worked with Konev, called Paulito in Spain, who was chief of terror for the Soviet apparatus. At the same time, he sent out information to his family – lists of names, lists of supplies, lists of the condemned. And scrupulous lists of all his own acts of terrorism which were undertaken to build and protect his cover. He lived both his roles fully, murdering efficiently to win the trust of those he was betraying.

('That is why he lived,' said Rodegas.)

Because Carlos had so many languages – Spanish, English, Russian, German, French – and had them so well, he was assigned to Madrid to the foreign community. Foreigners were pouring into the capital – journalists, spies, soldiers. Moscow wanted them watched; sometimes it wanted one of them killed. The Soviet controllers especially wanted a watch kept on Russians. It was better for a Spaniard to do it than a Russian, because Russians generally believed that Spaniards were children, and they would speak in front of them as they never would in the presence of others.

Carlos was assigned to observe and report on a young Russian poet who had been sent to Spain as a journalist. That was truly all he was, a journalist. He was brilliantly talented as a writer and he had been very brave as a boy soldier in the Russian Civil war. But he had no gift for intrigue. He was, perhaps, the one Russian in Madrid who was what he seemed to be.

236

('The Russian boy's name was Zhiɾalko,' Rodegas said, 'Kolka Zhigalko.')

Carlos was puzzled, before he met Kolka Zhigalko, that everyone called him a boy; according to his dossier, he was older than Carlos. No one thought Carlos a boy.

When Carlos met Zhigalko, he understood. Zhigalko, pink and curly and smiling, exuded sexuality. Even Spanish girls were eager to sleep with him. There was a wild light in him, which was his talent. He was prodigally generous with his body, his money, his thoughts. Carlos saw him, sweetly – and he supposed, when the time came, passionately – accept the advances of ugly girls. He saw him permit transparent knaves to cheat him, because he saw that it gave them pleasure. He composed songs for people he took a fancy to, played and sang them, and forgot them, he said they were for the person to whom he sang them and it would be wrong to preserve them. Zhigalko would go out to observe the fighting in the university city – remember, he was a journalist and a noncombatant – and he would join in, rescuing the wounded. He had type O blood, the most usable kind; he gave so much of it to wounded men that he became translucent. He had no fear of anything – not of embarrassment, not of disgrace, not of failure, not of punishment, not even of death. He had the gift of knowing, all the time, in his mind and in his blood, that he was alive. Carlos asked him, when he knew him better, how he could bear to go to sleep and lose touch with his waking self. 'But I dream!' Zhigalko cried.

It was no wonder that the NKVD worried about Zhigalko. To him, they meant nothing. Kolka Zhigalko was a Communist, almost an old Bolshevik, he had gone to war with the Red Army in his teens. But he had been formed, like all Russians, in the church and in the language and in those vast spaces of mystical Russia that everyone always uses to explain the fatalism of the Russian character. Kolka cared nothing for the secret police. How could they imprison him? He thought himself a beam of light. In one of his songs, he made it up in his room in the Gran Via for an English girl whose lover had been killed by a shell, he sang quite openly about God. Carlos never forgot the lines:

What is one instant of pain to a man, one passage through its darkness
When he comes from the bright face of his love for a woman
Into the heart of the Saviour?

237

What did it matter to Kolka if the secret police killed him? They had nothing to do with what he was.

Carlos understood that Kolka Zhigalko, living as he did, could not survive long. The temptation to protect him was very great, and for a while Carlos did. After all, Kolka was harmless by the standards of any sane man. He was a passionate Russian patriot, a passionate lover of the international working class. What Kolka did, everything he did, he did for love. He was the only Communist Carlos ever met – indeed, he may be the only political zealot who ever lived whose beliefs made him lovable because they rose from the truth and sweetness of his character in the same way that the actions of St Francis rose from his faith. That was the basis of his genius, and there was no doubt, even among the secret agents who were watching him and pondering whether or not to kill him, that he was a genius. His battle dispatches were extraordinary; every line he wrote was made flesh as soon as it was read by another person. Of course, what he wrote was not printed in *Pravda* as he wrote it. He cared nothing for dialectics, for jargon, for official terminology. Kolka thought that revolution had to do with life, and life with humanity, and humanity with language. The censors removed all that from Kolka's stories. The odd thing was, Kolka was a true peasant, the son of a lout and a slattern; one of those aberrations that crops up in all breeds of animals, the one random masterwork in a hundred generations.

Carlos was pressed for incriminating material on Zhigalko. He held back. The pressure was increased. Kolka was in the machine; it was impossible to release him. Anyone who has had to do with secret life will know that this is the unbreakable truth about it, that once a thing is started, once a case is opened, it can never be abandoned. The file must be completed. The spy longs for the final fact as the monk yearns for the last Host. Carlos, it must be said, lost his coldness where Kolka was concerned. He saw that Kolka was an artist, and that weighed. He saw that he was good, in the antique meaning of that word, and that weighed, too. But what weighed most was that Carlos was disgusted by the idea of having a hand in the destruction of such a creature as Kolka. Carlos, remember, was doing what he was doing because he was a Catholic, coming from fifty generations of Catholics. It is an interesting fact about Carlos that he prayed silently all the time he was doing murder, or betrayal, or whatever the day's work brought him. He thought that Kolka's was one death that God would not forgive him; Carlos was, after all, only the same age as Kolka. He thought in these terms.

The atmosphere in Madrid that winter was extraordinary. It was cold, Madrid is so cold in winter; there was no fuel to speak of, there was little enough food. One saw people in bandages everywhere, working and fighting. Shells were falling in the streets. The Moroccans and the Spanish troops of Generalissimo Franco were at the gates of the city. There were three great battles in November, and bombing by aeroplanes at night. The people were in something that resembled a religious hysteria. They went about the streets crying incessantly, '¡No pas-ar-án! ¡No pas-ar-án!' 'They shall not pass!' It was a murmur, a buzzing, like the chant of some primitive religion coming out of a sealed tomb. Carlos felt that he had come to the rim of existence. He was exhalted, against his will, by the bravery of these Madrileños, by their obstinate refusal to submit. On the other hand, always remember, he was their deadly enemy, a wolf among them. What in God's name would happen to Spain if those people – so courageous, so maddened by their hatred of all that Carlos was in his true self – should conquer? For a month or two in Madrid, in the winter of 1936, he thought that they might be irresistible.

At about this time, Carlos saw a way in which he might save Kolka Zhigalko from the secret police – or, if not save him, then at least prevent his death. A few weeks before, another journalist, travelling under a League of Nations *laisser-passer*, had come to Madrid and got a room at the Gran Via Hotel, directly below Zhigalko's. This man wrote for French and Belgian newspapers, and also sent feature stories to the English and American weekly papers. Like Carlos, he spoke a great many languages. He was ten years older than Carlos and Zhigalko, or perhaps a little more. A handsome man, a splendid conversationalist. He had a cynic's wit; faith and emotion in others amused him. He knew something about everything. Soon he knew everyone in Madrid. It was extraordinary how he got about. It was a gift quite as great, in its way, as that of an artist; this man could meet a man or a woman once, speak three sentences, and stay in the other person's mind forever. Had he been an American or an Englishman he would have become the head of government. But, as Carlos found out, this man had no country.

Naturally the NKVD was interested in him. They couldn't believe that anyone who operated as this man operated was not a master spy for some imperialist power. They opened a dossier on him. He went about, almost alone in Madrid, under the name on his papers, which Carlos took to be his own name. The NKVD gave him a code name. In their secret conversations he was called Kiril Alekseivich Kamensky. Sometimes, secret symbol within secret name, 'KAK'. But usually Kamensky. He maddened them; they could not get a grip on him. Who was he? Where did he come from? They learned some things about him – that he was a man of the Left, that he was *not* using his baptismal name after all. Finally they learned that he was a Russian. Before, they had been curious about Kamensky. Now they hungered for him. Carlos was told to befriend him, entrap him, take the bones out of his flesh.

Kamensky was the most approachable man in Madrid. There is a kind of intelligence operative called an antenna – he makes himself visible so that information will come to him. That's what the NKVD thought Kamensky was. They gave Carlos information to feed him, thinking that it would be transmitted to his masters. It was thought that he must be working for the British secret service; the Russians were, if anything, more convinced of the omnipotence of English espionage than Carlos's uncles. Perhaps, too, they thought, he was a Nazi agent, but they held that theory in reserve. Kamensky hadn't the Nazi style – he was too fine. His looks, his speech, his mind, his manners all argued that he could not be a follower of Hitler. So the NKVD, louts judging louts, looked at the matter. The information Carlos gave to Kamensky appeared in his newspapers. That, thought the NKVD, only proved how clever he was. They instructed Carlos to give him more information, chicken feed as they called it; Kamensky printed some of it, and told Carlos he hadn't used the rest because he hadn't been able to verify it. There was consternation. What deep game was Kamensky playing? If he didn't want our false information, what true information must he be obtaining for his masters, and how was he obtaining it? Kamensky became their obsession. Carlos urged them to consider the possibility that Kamensky was what he said he was, a genuine journalist. Impossible, they said. He must be trapped.

It was, in the end, easy. Through Carlos, Kamensky met Kolka Zhigalko. Kamensky had brought with him to Madrid a French girl, also a journalist, who was obviously in love with him. He, less obviously, for he was a man who masked his special passions with a general amiability, was fond of her. The four of them – Kamensky, Zhigalko, Carlos, and the French girl – fell into the habit of meeting in Kamensky's room during the bombardments. It was a gathering place for a large group of people, mostly foreigners, who wished to show their contempt for the guns and the bombers by refusing to take shelter. There was always a lot of French cognac to drink, the only supply of it in Madrid in private hands.

The language of this group was French, sometimes English. Zhigalko was no linguist. He limped along in Spanish. In French and English he was worse. But he liked the atmosphere, and because of his ear – most artists are able to learn languages rather easily, it has to do with their heightened powers of observation, perhaps – he understood a great deal more than he was able to say. He would sit there, golden curls and blue eyes, the ideal human form incarnate, his face shimmering with the heat of his interest in life, and listen to languages he could not really understand. Oddly, everyone spoke to Kolka – addressed their best remarks to him, as if he could apprehend meanings, even in foreign tongues, that others would miss. Kolka would smile his innocent smile, and sometimes make up a song. Sometimes, too, he would struggle with French or English, attempting to say what was in his heart. One night they had all had a lot to drink and the bombs had fallen quite near. Kolka made a song. Then he tried to translate it; it was in Russian, of course. He tried Spanish; no luck. Then French and English; worse and worse. Carlos had understood the Russian, but of course, drunk as he was, he dared not reveal his knowledge to the group.

Suddenly Kamensky, who up to this time no one had suspected (except Carlos, who knew) of understanding a word of Russian, addressed Kolka in that language. He spoke it beautifully; it was evident to all in the room that Kamensky was reciting a poem. At the end of it, Kolka, with Russian tears running over his cheeks, threw his arms around Kamensky and kissed him on the lips. Russians do that, or did. Kolka said something in Russian; Kamensky said something back. Carlos understood that they were proposing to go up on the roof of the hotel in the midst of the air raid. The Heinkels were flying over in the dark, dropping high explosive, the anti-aircraft guns were firing, shrapnel was falling back on the city. Enemy artillery shells passed overhead, gasping, and exploded in the streets. These two Russians, very drunk, of course, on cognac, raced together to the roof of the hotel. For the others in the room, that was carrying drunken bravado too far. It was the duty of Carlos to follow them; his drunkenness was excuse enough to do so.

On the roof he found them, standing at the very edge, facing the flashes of the rebel guns beyond the university on the horizon, shouting poetry in Russian. They remained there until the bombardment ended, and came back down, shivering – they had been sweating in the crowded room where the party was, and their soaked shirts were beginning to freeze – and with their throats scraped by their counterattack on the Fascist batteries.

Kamensky's French girl crawled in between the two of them, and kissed them both. When Carlos, the last to leave, departed, they were lying, all three of them, on the bed. Kolka was singing. After each verse, the French girl, her voice muddy with drink, would ask for a translation. Kamensky only smiled and stroked her hair.

They remained together all night. It was a thing that drunken people in a dying city might easily do. The French girl was desirable, and she belonged to that emancipated class of young women which existed in the thirties. These girls believed that they had absolute sovereignty over their own lives and bodies, that they could do as they liked, and deal with the consequences. That night she slept with both Russians. The next day she left, because during the night, out of Kolka's generosity and Kamensky's drunken release of his real self, the two men became lovers.

It was the French girl who told Carlos. She came to him to ask if he could arrange transport for her to the French frontier. It was early in the morning, Carlos had just awakened, and, yawning, he was removing the black-out curtains from the windows of his room when he saw the girl approaching in the street below. She wore the uniform of her type: belted raincoat, high-heeled shoes, a felt hat with a round brim pulled down on one side of her head, plucked eyebrows, lipstick. She was carrying a heavy valise and she teetered under its weight on her high heels.

Upstairs, Carlos gave her tea. Really, he thought, she is attractive, she would be something to subdue, with all that intelligence showing in her face, and all that unveiled hostility to men. There was a great deal of anger in her. She described, in a rush of French like a jet of bile, what had happened: the three bodies in the dim light, the two men caressing her, the strangeness of it and the terrible excitement, for this sort of woman lived for forbidden things. And then she opened her eyes to find the two men kissing not her but one another. They went on as if she weren't there, murmuring to one another in Russian. She was fascinated, the mysteries of the male body were being revealed to her in the way they handled each other. But she let it go too far. Kolka, after he had rested, came back to her and she admitted him, but as soon as he had satisfied her she was filled with disgust. Kamensky woke, he had fallen asleep, and found Kolka and the girl together; he had flown into a rage, speaking only Russian. The girl realized that it was Kolka he refused to share, not her.

Carlos heard the story with less surprise, and with much less repulsion, than would have been possible in most Spaniards. He had grown used to homosexual practices at school in England; he saw nothing wrong in them in others. He understood that most men, when they love most deeply, love other men, though not usually with a sexual dimension. The French girl, a woman scorned was less tranquil. She told Carlos she wished to leave Madrid, leave Spain, because she feared that she would kill the lovers if she remained. He arranged passage for her within the week; he could have sent her sooner but he wanted to know more about Kamensky. She told him all that she knew – willingly, sometimes with tears, sometimes with sudden shrieks of fury that burst from the depths of her body. She meant Kolka and Kamensky no harm – she was heartsore and she thought that Carlos was a friend.

Carlos told his controller in the NKVD about the love affair. Now the secret agents saw a way to use the man they called Kamensky. They let the affair between Kamensky and Kolka Zhigalko run on. The two were discreet – after all, there was nothing strange about a man becoming Kolka Zhigalko's inseparable friend. No one but Carlos, and the people to whom he sent his secret report, knew that they were secret lovers. The meetings in Kamensky's room went on as usual. No one much missed Solange, the French girl. Journalists, soldiers from the International Brigades, every class and type of foreigner came every night to drink cognac and talk. Now that Kolka had an interpreter, everyone loved him more. It became evident that he had, in addition to his body and his face, an incandescent mind. Carlos, of course, had known this all along, and everyone else had felt it; Kamensky made it visible to all, translating Kolka's long drunken speeches, interpreting his poems, explaining his silences.

One night, when Kolka had fallen into a melancholy mood, a little Frenchman, an officer in the International Brigades, wandered into the room looking for Kamensky. He'd been wounded and he carried his arm in a sling. Kolka had been lying on the bed with his eyes closed. He sat up and saw this Frenchman and leaped to his feet with a bellow of joy. It appeared that he and the Frenchman had fought together against the tanks of the White Army in front of Petrograd. They embraced and the Frenchman uttered a howl of pain as Kolka crushed his shot arm between them. Torrents of Russian ran between Kolka and Kamensky and this Frenchman, whose *nom de guerre* was André Girard. Soon André was a nightly visitor; when he was wounded again, Kolka gave him his room and moved down to Kamensky's room. Kolka nursed André, who had a head wound, by day. By night he slept with Kamensky. Soon the Frenchman was up and around. Kolka remained with Kamensky.

Carlos was ordered by the NKVD to make friends with him as he had done with Kolka and Kamensky. But André knew nothing of Kamensky, and of Kolka he would only say that he was the most important man in the Russian Revolution, because one day he would write about it. André had perfect literary judgement; he read languages as easily as Carlos and Kamensky spoke them, and when he saw genius he recognized it. Kolka, he said, was the sort of writer who appeared once in a century. Someday he would put Russia, all of it, on to the page. Kamensky tolerated the attachment between André and Kolka; André was a plain, small man, there was even something comical in his looks – you saw that he was going to be fat in a few years. He was no sexual threat; besides, André was ravenous for women. Oddly enough, he had a great deal of success. He was amusing, intelligent – and wounded. Girls came to him.

Carlos's controllers in the NKVD wanted to have access to Kolka's room. André was seldom in it at night, usually he went to a woman's room after the party in Kamensky's room. Kolka's, room, one will remember, was directly above Kamensky's. The spies made a hole in the floor, under the bed, and installed a microphone and a camera in such a way that they could not be detected. With the camera they took hundreds of photographs of Kolka and Kamensky on the bed below. Kamensky took such pleasure in the sight of his lover that he had him with the lamps lit. He made things easy for the photographer. A stenographer, one of those coarse-bodied Russian girls, sat in Kolka's room with a pad on her knees and earphones on her head, taking down in shorthand the things that Kolka and Kamensky said to each other in Russian when they were alone. Carlos observed this scene once; it was enough.

One day the NKVD man showed the photographs to Kamensky. While Kamensky looked at these travesties of his form and Kolka's, the NKVD man read him excerpts from the transcript of the stenographer's shorthand notes. Carlos was told that Kamensky sat through it all, unmoving. Then, like a snake, as the NKVD man put it to Carlos, Kamensky struck. He slapped the spy's face, a half-dozen rapid, stinging blows. As a boyar would strike a serf, Carlos thought; in the depths of the NKVD man's mind that image was awakened, too. Kamensky had made an error. Now the NKVD man, who had simply wanted to use him, had a personal reason to destroy him. He showed no sign, or believed that he showed no sign, that Kamensky's blow had stung him. He smiled at Kamensky.

'Done like a prince,' he said. 'When you've done what I am going to tell you to do, I will have something to tell you.'

'For you I will do nothing.'

'No? Someday, perhaps, you will go back to Russia. It is ours.'

'Not yours for ever.'

'Perhaps not. But Kolka Zhigalko will go back. You know how puritanical the government of the proletariat is. What if the Cheka' – he used the old term for the secret police, so that Kamensky would understand – 'were to have these pictures, these transcripts, our testimony?'

Kamensky saw that he was being made the instrument of Kolka's death. He didn't hesitate. He bargained: one act on behalf of the NKVD in return for the pictures and the transcripts, and for Kolka's safety. Of course it was a delusion; nothing would save Kolka now and Kamensky knew it. But Carlos, thinking on the matter, decided that Kamensky, abandoning himself to emotion, felt that he had to make the effort. He had to do something, and he had the sort of mind that would perceive the lasting damage to himself of committing an act of treachery and disguising it as an act of atonement. There was no question of Kolka staying in Christendom; he was an incurable Russian, he longed to return to Russia, he would never leave it once he did go back. Kamensky knew all that because he was the same. Later Kolka told Carlos that Kamensky had told him that he, Kolka, was the breathing apparatus that Kamensky needed to live in the poisonous air of a country other than Russia.

What the NKVD wanted was simple. Some time before, the secret police of the Spanish Republic had found several hundred bourgeois hiding in the deserted Finnish Embassy in Madrid. The NKVD had located another abandoned building, also a former embassy. They were going to hoist the flag of some remote Asiatic country over it, and hope that secret Nationalists would seek refuge there. There was a list of people, some of them Fascist agents, some of them Anarchists whom the Soviet apparatus wanted to destroy, some of them Social Democrats, some of them merely men the NKVD wanted to kill for their own reasons. Many of these last two classes were friends of Kamensky. The NKVD wanted Kamensky to warn them that death warrants were out for them, and to tell them where the false embassy was so that they could take refuge there. The bargain was struck; it would have terrified a man who had a smaller appetite for guilt than Kamensky, or who loved the man he was saving less than Kamensky loved Kolka Zhigalko.

Kamensky lured his friends to the embassy, one after the other. The NKVD listened to their conversations with hidden microphones. Then they killed them – twenty-seven murders altogether. The victims were taken into the basement and shot. Their last sight was the heap of the dead who had come down the stairs before them. Before each execution – the executioners had the condemned kneel in order to receive a revolver bullet in the spinal cord in the *descabello* style of the NKVD – they told the man who was to die that Kamensky was the one who had betrayed him.

At the end of it, the NKVD man delivered the transcripts and the pictures and the negatives to Kamensky. He told him what had been done in the cellar of the false embassy.

'Your class believes in God,' the NKVD man said. 'Think of it, highness – twenty-seven souls ascending to the Heavenly Father, cursing your name as they fly to Him.'

'Go away,' said Kamensky.

'Before I do,' said the NKVD man, 'I wish to tell you that you were entrapped. Kolka Zhigalko is, and always has been, our agent. He ——ed you on our orders and ——ed you, and ——ed you.'

As he spoke these words, the NKVD man turned over the photographs of the acts that he was describing with his obscenities. Another man might have attacked. Kamensky had already made his gesture. Now he sealed himself from the NKVD man. He stared at him, absolutely cold and absolutely silent, until he went away. Of course what Kamensky had been told about Kolka was a lie; it was payment for the slaps on the face he had delivered to the NKVD man. But how could Kamensky ever be certain? All Carlos's life he had heard the phrase, never knowing what it meant, but now he saw it in reality: Kamensky's heart was broken.

He stayed in Madrid for a few more days, until the siege was lifted. He remained with Kolka, who of course suspected nothing. He thought Kamensky's sadness had to do with the fact that he would be sent by his paper to some other city, and thus be separated from Kolka. But Kolka told him not to worry, he'd find a way to be sent where Kamensky was, nothing could part them. He pleaded with Kamensky to return to Russia; Zhigalko had powerful friends in the Party, even in the NKVD, he said, and he could make things all right. Kamensky knew nothing could make him acceptable in Russia, but to please Kolka he agreed that he would, perhaps go back.

Then Kamensky, one night on a dark street, walked up behind the NKVD man and shot him in the head. He immediately left Madrid. He did not say goodbye to Kolka, he took no clothes, none of his things. He just left.

Of course there was an uproar in the clandestine world. Kamensky was sought everywhere in Spain, but he got away. Kolka was inconsolable. He lived in darkness – darkness of two kinds, the despair of the loss of love, and ignorance of why the loss had befallen him. No one told him the truth. Not Kamensky, not the other Russian Communists, not Carlos. To console himself, Kolka Zhigalko, with manic energy, wrote a cycle of poems and short stories, beautiful things. André Girard read them and told

Carlos about them. He made copies for safekeeping. André did not trust the revolution; he knew that it would burn the books and slash the paintings of its artists.

Carlos read Kolka's work. It burned the page in his untidy, almost illiterate handwriting, tiny and cramped, as if no sheet of paper were large enough to contain all that Kolka wanted to put down on it. Out of this crabbed pen flowed the whole of human passion, the whole of the landscape of our time.

Carlos went to see Kolka, to express his admiration. The loss of Kamensky and, Carlos supposed, the expenditure of energy in the writing of the wonderful stories and verses, had left Kolka exhausted. He was translucent again, as he had been when he gave too much of his blood to the wounded. There was no gaiety left in him. To Carlos he said, 'I have lost everything.' Carlos asked him what he meant. In that innocent, reckless way of his, Kolka told him of the love affair with Kamensky.

'You may think it filthy, but I tell you it was love!' Kolka said.

'I know it was love,' Carlos replied.

Carlos had decided that Kolka, to be saved, must know the truth. Carlos took a hideous chance: he told Kolka what had been done to Kamensky, and what Kamensky had done for him. Kolka slumped. The life, the optimism, the force of hope – whatever it was he had that made him believe that he and his comrades had made a new world, ran out of him. Illusion drained from Kolka. It was like watching a man bleed to death from a heart wound. Kolka said nothing; he had no last words as the old Kolka. Carlos, by telling him the truth, had killed what he had been.

'The secret police,' Kolka said, and this was his only question, 'they must have had a code name for him. What was it?'

'Kiril Alekseivich Kamensky,' Carlos replied.

'Thank you, Carlos,' said Kolka.

Kolka Zhigalko took the pages of his stories and crossed out his own name. In its place, under each title, he wrote, in cyrillic characters twice as large as any others on the page, BY KIRIL ALEKSEIVICH KAMENSKY. Later he instructed André Girard to change the author's name on his copies of the works; he didn't tell André the reason, merely that he had decided to write under a pseudonym.

A month or two later, Kolka went back to Russia. He did have powerful friends, and through their intervention he changed his name in a Soviet court to Kiril Alekseivich Kamensky, which is the name under which he has been known ever since.

(Don Jorge de Rodegas ceased speaking; Cathy was sitting at his feet, gazing up into his face, over which no emotion had moved while he spoke. 'Go on,' Cathy said, 'don't stop. What happened to them all?')

Kolka Zhigalko published his stories, under his new name, in the Soviet Union when he returned there. In a matter of months his work was seized and burnt, and he was sentenced to prison. Most Russians who had been in Spain were shot or imprisoned in the great purge of 1937, the Yezhovschina, a bloodbath named for Yezhov, then head of the NKVD. Evidently not even Yezhov could bear to kill Kolka; he merely sent him to prison for life.

Carlos was arrested by the victors at the end of the war. He was sent to prison for an interval. There he learned a number of things, a prisoner's skills and tricks.

(Don Jorge folded a sheet of writing paper into an intricate pattern and made a little cup; he poured wine into it, held the paper cup over a candle flame, and showed Cathy that the wine was boiling while the paper did not burn.)

After a time, Carlos was condemned to death. He was taken out of his cell by the guards. The other prisoners saw a man killed by a firing squad in the prison yard. It was not Carlos. Elsewhere in the prison he was being fitted secretly into the uniform of a major in the Nationalist Army, and in those clothes he walked out of the prison and back to his true identity. He returned to the *estancia*. He rejoined his uncles. From them he heard the story of his fiancée's death, almost four years before. They thought it a most pathetic tale. Carlos was not much moved by it. He had lost the habit of judging people by the way they died.

Carlos wanted silence; he wanted to be alone. He remained on the *estancia*. He was haunted by the work he had done during the Civil War and tried to train himself not to dream. In 1941 he volunteered for the División Azul, the Spanish force that fought in Russia with the German Army, and was wounded again. Each time his troops liberated a prison camp on Soviet territory he looked for Kolka, but of course he never found him.

Carlos did have communication of a sort with Kolka. While he was recovering at the *estancia* in 1944 from the wounds he had received in Russia, he had a visitor. The man he had known as

André Girard walked up the drive one spring afternoon, carrying a child. André had seen a photograph of Carlos at a sporting event in a Spanish magazine, and had recognized him. He knew his true identity. There was no question of his betraying it; he was sick of revolution and reprisal. Like Carlos he had given up politics. The child belonged to the woman Solange, who had been Kamensky's lover in Madrid before Kolka. André knew nothing of what had happened between Kolka and Kamensky. Carlos told him nothing. Solange had told him nothing, even though she had taken André as a lover – the tale she had told Carlos when she was still hot with scorn is not one a woman would tell to a new bedmate. André said she had died in the mountains on the escape from France. André did not know what to do with the child. Carlos took it and kept it until the war was over; afterwards he sent it to France, to Solange's people. André made the arrangements.

Carlos asked André if he still had in his possession Kolka's stories and poems from Madrid. He did. Carlos gave André money, after the end of the European war, to have these things published in the West, in Russian and in other languages. They were, of course, published under the name Kamensky. Carlos was pleased to think that Kolka's work, some of it at least, had been kept alive.

'That can't be the end of the tale,' said Cathy. 'What about the original Kamensky? You haven't told us what happened to him.'

'Carlos never heard news of him.'

'What was his real name? Did he go back to Russia?'

'His real name was Prince Boris Donskoy. He was of the oldest Russian nobility. It was impossible for him to go back to his own country.'

Christopher spoke. 'Under what name did Carlos and Zhigalko and the others know Kamensky, in Madrid?'

'Otto Rothchild,' replied Don Jorge de Rodegas.

Eighteen

I

'All of them, one after the other,' Patchen said. 'Dick Sutherland, each time he had news of another killing, would lay a cable from Moscow on my desk like a cat bringing a dead mouse into the parlour.'

After the searing light of the Castilian Meseta, the August sun in Paris seemed feeble to Christopher; it hardly penetrated the cloth of his coat, but there was perspiration on Patchen's face. He had been waiting, alone with the consequences of their plans, for Christopher to return. As much as anything could be for Patchen, this operation was a personal matter. In the months since the death of Bülow, he had acknowledged to himself, bit by bit, that he had put his trust in the wrong people. His picked assets had gone bad. The worst thing that could befall an intelligence officer had happened to him.

Patchen had intellectual stamina and emotional control, but his body displayed the strain of sleeplessness and incessant travel. He had lost weight and the stringy musculature of his neck showed above his collar. He limped more than usual and sometimes he caught himself as he began to stammer.

'First there was Kalmyk,' Patchen said. 'You were right. That was the opening. Then they rolled up the other couriers, there were two of them. Sutherland has their names, not that it matters. They were patriots. One of them was even a KGB man of medium rank, a Scandinavian specialist, so that he must have been the one who mailed the letters from Helsinki for Kamensky.'

As a matter of routine, the KGB took Kamensky's girl, Masha, in for interrogation. She knew nothing of the courier network, nothing of *The Little Death*. Naturally her interrogators didn't believe her. Masha had been dealing with the KGB for ten years, since she was sixteen; she knew what they were. She held out for a long time. Sutherland's source said they used the soft method on her – kept her standing and sleepless, stripped, without food and water, with relays of interrogators repeating the questions, never stopping. What was her name? Her father's name? Her mother's? School? Who was her KGB trainer when she was recruited for special work? What were the names of the men and women she had entrapped for the KGB? What was her grandfather's name? What was the cover name used by her American case officer? What was her blood type? At what age did she lose her virginity? When was her last meeting with the Agency contact? Did she masturbate? How much did the Americans pay her? What was her grandmother's father's name? Where was she born? What did Kamensky's Agency contact look like?

Finally she broke. She had nothing to tell them. She had been cleanly handled by a good officer – brush contacts in the subway, dead-drops behind a radiator in an apartment building where her KGB handler met her. That particular insult, a typical Agency prank, infuriated them. They kept hammering away at *The Little Death* – how did Kamensky get it to the Americans? Masha must have carried it, handled it. She could tell them less than the couriers had told them – she didn't even know that the book existed. The couriers had had no contact with any American. Captain Kamlyk described Horst Bülow, but he couldn't identify him in the photo album. Of course he couldn't put a name to him. Kalmyk was an Army officer, not a trained observer. Bülow, from his description, could have been any of ten thousand shabby East Germans.

They killed Masha as they had killed the couriers; they knew that all of them were utterly wrung out, that they could not tell the KGB the one thing that would make sense of this whole shameful defeat for Soviet security – that treason had been committed, that the smuggling of Kamensky's manuscript and its publication in the West was an American operation. Even the surfacing of Cerutti did not tell them that; whatever else he had been he had never been an asset of the Americans. Now the Soviets put surveillance on him, replaced the wires that Wilson had removed. But Cerutti was in quarantine. He'd never see another American operative – not Christopher, not Joëlle, not a young man in a park, not anyone. Even under torture, Cerutti could not reveal that he had been dealing with the Americans, because Christopher had never disclosed his true nationality or his true name or his true purpose.

'Maria knew well enough what the Russians would be up to as soon as the news of Kamensky's death hit,' Patchen said. 'She picked a fight with Cerutti when he came around with his weekly bottle of champagne, threw him out. She called him a disgusting little fat Frog who made her skin crawl. Told him Otto had never liked him, thought he was a joke.'

'What was Cerutti's reaction to that?'

'He put the question to Otto: Is that what you feel, my friend? Otto said yes. Maria, he said, you didn't need to be so brutal, I asked you not to be insulting. She said, what other method would have worked with this cretin? Cerutti left. He made no reply to them.'

'So the opposition won't connect him to Otto at all?'

'Not unless they've done it in the past. He sure won't go back to the Île St Louis.'

Christopher asked about Kamensky's death. He and Patchen were walking slowly towards the Orangerie, with the morning light behind them and the greenery of the Tuileries ahead. Patchen was breathing more heavily than usual, suppressing the grunt of pain that rose in his throat each time he swung his wounded leg. Christopher had to ask him again for details. Patchen stopped by the stairs that divide the long riverside terrace and surrendered momentarily to his body; he sat down on a bench and stretched his bad leg before him. He looked around. They were quite alone, the city was empty of Frenchmen this month and it was too early in the day for tourists.

'What Kamensky did,' Patchen said in his toneless murmur, 'was to ask Masha to get him a death pill.'

Christopher, when he was examining data in his hotel room, had studied a photograph of Kamensky, the only one in the possession of American intelligence. It was a good clear picture, taken in strong sunlight, of an old man with the shaved head of a prisoner, sitting on a bench against an unpainted lumber wall. Now Christopher saw Kolka Zhigalko, young and passionate, moving within the old man.

'Masha was stung by the request,' Patchen said. 'She used her emergency procedure – a God-damned chalk mark on a Moscow wall her American case officer has to drive by on the way to work, wouldn't you know? – to ask for a meeting. She asked *us* for two cyanide pills.'

'She was going with him?'

'That's what Sutherland says. She told the case officer that she loved the old man. If he dies, there's no sense in scum like me living, she said.'

Of course Kamensky's request was never considered. To have him die and to have cyanide found in his body tissue at the autopsy would have been all the confirmation needed by the KGB that a foreign intelligence service was involved with him. Where else would he get cyanide? Besides, Kamensky's request shook the Moscow station. Did Kamensky know, somehow, of Masha's connection with our side? Masha said no – he must have assumed, as any rational man would, that she was a KGB asset. Why he thought the Soviet service would give Masha poison was not explicable. Perhaps he thought she had a sexual hold over a senior officer; perhaps he thought they'd be happy to have him out of the way. That was what she told the interrogators in the cellars of the KGB. She stuck to that point to the end. Nothing would make her accept the possibility, even, that Kamensky had a connection with an imperialist secret service. In the end she admitted everything, would have done anything. She was too tired to resist death, and she was only twenty-six years old. But she stubbornly insisted, up to the instant that she fell like a stone with a bullet in her spine, that Kiril Alekseivich Kamensky was incapable of treason. '*He is a Russian!*' she had cried over and over as they had pounded the question into her.

'It says quite a lot about Kamensky,' Patchen said.

'Yes. How did he die, finally?'

Patchen shrugged. 'Here Sutherland's magical sources within the Kremlin break down. We don't know. The Russians say heart attack. Of course, Masha was gone by the time he died, so we had no eyewitness. He may have killed himself in some more orthodox way.'

'He wasn't arrested?'

'No. Absolutely not. The Politburo was running the show after Kamensky's novel went on the air. It was a major policy decision – kill Kamensky as a lesson to others and take the punishment in the Western press, or let him live for a year or two and take the ten thousand lashes of his novel? They didn't know what to do.'

'Why would a man like that kill himself?'

Patchen held out a hand. Christopher took it and helped him to his feet. They watched a pleasure boat move down the brown river.

'I don't know, Paul. To do it himself.'

The state had permitted a funeral. Brave friends of the dead man had come to the grave. Some of them were writers, painters, poets, musicians who had been in the camps for decades along with Kamensky. No one had seen them in all that time, Kamensky had summoned ghosts as his pallbearers. Some of them fell to their knees in the dirt by the grave and prayed. One man recited a long poem of Kamensky's, written years before and suppressed in the USSR since the purges of the thirties. A secret policeman had taken motion pictures of the scene, standing on one side of the grave with his whirring camera while the mourners stood on the other.

There had been a long, emotional story about the funeral in the Western papers. In the Soviet press, Kamensky's death had not been noticed. Patchen, knowing that there had been scant coverage in the Spanish newspapers, had brought some clippings. Christopher read them while Patchen waited.

'The Russian text is out, the French will be published in three weeks,' Patchen said. 'Cerutti has made agreements for translations into English and all the European languages plus Japanese. He's sold serial rights in German and French. He's going to New York to offer your English translation to the big magazines.'

Christopher folded the clippings and gave them back to Patchen.

'So, from that point of view,' Patchen said, 'it's a picture-book operation, a Rothchild special.'

When Wilson joined them, by the Orangerie, Christopher repeated what he had already told Patchen about his findings in Spain. The Security man listened, inclining his head to catch Christopher's words; his low voice was lost sometimes in the sudden yowls of traffic in the Place de la Concorde.

'That's almost the last thing I would have guessed,' Wilson said. 'You're sure Rodegas is believable?'

'Either that or he's a better novelist than Kamensky.'

'But nothing ever showed up even to hint that Rothchild was queer,' Wilson said. He couldn't accept that twenty years of files, scrupulously kept by men like himself, could omit the central fact about a subject.

'He's not a homosexual. Neither was Kamensky. Something happened between them in Madrid – time and place and circumstance. What if they hadn't been drunk that first night? What if they hadn't spoken the same language? What if Solange had not aroused them sexually to begin with? What if, what if? It happened by accident.'

'And Rothchild has been paying for it in his soul ever since.'

This observation, coming from Wilson, startled Christopher. He looked sharply into the security man's face, to see if it was the joke he had expected from him, but he saw only an expression of pity.

'No wonder he eluded the polygraph,' Wilson said. 'The two unforgivable sins – a homosexual act that laid him open to blackmail and a past connection to the Russian intelligence service – were crawling under his skin, waiting for the machine.'

Patchen asked Wilson what he was going to do.

'Report.'

'Of course,' Patchen said, 'but when?'

'After Paul's report moves. This is your asset, and you two got him. Christopher did much more than I did. He was the one who flushed the bird and shot it. I'm just the retriever.'

Patchen, in the presence of Wilson, had covered the signs of his physical pain, and of whatever else he felt. Wilson had little to tell them. He had sent Joëlle and her companion on an operation in French Africa; they'd be gone for at least six months. 'We'll keep moving them as long as it seems wise,' he said, 'there's plenty for them to do in faraway places.' Patchen nodded; he wasn't really interested. He assumed that Wilson, having been instructed to do so, would clean up all the contacts with Cerutti. Joëlle, in her last report, had told Wilson that Cerutti had picked up the Soviet surveillance. 'I really don't think he ever noticed that we were dancing with him,' Wilson said. Somewhere, Christopher thought, a Soviet security man is telling himself the same thing.

'If I may ask,' Wilson said, 'what are *you* going to do?'

He knew already that Patchen and Christopher were on their way to call on the Rothchilds.

'Do?' Patchen replied. 'What is there to do? Talk. See what we can salvage.'

'There's this question – has Rothchild been working for the opposition all along, for the whole twenty years? It's unlike them not to move in on a man they've got something on.'

Wilson was addressing himself to Christopher. Patchen waited for the reply, as interested as Wilson.

'That's a question someone else will have to ask,' Christopher said. 'We always assume, about everyone, that the answer is yes. Everyone is considered to be opposition. If, then, it turns out, the one time in fifty thousand, that they really are, the safeguards are in place.'

'That's not really the assumption everyone made about Rothchild in your shop, Paul. He knows everyone.'

'Not quite everyone,' Christopher said.

Patchen and Wilson discussed technical arrangements. The exchange lasted longer than Patchen thought necessary, but he controlled his impatience. Wilson explained everything that had to do with equipment very carefully, and then repeated it. Men who lived with secret mechanical paraphernalia were like the natives of a great city – they didn't believe that strangers could find their way through lighted and well-marked streets. At another time Christopher might have laughed at the expression, somewhere between courteous patience and murderous exasperation, that flickered in Patchen's eyes as Wilson, staring at the ground, made sure that he understood the obvious.

There would be no need, after today, for Wilson and Christopher to see one another. Both knew it was possible that they could work for twenty years in their own compartments and never catch sight of each other again. Wilson, finished with Patchen, gave him an embarrassed little nod and walked to where Christopher was leaning against the base of a statue. Wilson put an arm across Christopher's shoulders and led him to the other side of the pedestal.

'I don't know what to say to you,' Wilson said. 'It's been a pleasure working with a professional. This ought to be a great moment for me. If it's worth anything to you, I don't feel any better about the way this has turned out than I imagine you do.'

'I know that.'

Wilson tapped, through the shiny cloth of his suit, the stack of index cards that he carried in his inside pocket. 'Nothing goes back to Washington from me except what's on these cards,' he said. 'Only what's relevant. Cathy's private life is not relevant.'

Wilson looked into Christopher's face, he had given up altogether the habit of avoiding his eyes, and began a phrase. He broke it off. 'I'll be glad to get home,' he said, 'it's been one hell of a long TDY. I miss my kids. I don't know how you do it, moving around all the time the way you do.'

'You get used to it.'

'I wouldn't.'

Wilson shook hands. Christopher was surprised – the act was insecure; Wilson believed that public contacts drew less attention if they were broken off without any sign of a goodbye. Wilson took a step away and then came back. He decided, after all, to say what he had to say.

'Moroni is back in Rome,' he said. 'The station sighted him with Klimenko. And there's this, from the German girl. Moroni's taking Dexedrine by the bottle, he's raving about Cathy; the German girl thinks he's crazy. Your wife did something to him in Spain, humiliated him somehow. He's looking for Cathy. If I were you, if I could find a way, I'd lock the door.'

Christopher nodded. He thanked Wilson, to make him feel less uncomfortable. Wilson touched him again, two soft punches on the arm. One for my agent, one for my wife, Christopher thought.

'Life's a bastard,' Wilson said.

Cathy, after they had heard Don Jorge de Rodegas's tale at the *estancia*, had taken Christopher into the gardens, and with the moon on one horizon and the dawn on the other, had enumerated for him all of her acts. He didn't try to stop her. Something in the story that Rodegas had told had released her from her idea that she must make a life for herself that was as dark as she imagined Christopher's to be.

'I don't want secrets, Paul,' she had said. 'I never wanted them. I never wanted lovers. I don't want someone telling my story when I'm old like Maria's husband, and trying to *guess* the truth. I want it known that it wasn't love with anyone but you. I want you to know why. You can bear anything, can't you?'

'Not very much more of this.'

'Say that again.'

'Not very much more of this,' Christopher repeated. He felt tears on his cheeks. Cathy watched their track on his face. Even she looked pallid and drawn after the long sleepless night listening to the dry voice of Rodegas. That I should cry, Christopher thought, and she should look less than beautiful – we must have escaped from the galaxy. She began a long, slow smile, and so did he; all around them the waters of Don Jorge's garden played, catching the light and breaking the silence.

Nineteen

I

Patchen went upstairs first, and Christopher, waiting in the street below, saw him come on to the balcony of the Rothchilds' apartment and look for a moment at the sunset. When he went inside again, he closed the french doors behind him so that the noise of the evening traffic would not interfere with the microphone Wilson had installed in his briefcase. Christopher waited a little longer, to give Patchen time to tell Rothchild that Kamensky had killed himself.

When Christopher entered the sitting room, Otto Rothchild pulled himself out of the depths of his chair and stood on his feet. The effort shrank his skin; his nostrils opened and his lips pulled back, exposing the teeth. The lamps had not been lighted and the room, filled with Rothchild's treasures, was in shadow except for two diagonals of sunlight falling through the west windows. Rothchild, leaving his walking sticks against the arm of his chair, groped his way across the dim room, moving from one piece of furniture to another like an exhausted swimmer floundering in the debris of a shipwreck. He seized Christopher's shoulders. There was real strength in his bony hands but no temperature. The two men had not been so close together for a year. Rothchild no longer smelled like a male, of liquor and smoke and sweat; his breath and skin emitted a bitter odour, not quite bile and not quite urine, that came from deep within his body.

'David has told me about Kamensky,' Rothchild said. 'You were right, Paul.' He swayed and tightened his grip; Christopher felt a tremor of physical weakness run through Rothchild's body like a shiver of disgust. 'But, Paul, *I* was right, too,' he said. 'Kamensky wanted his work and his name to live – believe me, that's the truth. We made that possible for him.'

Rothchild tugged at the cloth of the younger man's coat; he wanted to return to his chair. Christopher, his arms hanging at his sides, made no move to help him. Maria put down her glass and crossed to them. Frowning, she supported Rothchild, step by shuffling step, and when he was sitting again, smoothed his clothes and rearranged the things on his table – the Evian water, the crystal goblet, the reading glasses, the copy of the Russian version of Kamensky's novel, fresh and smelling of ink. Rothchild's place was marked by a silver paper knife.

Breathing in through his mouth and out through his nose, Rothchild waited until he had recovered his voice. Then he tapped the cover of Kamensky's book, printed on coarse yellow paper like that used in the packages of cheap French cigarettes, and pointed a finger at Christopher.

'If one had to die for a book, for one piece of work,' Rothchild said, 'would you say Kamensky chose well?'

'*Chose* to die?'

Rothchild's eyes, now that he was rested after his journey across the carpet, were bright with interest. Waiting for Christopher to speak again, Rothchild's gaze rested on Patchen, as if he could read the meaning of Christopher's words on the other man's face. Maria made a drink for Christopher and brought it to him; he waved it away. Rothchild watched; a smile came and went on his lips.

'Not drinking, Paul?' Maria said; and, smiling at Patchen: 'It's a bad sign when Paul doesn't drink his Scotch. It means he's going to stop being quiet.'

Patchen cleared his throat, as if he were going to spit. The noise seemed doubly rude, coming from this fastidious man, and Maria, still bent at the waist, turned her head to look at him. Her dark hair, heavy and gleaming from the brush, fell away from her cheek. She

261

frowned in puzzlement, then began to smile, ready to turn the sound Patchen had made into a joke. But when she saw his face, the expression drained from her own. There exists a device, used in safe rooms where secrets are stored, that senses the body heat of an intruder and sets off an alarm. Maria's nervous system worked in the same way. She waited, frozen, for Patchen to speak.

'Any other intelligence service,' Patchen said, 'would kill you both.'

Maria, Christopher knew, rarely smoked in Rothchild's presence, and never in this room where he kept his carpets and his paintings. But now she took a Gauloise from a package in the pocket of her skirt and lit it. Just as she always did, she inhaled one enormous·lungful of smoke. Her breasts swelled and her diaphragm expanded; she exhaled the rank smoke in a long, thin plume and snuffed out the cigarette. With the same gesture, she picked up Christopher's glass. Her face was no more than a foot from his. Her teeth clicked and Christopher heard this sound; he caught the scent of shampoo in her hair.

'Maria,' Christopher said, 'didn't you think it was odd, all these months, that there was no surveillance on you at all?'

Maria put Christopher's brimming drink back on the table. She spilled only a little of it. She walked away from him, backwards across the patterns in the carpet, and sat down in her own chair. She crossed her legs, the fine ankles, the swelling calves, the long straight bone of the shins. Her eyes widened and she gave a shriek of laughter. Rothchild flinched. Moments passed; Maria watched Christopher, the muscles in her face tight with the effort of suppressing another outburst of laughter.

'All right, Paul,' she said. 'What was the mistake?'

Christopher took the long butt of her cigarette out of the ashtray and showed it to her. 'Smoking like that, when you were setting up Horst Bülow in the Tiergarten,' he said.

Maria uncrossed her legs. She smiled – not her quick white smile but the slow, tight-lipped one that let her mind show in her eyes. She was concealing nothing now. Her body relaxed, she sipped her drink, and when she spoke there was a current of mirth in her voice.

'The man in the Tyrolean hat,' she said.

'In the Tiergarten, the week of Otto's surgery. Yes.'

'I thought he was opposition. Why would you have surveillance on Bülow? Otto agreed – play the odds, he said.'

Rothchild spoke Maria's name and then he coughed and spoke to her again in a stronger voice. Maria shook her hair, flushed, looked at herself in the mirror beyond Rothchild; he took the chain of mannerisms for an apology and subsided.

Patchen said, 'I want Maria to talk, Otto. We don't know quite everything yet.'

Neither does Maria, Christopher thought. She was enjoying the moment; her eyes, glowing with intelligence, searched the faces of the three men. She was flushed, a little short of breath. Christopher thought that she looked dishevelled, like a woman who had heard her husband's key turn in the lock as she lay in the arms of a lover, and, moments later, having thrown on her clothes and thrust the pins back into her hair, was making small talk with the cuckold. She gave Rothchild a look filled with mischief and Christopher saw why she loved him. No one had ever outwitted Rothchild. She thought he was invulnerable.

'Have you an accusation to make?' Rothchild asked.

'You murdered Bülow,' Patchen said. 'You caused Kamensky's suicide.'

Rothchild nodded his head, an abrupt movement, after each of Patchen's sentences. Patchen's voice was calm.

'You did what you did for reasons of ego,' Patchen said.

This time Rothchild made no gesture of assent. Maria gave Christopher a sardonic glance, to see if he realized how laughable Patchen's statement was.

'You lied to Paul, you lied to me, you lied to the outfit,' Patchen said.

Rothchild's throat was dry. Labouriously, he swivelled his torso, lifted his arm, picked up his glass, drank.

'On the contrary,' he said, 'I tried from the beginning to make you listen to the truth.'

2

'Maria will talk, I haven't voice enough,' Rothchild said. 'First, Paul, let me pay you the compliment of saying that you're a dangerous man. We always knew it. Maria and I saw that you'd be maddened by the idea of sacrificing Kamensky. Murder drives you crazy, everyone knows that about you. Evidently you can only cure yourself of the psychosis by solving the crime. It's a weakness, this refusal to let well enough alone. In the end it may kill you.' Rothchild turned his smile – undamaged teeth, square and white against his sallow skin – on Patchen. 'It *will* kill him,' he said, a reasonable man stating a reasonable proposition. He waved his hand, an apology for having taken up time in putting words to something they all knew. Maria waited, the smile of affection for Christopher lingering on her lips, until Rothchild told her to begin speaking.

'I can't speak for Otto,' she said, 'but what I thought was this: Kiril Kamensky, with his novel, had done his one last great thing. Why shouldn't Otto do his? As young men they were side by side, genius and genius. Let them end in the same way.'

When Kamensky's letter came in the Christmas mail, Rothchild had trembled with excitement. He had recognized the handwriting on the envelope as one would know the face of a friend seen by chance after many years – changed but still the same. Only days before, Rothchild had spoken to his medical specialists. They had told him that his blood pressure had begun to destroy his kidneys, that it could explode blood vessels in his brain, that it would kill him. They offered him a reprieve: the surgery in Zürich.

Maria said, 'The chief doctor told me this, I have the words by heart: "The body of Monsieur Rothchild, if he consents to the surgery, will be like a sleeping foot. His brain will be salvaged, he can live a life of the intellect, if not of the senses. Madame, at his age what do the senses matter?"'

Rothchild went out of the specialist's *cabinet* ready to choose death. For days afterwards, Maria watched Rothchild pass through spasms of drunkenness, sexual passion, eating; he commanded Maria to telephone to restaurants and order veal Orloff, tournedos Rossini, *Chartreuse de perdreaux*, sweetbreads *à la financière au vol-au-vent* – the glutton's dishes he had eaten at his father's table in his vanished Russia. To Maria he spoke only Russian. All his life Rothchild had lived in episodes, dwelling for a while in the intellect so as to be able to gratify the senses; he had always believed that his exceptional brain made exceptional pleasure possible. 'What I'm offered,' he told Maria, 'is a choice between two kinds of death, one where I will perceive light and one where I will not.'

Kamensky's letter, the image of Kamensky's novel, hidden like an infant cancer in the hated body of Soviet Russia, sending out signals to summon the blood supply that would make its growth possible, brought Rothchild back to life again. He would arrange the needed transfusion. 'This is too simple a way to say this,' Maria said, 'but Otto stopped seeing his surgery as the disconnection of his appetites. He began to see it – and how could anyone be more professional than this? – he began to see it as *cover*.' Rothchild saw a way to execute a brilliant operation, the last of his career, while he lay unconscious in a hospital. The elegance of it, the humour, were irresistible.

Rothchild had Maria arrange a date for his surgery. He thought no more about the invasion of his body. His mind was fully engaged in planning the operation that would bring Kamensky's book out of Russia, publish it in the West, put a seal on fame for both of them, overturn the security of the Soviet apparatus and the American service at the same time.

'For Kamensky,' Maria said, 'Otto wanted just what he's told you he wanted – his true place among the great writers. What I wanted for Otto, what I know he wanted for himself, was his own true place. After all he's done, David, after all he's meant to the world, Otto may lie in an unmarked grave. But some of us, the ones Otto cares about, ought to know where it is. That's not so much to desire.'

Rothchild told Patchen about Kamensky's letter. Patchen agreed to have the manuscript brought out. Rothchild suggested having it received in East Germany by an American asset; Maria, knowing the files, knowing that Patchen would trust no one but Christopher to handle the courier, knew that no agent except Bülow could possibly be used.

'We never spoke Bülow's name to David,' Maria said. 'Otto knew he'd give the job to Paul; I knew Paul had no one except Horst Bülow who could do the job.'

Otto and Maria, on the day before Epiphany, took the train to Zürich. Christopher imagined them: rising early, taking a taxi to the Gare de Lyon and then the express to Switzerland, Otto buying newspapers and magazines even as the train began to move out of the station, running after it with Maria pulling his hand, making incessant witticisms, eating too little and drinking too much, refusing to look out the window of the train as it passed through France because even the loveliest country in Europe was not worth looking at; he had not seen beauty, except in paintings, since he left Russia.

'David was resisting us, and we knew why,' Maria said. 'Paul was Otto's case officer, and David knew what Paul would say – wait, as Kamensky had asked, wait for Kamensky to die; keep him safe. Otto doesn't like scruples. Paul is too American for him. David is a little better – he's a scrupulous man who does unscrupulous things for practical reasons. He's under the spell of his ideals – America is the good guy, so anything goes as long as America wins. Paul *hates* ideals, he believes that nothing matters except keeping absolute faith with other human beings, each as an individual, one at a time. It's his strength, but Otto is right – one day he'll die of it.'

Maria was sitting on the sofa now, with her legs curled beneath her skirt, and she picked up Christopher's hand and patted it, as though her touch was necessary to take the sting from her words. 'Otto saw that we had to have a more powerful argument than the ones Paul would make,' Maria said. 'We knew that if Bülow was killed before Paul's eyes, even he would have to consider the possibility that the Russians had done the murder. I told Otto Paul would find out the truth in the end. He knew I was right. All Otto wanted was a few weeks of grace, so that we could do what had to be done, stay ahead of Paul if only by a step, run the operation right. It took cold hearts to do what had to be done. But we had to do it. Kiril Kamensky, alive, was an obscure ex-convict, living in a *dacha*, fornicating with a young girl. Dead, he was a martyr – and we could make him into an immortal.'

Maria was still holding Christopher's hand. 'We had to find a way to block you out, Paul,' she said. 'I'm sorry. I *hated* using you, using what's so good in you, this passion you have for the idea of trust, your conscience. But friendship is friendship, and business is business.'

Maria would have stopped here; she had replied at great length to Patchen's terse accusation. Christopher knew the Rothchilds; he knew that they had rehearsed this scene, divided their confession into segments. Maria wouldn't lie, but she demanded evidence of her own guilt before she would confirm it. She watched her face in the looking glass; she squeezed Christopher's hand. Her palm was damp, her fingers twisted in Christopher's, but these were her only involuntary reactions.

266

'Maria,' Christopher said. 'The transfer from Otto's numbered account to the Berliner Bank. The passports you got from the Abwehr forger in Zürich. Schaefer.'

Rothchild roused. 'All that was my work,' he said. 'The bank transfer wasn't much of a risk. You surprise me, Paul. Nothing is secure. That's the old, best rule.'

In Zürich, Rothchild went openly from the train to the bank and transferred the funds for Bülow to Berlin.

'Maria was taking all the chances,' Rothchild said. 'I thought I might die in the clinic, after all they were opening me up from pubis to jawbone. I wanted to leave a trace of evidence, not enough to be easily discovered, but enough to make it possible for you to think I'd done it all, for Maria to go away from this clean.'

While Rothchild was prepared for surgery, Maria picked up the false passports: one for Maria, one for Bülow. She sat in the clinic during the surgery. Rothchild was unconscious. ('I was riding on billows of morphia,' Rothchild said, 'I thought I saw Maria lean over me, kiss me, then go; it may have been a delusion. I was hallucinating. I thought they had disembowelled me, that the tubes in my arms and legs were electrical, that I had been made into a machine; I smelled ozone as if my breath were electrically charged. Sometimes I still smell it.')

While Rothchild lay in the clinic, Maria flew to Berlin. She took an early flight, leaving Zürich just after dawn; she had lunch on the Kurfürstendamm, too much vinegar on the beef, half-cooked potatoes, pale bitter beer. She took the S-Bahn to East Berlin and mailed Otto's frightening letter to Horst Bülow, typed on a German machine in perfect German. It mentioned names, a long neat list of them, men and women Bülow had sent to their deaths in France, names taken from records that Bülow had been promised would be destroyed. The letter told Bülow to await another contact.

Maria had to do the whole job in a single day. She had to be back at Rothchild's bedside when he regained consciousness, she had told the doctor she was going to sleep while her husband did not need her. She was, in fact, exhausted when she reached the Schaefer Baths. 'It wasn't a bad place to rest,' Maria said. 'I *ached*. The steam took some of the kinks out, and I slept for a while, waiting for Schaefer to come to work before the nighttime crowd. You can just stretch out on a bench, like a derelict.'

There was no difficulty in arranging for the murder of Horst Bülow. Maria showed Schaefer a series of 35 mm contact prints, photographs of documents that could send Schaefer to prison for life; he read them with a magnifying glass. He spoke Rothchild's wartime cover name, Jaguar. Schaefer ran his eye over Maria's body, cupped his hands in the empty air as if he were holding her breasts. 'I saw he meant it as a compliment to Otto, that Otto was still alive and had a woman as young as I, but God it was disgusting,' Maria said.

Schaefer, after he recovered from the shock of blackmail, was amused. Maria had never arranged for the death of another person before that night with Schaefer. 'When we first began talking about it, never uttering the specific words – murder, killing, what *do* you say? I wasn't trained by the outfit for this work – at first, I was a little sick. I knew Bülow from the files. It was odd, Paul, like going through the looking glass *into* the files and becoming one of the assets. Killing a paper man. The reality he had for me was the reality Gunga Din had for me when I was a kid, or Nigger Jim. I had no clothes on. This flabby German was staring at my breasts and belly. How could it be real?'

Christopher looked down at their joined hands, lying on the brocade of the sofa cushion. 'It was real enough for Horst,' he said, 'when he signalled your friends in that black Opel, and they broke him in two. You should have seen the blood running in the rainwater.'

Maria moved, tried to take her hand away. Christopher tightened his grip on her slippery palm. A pulse was beating in her forehead, her skin showed pink through her tan, her breathing had quickened. Patchen watched these signs of her agitation as if they were needles tracing jagged peaks on the tapes of a polygraph.

Rothchild spoke. 'Bülow was supposed to think that the black Opel contained friends,' he said. 'Schaefer's fellows showed him the car in Schiller Park – you know about that, I suppose – and a couple of other times. They wanted him to recognize it. Otherwise he might have jumped out of the way.'

Maria spoke Russian to Bülow, she met him at eighteen minutes after the hour, she made him use elaborate wasteful tradecraft, she controlled every moment, every code phrase. She used Christopher's name, she described Christopher's tradecraft, she named five men Horst had spotted and the Americans had recruited. He showed terror, then relief, then servility.

'Why the KGB tradecraft?' Patchen asked.

'We knew he'd recognize it. Otto hoped he might tell Paul the Russians were trying to double him,' Maria said. 'That would have reinforced the purpose of the op – made it seem certain that the opposition had killed him, that the smuggling of the manuscript was blown, that we couldn't protect Kamensky.'

'I'm surprised he didn't tell me,' Christopher said.

'So was Otto – he thought he'd run to you with it. Maybe if I'd been a man he would have been scared enough to tell you. What he did do, Paul, was ask for money. He thought we ought to snatch you, pump you out. He was willing to deliver you for ten thousand pounds. He insisted on English money.' Maria grinned. 'You'd be flattered at the value he put on you; he said he could tell from your manners that you were at least a colonel; I guess that's the highest rank Horst could imagine. I told him you were more than that, I couldn't resist. Then the price is fifteen thousand, Horst said.'

Rothchild laughed, a string of gasps like a tubercular cough. 'Few men were such obvious fools as Horst,' he said. 'He had a face like a bad actor's seen in an old nickelodeon – put a coin in his slot, put your eye to the window, and watch greed and fear and lust flip over like dirty cartoons.'

Christopher said, 'Is that how you felt about him when you knew him in Berlin in the twenties? Is that why you compromised him with the local Communists in the Jockey Restaurant?'

Maria stirred; she picked up Christopher's untouched glass and drank from it. Rothchild showed nothing.

'This business, Paul, is largely a matter of storing up fools for future use,' he said. 'You, of all people, ought to know that.'

'Were you storing him up in Paris, Otto? Did you give him

Solange in '44? Did you arrange for him to double her, give him the illusion that he was penetrating your network?'

Astonishment flickered in Rothchild's face. Then it vanished and something like anger came into his eyes. These facts from his past awakened his old mannerisms: Christopher might have been implanting nerves to replace the ones the surgeons had cut in Zürich. Rothchild had stopped closing his eyes between sentences; he spoke without rest and in a steady voice.

'You don't imagine,' he said, 'that Horst Bülow could have done it on his own, do you?'

'No more than you and Maria could have killed Kamensky on your own,' Christopher said.

Neither of them answered. They were going to go no further. Patchen had been sitting, as motionless as an animal, while the other three talked. Now he rose to his feet; he seemed taller than usual in the unlighted room and his spectacles, reflecting the final red sunlight of the day, were bright discs on his shadowed face.

'Kiril Kamensky killed himself,' Maria said. 'David told us so.'

Patchen turned on a lamp. He looked at Otto's Klee, the crude technique, the rudimentary colours.

'True,' Patchen said. 'But you killed Kalmyk, Maria, and all the other couriers, and their footprints led the KGB right to Kamensky's doorstep.'

'*I?*' She opened her mouth to laugh, then caught the sound before it emerged. There was enough light now to see into Christopher's eyes.

'No one but you knew Kalmyk's name, Maria,' Christopher said. 'Remember.'

Maria did. With tightened lips, shaking her head, she recalled the scene. 'Right here,' she said, 'in this room, after you'd knelt at Otto's feet, Paul, with that story about putting a pen name to Kamensky's work.' Christopher had given her Kalmyk's name, casually, buried in a meaningless sentence, as if she already knew it. Patchen had repeated it. Now she saw the trap, after it had closed.

'Oh, Paul,' she said, 'you *bastard*!'

She looked to Rothchild for permission. He shrugged. Maria was reporting now, in an even tone, in clear sentences. She had taken Christopher's bait, again, when they met by the Madeleine. She had stolen the Russian proofs after he told her where they were. She had taken them to Geneva on the night trian, mailed them to Munich, come back to Paris. 'Even then, you knew every-thing,' she said. 'I knew you must, there was no expression in your eyes, Paul.'

'And while you were in Geneva, called the KGB resident with Kalmyk's name,' Patchen said. 'You knew the Russian from the files.'

'You can't know that. There was no surveillance on me.'

'There was surveillance on Cerutti, surveillance on everyone else who might have done it. We know they didn't do it. Therefore, you did.'

Maria lit a Gauloise and put it out. The smoke brought water to her eyes.

'Kalmyk's name, giving it to me that way,' she said. 'I didn't see what you were doing, Paul. It was so simple a trick – it was almost an insult to Otto and me. You looked so tired, you were so upset, I'd seen how you mourned Bülow when I knew he would have sold you. I imagined, even Otto imagined, that you really wanted to save Kiril Kamensky. You *were* beside yourself.'

'Paul is never beside himself,' Rothchild said. 'Isn't that true, David?'

Patchen, before he answered, moved so that he could see all of them at the same time – Christopher and Maria and himself in the mirror, Rothchild unreflected.

'Very nearly true,' he said. 'But on that occasion, when he gave Kalmyk's name to Maria, he realized what you and she would do with it. He'd made it imperative that you kill him, or lose every-thing. Paul the death-hater was killing Kalmyk and Kamensky and, as it turned out, three others. It was quite a price, but he wanted full value – to know the truth.'

'Well,' Rothchild said, 'now he knows.'

4

Maria turned on more lamps. The rich colours of the room, returning with the light, revived her; she went to the window and looked down into the street. 'Wilson-Watson-Wharton's big black Citroën is parked below,' she said. 'When will we see him again?'

'When Paul and I leave,' Patchen said. 'He'll have some things for you to sign.'

'The transcript of this conversation?' Maria touched Patchen's briefcase with her foot; she was trained, she knew that it contained a transmitter, that Wilson's technician was minding a tape recorder in the Citroën.

'That, and an insurance policy.'

Maria frowned, looked to Rothchild for help.

'Confessions to murder,' Rothchild said. 'They'd want that. Blackmail insurance. You're an outsider now, Maria.' He held out a hand for her, but she did not take it. 'What love will do to us,' Rothchild said.

Rothchild was happy and so, in her way, was Maria. Anxiety had died for them. Christopher stood up. Maria touched the back of Rothchild's outstretched hand, trailed her fingertips over its veins and bones, and went to Christopher. She put her arms around his neck and pressed her cheek on his. He felt the sharp bone in her temple and her teeth beneath her lip.

'Oh, Paul,' she said. 'You and Otto are so alike.'

'Are we?' Christopher said.

Maria, flushed and still smiling, stepped away from him. She knew that nothing was going to happen to her except that she was never going to see Christopher again.

Christopher turned to Rothchild; Rothchild was smiling at him. Christopher waited for Patchen to notice the silence and turn around; he was examining the paintings again.

Christopher said, 'One last fact, Otto.'

Rothchild, still laughing, nodded.

'Did you believe Kolka was an agent? Did you believe what the NKVD told you when they showed you the pictures?'

Rothchild wiped his eyes. 'Of course,' he said. 'I'm a professional.'

Christopher told them Don Jorge's tale. Rothchild's face relaxed, he stared at a point in space, smiling in affectionate recognition as the story unfolded. Christopher stopped speaking. Maria clutched his arm.

'To use me for that?' she said to Rothchild. She shook Christopher's arm for a violent instant, as if she could change the patterns of knowledge in his mind, and so change Rothchild's past, like beads in a kaleidoscope.

'For *love*, Otto?' she said. 'After a quarter of a century, you had me murder your old lover? You were ashamed of love?'

'What other reason could have been strong enough?' Rothchild asked.

Maria went to the window again. Patchen went with her; they were on the sixth floor. Maria shuddered, Patchen put a hand on her hair.

'Kolka felt strongly,' Christopher said. He told Rothchild where Kolka Zhigalko had got his new name.

'Kamensky was the name the NKVD gave *me*?' Rothchild cried. His upper body sprang forward, he nearly lost his balance, saving himself by clutching the arms of his chair. 'Kolka took *my* name in Madrid?'

'Yes, and wore it like a ring back into Russia, and into the camps.'

Rothchild was transformed. He smiled without restraint, muttered a phrase in Russian. He was looking at an absent figure, hearing old conversations. For the first time since the NKVD had photographed him and Kolka together, Otto Rothchild's person was visible; his wife stared at him, rage rising in her face. He didn't see her.

'Kolka,' he said, laughing, speaking in Russian, 'Kolka – a secret marriage, a secret marriage.'

He went on laughing, as he had done when he had defeated the lie detector, until his voice fled and his cheeks were blistered with tears.

Twenty

On their last night in Madrid, Christopher and Cathy had gone to the Corral de la Moreria for supper. The flamenco there was not authentic; the girls were too pretty and their dresses were too new, they were décor not dancers. But the place made Cathy happy – a guitarist she admired was playing that night, and she liked the wine and the *paella*. 'The food in this country is so wonderful,' she said. 'You can either have *paella*, or all the things that go into *paella*, one thing at a time.' The simplicity of Spanish life made her feel free. 'The Spaniards never mix their colours,' Cathy said. 'Everything is what it seems to be.' Christopher gave her a look. 'So it's an illusion; I'll keep it,' Cathy said.

A new performer was introduced, a young girl wearing a round-brimmed hat, a male dancer's short jacket and high-waisted trousers. Her costume shocked the Spaniards in the audience, as it was designed to do. But the girl's voice, when she began to sing, carried them away. She had the voice for flamenco, ardent and true, with the hoarse tone, almost hidden among the notes of song, that Cathy called the scar on the heart. All fine singers had it, she told Christopher, and this girl had a wonderful one. The audience showed passion for her, and the girl was carried away by it. She sang the whole repertoire of flamenco songs, with the clapping hands of the company and the guitars playing behind her. Her limelit face, simple and homely, shone with sweat, and she listened with absorbed attention to the pitch of her own voice, as though she wished to be sure that it was fit for other ears before releasing it. She had no guile, and she made no attempt to hide her rapture. Cathy looked at the singer, and then into Christopher's face, and said, 'Me.'

Later, when Cathy catalogued her lovers in Don Jorge de Rodegas's garden, Christopher remembered this scene. She told him that she was finished with lovers. But Cathy's sexuality was like the flamenco singer's voice, an innocent thing of the body. He hadn't believed she had come to him a virgin and he didn't believe that she took no pleasure from her lovers. She carried too much of it back to him. The others had touched and changed her; he felt it in her body. They were both excited by it. Cathy, who had always wanted to talk about everything, would not talk about this. 'No one stays in my mind but you,' she said. 'It's *you*, Paul, whose memory is populated by old lovers; you never forget anything. If you remember phone numbers for twenty years, and you do, how would you forget the exact feeling you had with every one of those girls?'

The next day, they had driven over the Pyrenees, passing near the place where Solange had died, and down into the green valley on the French side of the frontier. Cathy wanted to go to Lourdes, she had never seen it. They agreed that she would drive back to Rome while Christopher went by train to Paris.

'Do tell Maria Don Jorge's tale of Kolka and Kamensky.'

'That's why I'm going to Paris,' Christopher had said.

2

Christopher, when he returned to Rome, found Cathy at home, listening to her tapes, with sheets of music spread over the tables and on top of the piano. The Siamese cat he had bought for her on their anniversary slept on the carpet, in a patch of sunlight. Cathy had found a frame, old and ornate, for the Goya drawing, and it hung above the bed.

She had been thinking about Otto Rothchild. 'I don't believe I saw all of Otto in that story of Don Jorge's,' she said. Christopher had involved her with Rothchild and used her against him; he told her enough of the truth to let her understand what Rodegas's tale had explained.

'But why?' Cathy asked. 'Twenty-five years of agony for *what*?'

'He was afraid of what had happened with Kolka. You say that lovers won't let you forget them. When Otto remembered Kolka – every day, I suppose – he remembered what he really was.'

'A queer.'

'No one cared about that. But his homosexuality, and his having done business with the NKVD in Madrid, laid Otto open to blackmail. That's the unforgivable sin – to be vulnerable. It puts everything in hazard.'

Cathy stroked the purring cat. Having it reminded her, she said, how much she loved animals, and she carried it with her from room to room. Now, on the terrace, it struggled to be put down and Cathy let it go. It walked along the balustrade, uttering a shrill mew. The sun was going down; Cathy and the animal were blank figures with the last light behind them.

'Why did you have to do what you did to him, Paul? It was so cruel, so awful a punishment. Why not just find him out, tell him you knew, put it in those files you're always talking about? Release him from the fear of discovery.'

'If he had told us the truth, we would have done that.'

'He made you angry by keeping silent? Paul – you?'

'No. He broke trust. We can't be what we are without absolute trust, Cathy. We live by it.'

'And you took it away from Maria's husband because he lost control of himself in 1936 and loved another person, and kept that secret from you? You have to know every secret?'

'You heard what Don Jorge said. He knows.'

Christopher looked at the sunset. The cat rubbed its back against his hand.

'Little by little,' Cathy said, 'I'm learning from you.'

Rome, in August, was almost empty. Cathy and Christopher were the only tenants in their apartment house who weren't out of the city on vacation. The building had once been a palazzo and now, with its cold marble halls and staircases empty and silent, it seemed like one again. Cathy opened the doors when she played sometimes, and the sound of the piano would fill the whole building. Christopher went to the top of the stairs to listen to her playing Haydn; the music was amplified through some trick of the palazzo's stone. As they always had done, they lived mostly in public. Cathy wanted to watch the sunset from the Pincio, to drink Negronis at Doney's, to eat spaghetti at Moro and artichokes at Piperno. When the food was before her, she ate little of it; she talked, telling Christopher stories of her family, of horses, of other animals she had owned. She made him laugh. 'It's funny, I remember everything that happened to me as a child, and everything that you and I have done together – every detail,' she said. 'But nothing in between. Will I remember anything that happens afterwards?'

She behaved like someone preparing for a voyage. In places where she and Christopher had been happy, she recalled the exact words spoken on the earlier occasion, the food they had eaten. Christopher saw that she was wearing the clothes that she had worn in the past to certain restaurants and theatres. He interrupted her reminiscences one night:

'Yes, I remember. You were wearing the same things you have on tonight – the blue linen suit, and your grandmother's pearls, and the same perfume.'

Cathy leaned across the table, they were in a theatrical restaurant called the Flavia where she was mistaken for a film actress, and kissed Christopher.

'Oh, it's a joy to love a man with a perfect memory,' she said.

'Why the costumes, Cathy, and all this time travel to the things we did together last year? What's wrong with now?'

'It was you who told me,' she said, smiling, 'that there's no such thing as the present. I'm just thinking of my future, storing up things.'

When, after a week, Christopher told her that he had to go to Africa, she showed none of her old temper. In his pursuit of Rothchild he had neglected his other agents; he would have to travel more than usual in order to see them. He told Cathy so, but didn't want to talk about it. She wanted to go to the Arlberg in the autumn, to walk in the mountains. She wrote to the manager

277

of the Mooserkreuz to book a room. 'Won't it be wonderful to be in the mountains?' she asked. 'There'll be snow on some of them, Paul; maybe we can ski, early in the day.'

Driving him to the airport, she turned and smiled as they passed Ostia Antica; it was the first time they had gone past the ruins together since the night they had gone inside, in the rain.

In the bar at Fiumicino she asked for champagne. It was after midnight, all flights to Africa left in the night, and they were alone with the bartender. The shriek of the jets and the stink of burnt kerosene activated Cathy's old feelings about Christopher's departures.

'Christ, I'll be alone,' she said, and bit her lips.

'So will I, and in the Congo.'

'There's a difference. You'll tell me nothing when you come back, if you do. Men go out like candles when they go away. You could die down there, a war is going on, without ever telling me what I've told you.'

'What do you call what you've told me?'

'Everything.'

Christopher's patience broke. Horst Bülow was dead, and Kolka Zhigalko and Masha, and he might find a dead man awaiting him in the Congo. What did Cathy know about being alone?

'Everything?' he said. 'Where is the other cat?'

3

In the Congo, Christopher found his agent, a man called Alphonse Nsango, sickened by magic. An enemy had put a juju curse on Nsango. His tribe believed that the liver was the seat of life, and within him Nsango felt his liver being devoured. He told Christopher, in a matter-of-fact tone, that he sometimes saw the spirit that was destroying him.

'It's a woman, all bones; I see her, just a wink of her, when she goes into me at night.'

Christopher didn't doubt what he was told. Nsango's face was haggard, the flesh was falling from his tall body. He was seized by violent fits of trembling. Outside the hut in the forest where Nsango now lay was an encampment of his followers. Nsango had been driven out of the capital, but many believed that he would come back as the head of his nation. Christopher had paid boys to write Nsango's name on walls in Leopoldville and Elisabethville; he had given journalists money to write stories about him. Nsango acted out the necessary legends, as he told Christopher in sardonic French, and Christopher transferred them into public consciousness.

Nsango had met him at a road junction, miles from his camp, and driven with him in a jeep through the dark trees. In an abandoned village the headlights had picked up something that did not have a natural shape. The two men walked across the beaten earth inside the circle of conical huts that had been the central place of the village. Nsango beckoned the jeep nearer. In the stronger glow of its headlamps they saw what they had found: a heap of human hands, the right hands of men, women, and children, with bloody stumps for wrists; the fingers were curved and delicate and except that they were black, might have been Cathy's, multiplied by mirrors, ready to strike a chord on a piano. 'Someone cut off all the right hands in the village, it's a punishment from the old Belgian days,' Nsango said. He put his hand on the pile of hands. 'Is this country an insane mind?' he asked.

It took a long time to heal Nsango. The local juju men could do nothing. Christopher knew of a man in the Ivory Coast who had powerful gifts. Nsango could not be taken there, as the kind of juju which afflicted him could only be cured at the place where the spell had been cast. Christopher was three hundred miles from the nearest American and he had no reliable communications. He went himself to Abidjan and brought the sorcerer back to the Congo. It took several days to drive the evil spirit out of Nsango's body and into the body of his enemy. There was fear among the Africans that Christopher's presence would diminish the powers of the witchman, and he remained inside a hut, some distance from the others. He heard drums and incantations in the night, and when he looked out he saw, outside the chief's house where Nsango lay, figures darting, like Cathy's jealousies, from the darkness to the firelight. By day, in the heat, he began to write a long poem for Cathy in his notebook.

Nsango, freed of his curse, regained his humour. 'What happened to me, Paul, will show you that I am still truly of my people,' he said. When he was within his tribe he wore its dress, spoke its language, and lived by its customs, but he had been educated by Christians and sent to a university in Europe. 'The Jesuits separated my mind from my body,' Nsango said; one part of his nature taunted the other. He and Christopher spoke about revolution. Nsango wanted guns. 'You and I have had enough ideas,' he told Christopher, 'the time for ideas has not come in this country.' When they first met and became friends, Nsango had spoken of something he called revolution without rage. Now he wanted to kill – he had changed more than Christopher.

Christopher gave the sorcerer gold and sent him back to his own country. Nsango did not thank Christopher or speak of the incident; he feared that the juju might not truly have been broken, because Christopher was involved. Without his friend and the gold Nsango would have died; but he didn't know what might befall him in the future in retribution for having brought an outsider into secret things.

4

Cathy's other cat remained, with her other clothes and her other jewellery and scent, in her apartment in the Piazza Oratorio. Christopher never went there. Sometimes, if he came home without warning, Cathy would still be in the other place and he would wait for her to call. She phoned their apartment at noon each day to see if he had returned, and when he answered she would hang up without speaking; in an hour she would appear, bathed and dressed in the clothes she kept for him.

Her hysteria recurred and grew worse. Christopher went back to Africa, and to Asia, and to northern Europe. Each time he returned she came to him from a lover. She went back to being the lover she had been at the beginning of their marriage, frenzied and taking what she wanted. She made love with her eyes open and watchful – waiting for the instant, she said, when Christopher would be drawn out of himself.

They went to the Arlberg as Cathy had planned and walked, with a picnic lunch in a rucksack, along paths in the evergreen woods. It snowed and they skied. Christopher was sick, he had relapsed into dysentery while he was with Nsango, and when he stayed in the room one afternoon Cathy found someone in the hotel to go to bed with. It was the first time this had happened. Always before she had kept herself to Christopher unless he was in another country. She was shaken by what she had done; she blamed it on drink – she had had wine with her lunch and cognac afterwards, and the man had begun to talk to her in bad English.

'I don't know what's happening, Paul, I'm beginning to want the others,' she said. 'I have to talk to you.' She told him again what she had told him in Spain: name after name. 'I always know their names,' she said, in a voice as brittle as Maria Rothchild's. Moroni, the first man she had taken, was jealous of the others, her other lovers had made him impotent. 'He's mad and bad, Paul, hard to control.'

Christopher listened to her as he would have listened to an agent's complaints, with the surface of his mind. He knew she wouldn't change. He told her that he wanted a divorce.

'Because I'm bad and mad, too? I love you, and I'm trying to ruin you.'

'Cathy, it's not me you're doing this to, it's my work. You think you can end my other life if you make a catastrophe of our life.'

'But it won't work?'

'No. The other is too strong, Cathy.'

'What if I stop now?'

She sat cross-legged at the foot of the bed with her hair capturing most of the light in the darkened room and a wreath of painted flowers behind her on the polished wood of the door; Christopher was always seeing her framed like a girl in a painting, enclosed by a window or by a space between trees or fountains.

'Cathy, you can't stop,' he said.

He kept speaking her name with every sentence, as if the sound of it would soften the rest of what he was saying. Cathy said she would stop. She was going to close her place in the Piazza Oratorio, sell the other clothes. She had used fictitious names with all of her lovers except Moroni: she could escape from them.

'When you come back from the Far East, it's only two weeks from now, all the traces of the others will be gone,' she said. 'I have a plan.'

5

In Indochina, while he waited for agents, Christopher worked on the poem for Cathy.

When he returned to Rome he found a bottle of wine cooling in an ice bucket. Cathy had left it on the low table where the cat liked to sleep, and both Siamese were curled up beside it. At the sight of Christopher, the animal that did not know him leaped down and ran into hiding.

There was a note from Cathy, two lines saying that she had one last errand to run. 'The Plan is working perfectly,' she wrote. 'The cure is complete.'

Christopher waited. He had flown from Saigon, nearly twenty-four hours in aeroplanes and airports. All that he had heard and done in the Orient was in his mind, intermixed with lines from Cathy's poem. He began to write his report so that it would not prevent him from listening to Cathy when she came home.

The phone rang, and when he lifted it he did not recognize the voice at the other end. It was Cathy; her words were distorted and she was taking great sobbing breaths. Finally a male voice came on the line; it was the waiter in the coffee shop on the Piazza Oratorio. He told Christopher to come quickly.

Christopher found Cathy leaning against the peeled wall of a building with a group of chattering Italians around her. Her face was bloody and swollen. She cradled her own body, half crouching when she moved with her arms wrapped around it, as if her pain was an injured child.

'I think something's pierced inside me,' she said. When she spoke, blood ran from the wounds inside her mouth. Her heavy hair was stained with blood and she had vomited on her clothes. Christopher carried her to the car and put her in and started for the hospital.

'Paul,' she said in her blurred voice, 'put up the top.'

Christopher took her hand and kept driving, very fast, through the streets of Rome – over the Tiber, through St Peter's Square, up the steep narrow road on the Janiculum, towards the international hospital.

'Put up the top,' Cathy said, 'put up the top. Paul, put up the top.'

At the door of the hospital he lifted her out of the car and she wakened, he saw intelligence come back into her eyes for an instant. She put a stained finger on his lips. She wanted him to kiss her. He did so, longing for her. Hours later, when he looked in a mirror, he saw the bloodstains she had left on his mouth.

Cathy's teeth had been broken, and bones in her face. Her spleen had been ruptured. Because she was a foreigner, the police did not investigate. Christopher sat with her, sleeping in her room for several nights, until she was able to let him leave without crying from fear. Mostly while she was still drugged, she told him what had happened.

Cathy had taken almost everything from the apartment in the Piazza Oratorio. She had gone back, on the day that Christopher returned, to give away her clothes; Franco Moroni had a German girl who wanted them. When she arrived she found Moroni in the flat with a dozen of his friends, including three or four foreign girls. They were seated in a circle, like a theatre in the round, in the room where the huge photographs of Cathy were hung. They were drinking *spumante*.

When Cathy entered, one of the girls slipped behind her and locked the door. Then Moroni, removing his jacket and shirt, beat Cathy with his fists while the other women watched and sipped their wine. She saw her own blood flying, little clouds of red droplets, and she realized why Moroni had stripped to the waist: he didn't want to spoil his clothes. At the end, he knelt beside Cathy where she lay on the floor, ran a finger into the blood on her face and, making certain that she was watching, licked his finger. Then he pushed her out the door. Through her ringing pain she heard him, inside, smashing the objects in the apartment.

Christopher could not find Moroni. He had the German girl's name from Wilson. He called her and asked her to meet him in Cathy's flat. Moroni had ripped the photographs from the wall and they hung in tatters. The furniture was overturned, the glasses smashed, Cathy's clothes torn and dirtied.

'Were you among the spectators?' Christopher asked.

The German girl stood with her hand on the doorknob, trembling.

'No. I would have warned her. I didn't know. Franco brought some Swedish girls.'

'Where is he?'

'Gone. I don't know where.'

The girl, a stranger to Christopher, shrank against the door. He realized that he had lost control of his face and he tried to smile at her. She saw the effort he was making, and spoke.

'There's a man Franco sees, a Russian,' she said. 'He went to see him afterwards, and he came back terrified. Franco just packed a bag and left in the car. He'd had a lot of dope and he was talking to himself. He kept saying your name. He was sobbing from fear. I don't know what the Russian told him about you.'

Christopher knew.

6

At the airport, they stood together by the glass wall above the tarmac and looked down at Cathy's plane. She made no effort to cover her injuries. Her face was still swollen and her eyes were distorted by the pull of the discoloured flesh. She was still bandaged from the surgery to remove her spleen and she moved apprehensively. She told Christopher she had no more pain. 'But I know it's still in my body somewhere,' Cathy said, 'waiting to come out again.'

Her mother would meet her in New York. Cathy had spoken to her on the phone about an automobile accident. She had said nothing, for the time being, about the divorce.

'I have this for you,' Christopher said.

He gave her the poem. She leaned against the wall in the thin light – it was a morning in early winter and it was raining – and read the handwritten sheets. As she read, grace came back into her body, and she stood for a while in her old dancer's attitude. She did not cry.

'That's the only copy,' Christopher said.

'I won't lose it.'

Her flight was called. Christopher carried her handbags down the ramp for her. Their ears were filled with the shriek of taxiing jets. They stood under an umbrella at the foot of the gangway with other people crowding by. Christopher put his arms around her to shield her from their jostling. Cathy's lips could not bear the pressure of a kiss. Their faces were very close together.

'There's this, Paul,' Cathy said. 'We've loved each other as no one will ever love either of us again.'

Her eyes were dry. Christopher wept.

'How much is that in real money?' he asked.